Triorion: Awakening

Book One
L. J. Hachmeister

D1115702

Novels by L. J. Hachmeister

Triorion: Awakening (Book One)
Triorion: Abomination (Book Two)
Triorion: Reborn, part I (Book Three)
Triorion: Reborn, part II (Book Four)

Forthcoming

Triorion: Nemesis (Book Five)

A Note from the Author

Sometimes I can't believe how long I've been working on this series, or how many different twists and turns it's taken over the years. It's been interesting to see how time and experience have influenced how I've shaped the characters, and how some things—Jetta's orneriness and Jaeia's quiet sweetness, Jahx's pursuit of the greater truths of the universe—have been that way from the day my pen first hit the paper.

I hope you enjoy book one and will continue on with Jetta, Jaeia, and Jahx in the following books as they travel across the Starways. If you would like to support this series, I encourage you to post your honest reviews and share this series with your friends and family. Your reviews and ratings make all the difference in this ever-changing publishing world.

All the best to you, and happy reading!

This book is dedicated to David, Jeanette, and Tim

For having to hear about it since 1988

Triorion: Awakening

The monster came at night, as he usually did.

Wake up, Jetta told herself as he body-slammed the front door of the apartment, taking it clean off its hinges.

Wake up!

Angry footsteps tromped toward the bedroom where Jetta and her siblings slept at the foot of their aunt and uncle's bed.

Not real. This isn't real.

Caught halfway in a dream, she couldn't rouse herself until she heard her uncle's voice:

"Get the children!"

Jetta sat straight up, panicked. In the confusion of her siblings' cries, she watched her uncle tumble out of bed and push the dresser in front of the bedroom door. *This can't be real. Please, oh, please—*

"Aunt Lohien—" Jetta started, tears already sliding down her face as her aunt rushed to her side.

Slender arms wrapped around her tiny four-year-old body. "Listen to me, Jetta. Take your siblings and hide."

A tender kiss from her aunt lingered much longer than usual on her cheek. In that moment, Jetta knew. *This is goodbye.*

"No, Aunt Lohien," Jahx said, tugging on their aunt's shirtsleeve.

"Please," Jaeia pleaded. "Hide with us."

"Here," Lohien said, prying off the air ventilation grate on the side of the wall. Fists beat against the bedroom door. A drunken howl signified a hunger that would not be satisfied with blood alone. "Hide in here. Don't come out until he's gone."

Her triplet siblings, just as emaciated as she, slid easily on hands and knees into the dark space of the air ventilation system. Wiggling in backward, Jetta went last, helping her aunt re-secure the grate on the wall as Galm and the wooden dresser lost their battle. Cheap clapboard splintered, and the monster got through.

Lohien poked her fingers through the slats of the grate, a smile trembling on her lips. Eyes, already burdened with a sadness Jetta could never understand, tried to convey one last sentiment of strength and love.

"Jetta, don't worry. You will find a way. You will survive," she whispered, then turned away.

"What are you doing?" the monster screamed, barreling straight for their aunt.

8

Jetta, what's happening? her siblings cried in the back of her mind. Biting her lip, Jetta shut out her brother and sister from the telepathic connection that bound them together, not wanting them to see the horror unfolding in the bedroom.

"Yahmen, stop, please stop!" Galm pleaded, backing into the corner with his hands held over his face.

Of course her uncle did nothing to stop his brother, Yahmen, from brutalizing him or their aunt.

Why won't you stop him? Jetta cried, angry and horrified as Yahmen landed blow after blow on her feeble adoptive parents.

Jahx pulled at the toes of her bare feet. In the back of her mind she heard his reasons and insights, but she didn't want them. It didn't matter that Galm was a timid, kindly soul who wouldn't hurt the lowliest creature on their rotten world. *Why won't he protect our aunt?*

(Why won't he protect us?)

Grabbing their aunt by the hair, Yahmen dragged her toward the front door, laughing and taunting their uncle as she screamed. "You did this to yourself, brother. This is your debt. If she doesn't satisfy me, it'll be those little street rats next."

"No!" Galm cried, hobbling after him, face bloodied from the beating. "Please, not my wife, please, Yahmen!"

Screams and laughter echoed down the corridor of their apartment complex. Jetta waited for what felt like forever before pushing out the grate and crawling back into the bedroom. The usual angry fights and drunken moans carried through the walls, but not the voices of her aunt or uncle, or the monster.

Stay here, Jetta said through their telepathic connection, instructing her brother and sister to remain in the bedroom.

"No way," Jaeia whispered, latching onto her sleeve. Their brother, eyes wide with fright, stayed plastered to Jetta's side.

Then be quiet, she said, tip-toeing through the living room and to the front entrance. With her siblings in tow, Jetta peeked around the broken frame of their front door.

A junkie, sprawled out on the stained green carpet of the corridor, caught her eye. "This place will take your soul," he mumbled.

Whatever he said next came out in a frothy babble, seized by whatever drug lit his circuits.

Not Fiorah. Yahmen, Jetta thought, but shoved her feelings aside before they had a chance to take hold.

A whimper and a groan came from the stairwell. The yellow, calloused hands of her Cerran uncle appeared on the top step. Grunting, Galm hoisted up his broken body to the third floor corridor.

Jetta weaved around the rest of the junkies and drunks lining the corridor to help Galm the rest of the way. Jaeia and Jahx followed suit, doing the best they could to assist their uncle.

"I'm sorry, children. I'm so, so sorry," he sobbed, leaning on the wall and limping back to their apartment.

Gleaning the answer from her uncle didn't keep Jetta from asking the question out loud. She wanted him to say it. Some ugly part of her, angry with her uncle for his weakness, needed him to stand accountable. "Where's aunt Lohien? What will Yahmen do to her?"

Stopping short of their apartment door, Galm slid down the wall, tears streaking down the clotted patches of blood on his face. "I—I...Why did I...? My fault, this is all..."

"Jetta," Jahx said, pulling her around to face him. Blue eyes would not let her look away. "Please. We're all upset. Let's go inside and help Galm get cleaned up."

There's no excuse for this, Jetta replied back silently, shaking with rage and heartache. *I want my aunt back. I don't want to be afraid anymore!*

"I know," Jahx whispered, cleaning off the tears from her face with his sleeve. Two other arms found their way around her body and pulled her in close. Jetta allowed Jaeia to hug her, needing her sister's strength.

"I won't let Yahmen take you, I promise," Jetta said, holding on tight to her siblings. Fear and hatred found their way into her words. "No matter what."

CHAPTER I

Jetta pressed her ear against the warm pipe running through the drillship's main engine core. "Sounds like there are minerals accumulating in the connector ports. We'll have to fix the cooling system or take the ship to the surface to fix it."

Her brother and sister looked up from the jigsaw puzzle of the subcoolant processor spread across the grated floor of the engine room, their eyes wide with fear.

"Yahmen will never stand for that. It'll slow business," Galm mumbled, staying hunched over a console with a readout of the overheated drilling modules.

Jetta disregarded her uncle and scooted over to her siblings, navigating around the intricate highway of pipework. "We can't just leave this—the main lines will rupture by first shift tomorrow."

Jaeia, her identical sister, sat back on her heels and wiped the sweat from her brow. It was getting late, and the heat from engine blasted down on them as fiercely as the midday Fiorahian suns. "I don't know how to fix this, Jetta."

"Jahx?" Jetta said.

Her triplet brother set down his tools and clutched his belly. Jetta should have known better. Fixing such a complex problem was out of the question, especially in their condition and without the proper knowledge.

"No, Jetta," Jahx whispered, reading her thoughts.

"We have no choice," Jetta said. *We have to risk digging inside someone's head.*

Subconscious protests arose from both her siblings. Hunger had collapsed all three of their bellies, and the dead heat from the machinery lent feelings of suffocation.

We can't, Jahx said, moping the sweat off his face with his shirt. *None of us are in any condition to—*

Then we're dead no matter what, Jetta snapped.

Everyone's already clocked out, Jaeia said, trying to reason with her. *Even the laborminders returned to the surface hours ago.*

Of course, Jetta thought bitterly. *Yahmen sent his work enforcers home because he knows we can't possibly complete this task. This is just another game to him.*

Old taunts and teases played out in her head: *"Fiorah is no place for Deadskins. No place for an ugly launnie like you."*

Jetta shoved close a nearby interface portal. *We've survived this rotten world, and we've taken Yahmen's abuse for years,* she thought to herself. *If only people knew what I could do, they would be a lot more careful of what they said to me—and they wouldn't treat me and my siblings like throwaway five-year-old kids.*

"Not everybody's gone home," Jahx whispered, still holding his belly.

Jetta followed her brother's gaze to Galm. Staring blankly at his workstation, their uncle's lips moved in a silent conversation with old haunts. With arthritic fingers curled in on themselves he periodically wiped his forehead, leaving a streak of grime.

At first she scoffed. *His mind is practically mush.*

Gently, Jaeia redirected her thoughts. *He wasn't always like this. Remember when he was a building maintenance manager? He fixed everything.*

"Okay," Jetta said, but her brother caught her arm before she could turn.

"No, I'll do it."

"You're not in any shape to—"

The intensity in his eyes betrayed the sickliness of his body. Any argument Jetta tried to put up dissolved. As the most gifted of the three siblings, Jahx possessed the skill and caution required to glean from their uncle. Jetta hated taking a back seat in the matter, but with her brother's pain and her sister's worry crowding her mind, she had no choice.

"Uncle Galm," Jahx said, crawling over to tug at his trouser leg. "Can you help me with this?"

Galm turned his head, but did not look at Jahx. "Is it time to go home?"

"This won't work," Jetta muttered. If they didn't get Galm focused on how to fix the coolant subprocessor, they couldn't steal that information from him, at least not without him knowing.

Jetta's stomach growled audibly, and Jaeia's followed suit. "Jahx, just let me do it," she said, trying to move her brother aside. Who really cared if Galm detected them? After all, no one took him seriously, and most of the time his sentences came out in toothless gibberish.

After grabbing a few pieces of the processor, Jaeia put them on the console in front of Galm. "Do you remember how these go together?"

Jahx put a hand on Jetta's knee, keeping her from interrupting as Jaeia continued to gently pry. "I know this part goes here, and this part goes here—but what happens when you have a broken routing wire?"

Galm stared blankly at the pieces, eyes withdrawn to some part within himself.

"Uncle," Jahx said, trying to coax him back. "You're always so good at fixing things. I remember when you helped me repair the refrigerator."

Jaeia chimed in. "I remember when you helped Aunt Lohien fix the air conditioner."

Jahx gave Jetta a nudge, trying to elicit her participation.

I can't remember anything like that, she grumbled through their psionic bond.

Jahx stood up on wobbly legs, his belly singing with pain. He placed his hand atop Galm's, blue eyes searching their uncle's wrinkled face. "I know you're tired, uncle. We are too."

Tears brimmed Galm's eyes. "I am so, so sorry."

"Enough," Jetta said, shoving her brother and sister aside.

Closing her eyes, Jetta dove into her uncle's head. The same chaotic whirlwind of sounds and images she had weathered many times before, but never understood, accosted her senses. Discomforting emotions, complex and laced with manifestations she had no way of coping with, played out in her head like a living nightmare.

Jetta blew past screaming matches with Yahmen and the forceful removal of their Aunt Lohien from their apartment. She tried to shield herself from his sorrow and anger, but as deep as she burrowed into his mind, she could not protect herself from the consequences of her telepathic invasion.

"You cannot take my wife!" Galm screamed, fighting to break free from his brother's hold. Trapping Galm's leg against the wall, Yahmen kicked down with all his might, shattering his kneecap. Pain exploded across Jetta's mind, and she bucked away from the memory.

14

Rising from the festering pits of her uncle's unconscious, new hells unfolded, drowning her in unconscionable miseries. Jetta squirmed away as Yahmen's menacing face appeared around every turn and bend in Galm's mind, his hulking figure eclipsing any other reality.

"You can never escape me," he hissed, black eyes bleeding into the shadows.

Panic rained down on her from all directions. She didn't know whose fear infused her with adrenaline reaction, or how many heartbeats pounded in her ears.

I should have known better! *Jetta reprimanded herself.*

Jetta clawed her way back through the clogged disorder of her uncle's mind, Yahmen—or some feral animal—cackling just behind her.

"You are mine!"

A blackened, gnarled hand shot out of the shadows. She narrowly missed the grasp of its growing fingers.

"Leave me alone!" Jetta screamed, fighting the reaching memories.

"You're okay, you're okay."

Her sister's words barely broke through. Some part of Jetta felt them before she heard them as the dizzy world of rusted pipes, engine parts and drilling machinery reformed before her eyes.

Pressing her palms into her eyes, Jetta tried to steady her senses and rid herself of the ghostly afterimages of their owner. *When did Galm become so unstable?*

"You shouldn't have done that," Jaeia whispered, helping Jetta to sit up.

"We had to do something," she said, not meaning to come off as gruffly as she did. "We can't just coddle him. Sometimes you have to be aggressive."

"But it has consequences," Jaeia said, turning so Jetta could see her brother. Jahx curled in on himself, face red and contorted.

"Jahx!" Jetta said, scrambling to his side. *How could I be so stupid?*

Although she bore the greatest risk entering Galm's mind, the telepathic connection she shared with her brother and sister dragged them along with her, inadvertently exposing them all to the nightmarish realm Yahmen dominated.

15

"Jahx, I am so sorry," Jetta whispered, afraid to touch him.

Of the three of them, Jahx feared Yahmen the most. Something about their owner terrified Jahx more than any of the other dark Sentients of Fiorah, and it usually took one or both of the sisters to calm him down.

Guilt kept Jetta at bay. *This is my fault. I should have known better—*

Luckily, Jaeia picked up the pieces. Wrapping her arm around Jahx's shoulders, her grey-eyed sister whispered into his ear. Jahx's face relaxed, and he slowly unfurled.

Blue eyes would not look at her. "I have what we need."

Jetta twisted the ragged ends of her shirt. "I'm sorry."

"I know," her brother said flatly. He looked to Galm. Their uncle sat limply at his console, lips once again moving in some broken conversation, completely unaware of what had transpired.

"H-how did you...?" Jetta started to ask.

Jahx crawled over the parts of the coolant subprocessor littering floor and started to fit them back together. "I picked up a stray memory. Just got lucky, I guess."

No, not lucky. Extraordinarily gifted. Jahx's sensitivities gave him insights Jetta could never have—and in many cases, want.

Jetta listened to her brother's thoughts and in seconds understood how they would fix the problem.

"I'm sorry," she tried again.

Jaeia gave Jetta's hand a squeeze. "Let's just put this back together. Then we can go home."

Jetta pretended to cough, giving her an excuse to wipe the tears from her eyes. "You know I would do anything to protect you and Jahx," she whispered.

"I know," Jaeia said, handing Jahx the tools he needed. Grey eyes looked solemnly back at Jetta. "That's what I'm afraid of."

***

Keeping Jetta's anger to a low simmer took almost all of Jaeia's energy. There was no arguing that their situation was dire, but if Jetta had her way, everyone Sentient in the galaxy would suffer her rage.

"She's only human," Jahx said half-jokingly as Jaeia helped him limp across the drillship toward the docks.

Jaeia chuckled. "Don't tell her that."

Staying up ahead, Jetta scouted around corners and down hallways for stragglers. The drillship felt empty, but some Sentient species eluded their senses. Any surprise encounter with a child labor gang, laborminder or adult, especially this late in the evening, could be disastrous.

"Let me go—I can walk on my own," Jahx said. "Concentrate on Jetta."

Jaeia frowned. "I can do both."

"Really," Jahx said, stifling a grimace while working his arm out of Jaeia's grasp. "She needs you. I'll be okay."

Glancing over her shoulder, Jaeia spotted Galm still shuffling along, bringing up the rear. Jahx could manage for a short while, and if anyone snuck up behind them, their uncle would alert them.

"Hey," Jaeia said, joining her sister's side. "We're almost to the docks."

Green eyes stayed sharp, sweeping the area up ahead. The narrow corridors of the mining ship provided plenty of unusual spaces packed between the machinery and pipework for enemies to hide. "This is where Sniffer jumped me two weeks ago."

Jaeia avoided Jetta's memory of the incident, trying to concentrate herself and her sister on better emotions.

"I'm going mapping again tonight," Jaeia said, brushing the back of Jetta's hand. "We're making progress. Soon there won't be any more surprise attacks or double shifts and dirty engines."

The sensation broke her sister's train of thought. Green eyes lost focus, shoulders relaxed. Jetta turned inward for a moment, but reemerged with a hardness in her thoughts. "No more topitrate," she said, wiping her hands on her shirt. Engine grease and the tan rock dust smeared together. "I hate it. It's always in my food, under my nails, in my eyes and mouth. It's starting to feel like a new layer of skin."

Jaeia agreed with her sister, but kept the rest of her thoughts to herself. She had grown more concerned over the safety of the drilling operation for topitrate when Yahmen doubled production demands and workers became sick. Hallucinations and vertigo were common if you breathed the rock dust in long enough, but Jaeia had

17

seen child laborers with lung infections, and even adults with new-onset dementia. Masks and filters were a rarity given out to laborminders and upper management, and certainly never afforded to her or her family.

Jetta's head snapped around, and her hands turned to fists. Immediately her tone changed. "No more Galm."

Jaeia looked back to see Jahx collapsed on the walkway and their uncle limping past him, oblivious to their brother's distress.

Does he just not see? Jetta yelled across their bond as she raced back to help Jahx.

"Not anymore," Jaeia said aloud, keeping up with her sister.

Kneeling next to their brother, Jetta touched Jahx's cold and clammy face. His mind squeezed tight around the lancing pains in his stomach, shielding his sisters from the agonies of his sickness.

Please Jahx, Jetta called across their shared bond. *Let me take your pain.*

No, Jetta, Jahx whispered back, curling himself in a ball.

Just for a few hours, I could—

"No, Jetta," he said, slowly unfurling. The look in his eyes startled her. "Let's just go home."

"What's the holdup?" Galm called back to them without turning around.

He's tired and sick, too, Jetta, Jaeia said, trying to reason with her sister as they helped their brother back to his feet.

"Not good enough," Jetta grumbled.

Jaeia saw Jetta's side of things, and couldn't deny that part of her agreed with her sister. Galm and Lohien were their adoptive parents—they were supposed to protect and look after them—not the other way around. But everything changed a few months ago when Yahmen took aunt Lohien away in some kind of debt.

"Galm's useless," Jetta muttered.

Jaeia looked for Jahx to back her up, but his energy waned with every step. "You don't mean that. It wasn't always like this."

"Don't do that," Jetta whispered, closing her eyes as Jaeia flooded her with memories from better days. Lohien, in the kitchen, humming as she cooked dinner. Galm, pretending to read the newsreels, chuckling as she and her siblings wrestled on the kitchen floor. One of them got outnumbered. He put down his pipe and

18

joined the fracas until the four of them were laughing so hard that the neighbors banged on the apartment walls.

It took everything Jetta had to firm up her voice. "That might as well be a different lifetime."

Galm stopped in his tracks and raised trembling hands in the air. Jetta immediately put herself in front of her siblings, spreading out her arms and making herself as big as possible.

"W—what's going on?" Jahx mumbled, head drooping off to the side.

Jaeia shared her sight with her brother as two soldiers in blue and black Dominion Core uniforms marched along the grated walkway, headed straight for them, plasma rifles in hand.

Galm cowered, pressing up against the guardrail, shielding his face.

This is it— Jetta projected.

(She's, right,) Jaeia thought, grimacing against her sister's reaction. *(It's too late to run, and none of us, especially Jahx, are in any condition for an assault.)*

Jetta's ferocity ransacked their connection. *I will use my secret talent. It's the only way!*

No, Jetta! Jaeia cried, calling out with her brother in unison. *It's too dangerous!*

Gritting her teeth, Jaeia drew from her brother's strength, and clamped down on Jetta's desire. Jetta could take down two armed soldiers—probably much more—but the price, even for the slightest usage of their individual secret talents, had already proven too costly.

Jetta glared at her siblings, but did nothing more than hold tight to her brother and sister as the soldiers passed Galm and tromped toward them.

Jaeia only chanced a glimpse of them. One, clearly human from his square jaw and blonde hair tufting out of his cap, griped to the other bipedal species resembling a lizard.

"Gods, I can't stand this heat," the human said. "I hope this is an in-and-out operation."

The lizard-looking alien, bifurcated tongue poking in and out of its mouth, spoke with a heavy lisp. "Not likely. The Sovereign's ordered another dropship this week."

"*Chakking gorsh-shit*. I didn't sign up for this. I'd rather be out hunting leeches."

The footsteps faded away toward the cargo hold. Jaeia slowly exhaled and peeked over her shoulder.

Thank Gods Jetta didn't use her talent—they were telepath hunters! she privately thought to her brother.

Jahx, barely holding on, returned the sentiment. *I couldn't read their minds, even the human.*

Then there's no telling what other tricks they might have had.

"Stop talking about me," Jetta said, lightly pinching both of them.

Jaeia tried to play it off. "You always say my thoughts are a nuisance. Aren't I doing you a favor?"

With a grunt, Jahx managed to lift his head just enough to give Jetta a wink.

Jetta looked back and forth between them, but any tension she tried to hold on to quickly dissolved. They were safe again, for now, and that's all that mattered to her.

"Let's get to the bus," Jetta said, slinging her brother's arm over her shoulder. "I'll even let you have the window seat this time."

As Jetta helped Jahx down the ramp exiting the drillship and to the bus depot, Jaeia went back to help her uncle still clinging to the guardrail.

"I'm afraid, Jaeia," Galm whispered to her, eyes wild with fear. "The Dominion are not supposed to be here. Yahmen will be angry—*very* angry."

Jaeia took her uncle's wrinkled hand in hers. His Cerran skin always felt so rough and calloused, nothing like the way she thought it should feel for such an infirm man.

"It'll be okay, uncle," Jaeia said, guiding him out of the mouth of the drillship and onto the bus platform to wait with her siblings for the next transport. She looked up the tunnel toward the tiny point of light that gave hints of the boiling surface. "Maybe things are going to change for the better."

***

Jahx allowed his sisters to help him into his seat on the bus, but only pretended to fall asleep. He closed his eyes, steadied the rate of

20

his breathing and let his thoughts drift until he felt the internal eyes of his sisters look away.

Keeping the seriousness of his condition from his sisters proved harder and harder each day. Sometimes his insides felt as hot as a blast furnace. Other times it was a cold knife-twist to the gut. He wanted nothing more than to allow his sisters to share in the burden, to barricade him from his miseries to allow him even the slightest reprieve, but he feared the consequences. *If they knew—if Jetta knew—how sick I am, there's no telling what extremes she'd go to.*

Jahx shuddered at the thought.

Fiorah had taught him about death since the very beginning, from the overdosed junkies clogging up the alleyways, gang victims stuffed in dumpsters, to the child laborers beaten to death by laborminders. He had seen and experienced death behind many sets of eyes, but no matter how much he learned, and no matter what he believed about what lay beyond, it provided little comfort as his belly continued to expand while the rest of him withered away. Death frightened him.

Jahx peeked open an eye. Galm and Jaeia dozed next to him on the same bench while Jetta, sitting across from them, stayed awake, watching out the window as they ascended the tunnel from the mining core station to Fiorah's red rock surface. Fatigue and the soft whir of the anti-grav engines lulled Jetta's mind, allowing him to see inside with singular clarity.

Stolen worlds unfolded within his sister: lush, green places with winding rivers and jagged mountains. A dark, nighttime sky studded with twinkling stars. White sand beaches and palm trees overburdened with drupes. Some of the rare, good memories they had chanced upon in their telepathic gleanings, places, for Jetta's own reasons, she usually kept locked away.

Hope, pure and genuine, arose from a place within his sister she seldom shared. Jahx relished the feeling, and for a brief moment, forgot about his pain.

Jetta's inner voice sang across the psionic planes: *Maybe we will surface on some other planet. Maybe I won't have to fight anymore.*

Something foolish and impossible; a thought Jetta would have never dared think in front of her siblings. Jahx had to keep himself from smiling.

The bus lurched forward, testing the strength of their seatbelts. Galm, not wearing one, pitched forward, nearly smacking his head on the opposing bench.

"Watch it, Drachsi," the operator called back, looking at Galm through his rearview mirror. "Wouldn't want to get hurt, would ya?"

Trembling, Galm worked his way back to his seat. Jahx let his senses expand, searching the other minds on the bus. Only two other workers had made the last bus to the surface, both too exhausted for any kind of altercation. If the operator hoped for a fight, it wouldn't happen today.

The transfer to the surface elicited its usual hisses and groans from the bus. The triple suns showed no mercy, even in the late evening hours, heating the bus in seconds. The operator blasted the air conditioner in his cab, but the rest of the main cabin quickly turned into an oven as they sped across the desert surface toward the protective airfield dome.

Jahx watched the scenery change through his sister's eyes. Windswept, hardscrabble surfaces whizzed by in burnt hues of red and orange. Mountains, off in the distance, looked like molten spires rising up to pierce the sky. When they reached the perimeter and transferred into the airfield, the circulators in the bus turned off, and the air from inside the dome filtered through. Taking in the first breath of the lone city's recycled pollution caused everyone to cough and sneeze.

Bars locked down over the windows as they passed through some of the roughest parts of the city. Jahx watched Jetta take it all in, pressing her nose and palms against the glass. Scanning the scores of homeless people waiting outside the social services office, Jetta extended her senses into the cloud of desperation hanging over each one of them. The vagrants had waited all day to see if the tight-fisted financial delegate—a friend of Yahmen's—would hand out the United Starways Coalition food stipends, braving the heat and Yahmen's watchdogs. Even though the plyboard doors to the social services office remained closed, and the city sanitation department had already come around twice to haul away those who didn't make it, they remained. Jetta couldn't understand why they would stay after all they had been through.

But I do.

They sped through scrap-yards, condemned refineries, and the ghostly high-rises that had once been slated to house rich businessmen back when investors thought that Fiorah might be worth more than its black markets. Condemned signs, graffiti and crumbling walls now gave sanctuary to the rats, and any unfortunate soul that wound up in the outskirts of the city.

Jahx kept himself tethered behind Jetta's eyes, curious to see her reaction as the bus entered the city's main drag. The hypnotic flicker of suspended neon ads and the electronic thunder of the stimulation boutiques jarred her from her lull. Forgotten were the impoverished outskirts of the city as painted streetwalkers paraded around in gaudy jewelry and fishnet stockings. Jetta pressed her face harder into the glass. Underhanders positioned themselves at each corner, throwing out hand jives to indicate what drug they were pedaling. Shop owners called out to vacant-eyed wanderers searching for something no guidebook listed. It wasn't anything she hadn't seen a hundred times before, yet it captivated her with fresh interest.

Jahx didn't understand why she was drawn to such sights, or why her subconscious yearned to know more of the dark secrets of the main drag. Then again, Jetta did not fear ugly truths of the Sentient heart. *Not like I do.*

The bus came to a screeching halt. The operator slammed his hands against the steering wheel. "Get out of the *chakking* road!" Expletives in Starways Common and his native language followed.

Jahx carefully shifted his attention behind the operator's eyes to see what had happened. Infuriated and distracted, the operator didn't notice his intrusion.

"*Chakking* leeches!" the operator shrieked.

"I know you're awake," Jetta whispered.

Jahx opened his eyes. Jetta scowled at him, arms crossed.

"At least let me see," she said.

Nervously, Jahx looked over to Jaeia. She remained fast asleep while Galm mumbled to himself, caught up in whatever his demons whispered in his ear.

"You're not going to like it," Jahx said.

"Try me."

With a big sigh, Jahx opened his mind to her.

A camouflage truck swerved into the middle of the street, blocking traffic both ways. Registration Security *was written on the* side. The back door swung open and a ramp extended, revealing a bed full of freezer cases. Dominion soldiers poured out the side doors, shockwands hot and crackling, silver insignia flashing in the neon sting.

Jahx bridged his attention between his sister and the operator. The operator laughed and cheered as the soldiers dragged a Sentient out of a taxi. Jetta recoiled in horror.

How do they know he's a telepath? Jahx wondered. The Sentient appeared to be of some humanoid ancestry, though his spiked vertebrae and yellow eyes indicated outerworld origins. Was it a false claim from an enemy? Or perhaps another demonstration of Eeclian Dominion authority?

"Serves 'em right, those chakking leeches," the operator grunted. "Only good thing the Dominion ever done."

Jahx wanted to look away, but his sister kept him grounded behind the eyes of the operator. She crowded the front of his mind, watching with fervent attention as they put a shockwand to Sentient's neck. Blue sparks danced off his body, and he immediately went rigid. By now a sizeable crowd had formed around the scene, though no one dared intervene. Some even began to cheer as the soldiers threw the Sentient's body into a freezer case.

Removing himself from behind the operator's eyes, Jahx found Jetta staring at her feet, sweat beading across her brow.

"You were right. I didn't want to see that," she whispered.

Jahx held back his thoughts from her. This wasn't the first arrest they'd seen—in fact, it was the third that week. Six months ago the Eeclian Dominion only seized telepaths who broke rules by cheating the casinos or manipulating the government with their powers. Now it seemed like even an accusation of telepathic talent warranted immediate arrest.

"Sorry, Jetta," he said as gently as he could. "I didn't want to worry you."

"Stop it. I'll take care of everything," Jetta said. Green eyes blazed with intense inner fires. "I promise."

***

The screams of the arguing couple next door rattled the apartment walls. Daring cockroaches skittered by. Usually exhaustion helped Jetta sleep right through the distractions, but restless nerves kept her awake. Something felt wrong, and she had learned over the years to trust her instincts.

She slowly uncurled, careful not to wake her brother sleeping fitfully next to her cot, and stepped onto the concrete floor. Walking on her tip-toes, she crept from their makeshift bedroom in the front hall and peered into the dimly lit center room where Galm sat staring at the television. The sound hadn't worked in weeks, and the flashing lights and wild colors of the infomercial did nothing to stimulate their uncle. He sat slumped in his chair, eyes unblinking, oblivious to the advertisements racing across the screen.

Jetta didn't recognize her uncle anymore. Cracked lips hung open beneath sunken cheeks. The little hair he had left tangled up into a greasy, knotted mess, and he hadn't bothered to shave in months. The only indication of life came in the shallow rise and fall of his chest.

Anger heated her limbs. *Why does Galm leave us to fend for ourselves?* She thought, biting her lip to keep from screaming. *Why doesn't he do something—anything—about our situation?*

Ugly memories shored upon her consciousness, reminding her of the truth. Before Yahmen took Aunt Lohien away, he played games with them, or at least taught them new skills so they stayed useful on the mining ships. *This is the best he can do; labor and sleep—and turn a blind eye to Yahmen's abuse.*

Grief tore down her scream and pricked her sinuses. Galm was still her *Pao*, her adoptive parent, and his love, and their aunt's, was their first understanding of family. No one else would have saved a street rat like her. Besides, she had never loved and lost like him, and in the face of his fiercest pain, she shied away.

Jetta weighed the consequences of trying to enter her uncle's mind again, but she immediately thought better. The failed attempt to extract information earlier that evening had only thrust her in a nightmarish morass of fractured emotions. *He's too far gone.*

A faint scraping sound pulled her from her thoughts. She turned around to see Jaeia kneeling at the edge of the vent in the hallway, unscrewing the grate cover. Her twin paused to look back at Jetta solemnly. A long moment passed before either one spoke.

"I'll be back before four. Don't wait up," Jaeia said as she began to wedge her tiny frame into the square shaft.

25

"Where are you mapping, Jaeia?" Jetta asked, glancing back at Galm. Their uncle sat frozen to his chair.

"I'm going back to the east side of town again. I think I found a parasitic area. I got too tired last week to make it past the latch-portal," she said as she dropped down into the shaft.

The eastern latch-portal, Jetta mulled, trying to remember the route. Thousands of subsidiary air ducts ran into every household and business structure, but parasitic areas typically fed off peripheral conduits, meaning tighter and more confusing passageways.

I hate that we have to crawl through the air system, Jetta thought to herself. *I don't want my sister risking her life trying to find a way for us to escape. What if she gets lost? What if she gets trapped in a juncture?*

"Wait," Jetta whispered. She ran to the small pile of clothes by her cot. After brushing away the Bulgis beetles that nested in its folds during the night, she uncovered one of her tattered socks. Reaching inside, Jetta withdrew the morsel of bakken she had won in the daily scramble for food with the rest of the child laborers.

"You didn't eat today," Jaeia said as Jetta offered her meal.

"If you're mapping, you'll need it. I'll be fine. I get to rest," she said with a half-smile.

Hesitantly, Jaeia accepted the gift. She let a smile touch her lips, sending wordless thanks to her sister before disappearing with a barely audible *swish* into the junction of the main ventilation shaft below.

Please be careful, Jetta thought, looking down into the darkness before placing the cover back over the hole. She then crept over to her brother's cot and, wrapping an arm around him as he moaned in his fitful state of topitrate toxicity, wished for sleep.

***

Pain triumphed over exhaustion, keeping Jahx from falling completely asleep. Even semi-conscious, he yearned for reprieve.

I need something, anything. Jahx squirmed in his cot as another spasm tore through his gut. *Gods, please—I can't take this anymore.*

Finding comfort or joy, rarities on a black market world, usually came through channels that made Jahx squeamish. He didn't want to feel nostalgic pangs after chomping on a human femur, or the

26

excitement of scoring an entire lot of fourth-class humans in another Deadskin auction on the Underground Block.

What is that?

Hope, though thready and faint, drifted by from the next room. Desperate for refuge, Jahx allowed himself to fall into the mind of the most unlikely of hosts.

Through his uncle's eyes, Jahx watched an infomercial where endless rows of children lined up behind desks, application forms in hand. Decorated Dominion Core officers accepted each child's form with a hearty handshake and a salute.

"This could be you!" announced the flashing script at the bottom of the television screen. A proud child with a beaming smile donned a Core uniform; a moment later he was sitting in a class taught by a Dominion officer, eagerly raising his hand to participate.

"Don't delay!" flashed across the screen, followed by a telecam number and signature.

Maybe this is my chance to do something right, Galm thought, eyeing the entryway where he believed Jahx and his sisters to be sleeping.

Memories came at Jahx in swirling heat.

A sunny, brisk day in the forests of Cerra. Galm clutched his rifle to his chest, shaking and sweating as he weaved through the trees. Even when the birdlike prawl appeared in a clearing, he couldn't take aim.

(I can't kill such a beautiful creature.)

Yahmen, moving through the bushes opposite of Galm, didn't hesitate, firing three arrows from his crossbow. The first speared the prawl through the neck.

(It was no accident!) *Galm's subconscious screamed, mind conjuring the bloody mess of his genitals. Yahmen, crossbow still in hand, did not bother to feign sorrow, instead revealing a sickle of brilliant teeth in some kind of deranged smile.*

Years passed by in heartbeat. Galm kneeled in front of his father, Co'Gin, head bowed and weeping.

"Your impotence is a disgrace to our bloodline," his father bellowed. "You force me to pass the family fortune to your younger brother."

"Please," Galm said, clinging to his father's pants. "Don't give it to Yahmen. He will destroy our family."

27

Flash-forward. Poor and desperate, Galm followed Yahmen to Fiorah.

"Don't worry, brother," Yahmen said. *"You and I will turn around the mining business. Then we'll be rich."*

That was never your intention, his uncle thought angrily. *You bled the trust dry on drugs and prostitutes, and when I found these children, when I finally proved that I had promising heirs to challenge you for the inheritance, you leave me nothing but debt.*

Still half-asleep, Jahx saw the frayed edges and over-processed colors of the torments that recycled over and over in his uncle's mind.

After all, what's left? Galm stared at his hands, but their decrepitude made him look away. *Soon leasing Lohien won't be enough. Yahmen will use her up and then come after the children.*

Uncle, please. More awake now, Jahx couldn't withstand the cramping pains of his stomach and groaned.

That's probably the boy again, he heard his uncle think.

"Uncle, no," Jahx whispered, too weakened to go to him or to wake his sister snoring by his side. In the far reaches of his mind he saw a future unfold in the muddy colors of death and destruction: *Creatures with mechanical limbs rising up from the sweltering pits of some hell-world, chittering in an ancient language that hurt his ears. A man with a plastic face holding up a martini glass, toasting to the bombs raining down on a city. Screams and cries as a monster, knitting itself together from spilt blood of his dead sister, called out Jahx's name.* "Don't sign us over to the Dominion. Gods, please…"

Galm, unaware of his son's pleadings, mashed together his gums and wiped the tears from his eyes. "Yes," he said to the television, clinging to his newfound hope. "This will fix everything."

***

Captain Mantri Sebbs popped *Military Combat*, the first of four videos, into the viewer.

"Pay attention!" he barked before he set the film rolling.

The children leaned forward in their seats, their eyes wide and mouths open as they viewed interstellar battles and air-to-ground combat. A few cried out in shock when an enemy was blown to bits, but after the initial scare, all of them hooted and cheered.

The booster tucked away in his sleeve called to him with each victory march and bloated admiral that romanticized the Eeclian Dominion's military.

There isn't enough methoc in the galaxy, he thought bitterly.

Not long ago he watched the same videos in awe, wondering if he could ever be a part of such an indomitable fleet. No, worse— that he would be the best of the best, leading the fleets of ships across the galaxies on a course of bravery and honor, just as the videos had told him.

"*Chakking* launnies," he muttered.

Ire and shame speared him. Here he was now, watching the children of Fiorah, their faces covered in ash and red-brown soot from the mines, knowing they dreamed of a future they couldn't possibly attain. Acceptance into the highly competitive Dominion Academy involved rigorous testing of both mental and physical competency, neither of which any of these children possessed. Most, if not all, had been born to substance-abusing streetwalkers who had somehow managed to keep them to term. The launnies who weren't completely damaged by all the harcok or methoc had one of two destinies—the mines or the Block, neither of which had a happy ending.

I could put that liver to better use, he thought, watching the child nearest to him chewing on his ragged shirtsleeve.

Despite the improbability that any of these kids had the capacity for military conditioning, he did as instructed.

"Seriously?" he muttered to himself as one of the kids wandered off into the corner and wedged his bottom as far as he could behind a power column.

"That is not a latrine!" he shouted. The little one didn't seem to understand Common and proceeded with his business. Sebbs rolled his eyes and turned away.

Everyone, even the degenerates of Fiorah, had to be indoctrinated. The Eeclian Dominion's military, known as the Dominion Core, would save the universe from disorder, righting the wrongs that the United Starways Coalition could not. Little did the people of Fiorah, or anyone else for that matter, know just what sort of order was coming.

The self-righteousness of the Sovereign and his Dominion sickened him, but little could be done about it. The Eeclian Dominion's power grew exponentially as the USC fumbled with the fragile Starways economy. Every day more star systems were drawn in by the Core's promise of security and wealth, and Sebbs knew that it was only a matter of time before the USC buckled. Sometimes he thought his habits and his side deals with Reht Jagger were all that kept him from losing his mind.

Out of the corner of his eye, Sebbs noticed the door of the classroom creeping open. Light from the hallway outlined three small figures. He pushed himself up from the corner projector as a Core soldier ducked his head in and nodded a silent command.

"*Chak,*" he muttered. More of Fiorah's backwash for him to condition.

And I will be the best of the best, leading fleets of ships across galaxies on a course of bravery and honor, just as the videos said. He swallowed the sour taste that filled his mouth.

As Sebbs walked toward the three new children, he noticed how weak and sickly they appeared, even more so than the others. Yahmen Drachsi abused the labor laws, but even he preferred his employees healthy enough to work long hours.

The two identical girls had deeply sunken cheeks, bony limbs, and knobby joints. Their clothing only emphasized their near-skeletal physique. The boy looked even worse, with neck muscles stretched taut like cables and a distended stomach that spoke of deeper sickness.

Sebbs closed the classroom door and faced the new three, towering at least a meter and a half above their heads. Not wanting to disturb the viewing of the video, he leaned down and whispered to them, "What am I supposed to do with you?"

He doubted they could speak, though they looked four or five years old. At that level of malnourishment and neglect their brain development was almost certainly impaired. They also appeared to be of direct humanoid descent, another strike against them. Most humanoids, including himself, were only able to survive on Fiorah a short while. He could only imagine what the heat and low levels of oxygen had done to them. But even if they'd been perfectly healthy, they were way too young to be drowned in this type of Core propaganda.

He muttered a command for them to stay and stepped outside to talk to the soldier who brought them in.

"Is this a joke, Lieutenant? I'm not much for humor these days," he said, pulling out a cigarette he had bought before duties that morning. The soldier averted his eyes as Sebbs lit up and blew a ring of smoke up toward the vents. Core regulations strictly forbade any activity that could impair their health, but most of Sebbs's subordinates knew not to challenge him, especially when he was in a bad mood.

"I received orders from Major Calcucci to pick them up during their shift today. Here is the report if you would like to read it, Sir," the soldier said, handing Sebbs a datapad.

Another personal message. Sebbs drew an irritated breath, and typed in his code. A note from Calcucci was either a matter of trivial importance, meaning more menial work for him, or an issue regarding his work ethic.

Captain, the note read, *these children are to be given a Priority Level 5. Test them by standard protocol and the new PCB. Notify me immediately of the results.*

Sebbs took a long drag and extinguished the cigarette on his boot. Why would Calcucci give Sebbs such a serious task? After his demotion and reassignment to the slums of Fiorah, his usual tasks required strict supervision by an operations officer and had never involved any assignment of consequence.

He muttered curses in his native tongue as he handed the datapad back to the soldier. The screen turned blank, orders erasing themselves as soon as it left his hands. This was surely a joke, a wild goose chase to prevent him from getting drunk that night.

When he reentered the class, he nearly tripped over the three new children. Still standing where he had left them, they ignored the video blaring its grand finale and studied the other children. Did they know none of them stood a chance? Had they seen through the careful editing to uncover the hoax that had drawn him in so long ago? Perhaps they saw that the Dominion did not want them to become part of their great officers' corps, only to turn their heads the other way.

One of the girls turned to examine Sebbs, the light from the hallway illuminating her face. Though nothing about her words or manner seemed rude, her eyes bespoke obstinance.

31

"We're grateful to be here, Sir," the girl said in Common, her thick Fiorahian accent grinding against the vowels. "Working the decks has been hard."

I didn't think laborers in her condition could learn the language of the Starways. Who are these three?

Looking closer, Sebbs couldn't help but notice her eyes. Brilliant green irises, haloed around dilated pupils, defied her pale and scrawny body.

Sebbs hid his curiosity with a scowl. *Deck work is for colonists with mechanical inclinations, not little children. They probably clean and install parts under the strict guidance of an adult.*

The little girl looked him up and down. "We did some duct work on the older drill rigs, but now we're doing engine repair."

Did she just read my mind?

"We do work with an adult," she continued. "Our *Pao* actually, but he just makes sure we don't get caught in the spindles. We've put in seventeen-hour days for weeks now with the second-class mining ships."

Pao, Sebbs thought, rolling the Fiorahian word over in his mind. He remembered hearing the term during the cultural briefings. One of the instructors had said that the closest Starways equivalent was "uncle," but Sebbs had heard the real definition on the streets. The launnies—street rats—mostly used it as a term of affection for a foster or adoptive parent, but the Underground definition equated to "rat keeper."

Sebbs sighed. "Fine. You can flip a few switches and hammer some nails. Can you even spell your name?"

"We can read and write in both Fiorahian and Starways Common, although some words, like *Pao*, don't really translate right, so sometimes we don't use them," the other girl explained, assuming a less abrasive tone than her sister. "We also know a little math and science, and whatever else our uncle could teach us."

What I wouldn't give for another cigarette right now, Sebbs thought, flitting his eyes away from their gaze. Though sizeably bigger than the lot of them, he found the children's self-possession strangely unsettling. *It's like their eyes are cutting right through me.*

"Seat yourself in the back," Sebbs grunted as the video came to a close.

He rattled off his scripted speech, inserting a few brief anecdotes he learned from his recruitment officer, and then finished in his most heroic voice.

"The hour of battle is upon us. Will you take up arms against evil and injustice? Will you defend your family, your people, against the Dissembler threat? Do you have the courage to raise your right hand and take the military oath to become the heroes and the leaders of this galaxy? Testing will begin tomorrow, so go home tonight and make sure to get some rest. Long live the Sovereignty."

The last line almost made him vomit.

When the other children had been escorted to their shuttles by attending soldiers, Sebbs turned his attention to Calcucci's mangy recruits. He took a quick glance at the digital readout on his sleeve: only three hours until the bars opened. He hated the thought of missing opening hour.

Irate, Sebbs yanked out the testing datapads from the filing cabinet and tossed them at the kids. "These tests are designed to measure natural intelligence, not acquired intelligence, to give those with no formal schooling a *slight* chance. You have six hours to complete the test; God knows if you'll even be done with the first section. Keep your answers to yourselves. I have you on video anyway," Sebbs said, pointing to the red light on each of the datapads. The cameras, designed to track the pupils of the student, alarmed if their gazes strayed outside the designated field.

"Questions?" They looked back at him with confidence, sitting straight-backed in their chairs, the datapads propped on their thighs.

"What will happen to us after we take this test?" the boy asked, voice raspy and strained. Sebbs hoped he wouldn't have to have another series of shots after having come in contact with him.

"You'll probably go back to playtime on your mining ships, so let's begin, okay?" Sebbs went around to each child and pressed the initiation button on the datapad.

With furrowed brows they fumbled with the keypads and holographic interface. He hadn't been fair by not going through the mechanics of the datapads with them, but he figured if their abilities interested Calcucci they'd be able to figure it out for themselves.

Quivering hands warned of impending sobriety. *Time for another hit.*

33

Ever since his back injury, he'd become secretly addicted to painkillers. He could have prevented it, but he found that a chemical romance took a little of the edge off his dismal life. Though the Dominion pharmaceuticals had cut off his supply of methocaine, the drug flowed freely in Fiorah's black market, and selling the information he had accumulated about the Core gave him a lot of bargaining power. In the last few months he'd landed himself enough methoc to live the rest of his life in a blissful haze.

He hadn't always been like this. Decades ago, his test scores indicated limitless possibilities, and he bought into the idea that his future had purpose, that he could make something of himself.

Not anymore, he seethed. Stripped of any control, the Dominion valued his willingness to perform every order over all else. Between the things he had seen and the information he had acquired about the silent movement within the Dominion, he realized that a future—any sort of future—was becoming less and less likely.

Wish I could just—

Turning his back to the kids, Sebbs removed the booster stashed in the inner sleeve of his uniform. He gave himself a quick prick and didn't hold back his exhalation of relief.

Drifting peacefully in and out of reality, Sebbs misjudged the passage of time. When the children set the datapads on his desk and left, he hardly noticed. He did however, snap to when a soldier leaned into his face.

"Are you alright, Sir?"

He fumbled with some papers in front of him, trying to make his jittery eyes refocus. Straining to see through the yellow haze, he noted the time on his sleeve: Only an hour and fifteen minutes had gone by, and he had taken enough of a hit to last him three.

Sebbs concentrated on every word that came out of his mouth. "Excuse yourself, soldier!" The soldier hesitated but eventually left, shutting the door behind him.

After a few steadying breaths, Sebbs stumbled over to the data processing port and downloaded the test answers. Within seconds the computer had analyzed the results and organized them in several different comparative modes: individually, to the current year's test-takers' scores, and to the rest of the Core scores.

Chak—*how much methoc did I take?* Sebbs thought, looking over the maxed-out scores. He couldn't help but laugh at the

34

unlikeliness of it all: Out in the farthest, dirtiest corner of the universe, he had discovered three Sentients of remarkable capabilities.

Gods, he thought, scrolling down the triplets' submissions. *They answered a lot of these questions just like I did on my entrance exam—*

Before Sebbs could put any more thought to it, Calcucci's scowling face appeared on the prompter.

"Sebbs!" he barked, "I want you to answer me honestly. If you don't, I'll make sure you end up on the Labor Locks of Plaly IV."

Sebbs took a step back. "Yes, Major."

"Are these test results accurate? Did you or anyone else manipulate these in any way?"

"No, Sir, I was with them the whole time. You can see for yourself on the cameras that they didn't have any help. But how did you get the results, Sir?"

"I patched into the network before you started to make sure it all went smoothly. Well, I'll be damned, Mantri—I guess the old fool was right! How about that."

"Sir?" Sebbs asked, trying to keep his gaze fixed on the display console as the room spun away.

"This morning some old rube claiming to be Yahmen Drachsi's brother came to me about those three kids. Claimed he bought them from the Underground flesh auctions about five years ago. He says they were orphans from some distant part of the galaxy or some *gorsh-shit* like that, and that they were brilliant—able to work the decks of the mining ships. The old man said if they hadn't been so smart Yahmen would have killed him and sold the kids to a harvester—something about a debt, but he didn't elaborate, and I didn't much care to know. I almost iced his *assino*, but for amusement's sake I thought I'd send them to you first."

The captain couldn't tell through the methoc haze if the major was being facetious or not. Instead he just nodded and waited for the major to continue.

"What's your impression of them, Mantri?" the major asked, crossing his hands behind his head. An amused grin plastered itself across his chubby yellow face. Sebbs couldn't help but look away; even with the numbing power of the methoc he couldn't stand the sight of the fat Jubon.

35

"They all have character, but they'll need to be broken in. Kind of a mangy, defiant little trio. I guess you'll be in well with the Sovereign now, Sir, after this kind of a find."

"Are you kidding? This will get me promoted and off babysitter duty. You'll have to find someone else to be chained to," Calcucci said with a long, hoarse laugh that made his belly jiggle. Sebbs felt his face flush, but the methocaine made it seem like a distant problem.

Calcucci continued, "I'll alert the Dominion Court to my find and have more orders for you. Make sure you intercept the children before their shift tomorrow. If we can piss off Yahmen Drachsi, it'll only make it that much easier to arrest him. The Sovereign will thank me for creating such a delightful opportunity. If you're lucky, I might mention your part in this. Maybe you'll be able to get a starpost somewhere—say, in the Varlous cluster?"

With that Calcucci broke into laughter again. Sebbs said nothing. He was just thankful that the fat Jubon was so excited about *his* find that he didn't notice Sebbs' methoc trip.

Sebbs signed off the terminal, swept the datapads into his briefcase, and scampered off to the sanctuary of the Underground bars.

***

The three siblings took shelter underneath the cooling unit of the old ore refinery as they waited for the midday heat to pass. The condemned structure had been converted into the base of operations for the Dominion, but the cooling unit was the same one the refinery had once employed. Whoever had been assigned to fix it had made a half-hearted attempt, enabling Jetta to peel back the protective covering and expose the cooling panel underneath. They alternated pressing different body parts against the panel as the suns reached their zenith, boiling the slabs of canted cement and red rock.

"That was weird," Jaeia mumbled, pressing her face up against the cool metal. Beads of condensation dripped down her cheek and neck, staining her shirt.

"Do you think it was a mistake to take that exam?" Jetta said. She didn't mean to sound defensive, but it came through in her tone anyway. Things had happened so suddenly, and decisions had to be made. Now she second-guessed herself.

"It's another option, I guess," Jaeia replied.

Jetta looked to her brother. His blue eyes focused on something beyond the planet's red-rock surface.

"What do you think, Jahx?" Jetta asked.

Jahx seemed bewildered by the question. "I... I don't know."

Jaeia looked at her, sharing her thoughts privately.

"Well," Jetta said, choosing her words carefully, "I hope we did well enough. We could use another escape plan if this one doesn't work, yeah?"

"Let's not count on it, okay? Fiorah I understand, dog-soldiers I understand. The Dominion..." Jaeia said, trailing off. "There are some strange politics these days."

"Yeah," Jetta muttered. The arrest she'd seen from the bus played out in her head again. She knew taking the exam wasn't a perfect solution, but it had gotten them out of work and it gave them an alternate escape route. Besides, when the Dominion officers showed up at their workplace armed with guns and official request documents, it's not like they had the option to refuse.

But by Jahx's silence, she knew that it was somehow wrong. He was only like this when he had a premonition, when he knew something big was about to happen.

Jetta hitched the twine a little tighter around her waist to keep her belly from whining.

"Whatever happens, we always get through it, right?" She took both Jaeia's and Jahx's hands in hers. "The Dominion can't be any worse than Yahmen. Besides, if we don't flaunt our talent, nothing bad'll happen. Those others weren't as smart as us—they slipped up."

Jaeia smiled weakly. Jahx was no longer paying any attention.

"You're right Jetta," her sister said, sounding as confident as she could. "It'll be okay."

***

"Jetta..." whispered Jahx.

Jetta strained to move the junkie out of the way, but she barely managed to lift his arm. He stank like ammonia and old vomit, and his eyes rolled around in his head like loose marbles.

"Sweet flavor, they say. Sweet, sweet Sapphire. Sweetness," were the only words either of them could make out as the junkie babbled to himself.

I don't have time for this. In a little while, more junkies would stumble into their apartment complex before the second big heat arrived. With a grunt she shoved harder, moving him just enough that she could see the crack in the corridor wall that exposed the third floor plumbing.

"Jetta," Jahx repeated, covering his nose.

Jetta removed a soda can from her trouser pocket and held it under the water trickling from the broken pipe.

"What?" she whispered back. Yahmen's watchdogs enforcing their house arrest were making their usual illegal transactions in the alleyway. Their five minutes of freedom were nearly up.

"Do you ever just know when something is going to happen?" her brother asked, looking at her sadly. Jetta stopped what she was doing and looked down the broken stairwell. Even over the shouting and clamor from the other units, she could sense the guards were still preoccupied with their deal.

"Sometimes. But it's because I've seen it happen before. A pattern," she said, offering him the first sip. He shook his head and tugged at the curl of hair on the nape of his neck.

"I know that Yahmen will kill me."

Jetta couldn't find her voice. Her brother had always been the idealist, the one who saw the good in any situation, in every person. But now when she looked into his eyes, she realized he knew something terrible.

"I would never let that happen," she said, taking his hand. Anger tightened her stomach and heated her muscles. Didn't he know that she would always protect him? That her siblings' lives meant more to her than her own?

He looked away with troubled eyes. "Promise me that you'll never put my life before yours and Jaeia's."

"Jahx—" she protested, standing so abruptly that she upset the soda can, spilling their polluted treasure. The front door slammed shut, and the guards' banter became audible in the foyer.

"Jetta," he whispered. "Please."

A lump swelled in Jetta's throat. She took his hand and said nothing.

As they crept back into the relative safety of their apartment, she felt that despite her tight grip she was somehow losing hold of her brother.

***

"Come on, Jahx," Jetta said, gathering up the rock dice off the floor and shaking them in up in her hands. "One more game."

Jahx yawned and started to take apart the fort they had made from their cots. "No. I beat you five times already. Why don't you ask Jaeia to play?"

"She hates our made-up game."

"No she doesn't," Jahx said, righting his cot and crawling on top. He brought up his knees to his chest and closed his eyes. "Besides, she could use a distraction right now."

Tilting her head to the side, Jetta searched for her sister's presence within the apartment. The kitchen and living room felt empty, but within the single bedroom came a steady thrum of pain and sadness.

"Go to her," Jahx said.

Jetta left her brother in the hallway and hurried to Galm and Lohien's bedroom. She found her sister sitting on the edge of the bare mattress, clinging to the only remaining picture of their aunt.

"Hey," Jetta said, walking over and hugging her sister. "I miss Aunt Lohien, too."

"I'm sorry, Jetta," Jaeia said, drying her eyes with her shirt and setting the picture back on the cement block serving as a table. "When uncle Galm leaves, it just makes it harder."

Jetta smoothed back her sister's hair and bit her tongue. It wasn't often, but Galm sometimes left them alone at night, claiming he was going out shopping for food. None of them really knew what he did, only that he returned with more cuts and bruises than when he left, and occasionally a bag of soggy vegetables or dried-up meat. Still, who left three five-year-olds by themselves?

He's desperate, she thought. *Or he knows we're not like other kids.*

Jetta stopped herself right there. Nobody could know what she and her siblings were capable of, not even their parents. *It's too dangerous.*

"Want me to make up a story?" Jetta asked.

Jaeia perked up a little, a smile nudging itself across her face. "Can you finish the one about the three kids escaping the monster's castle?"

"Haha, okay," Jetta said, taking her sister's hand to lead her back to their makeshift bedroom in the hallway.

I don't want to sleep in the hallway anymore. It's hot and cramped.

Jetta picked up her sister's thought, and shared the sentiment. *I know, but it's the best way to access the main vent without having to sneak around the apartment*

Shared worry resonated between them as they left the greatest risk unspoken. Sleeping in the hallway meant no time to hide, no chance to run, when unwanted visitors came crashing through the front door.

"Yahmen," Jaeia whispered, stopping in her tracks in the middle of the living room.

Yeah, I know. Let's think about something else, okay? Jetta replied. Fatigued and numbed to the countless drunks and junkies littering the outside corridors, Jetta didn't distinguish one intoxicated mind from the next until she sensed her sister's fear.

"Jetta—run!" Jaeia screamed.

The sound of cracking plastic shot through the apartment. Running to the hallway, Jetta turned the corner to see Yahmen tearing the door from its hinges. The bent door clattered to the tile, the low hallway light revealing his colossal figure.

Jahx!

No barriers, no protection lay between Yahmen and her brother. Jahx, too frightened to move, lay in a fetal position in his cot, breath caught in his chest.

No time to think. Jetta ran at Yahmen, smacking into his thighs, battering him with her fists. He grunted and hoisted her up by the collar.

"Oh, you got some fight in you tonight, eh?" he sneered. His breath reeked of booze, and she tried to wriggle away, but he only firmed his grip until she gagged for breath. "Good," he said, "I could use a fight."

Jetta pulled at her collar, trying to relieve the pressure against her throat, wildly kicking at his body to gain any kind of purchase.

"You have no idea," he slurred. "I am teaching you discipline. I am showing you what the real world is like. You should thank me!"

One of her kicks landed squarely on his chin, and he dropped her with a yelp. Jetta scrambled away, grabbing her brother and sister and pulling them into the living room.

"Hide!" she said, standing in the doorway between the hallway and living room.

"No, Jetta!" Jaeia protested. "Hide with us!"

Knocking the breath from her, Yahmen bulldozed through and snatched up both of her siblings.

With a savage smile, he delivered his retribution for the kick: "Choose one of them."

Pinned under his arms, Jaeia and Jahx cried out, only to have him squeeze them tighter.

Not again. Yahmen loved to make her choose her brother or sister to suffer his abuse, but he had never been this drunk before.

"Choose," he growled. "Or I'm selling the three of you to the flesh farms tomorrow morning!"

Jetta, please, choose me! Jaeia sobbed across their bond.

No, Jetta, choose me! Jahx argued.

"No," Jetta said aloud, picking herself up off of the ground. *Just let me use my talent—*

Yahmen stumbled, nearly cracking her sister's head into the wall. "You know you're nothing," he hissed at Jetta. "Your streetwalker mother begged me to take you in, said she couldn't stand the sight of your ugly faces."

Heat built upon heat behind her eyes and in her chest. Jetta shook, her fingers slowly curling into her palms.

"Look at you!" he laughed. "What the hell do you think you're going to do? You're weak—you're pathetic!"

Jetta, no! Jahx screamed, staking down her fury with panic. *You can't use your talents—you'll go too far!*

Yahmen didn't give her any time to counteract her brother's telepathic block. He dropped Jaeia and concentrated his malice on Jahx, wrapping his rough hands around her brother's neck.

41

He always chose Jahx first. Always. A dark stain formed around her brother's crotch, and Yahmen cackled. "Boy, you should thank me for this."

The blood drained from Jetta's face, adrenaline washing away her fear. Her siblings might be able to stop her from using her talent against him, but they couldn't stop *her*.

"Me, you want *me*!" she screamed, leaping at Yahmen and sinking her teeth into his calf.

Jetta! Jaeia cried across their bond, pulling at her feet to try and break her away. *Please, let go! He's going to kill you!*

Yahmen released Jahx, and her brother's tiny body collapsed on the floor in a heap.

You don't have to do this, Jetta, Jahx whispered, reaching to her as Yahmen removed his belt and grabbed Jetta by the hair. *You can't always be in his way—*

As Yahmen lifted his belt she whispered aloud, "For you, Jahx. I hope you'll understand."

***

"Come here, you little *ratchakker!*" Yahmen screamed as he chased Jetta around the living room, lashing her with his belt.

I've never seen him this out of control, Jahx thought as Jaeia wrapped herself around his leg, sobbing uncontrollably.

He won't stop, Jahx realized. Yahmen threw a lamp against the wall, eyes ablaze. *I have to do something.*

(I have to go into his head.)

Jahx cringed at the thought. Delving into Yahmen's mind meant not only weathering the rage and navigating through the murk of alcohol, but facing the dark undercurrents of his psyche.

Even passed out he's dangerous, Jahx thought, remembering his brush with death a few months ago. *I don't want to get lost in the trenches of his mind.*

Scooting out of the way, Jahx shielded Jaeia as Yahmen kicked over the armchair to grab at their sister. He couldn't be afraid now. Jetta's life—all their lives—depended on his ability to reach inside their owner. If he could connect with Yahmen, he could find the reason for their torment, and temper their owner's wrath.

And not resort to murder, he thought, feeling his sister's survival instincts overtaking rational thought. Jetta's secret power, drawn from a place of pain and terror, was vast in its scope and untamable when accessed. *Killing Yahmen would only be the start.*

Jetta crawled under the couch to protect herself, but their owner yanked her out and held her down with his boot, exposing her neck and upper back. The rhythmic blows from Yahmen's belt reverberated off the bare walls and drowned out the shouts of the arguing couple next door. Jetta's mouth formed a scream she held back as beads of her blood splattered the cement.

Because Jetta would not cry out, Yahmen hit her harder. "I want to hear you scream, launnie!" he roared.

Jaeia clutched his arm. "Do something, Jahx—before she does."

Jahx felt it too, the spreading shadow in Jetta's mind, the dark whisperings that became a seductive chant: *(Yahmen is weak, you are powerful. Take what is yours. Take his flesh. Take his mind. Take his soul.)*

He didn't know where such impulses came from; he refused to believe they originated from within his sister.

"Help me," he whispered back, sharing his idea with Jaeia through their telepathic bond.

"Not that way, Jahx—it's too dangerous!"

"Jaeia—we have to," he said, flinching as Yahmen kicked Jetta in the ribs. His sister's pain shrieked out across the psionic bonds. Green eyes narrowed, teeth bared. Jahx grimaced, tasting the copper of his sister's bloodlust. "Or we'll lose Jetta."

"Okay," Jaeia whispered. "But please, Jahx—you have to be careful."

Jahx tried to steady himself as sweat crawled down his neck and back. To go in now would mean sharing Yahmen's pleasure in hurting his sister, but he couldn't afford to think of all the reasons not to go.

(I'm afraid.) Jahx looked down at his soiled pants and flushed. He pressed his fists against his belly to keep himself from throwing up.

What if he feels you digging in his head? Jaeia pleaded as Jahx stretched out his mind.

He won't—he's too drunk. Please, Jaeia, you have to trust me.

43

Jaeia's worry persisted in his head, but she didn't try to stop him as Yahmen took another swig from his bottle. Rolling onto her stomach, Jetta's face suffused with blood, eyes portending brutal intent.

"Oh, little launnie," Yahmen chuckled, wrapping his belt around his fist. "You look like you're ready for round two."

Hold onto me, Jaeia, he called silently, rising to his feet.

Arms wrapped around his legs. *I won't let go!*

With Jaeia as his anchor, Jahx tore through the superficial layers of their owner's thoughts. Sifting through unmitigated anger was a daily chore on Fiorah, but being in this deep meant saturating himself in Yahmen's obsessive rage, and he couldn't prevent the backwash. His heart raced, and he bit back a snarl.

Jahx tried to fight back, to remind himself of who he was and who he was trying to save, but Yahmen's thoughts dominated his mind, their perversity intoxicating his senses.

I like the feel of tender pink flesh splitting apart, *Jahx heard himself say.* Alcohol warms my muscles, makes me feel stronger than I could have ever imagined.

Wait, *Jahx cried, trying keep hold of himself.* Is it Yahmen—or me—beating Jetta?

Any concern, any moral sense, twisted into the pure, raw pleasure of leather cracking against skin. He had never known that disciplining the weak could satisfy him so well, or how his ugly hands could become such beautiful vessels of pain and punishment.

Jahx no longer felt his own body or the pull of his conscience. I will finish her—

When he had all but given in to his new self-image, Jaeia called to him.

(Jahx!)

Memories, shared across a familiar bond, poured into his mind. Laughing with his sisters under a fort made from their cots, playing rock dice until Galm reminded them to go to bed. His aunt's warmhearted smile and soft embrace. Fixing engine parts with junkyard scraps and splitting bakken with his sisters.

And he remembered him. *The ruddy monster that reeked of booze and cigarettes who stormed into their apartment in the middle of the night. With Jaeia's thoughts, he surfaced from the drowning pool of Yahmen's mind, and he remembered what his mission had been.* (I will lose myself to Yahmen if I don't leave now.)

The shock of pulling his mind out abruptly threw him backward, taking Jaeia down with him. Vision swinging sickeningly, Jahx clung to his sister as he reoriented back into his own body.

I almost lost myself in Yahmen. Oh Gods, Jahx thought, horrified. He covered his mouth to keep back a scream. *I almost killed my sister!*

"What are you two doing?" slurred Yahmen. He stumbled over, dragging his belt along the ground. "Do you want a lesson, too?"

Jaeia's fingers dug into his chest as Yahmen tripped over the armchair and lost hold of his booze. The brown bottle shattered against the wall, spraying them with alcohol and glass. Closing his eyes, Jahx prepared for the blow. It never came.

With his heart thumping in his ears, he slowly opened his eyes to see Yahmen sprawled facedown across the carpet. His breathed loudly, snorting and mumbling, but appeared passed out.

"Jetta," Jahx whispered. Careful not to wake their owner, he crawled over to her. She didn't open her eyes, but when he put his hand on her forearm, she smiled.

"It's okay. It's not as bad as it looks."

Jahx felt the distant pain of her wounds, and the inner wall she had constructed to keep him from experiencing its full breadth. He didn't understand her unwillingness to let any of it be shared. "Thank you, Jetta."

Jetta's breath came in quick and shallow gulps. *Her body will survive, but I don't know about the rest of her,* he thought to himself, a chill running up his spine. He had heard and felt the dark pull of her secret talent before, but it had never been this fierce.

Joining him by Jetta's side, Jaeia helped dab the blood off their sister's back with the ends of her sleeves. *This is worse than it looks,* he heard Jaeia think.

"Jahx... if only you would let me. This could all be over with," Jetta whispered. "I could kill him now. We could just plug his nose and cover his mouth..."

The offer tempted him. *No more Yahmen. A chance to be a family again. I wouldn't have to be afraid anymore.*

Jahx hid his trembling hands underneath his knees and swallowed hard to keep the contents of his stomach down. He'd gone farther than he had ever before in Yahmen's mind, and it had only deepened his fright. However, he couldn't give up hope, in himself, or in others.

It's all I have.

"No, Jetta, we can't. There would be investigations; we'd draw attention to ourselves. And more importantly," he added softly, "we don't want to become a monster like him."

Jahx could tell she wanted to yell at him by the way her fist flexed, but she wouldn't risk waking Yahmen.

"There are evil people, Jahx; why can't you just accept that?" Her breath came faster now, and she squirmed onto her side. "We can kill Yahmen and be done with this—we can save our aunt and uncle and be free!"

"Jetta..." Jaeia whispered, placing her hand on her leg.

Jetta's eyes narrowed and she grabbed on to his wrist. "You're the one that's keeping us back. Even if you're right, that doesn't mean everybody's worth saving."

Jahx hung his head. *She can't be right—can she?*

A gentle hand lifted his chin. Grey eyes met his. *Don't give up, Jahx. On anyone.*

Thanks, Jaeia.

Closing his eyes, he helped Jaeia wade her way through Jetta's frustration, diffusing tensions with comforting memories:

The three of them crowding Galm's lap as he read them a bedtime story. Jetta and Jaeia playing with Lohien's hair, not appreciating their aunt's patience as they argued about how to style it.

In pain and too tired to fight their efforts, Jetta surrendered, tears brimming her eyes.

"I'm sorry, Jetta," Jahx said, carefully hugging her. He so desperately wanted her to understand.

She traced the tattoo on her inner arm. "Me too."

***

Two of Yahmen's watchmen appeared an hour later, searching for their boss. Yahmen, still fast asleep, snored loudly as they dragged him out of the apartment by the armpits. They gave no notice to the broken furniture or blood painting the carpet and walls.

Jaeia watched behind the safety of bedroom door. Her brother, too distraught, sat on the bare mattress, picking at the menagerie of patchwork holding the bed together.

"Jaeia, we need to talk," Jahx whispered, pulling up his knees to his chest. Jaeia scooted next to her brother, crossing her arms and leaning against him.

"Yes, I know," she whispered back.

"No, you don't."

"We told her not to go tonight. We can't make her listen, Jahx."

Jaeia peered over at the vent grate in the corner and shook her head. Despite her injuries, Jetta had insisted on continuing their nightly mapping mission.

"She thinks she has to take on everything and everybody herself," he said.

He didn't have to say anything else. She knew it too. Jetta was very different than the two of them. Stubborn and headstrong, she tried to keep her feelings locked away, but hers burned the fiercest of all. And she could never forgive anyone, especially herself.

"That's why we're here, remember?" she smiled.

Jahx nodded but still seemed troubled.

"What is it?" Jaeia asked, unwrapping herself and facing him squarely. She strained to sense his emotions, to see his thoughts, but he stared intensely at the vent grate, holding himself beyond her reach.

"She's not as strong as she thinks. Always keep her in your sight, or at least in your thoughts. Be her anchor. Do it for all of us, but especially for me, okay?"

"Of course, Jahx," she replied, kissing his cheek. She didn't understand his anxiety. At that moment, all she could think of was their uncertain future and their sister, who was about to cross into one of the darkest corners of the Fiorahian Underground.

***

The metal duct squeezed the breath from her lungs as Jetta desperately wiggled around a sharp juncture. Her struggle through the angled turn scraped the skin from her chest, but the pain barely registered. Most of her attention wrapped around the argument with her sister. Jaeia had wanted her to stay and tend to her wounds, but tonight proved they needed to get out now, at all costs. There was no time for coddling, especially after what Jahx had said the last time they had collected water together.

"I know that Yahmen will kill me."

His words echoed in her head, spurring her on, even though the shaft only got smaller. The walls smashed her from every side, squeezing her shoulders together, making it harder and harder to squirm forward.

Not too much further. The slatted vent covering lay just ahead. The smell of smoke and booze wafted into the air duct, and the telltale bar sounds of banter and metalcore music vibrated the walls.

Jetta bit back a sob. Yahmen had been drunk enough that his kick to her ribs hadn't been full force, but the crushing struggle through the vents ignited fresh agony.

Fear pushed aside pain. *I can't fail my brother and sister.*

Arms pinned to her sides, Jetta could not take in a real breath. Smaller and smaller gasps left her lungs screaming for air as tiny points of light obscured her vision.

Come back, Jetta, her brother and sister called out. *Please—you don't have to do this.*

Her one free hand fumbled with the rusted latch of the vent cover. Through the slats she could see the scene below. The barkeep yelled at the bouncers to remove a drunk patron while a busty waitresses passed out shots to a rowdy circle of mercenaries.

Can't breathe can't breathe can't breathe—

The vent covering fell off, into the bar. Not caring where she fell, even if it was right in the lap of a flesh-eating Toork, Jetta struggled frantically through the tight opening.

—I can't fail them—

She didn't feel the fall.

***

Reht Jagger, dog-soldier captain of the *Wraith*, licked his long incisors and took a swig of his brew. Scanning the Fiorahian bar, he couldn't help but notice the increased patronage. *That means the Core is shutting down more Underground hideouts.*

"Why the hell do they want this stink-hole anyway? It's the one decent place left in the galaxy," Reht muttered under his breath, sloshing his drink around his mug to the thundering beat of whatever metalcore band blasted over the speakers.

The joint was just how he liked it: seedy and rough, full of outerworlders and Sentients banished from regulated space. Even with the Core crackdown, it proved a decent place for business. Not a single cop or narc in the bunch. Besides, most deals that went on in the sublevels made his illegal weapons trade look like child's play.

How Mantri Sebbs, "the Jittery Joliak," got down to the bar without getting beaten or killed still amazed Reht. The *ratchakker* never even changed out of his uniform. Then again, Sebbs dealt within the ranks of the Dominion Core.

Even the rats can smell their own kind, Reht thought as Sebbs fumbled with his drink and continued his jabbering.

"No, no, really! I'm telling you the truth. They were no older than five. Identical girls and a boy—triplets. Brilliant. Look, I wouldn't believe me either..." Sebbs said, staring into his drink.

Reht sighed. Sebbs had spent the last half hour trying to convince him that some wild story about "genius launnies"—a laughable contradiction—was worth a trade for methoc. No one else took the bait either. His first mate, Mom, and Bacthar, the crew surgeon, sat with him in the alcove, listening to Sebbs' intoxicated drivel, looking perturbed.

"Why did I come here?" Tech mumbled into his drink, getting up from the table. Reht didn't bother to keep his nervous engineer from pacing just outside their alcove. The poor guy never felt comfortable around any other company than machinery.

Bored, Reht mindlessly picked at the bandages covering his scarred hands and looked around for the other members of his crew. Diawn, stationed in another corner, had already shed about half of her clothing trying to seduce a Froanan porter into a hot deal on the new phase inversion weapons system. Reht spotted Ro and Cray at the bar, gathering information and securing the allegiances they would need on their next run.

My Gods, those bastards are actually working, he laughed to himself.

"What do you think Billy Don't and Vaughn are up to?" he whispered to Mom.

His first mate growled, unappreciative of the tease. Leaving the unwelcomed crew members back on the ship without a chaperone was not Mom's first choice.

"Come on," Reht joked. "How much fun could a rehabilitated ex-con and pre-pubescent Liiker have in a dirty, sublevel Fiorahian bar?"

"Probably more fun than we're having," Bacthar sighed.

With a chuckle, Reht turned his attention back to Sebbs. "If Di didn't acquire us such fine upgrades this trip would be hardly worth it. Tell me you have something worth hearing or I'm postponing your shipment."

Sebbs' eyebrows shot up and lips peeled over stained teeth; Reht placed his hand over his gun. The Dominion officer was normally a bit edgy, especially when he was low on hits, but this was abnormal even for him.

"Oh, Gods—those launnies—if they fit the profile the senior officers have been talking about, we're *chakked*. What if this starts a new war?" Sebbs mumbled.

That got Reht's attention. "What profile? What are you talking about?"

Sebbs patted down his jacket, muttering to himself. Over the years Reht had watched the Dominion officer's personality splinter under the weight of addiction. Bright eyes blinked out, turning into wells of raw need. Sebbs used to enjoy a good hit of methoc once in a while, but now he used on a daily basis.

"Talk," Reht said, producing a booster from his pocket and pushing it across the table. Sebbs scooped it up and injected himself without hesitation.

"Jeez," Bacthar whispered, just loud enough for Reht to hear. Mom growled. None of his crew liked Sebbs, but they couldn't argue the profitability of their deals. As *chakked* up as he was, Sebbs had a knack for acquiring valuable Dominion intelligence to sell to Reht, who in turn supplied him with ample amounts of methoc.

"Start from the beginning," Reht said, shaking Sebbs' shoulder. "I want to know your source."

"General Duncan," Sebbs slurred. "I gave him a triple hit of Sapphire."

Even the thought of Sapphire made Reht shudder. He had seen plenty of flavors in his day, but nothing as viral and as toxic as the

50

Sweetness. Nobody could trace the rare drug's origins, but it was rumored that several Core officers were associated with its distribution.

"Ahh, good ol' Duncan," Reht chortled. "I didn't know the old bastard loved to party."

Sebbs shook his head. "No, that's not why he takes it. That not why any of the officers take it." The Joliak leaned forward, bloodshot eyes about to pop from their sockets. "Sapphire calms you down. It makes you not care."

Bacthar perked up, his giant wings scraping the top of the alcove. "A disinhibitor?"

Sebbs snapped his fingers. "Yes! The officers love it. Takes the edge off during combat."

"So?" Reht said. "You gave Duncan a loaded dose. Then what?"

"He told me about his orders to comb the galaxy for telepaths—and not just for Prodgies anymore," Sebbs said.

Reht shifted in his seat. Prodgies were once a revered telepathic race, with the unique ability to heal and restore almost any Sentient being no matter how severely injured or diseased. Over the years the Dominion Core had managed to shift reverence to fear by sensationalizing the Prodgy potential to Fall, or turn into a Dissembler with the power to destroy living tissue with thought. When the public had been sufficiently frightened, the Core introduced their new technological advancement: the telepathy inhibiting shock collar. The USC had nothing to match this new means of control and detainment, and Dominion gained support as the public demanded protection against the Dissembler threat.

Triel. Starfox. The Dominion is coming for you.

Reht could feel both Bacthar and Mom's eyes on him. It felt like ages since the crew had helped Triel return to her homeworld, Algar, to try and reconcile with her father. A day hadn't gone past that he didn't think of her. No woman had ever had such sway over him, but then again, a Healer's touch went deeper than any other.

"And?" Reht said.

"He said they're doing mass intelligence screenings on all telepaths. Like the tests I give the launnies, only he said that these were designed by somebody contracted by the Core," the Sebbs sputtered. Shaking, he reached for his drink and knocked it over.

Mom, standing up to avoid the spill, nearly took the table off its hinges.

"Sorry, Mom, sorry—" Sebbs said, cowering in his seat.

The giant blue Talian growled as he sat back down, using Sebbs's jacket—with the Joliak still in it—to mop up the mess. Sebbs didn't protest, but gave Reht a dirty look.

"Easy, Sebbs. You want to keep all your limbs, right?" Reht laughed. "So, what are they searching for? What possible connection could there be between smartass launnies and telepaths?"

"I don't know. Duncan says the orders are extremely vague, and he mostly just seeks telepaths out, imprisons them, and sends them off-world to some place I can't remember."

Reht ran a hand through the mess of platinum-blonde hair on his head and shrugged his shoulders. "You really aren't much help, Sebbs. What am I supposed to sell to the USC? That the Core wants smartass telepathic launnies? That won't buy me grandma's handbag."

"Look, that's all I know. If you had just seen them you'd get it. They were creepy. All silent, like they were talking to each other in their heads, I just know it. The Core could probably screw 'em up real bad—make them some sort of target or weapon—I don't know."

"Ahhh, Sebbs, there you go again."

"Don't *chakking* do that, Reht," Sebbs screamed. "Don't put me off! You know I'm right about these things."

Reht raised an eyebrow at him. Baring his teeth, Mom placed both of his hands on the table.

"Sorry, Mom—really I am," Sebbs said, eyes widening as the Talian dropped his claws. "I just think this is it. If the Sovereign has a new weapon that can take down the USC, then we're *chakked*. We'll all be under the Sovereign's thumb. We'll have to register to take a *chakking* piss."

Before Reht could respond, an eruption of laughter broke out from behind the main bar. Reht ducked his head out of their alcove and saw a large group huddled underneath the airshaft where a vent grate had been pushed out from the inside.

A tiny figure wormed her way through the crowd and took off running. Without thinking, Reht jumped out of his seat and nabbed her before the horde of criminals claimed their prey.

"Awh, come on. We was just playin' with the launnie!" shouted a drunken Vreaper stumbling toward Reht, his brew tipping as he knocked into a nearby table. Several others joined in and heckled the dog-soldier captain for interrupting their fun. Reht looked down at the tiny girl furiously fighting his grip.

"Enough, already. Go back to your drinks," he said, putting a hand over the girl's mouth to muffle her screams. The bandages around his hand protected him from her bites, but he didn't think they'd hold for long.

"She looks like a squealer. Maybe this be how the Dominion's been finding our jukes!" an angry voice cried out. "They run launnies through the pipework to figure out our adaptations!"

"Let her go, Jagger," the drunken Vreaper said, moving his free hand to the gun strapped to his hip.

Mom got up and stood by Reht's side. Towering a full meter above Reht's tall frame, the Talian warrior commanded the entire bar's attention.

"I've said enough. I'll take care of this. If anybody disagrees, they can take it up with my first mate," the captain said, smiling and nodding his head toward the Talian. The crowd froze as Mom's claws protruded from his hands and forearms, transforming his upper limbs into deadly, razored weapons.

"Alright, alright—call off your dogs," the Vreaper grumbled. The rest of the crowd muttered and cursed, but returned to their drinks and previous conversations.

After making sure his Talian had adequately tempered the Fiorahian crowd, Reht wrestled the little girl back to his alcove.

"Now what have we got here?" Reht asked, setting the child down next to his chair while dodging her scratching fingers.

Is she human? Reht didn't believe his eyes. *Fiorah is no place for a Deadskin.*

Barring Dominion soldiers, Fiorah's inhabitants were a menagerie of cutthroat outerworlders with the physical capacity to withstand the planet's hostile environment—and each other.

How can she handle the heat—the pollution? he thought, looking her over as she backed up against the wall. Cuts and bruises marred her face, arms and legs. *...Or the violence.*

"Just chill, kid," Reht said, taking his seat. "I just saved your scrawny *assino*, remember?"

53

Gods, she smells like she's straight out of the gutter, Reht thought, taking a closer inspection of the dirty child. Topitrate and sweat caked her face so that only the green of her eyes shone through. Barefoot and clothed in rags, the kid looked like she had just finished a bout in the fighting rings. He assumed she was a child laborer, though he had never seen one so banged up. How she had even made it down here was beyond him.

Reht looked over to Sebbs. The Joliak had gone white.

"You alright?" Bacthar asked, jabbing Sebbs in the ribs.

"That's one of them, Reht."

The girl's eyes narrowed as she looked the officer over.

"You two know each other?" Reht said, signaling the circulating members of his crew to join them at the table. If there was even a chance that what Sebbs had been bumbling about was legitimate, he wanted his crew there to protect the asset.

"Yeah. This officer gave us an entrance exam for the Core," the tiny girl said, her eyes flashing over each of them.

What a defiant little stinker, Reht thought.

"Aren't you going to introduce us, Sebbs?" Reht asked as Tech, Ro, Cray, and Diawn joined their party in the alcove.

Sebbs remained silent and his color ghostly.

"Changing diapers at a bar, Cappy?" Ro laughed as he slouched into the chair next to Mom and Cray.

"What gives?" Diawn said, glowering at the kid as she passed her by and sat on the other side of table with Bacthar and Tech.

"A wee one that manages to make her way into an Underground bar interests me. Especially since it looks like it was on purpose," Reht said, pointing toward the vent grate. He lit a smoke and signaled for the girl to talk.

"My name is Jetta. My siblings and I are indentured to Yahmen Drachsi. We can't survive much longer. We're looking to bargain safe passage on an outgoing ship," she said, her speech slightly rattled but deliberate.

"The street rat can talk?" Ro snickered. Jetta's brow furrowed. She inhaled and briefly closed her eyes before responding.

"The three of us can learn to do anything an adult can do, and if it weren't for size limitations, we could match any crew member on a starship. The only thing we have to trade is ourselves. Like I said, we won't survive much longer under Yahmen."

Only on Fiorah would a little kid be willing to trade her flesh for a ticket, Reht mused, taking a long drag from his cigarette to keep his conscience from weighing in.

"Yahmen Drachsi—what a *gorsh*-eating sellout. I'd love to kick that little *baech* in his lady parts," Cray said pretending to kick Ro in the crotch. Ro covered his mouth and acted faint.

"What's your problem with Drachsi?" Reht laughed. "You know he owns half this dump of a planet. And he's a bloody bastard. You're like soul mates."

Cray scowled and jabbed his thumb at the crowd. "Word's out that he's doing business with the Dominion. I don't sleep with the enemy."

"Only if she had triple tits like Veronica!" Ro laughed, spraying beer and spit across the table. Cray grabbed him by the ears and slammed his head into the table. Only Mom's intervention prevented things from escalating as he held them both by their throats until they waved their hands in submission.

Reht wiped his face and looked at the girl. She seemed shaken by their banter. He knew that Yahmen Drachsi was a vicious businessman who had a fairly nasty reputation in the Underground, but he was no different from any other scumbag he'd come across. But apparently, to this little girl, he was much, much more.

"Sweets, you're a launnie. A gutter kid. What makes you think you could handle a dog-soldier's life? Hell, do you even know what a dog-soldier is?" Reht asked, leaning back in his chair and glancing out of the alcove. Most of the bar's patrons had directed their attention toward his table, making him itch for his gun.

She took the insult well, keeping her tone in check. "Being a dog-soldier means you're a mercenary, but it's deeper than that. You have your crew, and that goes above all else, even profit sometimes. You hate organized government, military—whatever—and you're not afraid to screw over your own mother. It's Underground slang. Anybody knows that."

"Close enough. So what makes you think you could handle what we do?"

The little girl's face disclosed no answers, but her words were freighted with anger. "After surviving Yahmen for this long, I doubt there's anything we couldn't handle."

Reht studied her for a moment before checking the reactions of his crew. Diawn yawned and stretched her legs out on the table, inspecting her empty glass of ale. Bacthar completely disengaged, leaning his giant head on his arm and starting a low conversation with Mom and Tech.

A small part of Reht felt sorry for the girl. *None of them are taking this kid seriously.*

Cray shook his head. "If you came here for a pity party, you ain't gonna get it. This here is a table full of sob stories," Cray said, tipping his drink at his crew. Mom rolled his eyes. "There ain't one person here who's had the royal life, so your sad story ain't gonna twist our britches."

"That's not my point," she said calmly, though she stiffened at their indifference.

"Then what is it? Because you're making the whole bar go to jitters, and we'll off you sooner rather than later," Ro snapped, drawing a knife from his sleeve.

Reht raised a brow at her, curious to see her response.

"We already know what it's like to live life on the skids. We know all about loyalty and family because that's all we have. What don't we know about being part of a crew?"

"We ain't babysitters," Reht said. "Besides, why not just chance it with the Dominion? Probably do a lot safer under their belt than with criminals."

The girl looked at him with a careful eye.

"I'm young, but I'm not stupid. I hear what the adults say. Think I don't see the connection? The Dominion touches down and all of a sudden me and my sibs are working double shifts."

"And," she said, angling her head toward Sebbs, "I saw him dragging the other kids through Dominion propaganda *gorsh-shit.* Tell me that isn't a setup."

"Then why did you take the entrance exam?" Reht retorted, blowing a ring of smoke at her. She stifled a cough and continued.

"We never thought we'd be able to take that test 'cause of our age or 'cause of Yahmen. But we'd chance the Core over staying here if it meant regular schooling and three meals any day. Besides, you can defect or be discharged from the Core and have a chance. Defect from Yahmen and you and anyone you've ever known are iced. But still, we'd rather take our chances with you. I can't fail," she said, locking eyes with him.

"I don't know, kid. The Core ain't no playground. What if you've got talent? What then? You know they've got an unusual taste for telepaths these days. Nobody even knows what they do to 'em on the ships. They just disappear," Reht said, spreading his fingers out in her face.

Although the change in her facial expression was subtle, he caught it—the slight retraction of her lips when he said the word "telepath." *She's one of them.* The price tag on her head jumped by at least five digits.

"You think I'd put up with any of this *gorsh-shit* if I was a leech? We're just street rats—launnies—right?"

"Ahhh, girly, you can try to hide it, but the Dominion is all high-tech these days. Your talents don't have to be obvious for them to nab you. They may say they don't got a way to weed 'em out, but be sure that they do. Then they slap you with a shock collar and *bam*—you're either fried or in a freezer case."

"*Gorsh-shit,*" the little girl repeated, this time less fervently.

"Do you believe me now, Reht?" Sebbs interjected, glancing nervously at the girl.

"Yeah, I guess. So she's smart. All three of them are probably smart. What's the big deal? General Bersisa was smart and he caved an entire armada in less than two hours. Look, kid," Reht said, stabbing his smoke out on the back of his chair. "You're too hot now. If you're as smart as Sebbs says, you've already been tagged. My job is risky enough high-tailing it back and forth between Dominion and USC lines."

"But if we're taken away, there's always the chance that our Dominion superiors could find out about your private operation," she said, looking directly at Reht. Her face had gone cold and hard. "Given the number of crewmembers you have, I'd bet you're into illegal weapons transportation. I hear that will get you a lifetime on Plaly."

"Just give me the word, Jag," Ro snarled, lurching over the table and waving his knife dangerously close to the girl's face.

Without flinching, the kid kept her eyes on Reht. "You can't kill me," she said. "I'm too hot, remember?"

Reht stifled a smile. The way the launnie talked, reasoned—she was probably more intelligent than half the crewmen he had gone through in five years as captain. And her audacity was something he had never seen in a child. To risk everything crawling through kilometers of pipeline to the dregs of Fiorah took gumption, even if she was desperate or crazy.

Reht turned to Sebbs and grabbed two of the officer's fingers, twisting them backward. "Will the USC would pay hard cash for this intel?" He wanted to make sure Sebbs wouldn't lie. It's not that the Joliak did it on purpose. Sometimes the booze and drugs got the best of his mind and pain kept him focused.

"Duncan said—"

"Yeah, we went over that. Do you think they're the ones?"

"Please, Reht, my fingers—" Sebbs' eyes rolled back in his head.

What a useless assino, Reht thought, letting go of the unconscious Joliak's fingers. Whether or not to take the Dominion officer seriously would have to be a decision based on instinct. *If I'm right, stealing something so valuable to the Core will mean big profits with the USC.*

And big profits at high odds always made him smile.

Bacthar leaned over and whispered into his ear: "Hey boss—if they're really all that important to the Core, then we could hand them over to the USC. Maybe they can figure out why the Core's making such a big deal about registering or restraining all the telepaths. We could get Triel back."

My Starfox. Reht could still taste her kiss, feel his fingers brushing through her dark hair. *She won't leave Algar until the Dominion stops threatening her people. Maybe I can stop the war from happening. Then she'll come back to me.*

Agitated at Reht's noncommittal, the girl muttered something about getting back home before work call, but the dog-soldier captain caught her arm before she could duck under the table and run through their legs.

"My ship's engines never get cleaned well enough. Mom over there," Reht said, pointing to the giant Talian, "doesn't like the tight fit." The girl's eyes widened as the Talian half-raised a few of his claws and growled low in his throat.

"Maybe I could get some use out of you and your sibs. You'd have to stay outta the way and keep out of sight during our deals. I'll let Ro kill you at the first sign of trouble, yeah?" Reht cocked his head toward Ro, who tossed his knife from hand to hand. The girl nodded, her expression cautionary, as if she expected him to take it all back.

"Let me prep my ship and crew. Do you know a duct route to the old air transit station?"

"Yeah, but it's pretty far away; I've never been able to make it all the way because I always had to come back," the girl answered. "It'll take us a few hours."

"Then hurry up and get your siblings. Dustoff is in three hours," Reht said, giving her a hand up to the main deck of the bar. He walked her over to the air vent, accompanied by his crew and many shifty glares from the patrons around him. He hoisted her up to Mom, who lifted her to the edge of the open panel.

"Why do you trust me?" Reht said, his incisors gleaming in the low light of the underground bar. The girl paused before crawling inside the vent.

"I don't have a choice."

***

Despite her abilities, Jetta's couldn't easily read the dog-soldier captain. Still, she felt he would keep his word. She had sensed excitement, and something prospective leaking from his alien mind. A part of her questioned why, but hunger, pain and desperation kept her focused on the immediate victory.

No more Fiorah, she thought. *I will finally be able to see the stars...*

Even though the narrow passageway insulted her aching ribs, she breathed a sigh of relief. *It's better not to take any chances with the Dominion. I don't want to risk being sent to a telepath detainment camp—or just "disappear," like the captain said.*

As she wriggled through a complicated merging with three other air ducts, her thoughts turned to her adoptive parents.

There's a real chance me and my siblings can escape, she thought. *But what about Galm and Lohien?*

The question slid into her bones, making her shudder.

59

I can't leave them behind.

(I have to.)

Old memories percolated through the pain as she squirmed through the next juncture. Galm taking her and Jahx to the markets, holding their hands through the busy streets, making up grand stories about the odd species they happened to come across.

Lohien, tempering sweltering afternoons with her soprano song, her lithe figure always in movement, kept a watchful eye on them, even when Jetta thought her attention wandered elsewhere.

"My little warrior," Lohien said, gazing out the kitchen window. *"You are never far from my sight."*

Jetta shook her head until the memories faded back. *No, it can't be like this. I can't do it like this.*

Gritting her teeth, Jetta pushed the truth she needed to the forefront of her mind: attempting to take their crippled uncle along would only compromise their escape. He was too large for the air ducts, and Yahmen posted his personal guards outside their apartment. And Lohien—she was Yahmen's property now, caged somewhere in their owner's palace, brought out only on the rare occasion to torment Galm. Rescuing her was impossible, especially in her rapidly deteriorating condition.

The old pleas of her siblings washed up with fresh guilt: *We can't leave our parents, Jetta.*

No, Galm and Lohien are lost, she told herself, *but there is still time to save my brother and sister.* She would accept the consequences of her decision, no matter what, even though her siblings disagreed.

Jetta opened her eyes, ribs throbbing as she gazed into the dark shafts of the air ducts. *I must protect Jaeia and Jahx at all cost.*

Galm's gentle voice called out from a place within: *"Come, Jetta. Everyone needs hugs—even tough buggers like you."* The memory of his hug assaulted her; the way he wrapped his arms around her whole body, filling her with the same warm feeling that connected her to her brother and sister.

"Gorsh-shit," Jetta muttered through clenched teeth. *I don't want these feelings anymore!*

Bracing herself against the air duct, Jetta allowed her mind to fall away from the connection to her siblings. Outside their self-contained telepathic link lay the neuroelectric metropolis of Fiorah.

60

She searched for someone that would be familiar with the conflict boiling inside her, who would confuse her darkness with their own.

Jetta sank behind the eyes of someone possessed of a murderous intent. In the periphery of her senses, she felt the heaviness of his breath and tasted the burn of his cigarette as he took a long, slow drag.

"This is only half the Sapphire I paid you for, Vekry," he said, pointing his cigarette at a briefcase half-full of sparkling blue pills.

Jetta guessed from the windowless surroundings that they were in some sort of safehouse or bounty board, deep within the hidden underground network. A man tied to a chair under a flood lamp, already bloodied and bruised, struggled to free himself as her host approached him. Others, hidden in the shadows, watched his torture with hungry eyes.

"Hey—hey, put that down! Look, it's all I could get—the borders are closed off! The Core is everywhere—" Vekry pleaded.

"I'm tired of hearing you whine," her host said as he lumbered toward Vekry, spiked weapon in hand. She felt him smile, his lips retracting over jagged teeth.

"Seriously, seriously—put that away, alright?" the man tied to the chair pleaded. "You know the Core is impounding the supplies— it isn't my fault!"

"Demio," her host said, motioning to the shadows. "Get over here and help me with this. No more excuses from you, Vekry."

He lifted his arm, the weight of the weapon dangling in the air before he whipped it back down.

"No—no—please, please, PLEASE—!"

A crunching sound. Something warm and wet splashed her cheek.

Not wanting witness any more of Vekry's beating, Jetta closed her eyes, letting go of her anxiety, anger, and guilt and shoving it across the psionic plane. The assailant's mind, already swollen with bloodlust, absorbed her unwanted feelings without pause. His rage, magnified by her inner torments, only furthered his brutality.

"Hey, boss—he's had enough," Demio said, trying to take the weapon away from her host.

The attacker shoved Demio aside and brought the spiked weapon down on top of Vekry's skull.

I don't want see anymore— she thought, pulling back as pulpy yellow brain matter sprayed across the room.

When she opened her eyes, she found herself back in the air ducts, her body no longer hulking but small, hungry, and tired. The hum of the circulating air steadied her jangled nerves as she pieced herself back together. The people were gone and so were her unwanted emotions. Somewhere in the fading distance she thought she heard a man scream, though it died out as the rhythmic beat of her own pulse returned.

Her brother and sister didn't know she dumped her feelings onto others. She had learned the trick a few weeks ago by accident, resulting in a downed mining ship and an injured crew.

They would never approve.

Jetta choked down the lump in her throat, spurring herself onward through the air duct with new vigor. No, her brother and sister could never know her cowardice. They already thought her a monster for the talent she possessed.

(I am.)

"Stop it," she reprimanded herself.

Groping in the darkness, Jetta searched the metal housing for the scratches she and Jaeia had made in the unlit parts of the ducts, feeling her way through the junctures by the hash marks and arrows.

After rounding the final turn to the sub-conduit of their apartment row, she froze. A soft light glowed across the top of the vent, and she could hear voices. Usually at this hour she still had time to make it back before the lights were turned on and they dressed to leave for work.

Yahmen came back!

Jetta forgot about the pain of her ribs or the fatigue of her body. Her world narrowed into a singular craze as she frantically crawled through the last few meters of duct, scraping her shoulders and knees.

He's found Jaeia and Jahx!

Jetta gulped for air. Fear drowned out her perceptions, dampening her ability to sense her brother and sister, or anyone else. In the pit of her stomach, great and unmentionable things began to stir. The better part of her sensed danger, while ancient hungers bit into her mind and wrenched her back.

62

(Use your greatest power. Defend your siblings. Take what is yours.)

No, she thought, fighting the dark urges that longed for release. *Not yet. I have to see.*

Chest tight with panic, she poked her head out of the entryway vent and surveyed her surroundings. The light and voices came from the living room. She pushed herself out slowly, meeting the wide-eyed, nervous glances of her siblings sitting on their cots, shielding the vent grate access. She felt some relief until Jahx looked at her, face and heart full of worry. After replacing the vent cover, she crept over to them.

What's going on? Jetta asked. She could hear the voices of at least two other men besides their uncle, but she could not make out their words.

They're taking us away, Jahx replied, clutching his distended stomach.

Who?

Some Dominion officials. They're showing Galm the official order right now. We must have done something on that exam to make them want immediate acquisition, Jahx said.

The dog-soldier's warning played out in Jetta's head: *What if you've got talent? What then? You know they've got an unusual taste for telepaths these days. Nobody even knows what they do to 'em on the ships. They just disappear...*

Jetta hid her trepidation in the farthest corner of her mind away from Jaeia and Jahx. The dog-soldier captain didn't know everything. Besides, the three of them were resourceful and smart.

(This is a mistake—)

"This is good?" Jaeia asked, looking to her sister for reassurance. Jaeia knew of the danger on some level, Jetta decided. They all did. But there was no going back now. *It's up to me to lead us through it.*

Jetta couldn't stand the desperate look in her sister's eyes, but she forced herself to sound confident. "It will be."

"What about Yahmen? He owns us..." Jahx added.

"I don't know how they're doing it, but—"

A silhouette of a broad-shouldered figure appeared in the living room doorway. "Jetta, Jaeia, Jahx—congratulations, you have qualified for the Dominion Core Academy," the man said, motioning

63

for them to join him. Jetta froze, not knowing what to do. The man cleared his throat and said sharply, "Follow me."

When none of them moved, he added in a low voice: "Once you take the test you have committed yourself to the Sovereign."

Jetta probed his emotions, but his mind, tightly organized, prevented her from gleaning anything. *Why can't I read him? He's feels human—I should be able to pick his brain apart in seconds!*

Remember those telepath hunters we encountered on the mining ship a few days ago? Jaeia said. *I'm sensing the same blockade in this man's mind.*

Fear squeezed down on Jetta's heart. *(How are we going to survive without digging in our enemy's head?)*

Not wanting to alarm her brother or sister any further, Jetta continued to project assurance. *Don't worry—we'll come up with some new tricks.*

Jaeia locked eyes with her, but kept any reservations she might have had to herself. *Come on—help me with Jahx.*

Slowly they got to their feet, slinging Jahx's arms over their shoulders.

"What's wrong with him?" the man asked.

"He's been sick," Jaeia replied quietly. The man shook his head and motioned for them to follow him out of the apartment.

When they entered the corridor, Jetta saw the man they followed wore a Core high officer's uniform. Two soldiers fell in step behind them, bringing up the rear. The junkies and drunks huddled against the walls whispered and stared, but not one dared speak out.

Why aren't they heckling the military? Jetta thought. *Why are they so afraid?*

Her eye caught the smoke rising up from a junkie wadded up against the wall. As she passed by, she saw the black and red burn marks from shockwand strikes that scored the entire left side of his face and neck. The smell of burnt flesh threatened to upend the contents of her stomach.

Oh Gods—

"Wait, wait!" Galm cried out, hobbling out of the apartment as fast as he could.

The Dominion officer halted the procession and the soldiers raised their firearms.

64

No, uncle—don't do anything stupid! Jetta thought, wanting to break out of line and run to Galm. One of the soldiers eyed her and lowered the nozzle of his gun in her direction.

"Please... Please let me say goodbye," their uncle pleaded.

Jahx, voice pitched with calm entreaty, looked up at the officer. "Please."

"You have one minute," the high officer said.

When Jetta and her siblings approached Galm, he knelt painfully. He looked as if he wanted to hug each of them but was too afraid. Instead, he whispered, "Maybe this time I will do things right. I don't seem to be any good at it."

"I don't understand. Did you sign us up to take the exam?" Jetta asked.

Galm nodded, his eyes glistening. "Anything is better than this. *Anything.* Now I know you'll be taken care of—you're valuable to them," he said, squeezing each of their shoulders in turn.

When she tried to speak, Galm awkwardly grasped her hand in his. Disguising the exchange with a hearty handshake, she felt him press a folded piece of paper into her palm. In his eyes she saw regret and shame.

Is that what he's giving me?

Slowly, she withdrew her hand and let it hang at her side.

"What about you?" Jaeia whispered, gray eyes misting.

Galm forced a smile, just for them.

"Yahmen does not know of this yet, does he?" Jetta said.

Galm's eyes darted around the corridor as if he expected their owner to come crashing in at any moment. "N-no, I'm afraid they haven't informed him yet."

"This isn't right, *Pao*," Jetta protested.

"All Lohien and I ever wanted was to have a family. I am so sorry that I hurt all of you—that I could never protect you. I should have known better. Yahmen and I—what was once an old thorn between us has turned into something worse. I'm sorry you became involved."

"It's time." The officer put his hands on Jetta and Jaeia's shoulders.

"Promise me you won't come back. Not for me, not for anyone. Stay away from this place—from him," Galm whispered.

"Uncle Galm—" Jetta began, but the words she'd intended remained unspoken as the officer shuffled them away.

I can't leave him—Jaeia and Jahx are right. Even unsalvageable, she couldn't leave Galm. *Yahmen will kill him.*

Jetta tried to run to him, but the Dominion soldier clamped his hand down on her shoulder and spoke sharply: "Fall in line, cadet!"

Jetta kept her eyes on her uncle, watching as the other soldiers helped him to stand again, hoping to make their last few precious seconds stretch into an eternity. He smiled and waved at them weakly as they were hurried away.

"I'll come back—I promise!" Jetta cried out. One of the soldiers pushed her into line behind her siblings.

As she followed the officer out of the apartment complex and onto a shuttle, Jetta tucked the square piece of paper into her pocket, wondering what it could possibly be. But when the tears stung her eyes, she pushed the thought away. She couldn't afford to feel guilt and sorrow, not with an uncertain future in the Core Academy.

Any semblance of control came crashing down once she stepped off the shuttle and spotted the Dominion transport ship cycling on the launch pad. *This is really happening. What did I do?*

(I abandoned my parents.)

I don't care, she told herself, wringing her trembling hands.

A warm hand slid into hers. She looked up to see her brother's reassuring smile.

"Come on, you're not afraid of the launch, are you?"

He knows how I feel, Jetta thought, *but he's not calling me out. Why?*

"Guess I'm a little nervous," she replied, playing into the lie.

"Well, let's just make it through the countdown, okay?" Jahx said, shielding his eyes as he looked to the horizon. Through the smog and the layer of airfield glass they could see the suns and moons of Fiorah hanging low along the horizon, making the sky bleed orange and red. The roaring precycle of the transport ship's engines whipped fragments of rock and dust in their faces as they stood on the docking platform, but neither of them moved.

"I'm sorry, Jahx. I am."

Jahx hugged her, holding her as tightly as he could. "Everything will be all right."

"You're sure?"

Jahx tugged at her arm. "Let's go before Jaeia thinks we've ditched her."

"Is there a problem, cadets?" asked one of the soldiers manning the shuttle doors.

"No, Sir," Jetta replied, stepping aboard. She wanted to look back, but the doors sealed before she had a chance.

CHAPTER II

Even after the fifth day aboard the Dominion starbase, Jetta still couldn't acquiesce to the idea that there was enough food for everyone.

There are so many other cadets, she thought, scanning the mess hall packed with tables full of chattering, blue-uniformed pre-teens. Four different meal stations popped out tray after tray for scores of hungry children in a never-ending cycle. *Everyone is fed. Nobody's fighting.*

(I don't understand this world.)

"Jetta," her sister said, interrupting her thoughts as they reached their turn in line to use the food administrator. "Why do you think the teachers are so interested in our tattoos?" Out of the corner of Jetta's eye, she saw her sister's left hand automatically going to the inner part of her right arm. "One of them—Rogman—he questioned me about it for an hour."

Jetta pressed the dispense button. The scanner attached to the food administrator identified her fingerprint, and the chute dropped a prepackaged meal. The other kids complained that the food tasted funny, but neither Jetta nor her siblings cared. *This is so great.*

"I don't know. The customary defacement of unwanted offspring by Fiorahian streetwalkers must be a hot topic," Jetta replied, peeling back the plastic covering on her meal to inspect its contents. A pleasant odor of roast chicken and spices wafted up, along with a hint of something sharp, almost medicinal, reminding her of the smell of Galm's old pill bottles. She stirred the bright yellow potato mixture with her finger. *It must be the artificial additives.*

"Don't be sarcastic," Jaeia said with a frown. Her sister twisted her foot in her boot, not yet used to their rigid and confining feel. "I don't like the way they look at it."

I don't like the way they look at me, Jaeia added silently. *I can't read any of the Dominion personnel. We should be able to glean something from them, at least passively.*

To Jetta, their tattoo was a dead topic. Yahmen told them years ago that the symbol inked by their whore mother on the inner aspect of their right arms was some kind of price tag for the Underground Block. Neither Galm nor Lohien would answer anything more about the tattoo, or the triplets' origins; they just radiated shame and

69

embarrassment. That meant that for once, Yahmen told the truth, but only because it brought pain.

But the unreadable Dominion personnel is a problem, Jetta thought to herself. *How are we supposed to stay one step ahead?*

Lohien's last words to her leaked through locked-down memories: *You will find a way. You will survive.*

Yes, Jetta told herself. *I will not fail my brother and sister.*

"Look around. Almost all these chumps are from one of the Nine Homeworlds," Jetta said, waving her hand at the scores of humanoid variants. "I'm sure plain-looking, tattooed five-year-old kids from unregulated space are a lot more interesting than the privileged brats they get from the interior."

"Yeah," Jaeia said as a kid with polychromatic eyes and a prehensile tail walked by. "I guess we lack exotic flare."

"Let's catch up to Jahx," Jetta said, nudging her twin and picking up her meal.

We're coming, she projected to her brother. She reached out through their bond, feeling his frustration as he tried to find a place for them to sit in the packed mess hall.

A lot of the cadets are watching us, Jahx said as she and Jaeia joined his side.

Why? Jetta asked as they moved through the crowd.

"No one loves a rat," Jahx said, quoting part of the Fiorahian slum song.

"*Skucheka,*" Jetta muttered, sensing the surrounding tension as they directed themselves toward an open table.

"Gross—launnies!" one of the older kids said, turning around in his chair and sticking his foot out in front of Jetta.

"Be careful, Stempton," someone shouted. "They're probably diseased!"

Stempton, Jetta grumbled, hackles raising. She imprinted the face of her new enemy, from his red hair to the smear of brown freckles across his nose and cheeks. *Don't mess with me.*

"Move your foot," Jetta said.

"A launnie doesn't talk to a Crexan like that," he said, spitting dangerously close to her boots.

"Crexan?" Jetta said, rolling her eyes. Aside from mustard-colored eyes and nictitating membranes, Stempton looked like any other twelve-year-old human boy. *Who does he think he's fooling?*

Jahx's calm voice entered her head. *He's embarrassed of his human heritage, so he's targeting us because we're "lesser" humans.*

Screw the psychology, Jetta snapped at her brother. *He needs to check himself!*

"You got something to say to me, launnie?" Stempton said, rising from his seat.

Jahx grabbed her by the arm and pulled her in the other direction before she had a chance to react. *Don't even think about. We can't stick out, remember?*

"Are you kidding? If we don't establish ourselves we'll be killed," Jetta said, yanking herself away.

"That's right, just walk away, rat!" Stempton called after, rejoining his table full of cronies.

I could take him, she thought, looking back and sizing up her adversary. All of the other children at the table, including Stempton, outsized them, even the ones closer to their age. Then again, she had never been around well-nourished children before.

Jahx entered her mind, continuing to talk her down. *This is not Fiorah. There are different rules here.*

Fine. Whatever, Jetta relented, slamming her meal down on the nearest table.

Shiggla, one of the older cadet girls, turned up her nose when Jaeia took the seat next to her. "There's no room for little *launnies* here," she sneered, pushing away her sister's tray with her elbow.

Jetta hated them all. Why did they look at her with such disgust? The three of them had been on Core Starbase for less than a week, and already the other children had targeted them, even those who were in their same class level.

"Come on, let's find another table," Jahx said.

"The only thing you should find is the ejection hatch," Shiggla said, pointing her finger at Jaeia. "Since when did they let launnies from Fiorah into the Core? This is an *elite* academy, not a *chakking* shelter. I don't want some slum disease because I had to share the bunks with a Fiorahian."

"Yeah, you rotten street rats!" one of Shiggla's cronies said.

Other kids at their table joined in the haranguing, laughing and making faces:

"Scabs!"

71

"Lurchins!"

"Deadskins!"

Jetta clenched her teeth. Calling her a launnie or a street rat sparked anger, but being labeled a Deadskin boiled her blood. *I'm no fourth-class human,* she seethed.

Deadskins. The lowest of the low on the Sentient spectrum, nearly worthless if not for the price of their skin. Even if they had some remote human ancestry mixed with their telepathic bloodline, Jetta didn't think her or her siblings looked like the human detritus found in labor colonies, community projects and flesh farms.

Jahx looked at her, a warning in his eyes. *Jetta,* he called silently, *I hate it too, but we just have to let it go.*

But she couldn't. *What if Jahx is in a different class than me? What if Jaeia has to use the lavatories in the middle of the night? I have to make a stand now, before things get out of control.*

"I'll take on any one of you *passyes* right now," Jetta said, too angry to remember the Common word for "coward." She shoved her meal aside and stepped into the aisle, drawing the attention of the surrounding tables.

"Whoa!" Stempton laughed from the next table over. "Please, don't hurt me little rat! If you bite me I'll get the plague!"

This isn't right, Jaeia said across their bond as Stempton made gurgling sounds and pretended to keel over.

He's a lot stronger than you are, Jahx added. *He has too many friends, and fighting is strictly forbidden.*

Jetta didn't care. She growled, staring the Stempton down.

"Please, don't do this," Jahx whispered.

When she saw the steadfast look in her brother's eyes, her retort died in her throat. In the back of her mind she felt his stabilizing thoughts trickling in, combining with Jaeia's and diluting her anger. Unwillingly, her fists relaxed and her jaw unclenched. The realization that her brother and sister controlled her temper gave rise to one final wave of anger, but her siblings soothed the last of her tension with their own sensibilities until it became no more than a shade of resentment. A part of her knew they were right, and having sobered, she backed off.

"Go sit back down, launnie, before you mess your pants," Shiggla chuckled.

Stempton, Shiggla and their friends continued the taunts as they watched Jetta and her siblings pick up their trays and move to the table in the furthest corner of the mess hall. Jetta kept her brother and sister's presence at the forefront of her mind as food flew in their direction.

"You'll get your chance in basic training, you know," Jaeia said, wiping a noodle off her cheek.

"Won't be soon enough," Jetta mumbled, plucking a frensco leaf from her hair.

After a few minutes the other kids went back to their food and their previous conversations. Having entered the mess hall hungry, Jetta now stared at her food while her siblings ate.

Eat something, Jaeia called out to her. *You'll feel better.*

With a grumble, Jetta forked a meat cube. *I'll feel better when I can fight back.*

Listen, Jahx said, pulling her and Jaeia deeper into his head. Through his senses, Jetta eavesdropped on the conversations at Stempton's table.

"Yeah? Well, *my* dad brought twenty-two leeches into the registration office. He's a legacy now, can you believe it? No one has ever nabbed that many," Stempton said.

"Maybe he's got the 'talent,' too," somebody said.

"Hey—watch your mouth!"

"I'm just sayin'. I mean, how did he know they were leeches unless he was one himself?"

"'Cause they're weasels. If you're smart," Stempton said, tapping his head, "you can see 'em a light year away."

"Gods, I just want to see every last leech burn."

Stempton made a slicing motion across his neck. "I'd like to carve them up myself."

Jetta withdrew from her brother's mind to find that Jaeia and Jahx had stopped eating, their eyes cast downward, hearts hammering in their chests.

"I've never heard kids talk like that before," Jaeia said, fiddling with her utensils.

These aren't child laborers, Jetta shared across their bond. *They're not just concerned about day-to-day survival.*

73

No, the other recruits are something else entirely, she decided, scanning the mess hall. Behind every cream-smooth, cherub face hid a new enemy, one she had never encountered before.

"Let's go," Jahx said, taking her hand. Jetta dumped the contents of her meal into the waste disposal system. The light sensor blinked twice, processing how much she had consumed. She hated the thought of having a double-portion at the next meal to make up for this one, but at least someone actually kept them fed.

As she walked with her siblings back to their bunks, Jetta fought to keep her emotions in check. *I can't feel afraid, not when my siblings are struggling with their own fears.* She wanted to tell them she would keep them safe, but the words stuck in her throat.

"How long until we have to go to class?" Jaeia asked as Jahx pulled some datapads out of the storage unit at the end of his bunk.

"We have about fifteen minutes," Jahx said. "Want to go over this chemistry lesson with me?"

Jetta looked around the barracks. The kids milling around the long and narrow aisle between bunks seemed disinterested in their conversation. Most were catching a few extra minutes of rest or study time while others crowded around the more popular kids' beds, listening to the tales of their simulated battle victories.

"Ugh," Jetta said, waving her hand in front of her face as a cadet closed the door to the lavatories and walked past them. "I don't know if I can concentrate."

"These were the best bunks we could get," Jahx reminded her.

"At least we're all together," Jaeia said, sitting next to Jahx on his bunk.

Yeah, I guess, Jetta thought, eyeing the unoccupied bunk above Jahx. *No one wants to bunk with a rat.*

"Come on, Jetta," Jahx said, propping the interactive datapad on his knees. "I could use your help."

Jetta sat on the other side of Jahx, passing over his words and listening to his thoughts as he talked about the assignment.

We have to be forgettable. We have to be mediocre at best. Whatever happens, we have to be able to slip away unnoticed.

Jahx, Jetta thought, *is there any way that you could figure out what they're after—why they're going through all this trouble to register and screen the telepaths? If we don't figure out how they're doing it we're screwed.*

74

It'll be hard, Jahx conceded. *Everything's been classified, so it can't be accessed on the Dominion educational database. If we want to know more we'll have to watch the newsreels.*

But they're controlled by the Dominion media, Jetta groaned inwardly.

Exactly, Jahx replied. *I can still try the mainframe. They keep a tight watch on everything we do, so it'll take some time before I can circumvent their security measures.*

Jetta raised a brow. *When did you become such a techno-geek?*

Jahx raised one back at her. *One of the terminals broke down in my physics class. It took three techs to fix it.*

You gleaned from Dominion personnel? Jaeia and Jetta exclaimed in unison.

Yes, but only because they focused on repairs. All I could steal was that skill set, Jahx said. *Otherwise it was like trying to look through a brick wall.*

Well, at least we have some edge, Jetta remarked. *Lucky dig.*

"Not really," Jahx said aloud, voice paper-thin.

Jetta looked into Jahx's memory of the dig. Two of the technicians were completely incompetent, and copying their employed skill was about as useful as a broken thumbtack. However, the third, a Trigonian with a hawk nose and flinty eyes, had what Jahx needed, but his technical knowledge came with a price.

Vibrating algorithms of computer code and advanced programming concepts whizzed through Jetta's mind. At first Jetta didn't understand her brother's issue. Gleaning from another Sentient was never a clean imprint, and this man's essence was no worse than any of the Fiorahians they had stolen from. The man's hatred for women heated up her limbs, his appetite for greasy foods soured her stomach. The delight after framing another co-worker for data theft coated her insides with something slick and slimy.

"Elements in the same group tend to show patterns in atomic radius, ionization energy, and electronegativity," Jahx said. He paused, blue eyes flicking up to meet her gaze. Without moving, he redirected Jetta's sights, pulling her down and into his inner world.

Deeper than she had tread before, Jetta felt the undercurrent of her brother's psyche as he stole from the hawk-nosed technician. It was not this man's seediness, but the cesspool of Sentient ills Jahx had accumulated over the years.

75

There are some things I never wanted to know, Jahx whispered across their bond.

"I know," Jetta said, touching his hand and sharing his pain. "Me too."

Jaeia sighed, pulling her knees up to her chin. "Me three."

Clearing his throat, Jahx resumed his chemistry review and their internal conversation. *I will figure out why the Dominion is after telepaths. That will keep us one step ahead.*

I just don't understand, Jaeia thought. *Why are telepathic people so hated?*

Our abilities are hard for non-telepaths to understand, Jahx replied.

Or control, Jetta growled. *They envy our talents, so they spread lies to keep us under their thumb.*

Neither of her siblings could disagree.

Look, Jetta said, her inner voice firm and definitive, *we're getting out of here as soon as possible. I say we pass our classes but look for a way to escape. Jaeia, you and I will work on cracking their flight database and vehicle access codes while Jahx figures out what the hell is going on.*

That means we'll have to find a pilot to steal from, Jaeia said.

There are a couple pilots teaching a basic flight class down by the physics wing. We can hang out there after class. If you get one of them talking about launch protocols, I'll dig for something useful, Jetta said.

No way are you flying us out of here, Jaeia said. *You couldn't even reach the controls. You'd crash a ship in an empty dock!*

"Hey!" Jetta exclaimed, punching her lightly in the shoulder. *You were the one that crashed that towing cart in the mines, not me.*

Jaeia giggled and put her hands up. *Uh, yeah, if my name is Jetta.*

Jetta lunged for another attack, but Jaeia grabbed the pillow at the head of the bed and blocked her. They wrestled for only a few seconds before another cadet threw a datapad at them.

"Cut it out, *ratchaks!*"

Jetta grabbed the datapad and threw it back at the cadet a few bunks down. Ready for a fight, she jumped to her feet and put up her fists. The other cadet chuckled and turned back to talk with his friends.

"I miss Galm," Jahx whispered, closing his eyes and leaning against the bunk post. Jetta's fists uncurled, and she sat back down on the bunk.

"Me too," Jaeia said, pulling the pillow close to her body.

"I just wish we could tell him we were okay."

Jetta agreed with her brother. The Dominion Core forbade any contact with anyone outside the Academy for the first five years of training. Even if they could contact Galm sooner, Jetta didn't know what she would say.

"I'm going to be late to class. Gaming strategy is clear cross the base," Jaeia sighed, sitting up.

"Be careful," Jetta whispered. Jaeia managed a smile as she grabbed her datafiles, then exited the barracks to catch one of the flatbed, anti-grav lifts to her class.

"I've got to get to chemistry. Shouldn't you be getting ready, too?" Jahx said as he stuffed a few more supplies into his uniform pockets.

"It's an unfair trade, you know," she whispered as she passed him the pad. She projected her thoughts to him, sharing all the things she couldn't say with words. How happy she was that they could finally eat all they wanted—that they didn't have to fight for their food or search out water. How good it felt to be rid of that coarse tepper-cloth and the rucken worm infections that came with it. And the beds—they had never slept on real beds before, much less in a room with climate control and no infestations.

But most importantly, they all had a chance to be healthy now, especially Jahx. His belly was no longer swollen, and he breathed normally again. In fact, they had gained two kilograms each after only five days of regular meals.

And best of all, no Yahmen, Jetta thought. *No one could ever hurt us like him.*

"Please," Jahx pleaded, closing his eyes.

Feeling her brother's pained reaction, Jetta redirected her thoughts. "I'd better get going."

"Please—be careful. And be nice to the others," Jahx said as she grabbed her datapads out of her storage unit.

"I've always been nothing but sweet," she said, elbowing him in the arm on her way out.

"I'm sure," Jahx laughed.

77

***

As weeks turned into months of marginal performances in the classroom, no teacher paid any special interest in the triplets. Jetta even felt better about their social situation. None of the other students tried to befriend them after the incident in the mess hall, but the teasing had dwindled as she and her siblings grew. In less than a year they had put on so much height that they appeared to be eight years old instead of five, and with the constant influx of new students and the rapid graduation of older kids, the three of them disappeared into the mix just as they had hoped.

However, the Core monitored everything so strictly that they had gotten nowhere with their search for answers or opportunities for escape.

We have to graduate to the prep school. At least the students have semi-private quarters and their own terminals. We could request to room together. Then we could do it, Jetta communicated silently as she watched her siblings shovel down their dinners in the mess hall.

The first round of basic training had sparked their appetites, enough that they had each requested a third tray of food. Jetta felt uneasy every time she had to go up the next pants size or swap out for a bigger pair of boots. The occasional aching in her bones and constant hunger didn't bother her as much as looking in the mirror and seeing a giant staring back at her. Still, she couldn't argue with being stronger and faster.

Jaeia moved the food around on her tray as she mulled over the idea. *You're right. But that would mean we'd have to pass the prep exam, and that would seem a little weird, don't you think? I'm averaging a Pass in all my classes, and it would be a stretch if I just aced the exam.*

We could get tutors. Then there'd be an explanation for our improvement.

I don't know, Jetta, Jahx told her, taking giant bites of his meat roll. *We're doing okay now. We could ride it out a bit longer and take the prep exam in two years.*

"Two years?" Jetta exclaimed. She put her utensils down and lowered her voice. "We can't wait that long. I don't want to be here any longer than we have to be."

"We could always flunk out," Jaeia said.

"But they would send us back to Fiorah. We can't go back there," Jetta replied.

"No, we can't go back," Jahx whispered, setting down his drink. A look of puzzlement flitted across his face, and on its heels, terror.

"Look, can't we—"

Just as Jetta started to press her agenda, Rogman, Commandant of the Academy, entered the mess hall with soldiers in specialized uniforms flanking each shoulder. It wasn't unusual for teachers to visit the mess hall, but she felt her brother's anxiety spike. She looked over at Jahx and saw the line of concern across his forehead.

"What?" Jetta whispered. But Jahx remained silent, eyes trained on the new teacher, mind out of reach.

"Attention! We have an announcement to make," Rogman barked.

"Why is he here?" Jetta overheard someone say. She looked around and saw the confusion on the other students' faces. Jaeia nudged her. *Something isn't right.*

"There has been a change in policy regarding the Endgame competition," Rogman said. "It is now open to students of all levels. The overall winner at the end of this semester will be awarded the honorary rank of junior captain and acceptance into our officer training corps."

"What's the Endgame?" Jaeia whispered.

One of the other students overheard her and snorted. "Only the most important test of your command skills. Or in your case, *lack* of skill."

Jahx grabbed Jetta's arm as she whipped around to confront the student. *Just leave it be.*

Jetta grumbled and watched as the Commandant posted a signature and datareel code on the wall.

"Additionally," Rogman said, "the winner will be awarded a three day shore leave and fulltime access to the game room."

The second he left, students rushed for the front of the room. Soon everyone in the cafeteria crowded around the posting— everyone but the three of them.

"I don't like it," Jahx whispered.

"I agree," Jaeia replied.

Jetta watched the other students hurriedly file out of the mess hall. "They must be off to play that game. Whatever it is."

"Come on, let's go back to the bunks and study. I'm through eating anyway," Jaeia said, dumping her tray.

Jetta readied to leave when a hand gripped her shoulder. "Student, to my office, now."

Turning slowly, Jetta met midnight eyes and a hardened face without laugh lines. Despite Rogman's human appearance, Jetta could not glean any psionic reading. Instead, she saw the machinations of the Dominion Core in his perfectly trimmed mustache and his chest full of service decorations.

Soldiers with silver-sealed eyes stood a few meters back from Rogman, watching Jetta and her siblings. Eyes that could see more than just the beads of sweat collecting on her brow, but read her rising body temperature, the way her toes curled in her boots—

Don't be afraid, Jahx said, reaching out across their bond. *They may have infrared vision and can see through walls, but they can't see through you.*

Jetta released the breath she didn't realize she was holding.

I'll meet up with you in the barracks. Don't worry, Jetta whispered silently to her siblings, but both Jaeia and Jahx stayed present in her mind long after she, Rogman and the soldiers left the mess hall.

Neither Rogman nor the soldiers spoke as they boarded the lift. Cautiously, Jetta tried to probe their minds for even a hint of information, but a tightly knitted minds repelled her back.

How is this possible? she wondered.

A voice from within answered: *(They've been trained against telepathic intrusion.)*

But if they have their guard up, she thought, *that means they know about me. That means—*

Jetta held her breath until she thought she would faint. Gripping the railing of the lift, she forced herself to breathe. With each exhalation she buried the thought a little deeper.

One of the soldiers stopped the lift when they reached double doors at the end of a sterile, windowless corridor. *Commandant Rogman, Chief of Military Acquisitions,* was affixed above the control panel for the doors. Jetta had never been in this part of the Academy before.

It stinks like disinfectants, she thought, rubbing the medicinal sting out of her nose.

The soldiers showed Jetta into Rogman's office, and directed her to a chair facing a desk. She found the room sparsely decorated, with only a picture of the Sovereign and a display of war medals to lend color to the grey walls. The partition sectioning off the latter half of the room looked out of place, and the low lighting and intense humidity levels conflicted with Rogman's otherwise strict adherence to military protocol.

Although she couldn't be certain, Jetta sensed that someone—or something—lurked behind the partition.

What is that? she wondered, repulsed by the unnatural feel of the psionic vibrations.

Rogman excused the soldiers before locking the doors and closing the blinds. He took a seat behind the desk, sitting ramrod straight in his chair.

"Cadet Jetta Drachsi," he said, looking her over. "I have been monitoring your progress since your arrival on Dominion grounds. I have to say I am thoroughly disappointed."

"My apologies, Sir. I will study harder."

The smile that touched the man's lips vanished with a twitch of his mustache.

"The teachers believe you and your siblings lack the proper motivation to reach your full potential. I am here to motivate you."

The concern of her siblings mounted in the back of her mind as they sensed her fear. *I have to control myself,* she thought, trying to calm down.

Rogman wrinkled his nose again before he spoke. "Do you think any soldier would knowingly follow a human born and bred on Fiorah?"

Anger constricted Jetta's chest. She exhaled slowly and tried to let his words pass through her.

"In the Starways, Fiorahians are hardly considered Sentients, and unregistered humans are even lower than Fiorahians. Your kind are either streetwalkers or trade meal. Tell me, why are we wasting our time on you?"

81

Jetta tried to think of her siblings, but the fires of her anger spread with every breath. "You're not wasting your time, Sir."

"Well, that's odd, because according to this," he said, plucking a datapad from his front pocket, "all three of you are maintaining average grades. We only select the top twenty-five percent of each class to move on to the next level. The rest get sent to the front lines. Did you know that?"

"No, Sir, I did not."

"Well then," Rogman said, rising and circling the desk, "in case the threat of becoming cannon fodder isn't enough, I'll make things more interesting for you."

Jetta gripped the arms of the chair as he crouched down in front of her. The hot stink of his breath reminded her of Yahmen.

"All three of you will finish in the top three ranks during the next Endgame competition. No one would ever follow a losing *Deadskin* commander from Fiorah. If you want to stay, you will have to prove yourselves. You will have to be the best." His mustache twitched again, revealing a sneer.

I will tear that stupid mustache off your face! "Yes, Sir. I understand."

As Jetta left the office, she could have sworn she heard metal grating on metal, like a rusted engine struggling against itself. When she turned around, she only saw the commandant closing the doors to his office.

"Tomorrow morning do not report to your classes. I want to see you and your siblings in the game room or I will terminate your candidacy. Dismissed."

Jetta assured him of her compliance and boarded the lift back to the bunks. *Now there is no question of danger,* she realized. *The Core is monitoring us closely, and something else—something strange—is going on.*

***

When she returned to the barracks, she found Jaeia and Jahx on her lower bunk, watching a newsreel on one of their datapads.

"Dissemblers are a hidden enemy—know who you are dealing with. Register all telepaths; bring them in to your local Core embassy for screening. Protect your children. Protect your home. Protect your life," the newscaster said.

Jahx shut it off as soon as Jetta sat next to him. "They're broadcasting more and more of these warnings."

Jaeia whispered, "The Core is making it sound like all telepaths are like Dissemblers. They're getting fired from their jobs, kicked out of their homes. I don't get it. We have to figure out what the Core is trying to do."

"What happened?" Jahx asked, turning toward her.

Jetta couldn't find the words to tell them. When her siblings saw her face, they immediately reached out to touch her thoughts.

Jahx sighed. "At least we'll have complete access to the terminals in the game room. It'd be our best chance at hacking the mainframe."

"Shore leave would be nice, too," Jaeia added quietly. "We could see Galm, maybe even Lohien."

"Alright—so you two are onboard?" Jetta asked.

"I don't know how we're going to do it, Jetta. We've never even played the Endgame—and the only way to top some of the older kids' scores is to have a flawless record for the next month," Jaeia said. She switched topics for a moment as a Stempton and his friends walked past their bunks on the way to the lavatories. One of his cronies pretended to trip over Jetta's foot, elbowing her in the temple before catching himself.

"Watch yourself," Jahx gently cautioned the boy, pulling Jetta out of the way as he came back around.

"Sorry—didn't see the rat on the bed," the boy said. Stempton gave her a wink.

"Only for you, dear brother," Jetta said, gritting her teeth and allowing the *ratchakker* and his friends to walk away laughing.

"Come on, look at this with me. It seems complicated," Jahx said, pointing to the educational database on a datapad. He scrolled through a description of the gameplay and instructions for the Endgame. "It's played on a multidimensional field using hundreds of game pieces. In fact, it's a fairly accurate model of the war globe the Dominion Core uses. The only difference is that they've disabled the voice command feature for interschool competitions."

"Well," Jetta said, flopping back on the pillow, "we'll have to do it the way we did things on Fiorah."

83

"Yeah..." Jaeia and Jahx replied.

"But with a new trick or two," Jetta realized aloud. She continued on through their psionic connection. *We can't just reuse someone else's smarts.*

Her siblings nodded in agreement. Fixing a broken coolant loop on a drill ship didn't require much more than stealing knowledge from the right technician. Defeating an opponent on a battlefield went beyond gleaning from experienced players. They couldn't steal imagination and they couldn't steal instincts, two skills that played a bigger role in battle than anything else.

Closing her eyes and curling her legs up to her belly, Jetta wished back their life on Fiorah. *I could just kill Yahmen when he got too drunk and passed out, and then none of this would be necessary.*

No, Jahx said, soothing her tension. *We can do this. I'll be just like old times; we've always been able to figure things out together.*

An unnamable fear sent her heart into a flutter, making the breath catch in her chest. In that moment, Jetta looked back and forth between her siblings, wanting to remember every last detail of their faces.

"I hope you're right," Jetta whispered.

***

The more time she spent playing the Endgame, the more Jetta understood why the non-telepaths hated telepaths so vehemently. She had been right to assume it would take more than appropriating her opponent's knowledge to win, but she hadn't anticipated what would happen when the three of them were pitted against a single mind. Even though only one of them worked the gaming console, the other two could silently assist from the stands.

This is the first time the universe has ever given us a chance, Jetta thought as she and her siblings entered the game room. Newbies and veterans alike crowded around the different battle sims. Their faces, bathed in restless holographic light, seemed to belong to shifting ghosts. One second scarlet, the next azure. In a nearby console, a warship exploded in a golden flash, illuminating hungry eyes and gaping mouths.

On Fiorah, working together had been nothing more than a survival technique to keep them useful to Yahmen. Since most Sentients could sense some degree of invasive psionic activity, they each divided up the desired skill set they needed to learn so they weren't dwelling in anyone's head too long.

But as each of them entered the ranks of the Endgame, Jetta came to realize that even back then they had been sharing more than their stolen knowledge to fix broken-down mining ships—they had been using a combined perspective. Jetta remembered how she used her siblings' eyes to see new ways to solve old problems with one of the phasnoic drill heads that constantly failed. Jaeia immediately matched her own interpretation of the malfunction against Jetta's and narrowed down the solution to two choices. And Jahx, using both of his sisters' knowledge and perspectives, uncovered the crux of the problem and selected the right method to fix the rig. With that they had saved a ship—and saved themselves from being sold on the Underground Block.

However, solving complex engineering problems on mining ships did not compare to facing a live opponent who could adapt to their borrowed strategies and react to their maneuvers.

I'm going to have to dig deeper if I'm going to get in the top fifty, Jetta thought, eyeing the scoreboard on the far wall of the game room.

Somehow, through the thunderclash of sound and sizzling lightshow, Stempton zeroed in on her the second she and her siblings stepped into the main arena. His eyes lit up like some kind of animal spotting its prey.

"No way," he said, approaching them with a slow swagger. "I can't believe you'd even show your faces in here, *ratchakkers.*"

Jetta eyed Stempton's cronies breaking off from their games to join their leader's side.

"We came to play," she said, folding her arms across her chest.

Stempton rolled his eyes. "Yeah, I heard you three have been stinkin' the place up. Didn't anybody tell you? No rats allowed."

No, Jetta, Jahx projected, reading her thoughts.

It's the only way, Jetta said.

Of all the lessons she had learned on Fiorah, you never backed down from an opportunity to take out the lead bully. Strike hard and fast—and send a warning to everyone else.

Surprisingly, Jaeia sided with her. *He's got a good ranking.
He'd bump Jetta up in the stats.*

Okay, Jahx conceded. *Just be careful. He's real competition.*

Her brother had a point. Up until now they'd only faced lower-ranked cadets, and Jetta still fumbled with the complicated mechanics of gameplay.

I hate that I can't steal motor coordination, Jetta thought to herself. Such a shortcoming could easily result in defeat against a stronger opponent.

Jetta stepped forward, not letting her shorter and smaller stature stop her from getting in Stempton's face. "I'll take you, and everyone else in this Academy down."

"Whoa!" Stempton guffawed. "You're even dumber than you look."

"Burn her, Stempton," one of his cronies said.

"Stupid rat," another teased.

"Alright," Stempton said. "And after I beat you in the Endgame, I'm going to make sure you and your *ratchak* siblings pay for your lip."

Glimpsing the imagery behind his words, Jetta saw her neck in his grips, face bloodied and smashed to a pulp, begging for him to stop.

The dark undertow from within washed away Stempton's fantasy with a wave of unexpected confidence. *You will win, and you will make him pay.*

"After I beat you," she said. "You'll wish you'd never crossed me."

Stempton's cronies yipped and howled.

With a smug grin, Stempton pointed his hand toward an Endgame console. "It's on, little launnie."

Except for Stempton's followers, none of the other kids paid their game any attention. Besides, when Jetta took a seat opposite of Stempton, her entire body seemed dwarfed by the swirling holographic globe.

"This is going to be a slaughter," one of Stempton's friends snickered.

I can do this, she told herself.

Her brother and sister, standing behind her, sent her their assurances. With shaky hands, she logged into the console. A score of battleships, fighters, ground units, a warship and base of operations materialized in blue, facing off against Stempton's red fleet within the globe.

> "Little launnie in the gutter,
> No one loves a rat,
> Your momma's smoking jihja
> And your daddy's getting whacked."

Stempton sang the song of the Fiorahian slums just loud enough for her to hear as the game initiated.

That ratchakker, she fumed. *He learned that song just to get inside my head!*

Her anger only magnified as she fumbled with the controls. By the second verse of the song, she no longer heard her brother and sister as the fire roaring in her chest, and the intense need to win the game, dominated her senses.

> "Little launnie in the gutter,
> Broke and full of woe,
> Float downstream away from me
> To the Block where you will show."

After glancing at the score, Jetta bit down on her lip. *Stempton's already up by fifty points.*

Out of the corner of her eye she watched him deftly operate the controls, cutting into her forces left and right while she struggled to type in the commands to keep her fleet together. *It won't be enough just to imprint his knowledge.*

Rogman's face appeared in the holographics, his mustache twitching as the memory of his words played out in her head: *Your kind are either streetwalkers or trade meal.*

I will not be sent back to Fiorah. I will not be beaten by this Mugarruthepeta, Jetta thought.

> "Four and twelve you might have gotten
> If your face was not so rotten,
> Hurry up and die already
> So this all can be forgotten."

When Stempton finished the song, he directed his full attention toward the game. Sensing his vulnerable mind, Jetta saw her chance to use her secret talent.

I will only use a little, she promised herself. She couldn't help the giddy feeling tickling her stomach, or keep the smile from her face.

Pushing away from the connection to her siblings, Jetta traveled beyond the realm of Stempton's gaming knowledge, digging into the roots of his psyche.

"Come on, Stempton," she whispered. "Make this easy for me and maybe they'll ice you out so you can go back to Mummy and Daddy. Don't you miss them? Or do you think they forgot about you?"

Jarred by the mention of his home life, he accidentally ordered two of his ground units into her line of fire. Her smile broadened as a group of kids massed around their game and Stempton's cronies fell silent.

"Jeez, Stempton—it's not like a Crexan with a Deadskin Mummy is going to get very far anyway. You're human. You're weak. You've polluted the Crexan bloodline.*"*

She won the game in less than thirty minutes.

Red-faced, Stempton left without saying a word, taking his gaggle of followers with him. Jetta grinned. She wouldn't ever have to worry about him again, and if she did, she knew right where to hurt him.

None of the other kids congratulated her, and the crowd quickly dispersed as new games started up.

"I know what you're going to say," Jetta said, moving to the stadium seating with her brother and sister. They took a spot on one of the many rows of benches that formed a circle around the battle sims, with an excellent view of the main Endgame console, so they could watch—and steal—from the next match. *You're going to caution me about my methods.*

Jaeia and Jahx both looked at her, concern pinching their brows.

Just wait, she said, turning away from them. *Soon you'll be doing it too.*

***

A week later, when the teachers started to assign matches, Jaeia found herself pitted against Shiggla. Now a sophomore cadet with a solid Endgame record and a knack for getting under a player's skin, Shiggla was the toughest opponent any of them had faced.

"Uck. I have to play the rat? Come on..." Shiggla said, making sure to voice her disgust loud enough so Jaeia could hear it across the barracks. *"It's like pickin' on the handicapped."*

Jaeia remained quiet as she walked to the game room with her siblings. Trailing only a few meters behind Shiggla and her obnoxious entourage, she probed the sensitivities of her opponent before the match even started.

How am I going to do this? she worried, sensing the depth of her opponent's knowledge. *She's much better than me.*

"She's a jackal," Jetta warned her as Jaeia sat down at the Endgame console. "She won't go easy on you."

"Great pep talk," Jaeia muttered.

Jahx put a hand on her shoulder. "Just be patient. Your opportunity will come."

"Thanks, Jahx," she said.

Shiggla's Trigonian upbringing made her cocky and bold, and it showed in her playing style.

You can't keep retreating, Jetta called out to her as Jaeia pulled back her front line. *She's eating up your ground units.*

She's too aggressive. I can't keep up, Jaeia said, wiping the sweat from her forehead.

Another battleship blinked out on the holographics.

(I'm caving.)

Shiggla's followers cheered her on as she trounced Jaeia's moves, and she played it up to her hungry audience. "Time to send the launnie back to the gutters!"

No, Jaeia thought. *I can't lose. We can't go back to Fiorah.*

Keep calm, Jahx called out to her, trying to soothe her anxieties.

She didn't hear him, or her sister pushing strategies across their psionic bond. *I'm not losing,* she panicked, seeing Yahmen's face in the shadows of the shifting holographics. *(I have to use my talent.)*

Diving beneath the surface of Shiggla's consciousness, Jaeia unearthed the subconscious desires that manipulated her opponent's choices. *She wants to capture my warship to maximize her point total and boost her rank in the standings.*

No, that's not all, she realized, stripping away the darkest layers of Shiggla's past. *The secret behind her ambition...*

"You're pretty good," Jaeia suggested to Shiggla. Speaking in what sounded like normal tones, Jaeia worked her way inside her opponent's head with a heavy psionic push. "But I hear your brother Soling is the real competitor. Isn't he like fifty spots ahead of you? You'll have to beat me and everyone else by at least two hundred points for the next month to even hope to catch up."

No way, Jetta projected. *You get to use your second voice on Shiggla?*

Shiggla's cheeks bloomed red as she moved her ground units too aggressively against Jaeia's base, leaving herself exposed. Locking her fighters on Shiggla's ground units, Jaeia commanded the remainder of her fleet to target the warship.

"It's hard having a sibling who's better than you at everything," Jaeia continued as she set up for the final attack.

It's only a little push, Jaeia rationalized to her siblings.

We don't know how your second voice will affect her behavior, Jahx cautioned. *Not every species responds the same.*

And things usually get out of hand, Jetta added.

She won't even know I'm doing it, Jaeia downplayed.

"I know how it is," Jaeia said to Shiggla, voice ringing out across the psionic wavelengths. "You end up as an afterthought. Or just plain forgotten."

Shiggla's face contorted in bewilderment, her lower lip trembling. Jaeia put out her battleship in a seemingly open sector, and Shiggla, distracted, fell for the trap, her pieces demolished in seconds as Jaeia sprang her hidden forces.

"How did you do that?" Shiggla asked, watching her own rankings drop on the scoreboard. Panic reduced her voice to a whisper. "Do you even know what this does to me?"

Members of Shiggla's entourage gathered around her as she wept and wailed.

"Jeez… I've never seen her like this," Jaeia overheard one of the cadet's say.

"*Chakking* rat," someone else said.

Jetta pulled both of her and Jahx out of the game room before things got ugly.

On the verge of tears, Jaeia turned to her sister. *What did I just do?*

Jetta held the emotion out of her voice. "What you had to."

90

As he faced more and more upper-rank opponents, Jahx found himself no longer exempt from using his unique talent.

I don't want to resort to these measures, Jahx said, taking his seat at the Endgame for his next match. *This is dangerous.*

But you're not even trying, Jetta said, envy slipping through her words. *You know you could do so much more.*

Please, Jetta, he said, keeping his eyes trained on the console. He could see himself from within his sisters' sights as they watched him from the stadium seating. *I don't want to have this argument right now.*

"Jahx—what kind of *ratchak* name is that?" asked Teahvo as he sat down across the console to play Jahx. A hulking Sentient with multiple limbs and amphibian feet, Teahvo spoke through a translator since his species lacked the proper vocal cords to speak Common.

Beat him, Jahx. He's just another bully, Jetta said as she and her sisters watched from the stands.

No, he's not, Jahx replied, sending her images of his opponent's own torments. Ostracized and teased by the other cadets, Teahvo lashed out at others to protect himself from further harassment.

Of course Jahx sees things differently, he overhead Jetta grumble to Jaeia.

That's his gift, she replied.

Power gone to waste, Jetta said.

No, he thought to himself as the game started. *You don't understand my talent.*

Before Teahvo even made his first move, Jahx closed his eyes and reached across and inside his opponent.

I see you, he thought, touching the brilliant light within Teahvo's core. Weaving his fingers within the threads of Teahvo's being, Jahx saw every action and outcome of their game play out across the psionic plane.

When he opened his eyes, Teahvo moved his battleship above Jahx's base of operations, thinking he could launch a final attack. "Suck it, launnie."

"Good game," Jahx said, bringing about his hidden corvettes.

"What?" Teahvo exclaimed. "How could you—"

I know you, Jahx thought as Teahvo scrambled back to his defensive line. *I see every part of you.*

Still deeply entrenched in his opponent's mind, Jahx could not help but feel part of Teahvo's loss as the scoreboard tallied up the points.

"Want to grab dinner with me?" Jahx asked after nabbing the closely-fought battle.

"Go *chak* yourself, launnie," Teahvo said, spitting on Jahx's boot.

Jahx extended his hand. Having gleaned enough of Teahvo's native language of Gr'wy, he tried to speak a few words as a peace offering. "*Uk'ep id'p.*"

Teahvo wouldn't have it. Later on that evening, Jahx found his bunk trashed, the mattress torn to shreds and his datapads smashed.

We can't let him get away with this, Jetta said, kicking Jahx's bunk as Jaeia took an armful of ruined linen to the disposal.

Just let it go, Jetta, Jahx said, picking up the shattered pieces of his possessions.

Why are you always holding me back? Infuriated, Jetta tore into the deepest wound between them. *Why are you holding yourself back?*

Shoulders slumping forward, Jahx accidentally dropped his collection. *Jetta, I—*

No! You don't even know the ends of your own power because you refuse to explore it beyond your ridiculous need to help others.

What would have me do, Jetta? Jahx said, turning to face her. He matched her gaze, unfaltering even as she poured her frustrations into him.

Wordlessly, Jetta shared her darkest desires. *With even the slightest whim, you could unravel the very fabric of a person's being. But you don't. Not even against thugs like Teahvo or beasts like Yahmen.*

And you think I'm weak for that? Jahx asked.

Hey you two, stop it, Jaeia said, rushing back from the disposal. Taking each of their hands and linking them together as three, she flushed them each with good memories. *We're in this together, remember?*

Jahx looked in Jetta's eyes, past the barriers she believed would keep him out of her most private thoughts. *My empathy does not make me weak.*

Yes, it does, she said, arresting him before he delved too deeply inside her inner world. *And it will be your downfall.*

***

As the days turned to weeks, Jetta eagerly embraced her powers. With each game she got more used to seeing through three sets of eyes, and found her psionic voice becoming the loudest as her confidence soared.

When's my next match? she thought, sitting cross-legged on her bed and scrolling through her datapad for the latest game assignments. At least seventy other cadets had requested to play her, Jaeia or Jahx.

This is great, Jetta thought, seeing all the student names crowding her lineup. *I'll beat each one of you. Then you'll hang your heads like whipped dogs and whimper your excuse to any sympathetic ear.*

"Hey, where's Cam?"

Jetta looked up, surprised to see her brother back so soon from his gaming strategy final.

How do I tell him? she thought to herself as her brother eyed the empty bed above his.

Jaeia popped her head over the edge of the top bunk. *We have to tell him the truth.*

"Two soldiers escorted Cam out," Jetta said, keeping a neutral tone. "They said something about him cheating on the biochem final."

Jahx gripped the bedpost, knuckles turning white, and kept his response within their private link. *He never cheated. It's just an excuse.*

Jaeia swiveled around and dangled her legs off the bed. "Sorry, Jahx."

Cam, Iggie, Tomia, Jetta said. *Just a few of the cadets that showed us a shred of respect, even if it was just to share a bunk. Where are they now?*

Discharged or transferred, Jaeia answered.

93

Or they just disappear, Jetta said. Not to upset her siblings, Jetta kept the rest of her thoughts to herself: *Why do the teachers—why does Rogman—want to isolate us and keep us friendless?*

Jahx plopped down on his bed, resting his elbows on his knees. "Rogman is now offering a week's shore leave to anyone that can beat us."

"A *week?*" Jaeia exclaimed.

"Yeah," Jahx said, eyes losing focus. "As if we weren't targets already. As if anyone here needed an excuse to come after us."

Jetta showed them the text alert on her datapad. "And he's giving us exemptions from tests. Look here—he's authorized me skipping my calculus final."

"Special treatment. Great. Everyone will know," Jaeia sighed.

"Exactly," Jahx whispered.

After consoling her siblings as best she could, Jetta pretended to return to her datapad.

I don't care if Rogman is messing with us, or if we don't have friends. She lowered her datapad and gazed down the rows of bunks, seeing more than the cadets catching up on homework or getting extra rest. She saw the entire Academy and all the battle commanders of the Dominion Core lining up in front of her, even the Sovereign. A smile spread across her face. *I will beat you all.*

***

As the semester came to a close and the final battle was set to determine the Endgame champion, Jetta found herself pacing up and down the aisles of the game room, eager to meet their opponent. After securing the top three spots, Jetta and her siblings expected to play one another for the Endgame title, but once again, the commandant changed the rules at the last minute.

"None of your previous scores matter anymore, cadets," he told them earlier that day, his mustache poorly masking the smug look on his face. *"Lose this battle and you're all iced."*

Through an Academy-wide bulletin, the siblings found out that Rogman had selected a special opponent outside of the Academy for one of them to challenge. Some of the other students protested the triplets' perfect scores and wanted them to challenge each other to sort out the ranks, but their complaints didn't get them very far. Even

Jetta thought it peculiar that the teachers hadn't arranged a fight between them. *I'm glad I don't have to fight my brother and sister; I can't imagine anything worse than pitching our abilities against each other. Even if I won, it wouldn't be a victory worth celebrating.*

Students and teachers packed the game room while soldiers with silver-sealed eyes and loaded rifles lined the stadium staircases and gaming floor, keeping the excited crowd a few meters back from the central Endgame console. Standing on the far side of the console, across from their opponent and his entourage of older students, Jetta and her siblings discussed their strategy.

"Hey, Jetta..."

Even though Jaeia tried to mask her thoughts, Jetta already knew what her sister was going to say by the hesitant look in her eyes. Her siblings had been voicing their concerns about her growing obsession with the game, and Jetta knew they wanted to deny what was rightfully hers.

"It's our last game, Jetta," Jahx chimed in. "We can't afford to get greedy."

Jahx was right. She had been getting sloppy in some of her latest wins, focusing on the psychological torment of her opponents over the actual game.

"Don't worry—I'll be more careful this time."

Jaeia gave her brother a cautionary glance before taking over the conversation. "We were talking—we think Jahx should face him."

"Jahx?!" Jetta scoffed.

"Look," her brother said gently, "Drakken Varkanian is the Fleet Commander's son, and they brought him out of the officer's training corps for this battle."

"But why, Jahx?" Jetta said, trying to keep the hurt out of her voice.

"Drakken is a military prodigy, first of all, and he's damn hard to read. I ran into him in the mess hall," Jahx said, keeping his voice low. "He's got about as much personality as a rock."

"Jahx is probably the only one that can get through to him. You and I can still help," Jaeia said, careful to keep their conversation from being overheard by the other students milling around the arena.

"I'm the one that comes up with the best strategies," Jetta said through gritted teeth. "It should be me!"

Jahx tried to lay a hand on her shoulder, but she shrugged it off. "Trust me, Jetta—please. This battle is for all three of us."

"We need Jahx's perspective up front," Jaeia said. Silently, she added: *Think of what happened with Stempton.*

Jetta's hands bunched into involuntary fists. So what if she had gotten upset in past battles? Even if she got so emotional she could no longer hear or see through her siblings' eyes, she always had her secret talent.

We need to stay connected, Jetta, and fight as one, Jahx reasoned. *That is our greatest advantage.*

Her siblings' fear seeped into her head. No, they couldn't screw this up now, not with so much at stake. She could feel Yahmen's presence in the backs of all their minds, a hulking, shadowy figure in a lighted doorframe, bottle in hand, burning cigarette in the other, waiting for them to come home.

"You, the pacifist—you're going to claim the title?" Jetta said humorlessly. She could tell he took offense by the look in his eyes.

"I don't relish the victory, Jetta, but I will do what I have to do."

She crossed her arms and bit back what she really wanted to say to him. "Okay, fine," she relented.

Jaeia took her hand and they moved behind the spectator line as Jahx took his place at the game console across from Drakken.

The Commander's son is handsome, Jetta heard her sister think. *His strong humanoid features and deep-set eyes contrast nicely with the striped facial markings of his Zunnian bloodline.*

Gross, Jetta replied, sticking out her tongue. *He looks like a constipated thug to me.*

"I'll make this quick, launnie," Drakken whispered to Jahx. Her brother said nothing as the announcer took the stage.

There weren't too many in the Academy that didn't already know Drakken's reputation. Still, with a booming voice, the announcer impressed the crowd with Drakken's greatness:

The only other cadet to ever go undefeated in the Academy's Endgame!

Flawless record!

Top scores in every category!

Rolling her eyes, Jetta grumbled through the excessive praise until the announcer said something that caught her attention.

"... even after his brother, Xercius, was killed in battle," the announcer said, "Drakken chose to continue schooling despite his personal loss. He is a true Core soldier, brave, loyal, and honorable..."

Jaeia turned to Jetta and whispered, "Did you feel that?"

Though brief, a pang of emotion leaked from the otherwise glacial presence of the visiting command student.

"Yes," Jetta whispered back, hiding her smile.

The battle began.

Position the warship in engagement configuration alpha-beta-one. Send the fighters to mark 01045 and hold, Jetta thought. Hearing her, Jahx moved the pieces into position, but Drakken quickly pounced on her move. Jetta felt her brother worming his way through Drakken's mind, but they didn't have that kind of time. The stony-faced Commander's son was aggressive, but each move was carefully planned out and followed by an attack that left them reeling.

He's really good, Jaeia commented as Drakken downed one of their squadrons. *Not even Jahx can read him very well; it must be his mixed species. I don't know how we're going to win this if we can't imprint his tactics.*

Jetta glanced at the scoreboard; her brother had the lead by only one point.

But not for long, Jaeia said. *From the looks of Drakken's battleship formation, he's going to attack Jahx's warship while his fighters are busy scrambling with the mess he's made of the ground units.*

Skucheka! Jetta replied. *Jahx will have to abandon his ground units and base of operations or risk losing the warship.*

Drakken pressed his legions forward. The holographic display exploded with hues of green and red as pieces collided and disappeared. The crowd cheered, chanting Drakken's name as the legendary young man gained the edge.

"He's going to lose," Jaeia said as Jahx struggled to save the base of operations.

"No, he's not."

You could tease him about Xercius—throw him off his game, Jetta suggested to Jahx, but he quickly dismissed the idea.

I can win this without resorting to that.

97

You don't have the time! Jetta said, looking at the scoreboard. Shaking his head, Jahx put out another legion of air units that Drakken crippled within seconds.

Jetta grumbled and detached herself from the game and their connection.

"Jetta—no!" Jaeia whispered, grabbing her sister's hand. "What are you doing? We need you! You can't—"

"I can't what? You want to go back to Fiorah?"

Rendered speechless, Jaeia barely managed to shake her head.

"I'll make this quick, you bastard," Jetta muttered.

She closed her eyes. *The crowd disappeared, along with the arena, and her brother and sister, leaving her and Drakken alone in a sea of gray infinity. He remained unaware of her as she approached him across the psionic plane, inputting his final commands into the console. Reaching into his head, Jetta weaved the nerve cords of his eyes around her fingers and yanking back with all her might.*

(See him...)

Jetta opened her eyes again. Mouth hung open in a scream that never came, Drakken sat frozen in place, eyes dilated with terror.

Jahx only chanced a quick look at her before resuming his command. *What did you do, Jetta?*

As the soon as the teachers called the game, soldiers hauled Drakken away by the armpits, his face white and cheesy.

"Xercius... Oh Gods...what did they do to you?" he babbled incoherently. "So much blood. Put him back together—why can't you save him?"

Confused cadets whispered and pointed until the teachers told them to hush. Nobody in the stands saw the horror he spoke of, except for Jetta. Even so, she gleaned only a faint impression of the nightmare she caused: *A bloody, beaten corpse limped through the hollow core of the gaming projector, his eviscerated bowels smearing across the console as he cried out for his brother.*

I've never done anything like that before. Confronting people with their fears was one thing, but reconstructing their nightmares was another. *If only I had known about this back on Fiorah,* she thought, *I would have made Yahmen burn.*

As she celebrated her newfound talent, Jahx ran over to her, ducking under the congratulatory arms of some of the teachers.

A pained expression crossed his face. "You didn't have to do that. I was so close," he whispered, his voice constricted with both anger and grief. "You have no idea what you did to him."

Jahx pulled her into his mind, and her resolve quickly peeled away as she felt the depth of the damage she had caused the young man. She didn't want to lose, but she hadn't intended to completely destroy his psyche.

"You always go too far, Jetta," Jahx said. "I warned you before..."

"Do what you have to do, right?" she whispered. Tears stung her eyes as his disappointment sank into her, the weight of it crushing her ribs.

Jahx held her gaze for a moment longer before succumbing to the onslaught of praise from teachers and a few of the newer students not yet aware of the triplets' reputation.

One of the older cadets who had recently lost to Jahx stepped forward from the crowd. Behind him collected other sore losers, including Stempton and Shiggla. "That was impossible," he said. "No one—and no *launnie*—can defeat Drakken Varkanian. What are you—some sort of freak?"

Silver-eyed soldiers held their ground, not moving to intervene as the crowd of disgruntled students drew in around them. With so many adults around, Jetta concentrated on keeping herself in check, even when Stempton pointed a finger at her brother. "He's a damn leech."

Shiggla raised her arms up to rally the crowd. "They're all damned leeches! How else could lower levels win against the entire Academy?"

"Let's go," Jahx said, putting a hand on her shoulder, but Jetta shrugged it away. The older cadet stared her down, squaring himself between the console and the exit.

He's not going to let us just leave. And nobody else is going to help us, Jetta said to her siblings. Even the teachers had faded into the background, seemingly unconcerned that their top Endgame players were only moments away from being lynched.

Adrenaline surged through her veins, kicking Jetta's heart into overdrive and turning her hands into fists.

Let them be or we'll get in trouble, Jahx whispered through their silent connection. *Don't use your talent in the open.*

Jetta positioned herself in front of her siblings, directly across from the older cadet. Measuring a good meter taller than her, the kid tried to intimidate her with size. A smile lit her face. Yahmen was a lot bigger and meaner than this kid could ever be, and now that she knew what she was capable of, he didn't stand a chance.

He's not distracted—he will know you're digging in his head. Leave him alone, Jetta! Jahx said, sensing his sister's thoughts.

But I don't want just him, she said, eyeing the angry mob and gritting her teeth. *I want all of them—*

"That's enough!" a deep voice shouted. Out of the corner of her eye, Jetta saw Rogman and several guards in specialized uniforms fanning out at the entrance of the arena. "Everybody back to the bunks."

Jetta's hands remained clenched as the mob of cadets dispersed. Relief and a strange dissatisfaction diluted the rage pumping in her veins, but it wasn't enough to make her turn away just yet, even with her siblings tugging at her uniform sleeve.

"Jetta, come on, come on!" Jahx urged, pulling desperately on her arm.

"Not so fast. It's time to award our top finishers," Rogman said, coming up behind her.

When she turned around, her stomach dropped to her knees. Rogman's eyes glinted as the soldiers surrounded them. Spreading her arms to shield her siblings, Jetta realized her mistake. *We shouldn't have won. Oh Gods, please don't—*

Before she could cry out, something pierced the back of her neck. She thought she heard someone laugh just before she hit the ground.

***

"I told you they would beat Drakken. Didn't matter if he was the best."

Dreamlike voices, distant and filtered through the cotton stuffed in her ears, floated just above her head.

"Yeah, but did you see *how* they beat him? *Chak.* The kid's totally iced. The Fleet Commander wants to terminate Rogman."

"Right. Rogman is so far up the Sovereign's *assino...* hey—hand me that."

100

Something pricked her forearm. Jetta tried to pull away, but gloved hands clamped down on her, holding her still as a terrible itch worked its way up her arm and spread across her neck and chest.

"Gods, this one's a fighter. Give me a double."

The itching grew more intense until it became a flame held too close to her skin.

"You-know-who is going to have a field day with this one. Not one of those three is like the rest."

My skin—my skin!

She could feel her skin bubbling up and crisping under the terrible flame as it sizzled its way into her muscle and bone.

"Don't mention that name—I'm having nightmares about this whole operation."

"Yeah, it gives me the jitters, too."

Someone held her chin up, forcing her eyes open against harsh lights. Her entire body felt on fire, her insides boiling and exploding like an overheated furnace.

"Well, at any rate, this one ain't worth it. It's the boy that's special."

"No way. This here's the devil they've been looking for."

I'm not the devil, Jetta tried to say, but her lips seemed soldered shut. Somewhere in the distance she heard Yahmen laughing.

***

Jetta looked up. A man wearing a flight suit studded with colorful insignia sat across from her, his fingers drumming the armrest of his chair.

"You can't just assume that with an acceleration rate of 0.12 you can break free from the gravitational pull of the planet *and* pull off that little rotational maneuver. It just can't work outside a simulation."

Jetta looked at her hands grasping the controls of a flight simulator. Before her was the projected image of a complement of five fighters hovering above a ringed planet.

What am I doing?

Frustrated, the man pointed his finger at the playing field. "Let's do this again."

Where am I?

Only the gaming console and two chairs occupied the room slated in gray. Jetta looked for an exit and saw none until her eye caught a sliver of light leaking through a crack in the wall to her left. Black pods situated in the corners of the ceiling followed her every movement.

How did I get here? She tried to focus on the thought, but it kept slipping from her grasp.

"Pay attention!"

Jetta jumped in her seat. She knew she had to play against this officer, and she had to win. She didn't know why, but losing was very bad—very dangerous.

The playing field changed; an asteroid belt replaced the ringed planet. She didn't know what to do. How could she possibly play her five fighters against his warship and two mid-sized battleships? She considered employing a run-and-hide technique, praying that the warship didn't follow her deeper into the belt, but then she saw that the orders displayed on her console: destroy all enemy ships in under ten minutes.

Bewildered, Jetta looked to the officer. The light from the playing field distorted the features of his face, elongating his nose and jaw. No longer humanoid, the officer morphed into a large, hungry rat, waiting for her to fall asleep on her cot so he could nibble on her toes.

No, this isn't Fiorah, she told herself. *This is another place, another nightmare. Jaeia—Jahx—where are you?*

(No; can't think of them now. Concentrate. Winning is surviving.)

Using the holographic interface, Jetta commanded her five fighters to break away and dodge in and out between asteroids, buying some time. She didn't want to do it, but she looked into the predatory eyes of the officer attacking her fighters.

Bridging across the psionic boundaries, Jetta fell into a cold, controlled mind. Everything she needed to win pushed right up against her senses: what he assumed she would attempt, what he would do, and his fifty years of combat experience with the Dominion Core. But nothing else. Not a clue as to what she was doing, why she was here.

(This isn't right—)

102

Jetta wanted to keep only to the essentials to evade his detection, but without the aid of her siblings, she would have to take it all if she was going to stand a chance fighting him. And therein lay their greatest danger. Emotion and sensation intertwined with memory, as well as what she and her siblings feared most—reaction. Every Sentient was different, and every imprint was different, but there was always that one—the imprint that reacted to her talent, slipping under her skin and embedding itself within her so that it was indistinguishable from self.

"Kill all the prisoners."

"I don't care how you do it."

(The people need wholesome fear)

(They want someone to frighten them)

(They want to submit)

Jetta ignored the hollowed-out feeling in her stomach. She could feel his whole presence sliding into hers, his slimy impulses threading through her veins.

I don't want him inside me... Jetta pressed her knuckles against her forehead, forcing herself to focus on his knowledge.

The asteroids, she realized, concentrating as hard as she could. *Slingshot tunnel—the Battle of Greaod...*

The officer didn't consciously recall the feat—but she did.

Jetta flicked her left wrist very carefully, maneuvering her fighters out of range of the warship but drawing the battleships toward a large asteroid with a strong gravitational pull. She commanded two of her fighters to dump their plasma waste, overriding the computer's default safety measures.

"What are you doing?" the officer asked, smirking. "Giving up already?"

The two fighters, lagging behind to discharge their plasma waste, came into firing range. Since the waste evacuation didn't register on his monitors, he didn't see what was coming. After gathering her remaining three fighters near a large asteroid, Jetta ordered them to engage all engines at full capacity while in lock. It would do nothing against the asteroid itself, but everything would change when the battleships fired their ion cannons at the plasma waste.

"Stupid launnie. I thought you were supposed to be—"

He never finished his sentence. Fire from the battleships ignited the plasma waste, creating the effect that, after the Battle of Greaod, was termed a "slingshot tunnel." The blast from the engines of her three remaining fighters created the necessary directional push for the asteroid to rocket through the slingshot, demolishing her two fighters, but also his warship and two battleships.

It was over.

The officer fell silent, black pods in the corners chirped. Someone fumbled with a door handle, and she shielded her eyes as light poured in, outlining a tall figure looming in the doorway.

***

"You'll have two hours."

Jetta shook her head. *What's happening?*

Her brother and sister sat on either side of her at a supersized Endgame console, the enormous war globe swirling in front of them. Across from them were five rows of heavily decorated officers, each with their own interface modules linking into the holographic globe that spanned almost the entire arena.

The air popped and fizzed with electrical charge from all the machinery, making it smell faintly of burning plastic. Jetta squinted, trying to look through the holographic playing field to get a better view. The officers' faces, yellowed by the light, appeared indistinguishable one from another. *Is that the pudgy Admiral I played a few weeks ago? Or was it months?*

All of the senior commanders are here, Jahx shared within their bond.

Rogman came up behind her, writing something on a datapad, mustache in a twitch. "Watch your defensive line. You're losing points taking wild gambles to get their flagship. Keep your numbers tight."

Another game. *But this one is different.* Fighting seasoned officers was hard enough, but lately Rogman had been integrating some impossible obstacles to overcome, or handicapping them with damaged vessels and inferior weapons. This setup proved even more

104

demanding. Instead of one of them playing the game, they each controlled a separate legion of the fleet. The allotted game pieces had also been increased. Jetta's force alone numbered in the thousands, and as her complement tallied up on console, she held her breath until she thought she would pass out. *I've never fought with so many pieces before. How are we going to manage them and formulate a strategy against so many other players?*

Jetta slumped in her seat. *There are so many minds—how am I going to pick apart each one?* It took time and stealth not to get caught. They couldn't fight like they had in the Academy, and she couldn't be as stupid and reckless as she had been about Drakken. Winning now would require a different strategy.

I'm so tired... Jaeia thought.

Jetta agreed. She couldn't remember the last time she had slept—or eaten—or done anything else but play game after game. *It feels like this is all we have ever done.*

The idea of not playing briefly circulated through their shared thoughts, but it was universally dismissed as soon as it came.

We can't, Jahx said, inner voice racked with pain. *We have to play.*

Jetta dared a glance at the Commandant standing over her shoulder. *Rogman is dangerous,* she thought, feeling his midnight eyes at the back of her head. A feverish warmth took hold, and she pulled at her collar with a trembling hand, trying to get some air. *Not playing is dangerous.*

The game clock buzzed.

Within seconds, a swarm of enemy ships came crushing down on the triplets' front line. Jetta moved her fighters out of range, and seeing her siblings' positions through their eyes, matched their retreat.

Biting her lip, Jetta pushed back her anxieties and the drumming heartbeats of her siblings, and concentrated on the readings scrolling down her console. It didn't matter where she looked. Swiping through different angles of the battle, she saw only slaughter and defeat.

Look, Jetta offered as they pulled back their forces for a second time, *they're not like us. Their movements will never be as fast as ours; they can't see the game like we can. Let's use that to our advantage.*

105

Jahx's fatigue pulled at the back of her mind. *I can't fight anymore,* he said, loosening his grip on the controls. *I don't want to fight anymore...*

Please, Jahx, Jetta begged, eyeing Rogman coming up behind her brother. *Let's just win this one. He'll let us take a break after this—I just know it.*

She didn't know why she thought she could lie to her brother and sister like that, but they wanted to believe it just as much as she did.

"Get your fleet moving, cadet," Rogman whispered into Jahx's ear. Through Jahx's senses Jetta could smell his breath, making her lurch forward in a vain effort to get away from the stench.

Come on, come on, Jetta told herself. *Find something. Find their weakness.*

Jetta tried to rifle through all the easily accessible knowledge she had stolen, but nothing useful came to mind. The last thing she wanted to do was dig through the slimy experiences of the Dominion Core personnel and synergize a new strategy from their polluted memories.

Rogman appeared at her side as she flew one of her winged complements around the edge of the playing field to get a better view of the game. *He knows I'm stalling.*

"Why are you holding back?" he whispered in her ear. His breath reminded her of the stink of Galm's old dentures. "You have already mastered them. Stop playing like a launnie and think like the razor you are. Or maybe you are just a street rat after all..."

The playing field became a frenzy of electric color and sound. Seeing the battlefield from three sets of eyes, Jetta knew that it was going to take something radical to defeat the horde of officers. Outnumbered and outmaneuvered, she would have to face one of her worst fears to pull off a win.

Jetta bit her lip again, this time hard enough to draw blood. The three of them purposely locked away the darker memories of the Dominion Core personnel from their consciousness. Even glimpses of their acts of cruelty—torturing prisoners and slaughtering civilians—left her nauseous and hollowed. And that only grazed the surface of their crimes.

Shivers ran up her spine. *Some things just aren't worth experiencing.*

Wiping the sweat from her brow, Jetta told herself she would have to do it. She had weathered awful minds before—why would this be any different? *But never this many at once*, she thought to herself.

No, she decided after watching her brother and sister fumbling with their game pieces, *I can handle it; I'm not afraid of their evil.*

"No, Jetta—I'll do it," Jahx whispered to her.

"What?" Jetta exclaimed.

He turned to her, his blue eyes resolute and shadowed by the knowledge of the terrible undertaking he was about to endure.

"Jahx, no—it should be me—" Jaeia began, but it was too late.

Jetta's mind stretched backward as Jahx dissociated from his body and folded into their shared consciousness. She gripped the controls of her console with all her might as her vision telescoped beyond the room and into the space between.

Wait! Jetta screamed, her body shaking violently.

Jahx pulled down both his sisters as he sank into psionic limbo, tearing at the seams of corporeality. While he slalomed through the memories of the Dominion Core officers, Jetta shielded herself from the grisly backsplash.

Please, Jahx, *she pleaded.* I can't hold on—

Jetta only saw fragments of Jahx's ordeal as the visage of the past reverberated through their common bond. Thrust behind the eyes of an officer, she stood over an enemy soldier tangled in barbed wire. The dying man, suffocating as he thrashed to free himself, reached out to her. Jetta heard her own voice reciting the officer's favorite mantra: "Cruelty commands respect."

After giving the final order to her flight team to bomb the remainder of the city, Jetta watched from a safe distance as missiles rained down on helpless citizens. Men in blue and black uniforms bludgeoned surrendered soldiers while she sat nearby drinking tea and going over the spoils with other officers. She laughed as a mass execution concluded with cheers from her troops.

Lashing backward, Jetta yanked her mind away from her brother and sister before she experienced more. I can't bear their brutality—

She heard Jaeia's cry echo across the expanse, rising in ferocity until it suddenly stopped.

Jetta opened her eyes. Jahx leaned into the hologram, his face distorted by the lights of the projection field, eyes glowing red.

I can see them, he whispered through their connection.

Jahx—what did you do? Jetta said, surprised at her own tears. How could she have allowed her brother to risk himself like that? He shouldn't have had to bear the burden of so many evil minds. And how could she have abandoned her siblings during their darkest moment?

I'm weak, Jetta thought to herself, mashing her fist into her stomach. *It should have been me.* The pain felt good, but not as vindicating as she'd hoped.

"Follow my lead," Jahx said as he silently commanded them to restructure their attack. Looking beyond the field of play, Jetta sensed the buried gleanings her brother had unearthed and synergized into a cohesive, tangible strategy.

Jahx, my Gods—

Every move her brother commanded carved into the enemy forces effortlessly, every action and reaction met with indescribable perfection. He understood the enemy—he saw every possible outcome of the game—and he commanded their fleet to a victory in less than an hour.

Three to fifty minds—or more—and an improbable and unbelievable victory.

"Congratulations," Rogman said, terminating the game. The hologram canceled out with an angry whine from the soundboard.

Jetta touched her brother's hand, but it felt cold and unfamiliar. The detachment in his eyes stayed with her long after the soldiers dragged them away.

***

Time passed by in disjointed thoughts and splintered feelings. Through it all there was Rogman and the Endgame. The stupid game never went away, even after Jetta rebelled. When she did, Rogman separated them, and somehow made their voices disappear in her head.

Jaeia, Jahx, she called out, rocking back and forth on the edge of her bed. *Please, I need you. Where are you? WHERE ARE YOU?*

Silence. A deadness to the world that hollowed her bones and emptied her soul. She curled up in her bed and tried to remember her siblings' faces, but her mind couldn't recall a single detail.

Slowly and carefully to avoid the camera eyes in every corner of her grey prison, Jetta scraped her fingernails up and down her arm. She welcomed the pain, and its divine liberation. It provided something real to hold on to, and as a warm wetness trickled down her skin, she felt release.

Rogman didn't seem overly concerned no matter how many times she hurt herself. Nobody did. A trip to the infirmary patched wounds, and when she returned to her quarters, there were more cameras on the walls, and more frequent checks by the guards at her door.

With her arm screaming in sweet pain, Jetta comforted herself with the only hope she had left. She would see her brother and sister again at game time. Rogman still allowed that. A fragile smile trembled its way across her lips.

For now, the voice inside her whispered.

Jetta's smile collapsed, her teeth setting upon teeth in madness. Scrambling to her feet, she tore the sheets and mattress from the bed. After overturning the frame, she stomped and kicked the metal bars until they split apart at the junctures. With no other furniture to destroy, she attacked the grey paneling, repeatedly slamming her fists. She didn't recognize the metal material, but some part of her knew that she shouldn't be able to punch holes through the wall.

Exhausted and spent, Jetta finally sat down on the cold tile floor, surrounded by her bloodstained destruction.

Jetta braced her head in her hands. *Why is this happening? Where did I go wrong?*

On Fiorah she always managed some kind of plan, even if implausible, but concentrating on escape—on anything—seemed impossible. Things only made sense when she played the Endgame. Putting her mind to anything else resulted in more confusion.

This is all my fault...

The lock clicked over, but she didn't lift her head from her hands. It would probably be the guards and a nurse with a tranquilizer to take her to the infirmary. *While I'm gone they'll repair the damage, and things will just start all over again.*

Lights dimmed and heating ducts groaned with strain.

"What the hell?" she said, standing up as a rank miasma impregnated her room. She backed up into the overturned bed when she saw the creature hulking in her open doorway. At first she thought it was a machine—and then she saw the decaying fragments of flesh stretched over the segments of its mechanical body. One bloodshot eye bulged from its organic socket, white jelly spilling from the inner canthus.

She recognized the same psionic energy she had sensed the first time she had visited Rogman's office. *Was this thing there when the Commandant threatened me?*

Its spidery feet made a *clickety-clack, clickety-clack* as it entered her quarters. She shielded her face, thinking the thing would attack her. Instead, it extended one of its legs, offering her something. At first she didn't accept the ear bud dangling from its pincers, but when it started to speak, its voice shrill and grating, she nabbed it. Wedging the remote translator in her ear, she wrapped her arms around her head to protect herself from the sound of its voice.

"I am M'ah Pae, Overlord of the Motti," he began. As he reached up with one of his mechanical legs and deactivated the cameras, Jetta noticed that he bore no Dominion insignia. "You are Jetta, one of three. There is respect for you among us."

Jetta didn't know how to respond. She couldn't understand exactly what he felt—or if he even possessed conventional emotions—and the expressions on his face were twisted by the mechanical implants.

"You are a humanoid I do not despise. You are different from the others. You share my disgust for the infectious impurity of the Sentients, for the lesser beings that try to control you."

"What are you talking about?" Jetta asked, digging her nails into her thighs just to keep from hyperventilating. *Jaeia—Jahx—where are you? Help me—*

"I know your blood—you are a telepath. And you are Fiorahian. There is nothing you can do to escape your persecution."

Jetta heart stopped in her chest. *He knows our secret.* Did that mean that the Core knew about her too? If so, that meant that—

—the thought disappeared. *What is happening? Something about a shared disgust.*

110

"The Motti are the same. They call us the Deadwalkers. The Core uses us for our technology, but we are nothing but slaves to them. Just like you. They are using you, too."

"Why are you telling me this?" Jetta asked.

He smiled, revealing a row of metallic gums and black nubs for teeth. "Play the games as I know you can, and I will give you the power to defeat your enemies and claim what is rightfully yours."

Jetta gnawed on the inside of her cheek, trying to think clearly. *Who or what is this thing and why is he telling me this?*

"No... I can't. I can't," she said, shaking her head. "Rogman is watching."

The Motti Overlord emitted frenzied mechanical chatter. *Is he laughing?*

"You only need to be shown the power in your grasp. I will show you. Then you will not stop until the universe is cleansed."

This is a trick. It has to be a trick. Everybody lies. "No," Jetta whispered.

His face contorted in the oddest way, causing blood to ooze out from the corner of his eye. "If you don't, I know someone else who will."

"Stay away from my brother and sister!" Jetta shouted.

She lunged at the creature, but he caught her by the neck with one of his mechanical legs. As she struggled to breathe against the metal grip, he drew her close. His cadaverous flesh reminded her of the bodies she used to find in the dumpster on Fiorah, and her stomach threatened revolt against the stench.

"I do not understand your resistance. Do you not understand what you are? You are better than them. You are the next evolution. But if you will not see, then I will make you see. General Volkor. He will be your eyes. Through him you will find your destiny."

When he released her she fell and cracked her head against the tile floor. She tried to reach out to her siblings, but the world faded to black before she could find them.

***

"I understand your concern, but we cannot wait for any more of your trials. They've already shown considerably less resistance when separated. There is no need to destroy the other two."

A voice, shrill and grating, responds.

"The Sovereign himself has issued this ruling. I must follow orders."

That voice—it hurts my ears.

"Your insistence leads me to believe that you've invested too much interest in this project. The Sovereign is paying you for your technology, not your *suggestions.*"

Rage heats the room. A long pause. *Clickety-clack-clickety-clack* fades into the distance.

I remember that sound, Jetta thought.

"Filthy abominations."

Another voice, much deeper and filled with concern. "Commandant Rogman, Sir, this is not the first time that—"

Pause.

"—has *suggested* that the one of candidates be, uh, 'converted.' I think they're up to something."

The first voice is filled with confidence—*arrogance.* "What are you getting at, Temmins? The Deadwalkers are nothing. They're puppets. *Our* puppets."

Doubt, suspicion. The first voice becomes irritated.

"I don't have time for this—General Volkor is long overdue. I need a full report in three hours or it'll be your *penjehtos* that I'll send as restitution."

Oh Gods, what is that crawling up my arm? It itches—no, burns—

Make it stop, MAKE IT STOP—

***

Where am I?

Jetta lifted her head from the gaming control console. Looking around, she couldn't decide if she was awake, or if it was a continuation of the nightmare.

Rogman appeared in her peripheries, bending so his eyes leveled with Jetta's. Frightened and disoriented, she knew enough not to return her gaze, keeping her eyes fixed on the war globe in front of her as she straightened in her chair.

"This war globe module is modified to anticipate your command based on your previous strategies," he said, pointing to the rotating sphere in front of her. Jetta's eyes diverted to the supercomputer feeding into the opposing console. Expansive, with entire columns of lighted data processors humming and blinking, it spanned half the war room. "Listen to yourself, and listen closely. You have all the training you need. Rely on your eyes. Rely on your *intuition*."

Rogman leaned in for the final delivery. "Or I'll send your brother back to Fiorah. Alone."

Perspiration drenched her uniform. How was she supposed to play an opponent who had no psyche, nothing for her to glean—or nothing for her to frighten? Those were her best tricks—her only tricks for winning—for surviving.

Attack Rogman.

Jetta weighed the option, as she had a thousand times before. Though bricked from her sights, Rogman's mind was not impenetrable. She could sacrifice exposure and dig behind his eyes, tear out his worst fear, and force him to relive his greatest nightmare.

A smile played at the corners of Rogman's mouth. "Mind yourself, cadet."

I could kill him, she thought angrily, *but could I kill all the soldiers in time to save my siblings?*

Jetta eyed the silver-eyed soldiers guarding the exit, fear snaking into her stomach. The answer was always the same. *I have to play.*

"Bring the other two in," Rogman said into his sleeve com. Soldiers escorted Jaeia and Jahx into the war room.

Jetta could barely stay seated. As soon as her brother and sister came within a few meters, she could hear them again in her mind.

I missed you—how are you—what have they done to you?! Jetta blurted.

Jahx's eyes remained downcast as he logged in to his station. *I'm fine.*

Face gaunt and pale, Jaeia sat in her chair and brought up her ancillary holograms for the match. She looked like she had lost another two kilos.

Jaeia, Gods, they're going to start force-feeding you again! Jetta thought, but her sister had no reaction to her outreach.

Rogman placed a hand on Jetta's shoulder and squeezed. "Let's begin, shall we?"

113

The game was slated against them from the start. Vastly outnumbered, Jetta didn't know how she would gain any advantage, especially with the opposing forces spread out behind two planets, an asteroid belt and dwarf star. Far more crippling was the enemy itself. Cold and emotionless, Jetta didn't know how to attack a supercomputer.

Bring the fighters around to mark 01-1, Jetta instructed her sister. *We can draw fire from their battleship and move the warship into position.*

No, that won't work. We'll forfeit our defensive line, Jaeia replied silently, swiveling in her chair and calling up different holographic views of the fight.

Jetta heard Rogman impatiently tapping on his datapad. Looking to her left, she only afforded herself a quick glance at her brother. Blue eyes, ringed with dark circles, weathered storms she could not see.

I have to win this. He can't go back, Jetta thought privately.

Losses tallied up quickly on her console. In less than a minute, she had lost a battleship and a legion of fighters.

I can't do this, Jetta thought, watching the enemy fighters descend upon their warship.

No, but we can, her brother whispered across their bond.

Not knowing what else to do, Jetta yielded, allowing her brother's perspective to take hold. The game pieces in the display came to life, lighting up across the globe. Impossible numbers and variables projected on every holographic access. Panic dissolved, and something new, something beyond her steadied her thundering heart and expanded her sight.

"I see..." she whispered. Her arms reached out to touch the holographic interface, tentatively at first, but when she selected the first attack, a warm wash of confidence filled her, and her hands, as if working on their own, found the next move.

"Beta team in flight pattern Nova," Jaeia commanded across the console.

"Move all ground units to position 1-1-9," Jahx added.

Jetta licked her lips. Hands moving faster now, her voice called from within, projecting her ideas to her siblings and receiving their augmented perspectives in blasts of wheeling light. She felt

114

perfection, a flawless intuition she had never experienced before. Impossible against a non-Sentient opponent, but somehow—

"Yes," Rogman said, coming up behind Jetta as they flanked the enemy warship and prepared for the final assault. "Finish the job."

Torn between two realities, Jetta mouthed Rogman's orders, barely aware of her body already reacting to the command.

"Fire all weapons," Jetta said.

"Firing all weapons," Jaeia echoed, locking in the enemy target.

"Target destroyed," Jahx announced as the enemy warship exploded. Wreckage spewed across the holographics as the remaining enemy fighters retreated.

What was that feeling? Jetta wondered, reaching out to touch the war globe. The lights reacted to her touch, burnt oranges and sun yellows dancing around her fingers. *Connection like I've never felt before...*

"Well done, cadet," Rogman said. "Better than projected."

Jetta shot out of her chair as soldiers, armed with shockwands, yanked her siblings from their seats and shoved them out the door.

"Why are you doing this?" Jetta screamed, lunging from Rogman.

Rogman faded back, allowing the soldiers to tackle and pin her down.

One shock, then a second to extinguish all the fight from her. Jetta lost focus, though she recognized the smell of charred flesh wafting up to her nose.

Standing over her, Rogman gazed down at her, his hands clasped behind his back. "Don't worry. We're almost through with you."

***

Reht Jagger found the Healer in the black hills of Algar, five kilometers from her village. Barefoot and clothed in only a bloody, ripped nightgown, Triel sat in a bed of wildflowers.

"I came as soon as I heard," he said, approaching her cautiously.

"It all happened so fast," she whispered, still looking out toward the bright flames that consumed her village. Tears ran steadily down her cheeks as she shivered in the cold night air. "Everyone is gone."

"Not everybody," he said, offering her his jacket.

115

The Healer took it absently, but did not pull it around her shoulders.

Her tribal markings haven't faded, Reht said, remembering what she had told him long ago about Healers turning into Dissemblers. *She hasn't Fallen...yet.*

Reht glanced down the hill where the *Wraith* idled a few meters off the ground, his crew ready to depart at a moment's notice.

"Ro, Cray," he whispered into the com on his shirtsleeve. "Anything?"

"No," Ro said. "Not a single *chakking* warship on the scopes."

Not that there would be. By the swath of destruction, Reht couldn't imagine the Dominion had anything to stick around for. Still, he didn't want to take any chances.

"Keep on it," Reht ordered. "Those bastards use autodroids and robotic surveyors to comb the debris for survivors."

"Aye, captain," Ro and Cray said in unison.

Reht clicked off the com. Not yet knowing what to say, Reht fiddled with the bandages on his hands. He had no ties to Algar, but still, the flames, the peaceful blue and green world gouged and gashed, reminiscent of his own pain—

Elia. My own world, destroyed.

"Reht," Triel said, pulling him from his thoughts. She hugged his jacket into her chest. "How did you find me?"

"You said you always ran to the hills when you got in a fight with your parents," Reht said, braving a few more steps toward her.

Finally, she looked at him, blue eyes searching him for answers he didn't have. "I ran away. I hid. Again. I couldn't just let the Dominion take me."

Carefully, Reht laid a hand on her bare shoulder. The coolness of her skin worried him, but when she placed a gentle hand on top of his, his concern evaporated. He knelt down and took her in his arms, kissing the top of her head. "My Starfox, oh Gods, I was so worried."

The Healer's tears soaked through his shirt. "There's nothing left for me here."

"You're coming back with me," he said, squeezing her tight. "You'll still have your family."

She pulled back, looking him in the eye. "You know I can't go with you. Not now."

116

Guilt and sorrow tore down the illusion of his words. "Okay," he relented, cupping her face. "But I'll take you somewhere safe until this Scare is over. I know a safehouse in the Polaris system."

Triel of Algardrien looked back to her village. Buildings, caving in, gave rise to reaching flames and plumes of smoke. "Volkor must pay for this," she whispered.

"Yes, baby, he will," he said, still holding her tight. "I'll make sure of it."

"No," she said, voice cold as ice. "I will."

***

Jetta knew it hadn't always been like this.

Wasn't there someone else?

She felt as if someone was missing

Who?

(I can hear them—there are others here, listening.)

(I must tell them what to do.)

Too hard to think too hard to think. Think. Think. Must finish, then I can drink again.

This cannot be—

So hot, thirsty.
Not water. Something else.

My eyes, what do they see?

Holographic

Full of voices needing answers right away

Whole body skin crawling

Command. COMMAND. Come in, command.

Yes, that's right. Command them and drink

117

Scratch away this terrible—

No. This is wrong. THIS IS WRONG.

***

Scraping and scratching sounds surrounded her on all sides. Something warm and gooey dripped down her cheek. Jetta's left ear hurt; something had been crammed into the canal. She felt cold, wet breath on the same ear and smelled the musty tang in the air. Jetta wanted to open her eyes, but they stayed shut.

"Awaken, now. See them. Awaken now, and let them taste your power."

***

The alarm shrieked in Jetta's ear, but she laid in bed, breathing hard, her mouth full of sand. Her mind chased after her most recent nightmare, but it receded from her consciousness, leaving behind only the distinct sense of dread that had poisoned her sleep. She spread out her fingers and toes, arched her head back and held her breath, trying to steady the thumping in her chest.

Breathe, calm down, she told herself.

Still shaky, she untangled herself from the covers and placed a foot on the icy floor. The unpleasant sensation jarred the image of a machine creature with a burning red eye from her dream. Her stomach knotted, and she bent over, catching herself on her knees.

I have to get it together. What if we have games today?

As she dressed in the limited space of her quarters, she tried to avoid the stare of the mustached man pictured on each of the four walls. His martial scowl and hardened features frightened her, reminding her of the cruelty in Yahmen's face. Rogman told her that his name was General Volkor, and he was the newly appointed chief commander of the Dominion Core's fleet. His face infected every centimeter of the ship—on posters, news banners, and even in holographic tributes before game time. But it seemed like she'd heard the name before, somewhere, somehow, before his popularity exploded across the Starways.

As she left her room, the two guards stationed outside fell into step behind her. The mustached man and his dead black eyes followed her too, staring at her from the propaganda posters lining the corridors. The soldiers passing by barked the new Dominion salutation.

"Hail Volkor, long live the Sovereignty!"

As she boarded her lift, she wondered what Endgame scenarios they would be playing today. In the latest iteration, Rogman ordered for the Endgame controls to integrate voice command like the real war room, as if he wanted her to feel more like a real commander and less like a pet.

This is it, she thought as they sped down the corridors. *This is the last time I play, I can't—*

Nausea licked at the back of her throat. She grabbed the siderail of the lift panting for breath, cold sweat beading on her forehead.

Maybe just this one last game. I'll play this one last game.

The nausea subsided, her heartrate slowed. *Yes, I'll play.*

Excitement tingled down her arms and into her fingers as they came to a stop and she exited the lift. She licked her lips with anticipation. *I'll play, and I'll win.*

Yes, play and win. Winning kept her brother and sister alive, and could be so fiercely satisfying. No reason to dissent or rebel, not with such power at her fingertips.

Jetta stopped mid-step, her brow knitting on her forehead. *What was I...?*

It wasn't until the guard nudged her with his rifle that she picked up her pace again.

When she reached the war room, her brother and sister were already in their stations, with an entire room full of people crowding the staging area. Observers weren't uncommon, but never this many.

Ecstatic to be with her siblings, Jetta headed straight toward her brother and sister, taking a seat in between them at the console.

Jaeia, Jahx, she thought, trying to hide her smile.

Hello, Jetta, Jaeia replied wearily.

Jahx said nothing, and would not make eye contact.

What's wrong with him? Jetta asked her sister.

Jaeia kept her eyes directed to her console. *I don't know. I can't get him to talk to me, either.*

119

Jetta wanted to reach across to her brother, but Jaeia pulled her attention to the readouts. *Jetta, look at this. The last twenty games have gotten progressively easier. The computer is using fewer game pieces and more defensive strategies.*

It's a trick, Jetta replied. *Some sort of test of character. I don't know. Rogman would never make things easier.*

Jetta shook her head. She hadn't felt doubt or suspicion like this in a long time. She looked around; her observers were still mulling over their clipboards and datafiles for the game.

Jetta sucked in her lower lip. *Something's different. Something's out of place.* Normally she felt more focused, more adrenalized than this.

Daring a glance over her shoulder, Jetta spied Rogman talking to another man in a lab coat, his words heated. After the man in the lab coat hurried off, Rogman approached her and gave his orders through tightly compressed lips: "Get your secondary fleet out faster today. I want a quick victory, not a pretty one. Their forces will surrender once you cross the Front."

Jetta was supposed to nod her head, so she did. Rogman resumed his previous post next to the other decorated officers on the observation deck just behind her station. She didn't let her gaze linger long, but she realized that she knew each of the officers standing with Rogman; they were the high commanders she had been forced to play in the Endgame so many months ago. Why were they all here?

Jetta's hands trembled as the playing field downloaded onto her console and projected the blue and red lights of the game pieces across the war globe. Normally she would ring in to her fleet on the headsets, but she hesitated.

I don't have to.

Frightened at the thought, she rang in her fleet anyway and gave out her orders to start the game. After seeing that the initial assault was working, she sat back in her chair and extended herself to her siblings.

What is happening? What are we doing?

I don't like this, Jaeia answered. *I don't like the way the others are watching us. They're so anxious. There's a lot riding on this game.*

120

The thought repeated in her head several times: *There is a lot riding on this game.*

"Game..." she said aloud.

The compulsion hit her quite suddenly. She looked down at the sleeves of her uniform. *Oh Gods—*

Parts of her uniform penetrated her skin. On closer inspection, she could differentiate the threads of her sleeves from the tiny cannulas that pumped a milky white substance into her body.

"What is happening?" she whispered. *Why are my thoughts so clear?*

She didn't dwell on the question for long. *Something's happening to us, something bad.*

Resist. We need to resist! she cried out silently, feeling the pitting nausea in the bellies of her siblings as they too backed off of their command duty.

She perceived the reverberation in her own voice, and the shadow behind the psionic presence of her siblings. *There are others listening...*

Her idea of resistance resonated farther than the scope of the room, or the span of her siblings' minds; she felt like it echoed across the stars.

Game pieces stopped moving, sending ripples of satisfaction and terror coursing through her veins. *Did I just turn off the entire fleet with a single thought?*

"What is happening down there?" screamed Rogman. Men in lab coats rushed over to peer at a nearby data display. Her arms tingled, but she barely noticed over the overwhelming shift in her superiors' minds from anticipation to fear.

"We're in the dark, command base—we need your orders," a voice said into her headset.

She didn't move. She realized that if she could stop the army she commanded, she could do more.

"All the relays are down!" one of the techs shouted over the commotion. "There's a network blackout!"

"The White—the concentration doesn't seem right—" one of the men in lab coats shouted.

"Get that *thing* up here *now!*" Rogman yelled.

As the red and blue orbs of the game pieces rotated on the screen, anger swelled inside her. *The Core places such importance*

121

on this stupid game. What's next? Real battles? I don't want that—I never wanted any of this.

"We need your orders—they're mounting a counterattack!" the voice in her headset repeated more urgently.

Jetta watched as the enemy ships zeroed in on her game pieces. The tingling sensation intensified to burning, and her vision narrowed.

I'm losing control, she realized, grabbing the armrests and squeezing as hard as she could. The veins on her hands and arms bulged, and the catheters running underneath her skin backfilled with blood.

And then it came down on her like an invisible sledgehammer. Fiorah. Yahmen. The other child laborers. Laborminders. The Dominion. Cadets and teachers. Rogman. The thing with the burning red eye. Her persecutors, her tormentors. Tasting copper in her mouth, Jetta ground her teeth together as if biting through lead.

I want to eliminate them—all of them. Both sides. We could do it— Jetta thought to her siblings. *I'll end this game, and then every last person that's hurt us, every last living thing—*

Don't, Jahx whispered. *It's a trick.*

I don't understand— Jaeia cried.

I will kill them all!

But before she could act, two soldiers grabbed her by the armpits and dragged her away from her console. Chaos swarmed around her as officers shouted orders and soldiers frantically worked their stations, but it didn't bother her. The milky white fluid had resumed infusion. Her anger, once ripe and visceral, dissipated in a cloud of serenity as she floated away from herself.

The soldiers held her tightly while white-coated men shouted at each other. She tried to contact her siblings, but fog smothered their connection. What did she need to do?

What is happening to me?

(It is all my fault—Jaeia, Jahx—Galm, Lohien—I am so sorry—)

As she struggled to free herself from the soldiers' grip, something stabbed her in the shoulder. She tried to swat at the pain, but her arms were too heavy to lift. The world went upside-down, and her feet were no longer on the walkway. As her consciousness waned, she heard Rogman shout above the clamor:

"Terminate them immediately!"

***

There was no telling the difference between yesterday and the day before. For all Jahx knew, ten years could have passed just as easily as one week. There was the momentary clarity of the last Endgame and Jetta's revolt, and then today. Everything else was a blur of needle sticks and machine laughter, dissociation and terrible loneliness.

How or why he woke up again from the nightmare, he wasn't sure, but when he heard the gunfire and saw the guards leave the post outside his door, he didn't hesitate to make his escape.

Blast fire and blood painted the ruined corridors. Lights, torn from the ceiling, sparked and sputtered. Running as fast as he could through the rubble, Jahx noticed deep gouges in the walls and floor.

The monster—Jahx panicked, and tripped over a fallen beam.

Scrambling back to his feet, Jahx spotted the sign next to the door just in front of him. *Environmental Control Tower B.* Reason took charge of panic, and he kicked aside debris to get inside the control tower.

With limited power still routing into the terminals, Jahx punched up a keyboard interface. He searched the base files, trying to figure out what was going on, who had attacked the Dominion base.

(You already know who.)

The console blinked red. *Error code: 177-01*

"No," he muttered to himself. Something or someone had corrupted all the Dominion files.

Did the Dominion do this? he wondered, tracing the pattern of code destruction. He had gleaned from one of the high officers that it was a Dominion failsafe if all hell broke loose.

It must be really bad out there...

Gunfire popped and rattled off down the hall. He didn't have much time.

Working as fast as he could, Jahx found an unlaunched jump-ship still sitting in one of the lesser docking bays while he queried the location of his sisters on another terminal.

Subjects in termination holding cell 2.

The text recycled itself on the terminal three times before it sank into his bones.

"Termination..."

I can't do this, he thought, looking back at the flickering image of the jump-ship. One keystroke to prep the engines and lay in a course to anywhere but here. But he would do it alone, which meant he couldn't do it at all.

He searched for the curl of hair at the nape of his neck, not realizing his head had been shaved. Instead, his fingers found stubble, and closed lacerations at the base of his skull. The square lump jutting out of his cervical spine made him retract his hand with a stifled cry.

I am changing.

Focus. Jahx closed his eyes. The only other course of action involved a time-consuming hack into the Core sub-systems. Letting his mind expand, he saw a burgeoning putrescence, and heard the screams and cries of those who had fallen before him. Darkness was coming, infectious madness at its heels.

I can't think of what is to come for me, he thought. With tears squeezing through closed lids, he clung to memories of his sisters while his mind was still his own.

Jaeia, the quiet one, who always looked out for him in the little ways that meant so much. Cleaning out the entryway so the rats would leave them alone. Making sure that nothing was laying around the apartment for Yahmen—or Jetta—to use as a weapon. He didn't have to tell her anything—most of the time she already knew.

Jetta, the fighter. Between their minds it was always a tug of war, but he couldn't imagine a better friend or sister. He remembered when Jetta risked a beating to pick a drunken miners' pocket for his stash of red opium and then slipped the ground-up weed into Yahmen's drink. Her success bought them all a day of peace. No matter how ugly things got, Jetta always pulled through for him and Jaeia.

Jahx licked his lips, wishing he could quench his maddening thirst, but the gunfire outside his door became more sporadic as the Core's resistance dwindled.

He had to make the decision. Scratching at the dry skin on the base of his neck, Jahx looked longingly at the secondary shaft that could lead out of the utility room and drop him into the docking bay.

124

It would be so easy. He could hide out on one of the far moons until things settled.

"Jetta," he whispered under his breath as his fingers worked furiously to access the sub-systems, "I hope you'll understand."

***

A boy with black hair and bleached-blue eyes stood in front of her against an endless black mirror. His lips did not move, but he spoke to her in a language that did not need words.

Jetta felt his sorrow and his love, but it receded like the boy himself, wavering, vanishing into shadow.

He had traded his life for theirs.

She screamed, but sound was not possible in this place. She had failed him.

He was lost.

CHAPTER III

Black smoke, pumping out from the broken engine of the escape pod, blotted out cloudy skies.

Is this real? Jetta thought, trying to lift her head off of the ground. *How did I get here?*

She remembered being afraid, trapped inside grey walls with men in uniforms holding her down.

A blue sky with white clouds. Grass and trees. Somewhere new—

The noxious smell of burning fuel irritated her lungs. Coughing, Jetta tried to roll onto her side, but the broken door from the escape pod pinned her legs.

Oh Gods, I can't move—

Taking fistfuls of grass and tugging with all her strength, Jetta tried to free herself. The door creaked, but didn't budge. Bolts of pain shot through her legs and up her spine, and she collapsed, panting for air.

"Jaeia? Jahx?" she called out. The trees, swaying in the light winds, answered with a rustling of leaves.

Propping herself up on an elbow, Jetta scanned the surrounding forest. The crash landing stripped limbs from trees and set fire to branches. *Jaeia, Jahx—where are you?!*

Head spinning from the fumes, Jetta spotted her sister shaking violently on the ground ten meters to her left.

"Jaeia!" she croaked, stretching out to reach her. The shift in her weight caused the escape pod door to come crushing down on her legs.

The pain, oh Gods—I can't—

A feverish heat seized her body. With each breath she took, an invisible vice tightened down around her chest. Fresh blood dribbled from her mouth as she clawed wildly at her throat, trying to pull air into starving lungs.

As the world gave way to suffocating darkness, she tried to call out to her siblings one last time.

***

"Not so fast or she'll choke," said a gruff voice overhead. Strong hands forced Jetta's jaw open, and a thick, tasteless liquid

127

filled her throat. When she spit out the contents of her mouth, the hands gripped her more tightly. Finally she swallowed, defeated.

"Enough. Let her rest," the voice said. The hands went away, and she collapsed into something soft and warm. She slept.

***

Voices, above her.

"Wait—I've seen those markings before."

A hand gently turned her right arm outwards.

"And?" another voice inquired.

Silence. *Reflection.*

"How unusual. This was spoken of when I was with the Order."

Silence. *Fear.*

"Gather the others quickly. We must prepare."

***

Blurry images hovered above her in the low, phosphorescent light. A thick, metallic taste lingered in her mouth. She tried to sit up but couldn't.

"You're still weak, dear," an old, raspy voice said. A calloused hand came to rest on Jetta's shoulder, and she shrugged it away. "Please—I mean you no harm."

"Where are my brother and sister?" she managed to say, though her jaw felt stiff and sore. The image overhead solidified into the face of an old man stroking his bedraggled length of white beard. Withered brows overshadowed dark amethyst eyes.

"Your sister is right here." He leaned back so she could see the rocky outcropping where her sister lay. She seemed to be sleeping, peaceful and safe.

"How did...?" Jetta muttered, squinting to see in the dim light of what seemed to be a cave. Bundles of glowing orbs clustered on vines winding along the cavern ceiling and walls, illuminating massive pillars and stalagmites.

Wasn't I just outside?

No, the air here smelled thick with moisture and mildew, reminding her of the inside of an engine coolant mixer she had fixed on Fiorah.

128

"Where is my brother?" she asked, trying to leverage up on her elbow. Her side screamed in pain, and she fell back into her bed made of animal skins.

Confusion bunched together the old man's brows. "We found only the two of you by the escape pod. There were no others."

Where is Jahx? Why isn't he with us?

Closing her eyes, Jetta thought back to the Dominion ships, but the last thing she remembered was playing Drakken Varkanian in the Endgame. Beyond that, there was nothing. Nothing at all. Her mouth went very dry and her stomach ached.

"Who are you? Why are you hiding Jahx from me?" Jetta demanded.

The old man looked shocked. "Goodness, child. I am the Grand Oblin, and I am not hiding anyone."

Jetta rolled on her side and bent at the waist, but every fiber in her body protested against the effort until, exhausted, she lay back again. She could sense Jaeia's thoughts but not Jahx's. *He's not here.*

"My child, you've been through so much," the old man said, gingerly patting her shoulder. "I'll let you rest and come back later."

He tried to get up, but his knees locked. When he strained, his eyes almost disappeared between the folds of wrinkles.

"No—" Jetta shouted, reaching out and grabbing him by the sleeve of his robe. His memories exploded across her retinas, thrusting her headfirst into his most recent thoughts.

Through his eyes she saw men in fatigues carry her and Jaeia's broken bodies into the cave. Someone waved a bioscanner above her chest while another bandaged her leg. Meanwhile, a muscular man with a red facial tattoo yelled at the Grand Oblin, challenging his decisions. He was afraid of Jetta and Jaeia and the marking on their arms.

"Gods," Jetta said, retracting her hand and covering her eyes. Someone else's memories never came rushing into her with just a touch.

"Be careful, child—you've been through a lot." His forehead creased in concern. "Things must seem drastically out of place."

"Where is Jahx? Where are we?" she said, her voice rising in intensity.

The Grand Oblin leaned on his walking stick and stroked his beard. "This is Tralora, former home of the Narki, in the Elaraqui system. Do you remember why you were sentenced here?"

Sentenced? Jetta thought. *Wake up, Jaeia!* she called to her sleeping sister. *I don't understand what is happening!*

With frustrating deliberation, the old man felt around in the pockets of his robe. Finally he withdrew a bright red plant root and placed it in his mouth, chewing with exaggerated bites.

Since Jetta didn't answer him, he probed further. "Do you remember how you got here?"

His words triggered a hazy memory of the crash and she flinched, but she fought through it, trying to think harder about the question. *What's happened? How did we end up here? Where is Jahx?*

When she tried to focus her energy on her brother, it seemed to rebound. Her mind raced with disjointed thoughts and images—
Escape

Resistance,

Thirsty, so thirsty,

Must escape

MY SKIN

Jahx?

Jetta held her throbbing head in her hands. Something terrible lurked just beyond her grasp.

The old man nodded as if he understood and removed the root from his mouth. He broke it open, and an orange-colored gel oozed from the tip. He held it by the thick end and leaned toward her.

"Stay away—" she warned, scooting backward on her elbows. She bit her lip against the pain.

His tone, which had been warm and lighthearted, turned serious. "Sometimes when bad things happen, we start to see the enemy all around us. I assure you, I am not your enemy."

Jetta's hands clenched into fists, but tears welled in her eyes. She blinked them away. She wouldn't cry in front of this stranger.

"If you are not my enemy, then who is?" she asked.

The Grand Oblin placed the root next to her. "This is only to help with the pain, help you sleep. Rub the gel on your skin until it's completely absorbed. But if you don't want it, you don't have to have it. We'll talk more tomorrow."

His knees made a cracking sound as he rose from his perch on the rocks. He paused for a moment, seeming to take in more than just her image.

"Sleep well, my friend," the Grand Oblin said, lifting a weathered hand. He slowly shuffled out of the cave, the soft tap of his walking stick eventually fading into the darkness with him.

"Jaeia," Jetta called. When her sister did not rouse, Jetta tried more firmly, using her inner voice to augment what she said aloud. "Jaeia!"

As she struggled to free herself from the bedding, her hand slipped, and her elbow landed in the orange gel.

"*Skucheka!*" she cursed in Fiorahian, trying to rub it off.

Within seconds her heart rate slowed, and the need to rush over and wake her sister replaced by the irresistible desire to sleep.

"No, Jaeia—Jahx," she mumbled, her head very heavy—too heavy to hold up.

She haphazardly rolled out of bed, falling to the ground in a crumpled heap. Her eyes, weighted, could barely stay open.

Can't fall asleep.

Jetta crawled and clawed her way over to her twin, injured leg screaming in pain as it dragged along the rocky floor. With a grunt she lifted her arms and pulled herself with the last of her strength atop the rock pile next to her sister. There, concentrating on the presence of her sibling and the steady pulse of pain in her leg, she fought the urge to sleep.

***

Hours passed in dreamlike realness. Still perched on the rocky outcropping next to her sister, Jetta chewed her thumbnail, rocking back and forth, waiting for Jaeia to wake up. She had fought off the sedating effects of the root, but as tired as she was, she couldn't stop herself from drifting in and out of sleep, and she awoke to Jaeia tentatively shaking her by the shoulders.

"Jetta," she croaked. Her eyes were wide and frantic in bruised-looking hollows. "Where's Jahx? I can't feel him."

131

Jetta held her head and tried to push back the despair that rushed in with Jaeia's words. "He isn't here. I don't know what happened. We'll find him, just as soon as we get out of here."

"But where are we?" Jaeia asked. She wobbled as she tried to stand but managed to catch herself on a nearby stalagmite, gasping at the pain. Her ragged shirt gaped, and Jetta sucked in a breath at her first sight of the deep, scabbed lacerations on her sister's torso.

"What's that?" Jaeia asked, pointing to where Jetta's pants had rucked up, exposing wounds of her own. Jetta rolled her pant leg up further, wincing as it brushed the bloodied lump just below her knee.

Seeing her sister's wounds and some of her own, Jetta's heart raced. She didn't want to know any more, but before she could stop herself, she pulled up her shirt.

"Gods..."

Some of the wounds were fresh, like the lump on her leg and the dark bruises that discolored her side. The others, though, had healed as much as they ever would, crisscrossing her chest and abdomen with surgical precision.

"These aren't from the crash," Jetta mumbled, tracing the marks with a finger.

Lines of worry pinched the corners of Jaeia's mouth. "Do you remember?" Jaeia began, but she stopped when her fingers found the scar that zigzagged across her inner forearm.

"The last thing I can really remember," she continued, pulling her sleeve down over the scar, "is beating Drakken."

Jetta looked at her solemnly and whispered, "Me too."

Jaeia nodded, her facial expressions carefully neutral. Feeling that her twin tried to control her psionic projections to not upset her further only made things worse.

Jahx—oh Gods—where are you? Jetta thought, panic kicking her heart into overdrive.

The Grand Oblin peeked into their cavern.

"Feeling better?" he asked gaily as he hobbled inside, leaning heavily on his walking stick. In his other hand he carried a milky-white, semi-spherical object with luminous green roots. It glowed softly, the light changing in intensity with the Oblin's uneven movements.

It's just like those glowing orbs on the ceiling and walls, Jaeia shared across their bond.

"What do you want?" Jetta said sharply, mind still on her brother. The old man appeared far too frail to be much of a threat, but that did little to ease her tension. Out of the corner of her eye she saw Jaeia sit back down and slip her hand beneath her blankets. In her own palm, Jetta felt the rough edges of the rock that Jaeia grasped.

The old man winked at Jetta, and for a moment she felt that he knew about the rock and found it amusing. She dismissed the thought. *There's no way he could know.*

"Do not be alarmed, my friends. You must trust me when I tell you that neither I nor my companions wish you any harm. If we had, we wouldn't have bothered saving you in the first place. Now," he said, edging himself down onto the boulder in the center of the room, "at least tell me your names. I have already introduced myself—I am Oblin."

"You said 'Grand Oblin' before," Jetta corrected.

He chuckled. "Yes, sometimes I forget my title. Sometimes I even forget what day it is. Another consequence of old age, I suppose."

Jetta silently questioned his sanity. "'Grand' of what?"

"'Grand' is just an honorary title that comes with age and debatable achievement where I'm from," he replied, raising an eyebrow and sporting a goofy grin.

Jetta felt her sister's grip on the rock loosen, and the knot in her own stomach slackened. This old man was daft, senile, and as much as she tried, she couldn't keep hold of her anger.

"Can you tell us where we are?" Jaeia asked, her gray eyes fixed on his every move.

The old man combed his beard with his fingers. "As I told your sister yesterday, this is Tralora, once home to the Narki."

"What quadrant?" Jetta asked. "What are the exact coordinates? Are we near the Homeworlds, or are we in deep space?" If there were people here, she reasoned, there had to be ships, and she could find her way back to the Dominion, and Jahx.

The Grand Oblin eyed her again and brought the walking stick to his shoulder. "My dear, what use is that information to you?"

Jetta huffed. "You don't expect us to stay here, do you?"

The old man shook his head. "Child, there is no escape. You're lucky enough to be alive."

133

"What do you mean?" Jaeia asked, approaching the Oblin cautiously. "What is wrong with this place?"

The old man's watery eyes seemed troubled by the question. "Do you know what the USC is—the United Starways Coalition?"

Jetta lurched forward. *The USC.* She looked to Jaeia, but her sister held her breath, staring off into the distance.

"A few years back the Narki invented a transport system that could move massive amounts of cargo, people—entire armadas—instantaneously from one area to another. When they opened up trade communications with the USC instead of the Dominion, the Dominion made use of their bioweapons department."

"Bioweapons?" Jaeia repeated.

"They sent a plague. Their idea was to neutralize the Narki and then raid the planet for the transport designs, but they never thought the Narki might try to combat the illness with their own bioweapons. Unfortunately for both the Narki and Dominion, their attempts at a cure caused the plague to mutate. The Dominion had no means of neutralizing it, and the planet became—for lack of a better term—poisoned."

"So why didn't they send a probe or an autodroid to take the designs?" Jetta replied skeptically.

"The central city's defense perimeter is still active, even after all these years. No alien vessels, manned or not, can enter the city."

"So... are we infected then?" Jaeia whispered, her eyes widening as she turned over her hands.

The Grand Oblin lifted his arms. "Yes—it's everywhere."

"What?" Jetta exclaimed, looking over her body. She didn't feel sick, just bruised and banged up, and she didn't have any rashes or other signs of illness.

The old man chortled. "Well, as far as we know, these caves have the planet's only known source of suppressant. We've been dosing you since you arrived."

Jetta's forehead knitted with all the questions running through her head. "So—what is this place then? A dumping grounds for enemies of the Core?"

The Grand Oblin tapped his forefinger on the tip of his nose. "Precisely. Sometimes others come along, too—the unfortunate souls who have wronged the right people."

Jetta pursed her lips. "A lot of this doesn't add up. Why can't you just go to the city, send out a signal, and get rescued?"

The Oblin shook his head. "Even if we could get past the animals that have been transformed by the plague—and there are plenty out there—nobody would come. What we have is incurable and highly contagious. Most people die within weeks or even days, depending on the species. The fact that we've discovered a way to keep the disease in latency is very lucky. Even if the Core knew about our ability to stave off the infection, I don't think it would matter to them. We're trapped."

"How do you know all this?" Jetta questioned.

He smiled and replied softly. "There are a few USC officers here among us. They knew about what happened to the Narki and were some of the first Sentients sentenced to this place by the Dominion."

There are USC officers here. Jetta filed that information away for later, knowing she would need to pursue it further.

"Are we safe here? What do these infected creatures look like?" Jaeia asked.

"You are quite safe here in the caves. The only working entrance at this time sits high atop a mountain ledge which 'the altered' have never been able to reach. We've also salvaged a high-frequency bioshield from a cruiser wreck to act as a backup."

Shifting uneasily, Jetta allowed her twin's emotions to enter her mind. She shared the same concerns: a nasty pandemic, mutated fauna—at least according to this strange old man. *Is this just another prison? Is he our new warden? What does want from us?*

Jetta looked at the spherical object in the old man's hand. He noted her gaze. "Yes, this fruit is the source of the suppressant. We call it 'Macca.' It's the only means to keep the virus inside all of us in latency."

"How do you know that?" Jaeia inquired.

"One of the Exiles in our band is a scientist from Oriya. A long time ago we were able to recover some lab equipment from the Narki city so he could work to find a cure. As of the moment, however, he is unable to replicate the fruit's suppressant properties."

"Why not just stash a whole bunch of that fruit, dodge the monsters, nab a ship from the city and blast off this rock? I'm sure somebody could freeze you up there, at least 'til they can find a cure," Jetta said.

The Grand Oblin used his walking stick to draw a circle in the dirt. "You're not the first to think of that, and many have tried. Things are a bit more complicated than they seem."

Emotion weighted his words, forming images in Jetta's mind. She saw a vast city entombed in ashes and debris, and the remnants of disabled starships. Macca, plucked off the vine in the morning, withered and rotted before sunset. Regret and sorrow filled her heart as the faces of old friends, foolish souls who tried to survive without the Macca, turned to dust.

Skeptical, Jetta tried to look deeper and root out the falsities, but the Grand Oblin's mind seemed out of reach. This whiff of emotion and memory, bland, and worse yet—filtered—was not helpful.

An old thought resurfaced: *(Control. All of their minds are so controlled. I can't read them.)*

She placed a hand on her head. Something like this had happened before.

We have to get out of here, Jetta called to her sister, searching for anything around her that could serve as a weapon.

Wait. We need to know more, Jaeia said, her presence rising in her mind. *We can't make any enemies right now.*

Jaeia's sensibilities diffused her urgency. They were lacking enough information to escape, and if Jetta assaulted the old man, the other Exiles would come after them.

"How many Exiles are there?" Jaeia inquired.

The old man looked up to the rocky ceiling as he thought. "There's been some trouble, so our numbers aren't what they used to be. We're down to seven right now, with you two included. The others are Rawyll Cay and Crissn Ere from Oriya, and Commander Dinjin Lorkan and Lieutenant Senka Cordjha from the USC."

"Trouble? What kind of trouble?" Jetta asked. She sensed the Oblin's caution now and noted how carefully he chose his words.

"Well, there are other Exiles on this planet that we do not get along with very well. Sometimes they attack us for our supplies from the city and also our Macca. We have tried to live harmoniously with them, but things are not always as simple as they should be."

"But no one can last without the Macca, right?" Jetta said, righting herself. "So how the hell are the other Exiles still alive? Are you attacked every night or what?"

Although barely perceptible, Jetta caught the Oblin grinding his teeth. *Just like Galm used to do when he concocted wild stories to get out of talking about his history with Yahmen.*

"The suffering from their sickness is unimaginable," was his only explanation.

He obviously didn't want to tell them more, and Jetta knew that asking would get her nowhere. She reconsidered grabbing onto him again and stealing his knowledge, but before she had a chance he swiveled off his perch, brushing the dust off his robes. *That's the fastest I've seen him move.*

I think he's telepathic.

Jetta heard her sister's thought in the back of her mind but didn't know how to respond. They had never really interacted with another telepath before, so she didn't know what to expect. However, his responses to them were always a step ahead, like he had an unseen advantage.

Fearful of vulnerability, Jetta shrunk inside herself, guarding her thoughts like she did when she didn't want her siblings to know how she felt.

"Speaking of the Macca," the Grand Oblin said, "it's about that time." Despite his frailty, the Grand Oblin took the fruit and cracked it against his bony knee. It broke evenly, and a gelatinous gray substance jiggled in each half.

"I admit the taste leaves something to be desired, but it's filling, and it keeps us alive," he said, setting down a half next to each of them. Jetta looked at the melon, the Grand Oblin's memories whispering warning.

Death will come.

Jaeia, overhearing her thoughts, added her own: *The Oblin's fear is real. I see it in his eyes. We can't survive without the Macca.*

Seeing their hesitancy, the old man reached over to drink from Jetta's half. He swept the gray, gooey trail from his mouth with the back of his hand.

"None too appetizing, but vital nonetheless. I need to go meet with the others now. If you need anything, well, I will be back soon enough," he said. He levered himself up with his walking stick, a grimace crinkling his face, and carefully ducked out of the cave.

"Something's different," Jetta said when she was sure the old man was out of earshot.

"What's that?" Jaeia asked, timidly licking the rim of the fruit, her lips pursed against expected unpleasantness.

"I can hear you—*really* hear you. It's like you're shouting in my head."

Jaeia stopped, cocked her head, and let her eyes relax. "Your voice is stronger in my head, too. Not just that, either. Everything feels more vibrant. Like the Grand Oblin—I couldn't get inside his head, but I still got an impression. What do you make of it?"

"Don't know," Jetta replied, slurping up a small mouthful of the Macca. The thick jelly slid down her throat, leaving a metallic aftertaste. "But I do know he's not letting on to everything he knows—about us or about how to get outta here. He's being really careful about everything he says and thinks. I think he wants to use us."

Jetta could tell by her sister's thoughts that she didn't want to concede to her skepticism—she couldn't concede. *Why is Jaeia always so afraid to fully align with me?*

"It's going to be difficult to trust anyone until we can remember everything that happened to us," Jaeia said, tracing the rows of scars on one of her legs with her finger. She winced, not in pain, but at the ugly testament of violation.

"Jaeia, we need to find Jahx," Jetta said, setting down the fruit and scooting closer to her sister on the rock shelf bed. *I couldn't live with myself if something happened to him.*

Jaeia shook her head, tears welling in her eyes. "Jetta—I'm afraid."

Jetta laid her head on top of her sister's thighs and squeezed her eyes shut. "I swear on my life that I will never let anybody hurt you again."

***

"You can't be serious—they're kids!"

138

Sharp words came between dreams and reality. Emerging from sleep, Jetta expected to see red and gray apartment walls, and Galm and Yahmen fighting in the living room.

I don't want to work in the mines, Jetta thought. When she felt the cold dampness of the rock against her hands as she tried to sit up, she remembered where she was.

Another time, another prison. With a heavy heart, Jetta flipped off the animal skin covers of the rock shelf bed and checked her wounds. The soreness in her chest and leg had diminished to an ache. *Maybe I can stand?*

(Maybe we can escape—)

Jaeia, curled up next to her in the same bed, lay in fitful sleep, her arms and legs twitching.

"Hey," Jetta whispered, nudging her shoulder.

Jaeia mumbled something and slowly opened her eyes. Jetta placed a finger to her lips and looked toward the source of the angry voices.

Let's see what we're up against, Jetta thought.

Afraid, but following her sister's lead, Jaeia silently agreed.

Jetta crouched low to the floor, leading her sister to where their cavern tunneled into the next. Larger and better illuminated by huge clusters of Macca, the adjacent cavern appeared to be some sort of central meeting area. A circle of rocks surrounded an extinguished fire pit, and tools and clothes lay scattered in messy piles as if a project had been interrupted.

Five adults stood inside the circle of stones, arguing in low voices that occasionally rose. Jetta blinked in confusion. The Grand Oblin had mentioned only himself, three other males and one female, but the old man did not appear among the arguers.

Jetta recognized the large man with the red facial tattoo from the Oblin's memories. His serrated nose and large, pinned-back ears were echoed in the smaller man wearing wire-rimmed glasses standing to his right. Yellowish skin and bristly hair marked the third, uniformed man as Kulu. The woman standing next him wore the same faded uniform in a different color, but Jetta wasn't sure of her species. Pointed ears and high, arched brows, suggested she probably hailed from the Vreaper colonies, but her pink skin and delicate hands seemed more human than Vreaper.

"—we can't try the city again, Rawyll—we barely managed to save the children before the infected found us, and that was only a kilometer away from the caves," a plump woman said.

Jetta shared her sister's confusion. The middle-aged woman wore the same robes as the Grand Oblin's, though they dragged on the ground as she waddled around the fire. Only her gigantic breasts kept the cloth from getting completely underfoot.

Where is the Grand Oblin? Jaeia thought.

"We need more supplies. The Prigs stole our last ammunition box, and we've used up all the medical kits on the launnies," said the tattooed man.

"Don't call them that," the Vreaper woman insisted. "That's the ugliest word in the Starways."

"That's debatable," one of them said, but Jetta couldn't see who.

The tattooed man grumbled. "The Prigs are going to raid us any day now. Grand, you know better than anyone that we're in danger."

Bewilderment echoed between the sisters. *Why is the tattooed man addressing the fat lady as Grand? Is she wearing the same robes as the Oblin?*

"And what about those kids anyway? Are they dangerous? Why were they sent here?" asked the uniformed Kulu.

The plump woman held up her hands in the same strange fashion as the Oblin.

"Please, listen," she started, then stopped, turning her head sharply in their direction.

Oh no—

Jetta ducked down behind the rock, but it was too late.

"Come out," commanded the tattooed man. The adults kept their eyes trained on Jetta and Jaeia as they came out from their hiding place.

"What are you doing up?" he demanded.

He's concentrating very hard on keeping his thoughts in check, Jaeia shared across their bond. *I can barely detect anything.*

Jetta probed the rest of the adults, but came up against invisible brick walls. *It's like they've been trained.*

Jaeia shuffled closer to her sister. *They know.*

The plump woman muscled her way past the others and planted herself in front of the tattooed man.

"Don't start with them. I told you to leave them alone."

"Men," huffed the Vreaper woman. She walked around the circle and knelt down a few meters away.

"My name is Senka. I'm an officer in the United Starways Coalition. What are your names? Where are you from?"

While Jetta couldn't detect harmful intent, Senka still reined in her thoughts just like the other adults, though not well enough to hide her underlying apprehension.

But if you answer her, maybe we can gain more answers, Jaeia said, feeling her sister's resistance.

"My name is Jetta," she said, her voice just above a whisper. "And this is my sister Jaeia."

"Jetta and Jaeia. I like that. You're identical twins?" Senka asked, trying to be sweet. Jetta couldn't help but frown.

The Vreaper woman looked them over more carefully, eyes searching beyond their faces. A stray pang of loss escaped Senka's keep, surprising Jetta.

We remind her of someone, Jaeia observed.

Jetta only saw the advantage of the Vreaper woman's vulnerability, but kept it to herself.

"Your eyes and hair are different colors," Senka said, looking as if she wanted to reach out to them. "And you're a bit taller, aren't you, Jetta?"

Jetta wondered why adults talked down to kids like this. She found it insulting, but for some reason Jaeia seemed to enjoy it.

"My eyes are gray and my hair is lighter than Jetta's because I used to work with chemicals that altered certain pigmentations," Jaeia replied. Jetta shot her a warning, but Jaeia ignored her.

"Chemicals?" Senka exclaimed. "What are kids your age doing using chemicals?"

Jetta sent a string of disapproving thoughts Jaeia's way for leading this officer to question them about their past. *They know too much already.*

We have to give them something, Jetta, her sister replied firmly. *We have to gain their trust if we're going to survive this place.*

"We used to work aboard mining ships," Jaeia answered. "But that was a long time ago."

"Is that where you got that mark on your inner arm?" Senka asked, pointing to Jetta's right arm.

141

Face flushing, Jetta crossed her arms across her chest. "Why does that matter?"

Senka stood up and reached for her arm, but Jetta moved out of the way. "Your wounds seem to be healing at a remarkable rate," the Vreaper woman said. "I've never seen that in a human."

"We're *not* human," Jetta replied curtly.

"Oh, I'm sorry. You just look—"

"Like Deadskins?" Jetta snapped. "We're not."

Jeez, Jetta—she's not attacking you. Give her a break, Jaeia thought.

Jetta pushed back angrily, dumping her frustrations on her sister, but Jaeia stayed resolute in her assertion.

Senka backed away, and kept her voice neutral. "How old are you?"

Jetta did not like that this woman continued to prod, but Jaeia answered before she could stop her.

"What is the star date?"

Senka looked back toward the adult group as they decided between themselves.

"We think it's 3184.21. It's hard to tell. The days are unusually short on this planet."

"3184.21?" Jetta said incredulously. The woman had to be lying.

I don't think she is, Jetta, Jaeia said, sensing no deception.

We can't be seven years old, Jetta thought. That meant that just two years had passed since they joined the Dominion Core, one of which she couldn't account for.

Jetta looked at the size of her hands. They were strong and calloused, and belonged to someone twice her age. *No way.*

How could she and her sister could have put on so much height and muscle in such a short stretch of time? *I feel like an intruder in my own skin.*

"She asked how old you are," the tattooed man demanded.

"Oh Rawyll," Senka said, standing up. "And you wonder why Jaimey and the rest ran off."

The tattooed man looked at her contemptuously, but the plump lady stepped between them.

"If your calculations are correct about the star date," Jaeia said, "then we're seven years old."

142

Every single adult looked them over. Jetta felt like she was on the Block about to be auctioned off to the highest bidder, but her resentment quickly spun into fear. *Why are they looking at me like that? Are they sizing me up? What do they want?*—

Yellow gloved hands reaching,

> *(Everything*
> *hurts, IT BURNS)*

(I can't control my—)

Voices, everywhere

(They're all listening)

Jetta closed her eyes as a feeling of dread settled heavily in her stomach. *Jahx, oh Gods, where are you? This is all my fault—THIS IS ALL MY FAULT—*

"Let's get them back to their cavern," the Grand Oblin said, trying to catch her arm as she stumbled away.

(Come in command)—

—"ready for your orders, Commander."

Breathing hard, she grabbed on to Jaeia to keep her close. Shadows collected off the rocky floor, giving rise to dark figures. Stempton. Rogman. Yahmen. Enemies circled, readying for the final attack.

"You... will... pay," Jetta threatened, staggering into the cave wall.

Jetta! Jaeia cried, trying to pull her sister back up. *Come back to me!*

"It's too late," someone said.

Jetta lunged into darkness.

***

When Jetta awoke, she found herself on her back with a damp cloth pressed to her forehead. Animal skins provided warmth and comfort on a rocky bed, with stalactites keeping watch from above.

How did I get back in our cavern? she wondered.

She tried to rise, but nausea quickly pinned her back down.

"You are the worst patient I have ever attended to."

Jetta looked to her right to see the old man on a rocky outcropping, chewing on a plant root. He beamed at her, his gap-toothed smile wider than ever.

"You're not what you seem, old man," she said, trying again to sit up. Her limbs, wobbly and weak, gave protest but she managed to stay upright.

"What do you mean?"

"You're that fat lady, aren't you? I don't know how you do it. Are you a changeling? A Spinner, perhaps? What other tricks have you got up your sleeve?"

Jetta tried to find Jaeia for support, but she was not in the cavern.

"She's safe; she's helping the others wash our dinner. We're vegetarians here, I'm afraid. The only food besides the Macca is what we can forage for in the valley. And an occasional cave-dwelling insect or two."

Did that chakker *just read my mind?*

"Are you some kind of bloody leech?"

The Grand Oblin raised his white eyebrows and laughed. "That is the first time I've heard that from another telepath."

Jetta brought her knees to her chest. *Oh Gods, he knows—*

"Don't be afraid," the old man said, taking the root out of his mouth. "You're safe here."

"Who are you?" Jetta asked warily.

"I am a Taurian priest from the Order of Cress. We are Moro telepaths; we use our talents as a means of spiritual connection with other beings."

The emotion seeded in his words gave Jetta glimpses of a past life. Stone temples carved into lush mountainsides, with moss-covered stairs leading to the peaks. Incense burning atop wooden altars. Prayers, chanted in great sanctuaries, hummed in her chest.

"I am also a Berroman," the Oblin said. "Because of my age, I can no longer control my shape. My appearance changes with my moods. I guess you could say my shape is congruent with the emotions I experienced at a certain period of my life."

"You were a fat woman—on purpose?" Jetta said, not mindful of her rudeness. Why anybody would elect such a physically inefficient form defied her logic.

The Oblin chuckled. "In my middle years I was in charge of a refugee relief program on Thowhaus VII."

Orange and red robes wrapped loosely around her body, tied around the waist with beaded belts. Hands, spotted and wrinkled, smoothed pink when handing a child a bowl of rice.

"There were many children," he said, "and it was that form they liked best. Something soft is always nice to hug."

Beaded belts stretched to the limit as her waistline ballooned outward. Little bodies collected around her, faces pressed into her soft belly, seeking comforts only a parent could provide.

Jetta pulled away from his memories with a frown. There had to be something more to this old man than what he showed her. *No adult can be trusted.*

"Tell me what you mean when you say that you 'spiritually connect' with other beings. Do you invade people's minds? Do you steal from them?" Jetta asked, slowly sliding off the bedding onto her unsure feet.

Get back here, Jaeia, she silently called to her sister. Feelings of contentment and ease drifted back. Infuriated, Jetta couldn't understand how her twin could be so unconcerned about the adults or their situation. *Come back now! We need to figure out what the old priest is really after—what they're all after—and why they're keeping us from Jahx!*

"The Moro act as a bridge between the mind and the spirit," the Oblin said, unfazed by her tone. "I have helped many people rediscover their true selves."

"So," Jetta said, using the stalagmites to steady herself as she circled him, "have you been in my head?"

The Oblin's fingers twined together, his old knuckles knocking against each other. "Yes, I have."

"Why?" Jetta said, her voice just below a yell.

"When we found you at the crash-site, I felt incredible pain, and I speak not of your physical injuries," the Oblin said, rheumy eyes not bowing to her glare. "It went beyond anything I'd ever felt before. Within you and your sister lies a great suffering. A

145

culmination of agonies no Sentient—no child—should be forced to bear."

Jetta stopped in front of the old priest and squared her shoulders to him. "That doesn't mean you can dig in my head."

The Oblin nodded. "I did what I thought was right. I have been trying to help you."

Feeling the edge of his words, Jetta inferred his meaning. "You've been keeping us from remembering everything," Jetta said, her hands balling into fists. "You know what's happened to us. You know where my brother is."

Jaeia rounded the corner, followed by Senka, a worried look spread across her face. "Jetta, wait—" her sister said. *Don't do anything stupid!*

"As much as you refuse to believe it," the Oblin said to Jetta, motioning for Senka to stay back. "I am your friend. You know this—you have felt my intent. I only wish to help you."

"Then give me back my memories!" Jetta demanded.

"You must have patience," he said calmly. "The mind is not a simple thing. You must give me time to help you through each step, teach you to control—"

Enraged, Jetta grabbed the Grand Oblin's vein-riddled hand and held on tight. Jaeia cried out, but before she had time to react, Jetta slipped inside his mind.

The walls of the cave disintegrated as the cold confines of a starship boxed her in. Sitting before a flickering hologram of a battle, Jetta's hands worked furiously at the controls of the console, changing the angle of the projection to better view the battlefield while typing in commands for the secondary and tertiary fleets.

She licked dry lips and glanced at the scoreboard. She had to win, no matter what. It was the only way to make the stabbing thirst go away, to stop her skin from catching fire.

The shadowy face of Jetta's enemy peered at her through the blue light of the simulation. Yet another pompous, egomaniacal officer Rogman had pulled from duty somewhere across the star systems to try and beat her. He resented her, muttering to himself and barely making eye contact. After all, who would want to waste their time playing a launnie?

"Show no mercy," Rogman said, squeezing her shoulder with his gloved hand.

Jetta grimaced as she slipped into her opponent's mind. Cheap thrills and unsavory penchants interlaced with her enemy's combat experience, making her skin crawl. She didn't want to know the sting of whiskey, or the touch of a streetwalker, but his weakness coalesced within the memories of all-night motels and binge drinking.

(He is easily distracted)

Jetta opened fire on his air units, raking swaths of destruction across the electronic playing field. Her opponent cursed as the wreckage scattered through simulated space, forming navigation hazards he wasn't prepared to deal with when his warship entered the fray. Seconds later his warship caught in the planet's gravity well, making him easy prey for her battleships.

Cheers erupted from all around. The terrible thirst went away, and euphoric warmth filled her body. It felt so good to win.

Something metallic caught her eye, and she looked down at her uniform, her vision distorted and milky. She saw the tracks into her arm where her uniform threaded into her body.

Somebody laughed at her. They were all laughing at her.

(No, NO, NO, please STOP—don't take him! Not Jahx, please, not Jahx. Take me, TAKE ME!)

"Jetta!" Jaeia screamed.

Jetta gasped as her sister pulled her away from the Oblin, severing the psionic connection. The cave reappeared, spinning out of control. Off-balanced, she came down hard on a pile of rocks and clutched her head.

"*Tre causos,*" she whispered in Fiorahian.

Tears filled her eyes as the memories came flooding back. Rogman. Endless hours of playing the Endgame. The alienation of imprinting officer after officer. Separation from her brother and sister. Punching holes in walls and gouging herself with anything sharp to fill the void in her heart.

Then time fragmented. She wanted—no, she *had* to—play the games for that wondrous fulfillment she could only get by winning. Even when she was tired and hungry, she still wanted to play. And when she went for too long a time without playing, the *thirst* and the *burn* took over, and she nearly went out of her mind with the pain.

Jetta squeezed her eyes shut. Something else needed to be remembered, beyond the elation of playing, beyond the fog of her

147

last few months. Her eyes shot open. She remembered their last game as if it had happened only moments ago. The memory hit her like a transport freighter at full speed, knocking the wind from her. She turned away from her sister to hide her face, and the truth.

"What did you do?" Jaeia put herself between Jetta and the Grand Oblin.

"No, don't," Jetta managed to say, holding onto her sister's arm. "I remember now. The Core hooked us on something," Jetta choked, trying to wipe away her tears. "It can't be real..."

"Jetta, oh Gods—" Jaeia whispered as her own memories reawakened. Her entire body lurched forward, gray eyes seeing much more than the dirty rock floor.

"They separated us when we were trying to lose," Jaeia said, breath sharp and fast. "I remember trying to resist—"

"—but the thirst and the burn, that *need*—we couldn't resist. We had to play their games," Jetta finished.

"If they addicted you to something, why aren't you showing any signs of withdrawal?" Senka asked, approaching cautiously. Jetta couldn't answer. Some of the street junkies on Fiorah went crazy without their chemicals. She remembered watching them crawl on their hands and knees, talk to people who weren't there, even tear at their own flesh. It would make sense that she should have gone crazy too.

"I remember... pain. And a cell of some sort. I remember feeling like we did when we wouldn't play their games—but much worse. It's one of my last memories before waking up here. I feel like we were supposed to die there, but we didn't..." Jaeia said.

"Sounds like you survived detox," Senka said.

Jetta pursed her lips. *To hell with the drugs and games—all that mattered is finding Jahx.* Mind racing, she found new hope: *The Core's manipulated our telepathic talents before, so that has to be why I can't feel him now.*

Revitalized, she cried out as loudly as she could across the psionic planes. *Jahx, I'm coming!*

"How did the Core know we were telepaths?" Jaeia asked the Oblin, fiddling with her shirt sleeves. "We tried to hide our abilities."

"It is hard to understand, but there are those that would turn against their own," the Grand Oblin replied softly.

148

"Why?" Jaeia said.

Jetta silently chided her sister for playing ignorant. "For the right price."

The Oblin nodded. "Yes, Jetta. Lab work isn't always conclusive with some gifted Sentients, so the Core hired telepaths to weed out other telepaths."

Leaning heavily on his walking stick, the Grand Oblin rose from the rocky outcropping. Senka trailed behind him as he approached the twins.

"You surprised me, Jetta," he said, dabbing his forehead with his sleeve. "Ever since I first laid eyes on you, I knew you two possessed some type of telepathic ability. I felt an indescribable bond, well beyond the norm for telepathic connection. At first I thought it something unique to you, because you are twins, but there's more to it than I originally thought. What kind of telepaths are you?"

Core propaganda posters listing the four known types of telepaths filtered through Jetta's mind.

Do you have a tickling feeling in your head? Do you feel like you're being watched?—The Si!

Have you been feeling emotionally vulnerable lately? Do you feel manipulated?—The Moro!

Has someone been stealing your dreams?—Tre!

We aren't any of those, Jetta thought. *We are so much more.*

Jaeia silently agreed.

But as easily as either of them could dismiss the first three types of telepaths, Jetta couldn't quite shake the fourth.

Blue eyes and indigo tribal markings—Prodgy! The most dangerous!

Dissemblers, Jetta thought, turning the word over in her head. *Liars. Deceivers.*

The posters and billboards on Fiorah painted them as black-skinned monsters born from the fires of hell, able to convince the mind and body to turn upon itself. Evening infomercials featured entire crowds murdered under the gaze of a Dissembler, intestines exploding out of their abdomens, eyes melting in their sockets. *The most horrible death! A raping of the soul! One Dissembler can annihilate an entire world!*

We are not that, Jetta said, but wasn't as convinced this time.

149

(I've hurt so many people—)

Jaeia, moving to stand next to her sister, touched the back of Jetta's hand. *No, we are not that,* she affirmed.

The Grand Oblin studied Jetta's face. "You don't see yourself as Si, Moro, Tre or Prodgy, do you?"

What is he trying to do? Figure out how to control us? Jetta thought angrily, fighting back unexpected tears.

He's trying to understand us, Jaeia replied, looking behind the Oblin's eyes.

How can you believe that?

Listen to him, Jaeia thought, squeezing her sister's hand.

Jetta resisted, but with her sister's guidance, tentatively probed the Oblin's thoughts. *He isn't Yahmen, and he isn't part of the Core.*

Searching further, she found his surface emotions accessible, and they didn't hurt to listen to.

He's still holding back, Jetta observed.

He still has reason to, doesn't he? Jaeia said.

Jetta ground her fists into the cave wall and averted her eyes. The thought of trusting someone else frightened her. Jaeia and Jahx were the only ones who had never let her down. Everyone else wanted to exploit her and her siblings' abilities for their own self-serving motives. *So what is the Oblin really after?*

Jetta looked at her fist where she had scraped away some of the skin and little beads of blood had surfaced. No, he couldn't be trusted, but there was an advantage to gaining the Exiles' trust. Besides, even if she told the Oblin and Exiles about some of their powers, they couldn't control her. No one, she vowed, would ever run their lives again.

"We are not like other telepaths," Jetta said. "I know what people fear. Jaeia can talk a certain way so people listen, no matter how upset they are."

"And our brother," Jaeia said, urging Jetta to continue. Jetta couldn't find words. Pain surged in her chest, and her limbs tensed.

"Go on," the Oblin whispered.

Feeling her Jetta's distress, Jaeia answered for her sister. "He has the most talent of the three of us, but he never really talked about it much."

"Or used it," Jetta mumbled.

Jaeia shot her a look before continuing. "He could see into people—I mean really *see* into them. A lot of times he knew more about them than they knew about themselves."

"Your brother—where is he now?" Senka interjected.

Jetta exchanged glances with her sister. *Why do you trust them?*

"We think that he's—"

Jaeia's voice cracked, and she looked down at the floor. Jetta dug her nails into her arms and bit her lip as hard as she could stand.

"We don't know what happened to him," Jetta said. "So there's no use guessing. We just have to go find him."

Jetta hated the way that Senka and the Grand Oblin looked at her—as if they didn't believe her, as if they knew she had left her brother to the Dominion Core. With trembling hands she covered her face and wished she could stop thinking, stop feeling.

Jaeia pulled Jetta's hands away, her gray eyes connecting with Jetta's, refusing to let her withdraw. Without speaking, Jaeia took her hand and reached beyond their touch, taking the edge off the crushing feeling in her chest. *Jaeia is always there for me—I can't forget that.*

The Oblin sighed and wrapped his robe more tightly around his thin frame. "Perhaps you are something entirely new. Has anyone ever taught you how hone your senses?"

Jetta frowned. "Nobody has ever helped us."

"I see," the Oblin said skeptically.

Senka knelt down in front of Jetta, tears in her eyes and an expression of sympathy, only furthering Jetta's agitation. "How did you end up in the Core?"

Jetta wanted to crawl behind a rock. She didn't want them to know how she had stupidly allowed them to take that entrance exam.

"It's okay to tell me. I know how they recruited little children into their Academy. It wasn't your fault."

"Not now, Senka. Let them rest," the Grand Oblin said, walking stick scraping against the ground as he put himself between them and Senka.

"All we do is rest," Jetta grumbled, scuffing her foot against the floor. She glared at the Oblin, but the hot feeling in her stomach diminished in the face of his smile.

"I know you both are terrified of your past as well as your future. If you can continue to trust me, I can help you realize your abilities and overcome your fears," the Oblin said softly. He put on a hand on Senka's shoulder, and they both turned to leave.

Jetta held her breath as she tried to pick apart the Oblin's words and find further evidence of their deceit.

He isn't lying, she realized. *That can't be possible....*

Exhausted and not knowing what else to do, Jetta moved to her bed, and her sister crawled in by her side, wrapping her arms around her like she used to after a bad night with Yahmen. Out of habit she looked around for Jahx to bring him in close, only to be reminded again of his absence.

Jahx, please be okay, she thought, pressing her hands against her chest. *I'm coming, I promise. I'll do whatever it takes.*

Hearing and empathizing her heartbreak, Jaeia hugged Jetta even tighter. *Be with me here, Jetta. We will survive this and then find answers.*

Jetta wiped the tears from her eyes, allowing her sister's hope to fill her. Maybe they didn't have to fight this battle alone. Maybe, after all the years of relying on each other, fighting the prejudices against Fiorahians, humans, and telepaths, there was a chance to make an ally—a friend.

As she drifted off, she held onto the idea, too afraid to realize it and too afraid to let go. Somewhere, beyond the callused layers of her armor, was a longing for the Oblin's words to hold truth.

***

Concern reshaped the Grand Oblin, causing her to shrink and expand as her voice lost its frail rasp and tightened up into a no-nonsense motherly gruffness. Adjusting and re-adjusting her robes proved aggravating, but at least in her female, middle-aged body, her joints didn't bother her as much.

"Dinjin was already suspicious, and Rawyll and Crissn, even though they're not military, aren't stupid. If you know anything more about what happened to them and why they're here, it would be helpful," Senka said, folding her arms across her chest. "We're getting raided every other day now, and we can't afford to lose anyone else. If those kids are dangerous, we need to act."

"Keep your voice down," the Oblin said, collecting her long, stringy hair and tying it in a bun above her head.

The Oblin peered down the tunnel. Privacy was hard to come by in the caves, and trying to have a discussion in the tunnel connecting to the main meeting area would only arouse suspicion. She didn't think the others would be ready to hear what she had to say, and even telling Senka was going to be difficult.

"We've confirmed that they're telepaths," the Oblin said.

"Yes, I know. You knew that right away. You made us go through all that mental conditioning. Tell me what I want to know. What we all want to know—are they trained by the Core? Are they spies? Are they in any form related to Dissemblers?" Senka asked.

"If they were Dissemblers, we'd already be dead. Truthfully, they are like no other telepath I've ever encountered. And no, I don't think they're spies, but I do think they were conditioned by the Core. They are more dangerous to themselves than anything," the Oblin said as she pressed the palm of her hand against her forehead. Her mind still ached from Jetta perforating her thoughts.

Senka's moved her hands to her hips. "I want to know what you know of their experience with the Core."

The Oblin sighed and tried to loosen the robes around her blossoming chest. "Senka—what details do you know about the recruitment of children for the Core Academy?"

"Are you saying that they were part of the Roundup? Dinjin and I suspected that, but at the same time, they don't act like the children we encountered. All the others... well, you know what happened."

"These survived," the Oblin said in a hushed voice.

Footsteps echoed in the tunnels. With a sigh, the Oblin grabbed Senka by the hand and led her to the main cavern to circle of rocks around the fire pit.

"Please," the Oblin said, motioning for Crissn, Rawyll, and Dinjin to join them around the crackling fire.

"It's time for answers," Rawyll said, refusing to sit. Dinjin chuckled at the tetchy weaponsmaster and took his seat next to Crissn and Senka.

The Oblin scooted over to a rock and sat down between Senka and Crissn. She laid her walking stick across her lap and, taking a deep breath, elected to tell them as much as she could. "The tattoo on their arms—do you remember how I reacted to it?"

"Yes," Senka said, leaning forward in her seat.

"I knew it. I knew that symbol. About a year ago I met a fugitive of some sort who had found his way to Tauri-Mone by illegal transport, hiding in shipments of spice or running drug errands for shipmates so he could stay in their pens. He never did tell me his name—only that he sought redemption for a horrible crime he had committed. I listened to his confession, and I must admit, at first I doubted his credibility. He claimed that he could have prevented the tragedies that had befallen the galaxy—that he was responsible for the Raging Front and the annihilation of several interior star systems. I asked him how he could have done this. He said that the 'weapon' had been right in front of him during the Roundup, and he let it slip past him into Core hands. Wild-eyed and smelling of drink, he traced a symbol in the garden's dirt for me, over and over, and repeated the name 'Kyron.' I tried to reach out to him, but he fled the Order's sanctuary. I never did see him again, but I had a feeling, one that I couldn't quite place at the time, that I would somehow draw upon this knowledge once again," the Oblin said, staring into the fire. "That symbol that he drew is the tattoo we uncovered on the girls' arms."

"So what does that mean?" Crissn said, pushing his spectacles up the bridge of his nose. "If those kids were really that important, why would the Core sentence them to rot here?"

"Yeah," Dinjin interjected, scratching his forehead. "The Core is exact about detaining or eliminating their enemies."

"Please tell us everything," Senka whispered, resting her hand on the Grand Oblin's knee. "We can't afford not to know."

If I did, the Oblin thought. *You wouldn't believe me. Or at least you wouldn't want to.*

"There is still a lot I don't know, my friends. Whatever drugs the Core gave them are holding back their memories, and I can't access everything. But it's all there, and it is not good. I fear that if I help them remember all of it right now, while they are still so vulnerable, I will cause them irreparable damage. They already know too much as it is."

"But you are saying that they're important, yes?" Dinjin inquired.

The Grand Oblin nodded. "They are telepathic, and they were involved with the Dominion."

"Great. Just great," Rawyll huffed. "What now—were they in league with General Volkor?"

The Grand Oblin said nothing. Flashes of the Slaythe appeared in both Jetta and Jaeia's mind, though she couldn't discern much through the jumble and distortion of their memories.

Crissn pinched the bridge of his nose and laughed hysterically. "Come on, you've got to be joking. No child is capable of that kind of evil. Volkor killed more people than all the other intergalactic warmongers combined—I can hardly picture those kids bloodying their hands for that bastard."

The Grand Oblin gripped her walking stick more tightly. "They were involved with battles fought by the Core, but at this time, I'm not quite sure how."

"All right, let's assume the impossible," Senka said, "that those *girls* were somehow involved in the war and with General Volkor. It wouldn't be right for them to be sent to a low-profile prison, even this cursed place."

"But Grand Oblin, you were revered for your telepathic skills, and you were sent to this place," Dinjin pointed out.

"Yes, but remember that I was never in Dominion hands—my coming here was my own doing," the Oblin replied.

"And the Core *knew* about the girls' talents, so they wouldn't just exile them here, even with our inability to be rescued. They'd keep a tight grip on them, and if anything, they'd kill them so nobody else could have their secret weapon," Senka added.

"I don't know how they managed to get here, be it by escape, accident, or some other means. That is still repressed within them," the Oblin said, rubbing her temples.

Crissn paced the circle. "But if it was a mistake or accident that they were sent to Tralora, that means that somebody—be it the LaTannian mafia, the Oriyan guard or the USC—would come after them if they somehow got word."

"Or the Dominion. If the launnies escaped and accidentally landed here, then maybe the Core will be back," Rawyll said, hitching up his weapons belt.

"*Stop* using that word," Senka said.

"Or maybe the war's ended. Maybe the Core fractured if the launnies were able to escape," Dinjin interjected.

155

"Something isn't right about those—those *kids*—about any of this," Rawyll grumbled, sheathing and resheathing several of the knives on his belt. "I don't like it."

"They're not bad, Rawyll. I can't see them being in league with Volkor," Senka said. The Oblin smiled. *I'm glad I'm not the only one who believes in them.*

Rawyll gritted his teeth and made slicing motions with one of his blades. "Either way I think that they need to be controlled. And if they're truly that powerful, we have to keep watch over them."

"They're just *kids*—"

The Oblin raised her hands once again to silence them. "I am trying to find out more. I know you are concerned. But it is very difficult to protect them and at the same time help them remember—"

An unexpected apprehension seized her. She looked down the dark tunnel that led to where the girls should have been, and her stomach dropped.

Fear. Desperation.

She grasped Rawyll and Crissn's wrists, her amethyst eyes glowing. "They've left the protection of the caves."

***

"We need to find a way off this planet," Jetta said as she exited the cave system with her sister.

The cool night air greeted them as they stepped onto the mountain ledge overlooking the valley. Jetta inhaled deeply, filling her lungs until she thought they would burst. After years of living in the recirculated pollution of the Fiorahian airfield and then the sterile spacelock of the Dominion starships, the lush foliage and rich outdoor smells of Tralora tantalized her senses.

Not a single stolen memory compares to this, Jaeia shared.

No, not even close, Jetta thought, not able to stop the smile that spread across her face. Tralora, raw and untamed, disease ridden and dangerous. *This place is real...*

"Look, Jetta—can you believe it?" her sister whispered, looking up. "Only two moons—not enough to drown out the night sky."

Jetta looked up and gasped. "My Gods..." she said, marveling at the star-speckled sky. It had been so different on Fiorah. The triple star system and eight moons had drowned out any other celestial light. The Core ships were no better: windowless prisons denied even a glimpse into the heavens.

"Finally," Jetta whispered as a strange elation tingled through her chest and into her fingers and toes. She couldn't help the giggle that slipped from her lips.

Jaeia took a step back. "Am I crazy, or are you a little giddy?"

Jetta tried to wipe the smile away and look serious, but it came right back with a vengeance. "*No,*" she insisted, socking Jaeia in the arm.

"What's that?" Jaeia said, pointing to the east. It took Jetta a moment to see the shining mote speeding across the sky.

"Don't know. Maybe a satellite?" Jetta said, dampening her excitement with the reality of their situation. *I should be ashamed for enjoying this without Jahx.* "It doesn't matter. We need to get going."

With the aid of the moonlight, they carefully made their way across the razor-thin ridge of the granite mountain to a small plateau. The surf of trees below swayed and bowed in the wind, crescent leaves trembling.

From their vantage point, Jetta spotted a precarious-looking trail that wound its way down the talus fields of the mountainside into a green valley that separated them from another jagged mountain range. From its wear patterns, Jetta guessed it was the only route to and from their cave system.

She looked back up the mountain face and tried to spot any other openings to the caves. What might have been old entryways had all been blocked from the inside with boulders and rock slabs, as if someone hadn't wanted whatever was outside to get in.

Her sister crouched down and gazed at the forest below them. "It looks so peaceful from here," Jaeia said. "Seems hard to believe what the Oblin told us about this place."

"It's quiet," Jetta noted, crouching down with her sister. "Like there isn't any nocturnal life.

"Hey, look—you can see the edge of the Narki city," Jetta said, pointing to the distant horizon. Just before the mountains jutted the rim of the city's alabaster wall. Several buildings peeked above the protective barrier. "Let's go now."

"No, Jetta," Jaeia said, grabbing her by the upper arm. "That wouldn't be right. We're not in any condition to travel, we don't know enough about this 'disease' we carry, and I don't want to leave these people. They risked a lot to help us, and we owe them."

"That disease talk is just *gorsh-shit*," Jetta said, wrenching her arm away. "And these people chose to save us—it's not our duty to stay here and rot along with them. We need to get a ship from the city and find Jahx."

Jetta tried to turn away, but her sister pushed her to the ground and held her down.

"I can't feel him. Can you?" Jaeia asked.

Jetta struggled to get up, but her twin held her down with remarkable strength.

"Does that matter?" Jetta said, trying to get an elbow lock on her, but her sister evaded her attempts. "I would have thought that wouldn't be enough. He's our brother—doesn't that mean anything to you?"

Jaeia let go and sat back, pain spreading across her face, but at the moment Jetta didn't care.

"How could you even think that?" Jaeia whispered. Her breath caught, and she looked away. "I love him just as much as I love you. It kills me to think that something may have happened to him, but we can't just rush off, Jetta. There are still holes in my memories, and I know there are still holes in yours. We don't know what kind of danger lies beyond the horizon. I want to look for him, but my gut tells me that we need to remember everything first."

"This is not the time to wait—it's the time to act," Jetta replied angrily.

Jetta vaulted over the ridge and onto the narrow trail below, tuning out her twin's protests as she climbed down the mountain base. *If Jaeia won't help me, I'll do it alone.* She might not be able to feel Jahx, but once she got a ship and left Tralora she'd somehow find her way back to the Dominion and figure out where they had taken him.

Excruciating pain hammered her legs each time she leapt from rock to rock. She had pushed her body through tougher times, and there was no room for self-pity. *I will find my brother.*

Jaeia screamed. By the time Jetta managed to interpret Jaeia's scattered mental impressions, a high-pitched shriek erupted from the forest ahead of her. Wood groaned and split beneath heavy footfalls. The leaves shook violently, and bits of foliage flew away in the wind.

Jetta stepped back when she saw the huge shadow-toppling mammoth timberwood trees in its path.

"*Oe Vead*," Jetta cursed in Fiorahian.

Moonlight revealed the colossal monster charging toward her, a deformed, agitating mass of wildly proliferating organs and appendages that she couldn't have imagined in her worst nightmares. Misshapen eyes bulged from bloody sockets. Clumps of hair decorated grainy, discolored skin hanging like drapes in some places and stretched taut in others.

The disease, she thought as the sight of a gaping mouth full of razored teeth soldered her in place.

Run! Jaeia yelled in the back of her mind.

Jetta commanded her body to run, but nothing happened; she couldn't even breathe. Points of light dotted her vision, and she swayed on her feet.

"Stupid launnie—run!"

A rough hand grabbed her by the shoulder and threw her backward. The tattooed man stepped in front of her and withdrew a firearm. He fired a few rounds into the beast, knocking it back.

"Come on!"

Senka took her hand, helping her to scramble up the trail as fast as she could. Still dazed and numb, Jetta fell twice, dislodging rocks that narrowly missed hitting Senka.

The tattooed man bellowed. Jetta looked back in horror. Smoke from the blast rounds rose from the creature's crisping flesh, but the creature did not notice or care as it continued to advance.

"His clip is empty!" Jetta said, tugging on Senka's sleeve.

"*Chak,*" Senka said. Putting her hands to her mouth, she shouted down the mountain: "Hold on, Rawyll! Dinjin and Crissn are coming!"

They're not going to get here in time, Jetta thought as the two other men stumbled down the mountain, bag full of weapons in tow.

Jetta looked back down to the tattooed man. *Gods, what am I doing? I'm running away. Again. I'm leaving someone behind.* The faces of her aunt, uncle and brother flashed before her eyes.

Fear and angered warred within. *No,* she thought, hands balling into fists, trying to convince herself that the tattooed man meant nothing to her.

(I will not run anymore.)

She had to go back.

"Hey, no!" Senka cried as Jetta leapt off the trail and scrambled down through the brush to the forest floor.

"Jetta!" Jaeia screamed as Jetta came to a standstill before the abomination. The creature slowed and dropped down onto all five of its appendages, readying its attack.

A sense of calm spread through her, much like the calm she'd felt all those times she faced Yahmen, allowing her to absorb his taunts and blows without flinching.

"Get back up that mountain!" Rawyll growled, backing away as he unsheathed a bladed weapon from his belt.

The creature let loose a deafening roar and reared up on its hind legs. Ribs cracked apart, and its chest blossomed like a flower, revealing rows of hollow teeth and a mucus-lined gullet. It lashed out at Jetta with a fleshy tentacle, but she threw herself to the left, narrowly avoiding its attack.

"Take this!" Rawyll shouted, tossing something silver toward her across the forest floor. The weapon, with its three blades and large handle, was like nothing she had seen or used before, but felt light for its size.

When the creature lashed out at Jetta again, she swiped at it with all her might. She missed, teetering backward, barely managing to stay on her feet.

"Mind your balance!" Rawyll shouted, sinking his blade into one of the creature's arms. It shrieked and retracted.

Seeing that it directed its attention on Rawyll, Jetta tried again, this time managing to connect. The center blade on her weapon sliced through one of the creature's smaller tentacles, cutting it cleanly off. As it whipped back its stump, the creature doused them in black fluid.

Jetta took a step back. The severed tentacle writhed and wiggled on the ground, then lay still. She was about to turn away when little red feelers erupted from the felled tentacle, searching for something to grab onto. As the creature pulled itself up on nearby branches,

Jetta realized with a mixture of disgust and horror that the thing couldn't be stopped unless it was completely destroyed.

"Get up the mountain, *now!*" Rawyll screamed, taking off toward the trail.

She knew she should follow his order, but something inside wouldn't let her leave. At first she thought it was curiosity, but as the feeling grew in intensity, she realized it was more than that. *I want to kill it.*

Oh Gods no, Jetta—come back—please!

Jetta pushed her sister's thoughts aside with a burgeoning smile.

As the other Exiles screamed at her to run back up the trail, the creature lashed out again. Jetta ducked, avoiding the first tentacle, but the second and third slapped down around her neck and leg, yanking her to the ground and dragging her toward its maw.

Jetta! Jaeia screamed across their bond. *Please, Gods—you have to fight!*

Mucus and saliva flung across her face as it pulled her leg over its lips. The edge of its teeth shredded into her pants as she bucked and thrashed, lacerating her skin.

It's going to eat me! Jetta panicked, clawing at the tentacle tightening around her neck. The monster's putrescent breath steamed on her face as it pulled her deeper into its gullet, teeth cutting into her legs and hips.

(No.)

A dark voice, assailing her from within, called forth. *(There is no one to hold you back. Kill it.)*

There is no one to stop me, Jetta repeated. No siblings to intervene, no conscience to cripple her fight. This was life or death battle against a festering monster.

(Use your greatest power.)

Without bonds, Jetta ground her teeth together, digging down into the darkest places within herself, bringing to the forefront of her mind her all the hatred she had ever known—for Yahmen, Rogman, the Core—for all those that had harmed her and her siblings—and hurled it at the monster. The creature paused, breathing halting and frothy, but resumed its attack.

In the back of her mind, she heard Jaeia cry out as it swallowed both of her feet. The walls of its throat contracted and relaxed, trying to pull her further down the digestive canal.

161

Razored teeth came closing down.

I'm not dying like this, Jetta though, concentrating harder. She channeled all her negative energy, undamming every emotion she had ever buried away, invoking her darkest fantasies.

She saw herself on top of Yahmen, striking him repeatedly in the face until it was nothing but ribbons of blood and flesh. After pulverizing his face, she took his fat neck in her hands, wringing it until he turned blue and his feet kicked helplessly against the ground.

She imagined each Core officer, teacher, and soldier—even the cadets—lined up against a wall, where she systemically exterminated them with the same precision and indifference that they had used to deconstruct her and her siblings. She ended the mass extermination with Rogman, taking the time to broil every last nerve fiber before she tired of his pathetic pleading for the mercy he had never shown her.

The child laborers were there, too, the ones that had beaten them for their food, for being human, for being smaller—for existing. In her mind she landed blow after blow on their smug faces until they were bloody pulp, leaving enough breath in them for the ship rats to finish the job she had started.

Jetta opened her eyes. Razored teeth froze millimeters from her face. The creature gagged and spat, a wet tongue pushing her from its mouth. She landed hard on the ground, slathered in saliva and blood, but undigested.

Die, she shrieked across the psionic planes.

The creature's body trembled and curled in on itself. Reveling in her newfound power, she poured every part of herself into reviving the terrible imaginings she once restrained, feeling the power surge through her body like an overcharged circuit. Electrified, she wanted more.

She felt his soft eyes squish and erupt around her thumbs as she dug her fingers into his face, screaming at the top of her lungs. Yahmen pleaded for her to stop as she kicked him in the stomach, lashing him with the same belt he had used so many times on her and her siblings.

(You're nothing! Don't you understand? You're nothing!) *she cried over and over again until his body disintegrated into the bloodied floorboards.*

(Jetta—get back!)

The voice penetrated through her illusion this time, jarring her concentration. She looked up to the ridge to see Rawyll taking aim at the creature with a modified firearm the others had brought him. Jaeia stood with them, motioning and screaming for her to run to safety.

Jetta did not want to stop, but Jaeia called to her again, this time using her second voice.

Jetta—GET BACK.

Jetta found her desire waning as Jaeia's manipulation eroded her bloodlust. She could still feel the phantom outline of Yahmen's skull in her hands, but it faded like a dying fire with every breath she took. Dazed and unsatisfied, Jetta ascended the mountain trail, chased by the wheezes and agonies of monster writhing on the ground.

Once Jetta reached the first ridge, the tattooed man fired what appeared to be a badly damaged double-barreled hand cannon. The discharge seemed louder than it should have been, and Jetta covered her ears and dropped to her knees. When the quaking ground settled, she looked up to see the smoldering remains of the creature embedded into a crater in the forest floor.

Hands shook her shoulder. Jetta turned around to find Rawyll, Senka, and Jaeia standing over and yelling at her, but she couldn't hear them above the ringing noise in her ears. She could, however, hear the barrage of reprimands sent by her twin telepathically.

*How could you do that?—you should never use your powers like that—what if you had been injured?—never, never again—*streamed into her head. It sounded not just angry, but rattled—almost shattered—something she never would have expected from Jaeia.

Jetta wasn't sure why this was so different. She had done plenty of things that weren't exactly safe—fighting with larger child laborers, stealing from the miners' food supply, even attempting to snatch a gun off one of their guards outside their old apartment. Using their talents was a means to survive, so why not use it aggressively, especially when everybody already knew what they were?

The tattooed man grabbed Jetta by the arm and tried to yank her to her feet, but Senka pulled him off her. The two adults shouted at each other until Rawyll, scowling down his ridged nose at Senka and palming his fist, stalked back to the main entrance. Senka shot Jetta a

163

look of disappointment before motioning for the two of them to follow her.

By the time they reached the main cavern to reconvene, the ringing in her ears had dissipated to a dull buzz.

"Sit," Rawyll commanded, pointing to two of the seats around the fire pit. Jaeia sat immediately, but Jetta refused.

"What kind of stunt was that?" Rawyll yelled, throwing down his weapons belt and ripping off his furskin, which had been torn to shreds during the fight. Jetta hid her astonishment as Rawyll revealed a muscular, athletic body covered in battle scars and intricately woven tattoos. Whoever Rawyll was, he had clearly been an important person where he came from.

Senka and the others didn't move to intervene as Rawyll chewed her out, and the Grand Oblin, still in the form of a middle-aged woman, paced behind the group. "You are not allowed leave the cave system, let alone mess with the bioshield," Rawyll shouted. "We have risked our lives to take you in, and you just throw it all away for what? There is only death outside!"

"You could have gotten us all killed," Senka added sternly.

Jaeia's voice bulldozed its way back into Jetta's head. *You can't run off like that ever again. I need you here, with me. If we're going to get through this, we have to work together.*

With her sister's anger and fear rattling in the back of her skull, Jetta found her confidence floundering. She had been so sure that she could get to the Narki city, find a ship and escape—and then when the monster came along, she was sure that she could defeat it using her talents.

Gods...that thing almost ate me, she thought, looking down at her pants, torn and wet with blood and mucus. *What would have happened to my sister?*

—what about Jahx?

Jetta tried to sound assertive. "I need to get a ship—we need to get out of here. My brother's life depends on that."

The Grand Oblin pushed through the center of the group. "Now is not the time to act hastily. We can help you if you will let us, but we will have to come up with a plan."

Why are they always so eager to keep us here? Jetta thought, eyes narrowing. "I don't trust you—any of you," she growled.

Mind yourself, Jetta, her sister bade. *They're not our enemies.*

Disregarding her sister's caution, Jetta eyed what looked like a utensil for cleaning furskin next to her. It was short, but sharp. "So why should I stay?"

"We could put her in the hold, Grand, keep her there a while 'til she settles. We can't risk her going on another adventure and leaving us vulnerable," Rawyll said through gritted teeth. Dinjin lowered his head to hide his smirk.

"No—that won't be necessary," Jaeia said, wrapping her hand around Jetta's arm and pulling her against her side. *Don't even budge.*

Surprised at the ferocity behind her sister's words, Jetta complied.

"Just give us a night alone to cool off," Jaeia said, words coming across soft and even. "Is it okay if we meet in the morning? We're very sorry—about all of this."

Simmering, Jetta couldn't believe her sister's hypocrisy. *She's using her second voice again! How can she reprimand me for defending myself when she's using it for control?*

"That's fine," the Grand Oblin said, holding her hand up to keep Rawyll from further antagonism. "See you in the morning."

The Exiles talked heatedly amongst themselves as Jetta and Jaeia returned to their cavern. The doubt and frustration that lingered in their thoughts echoed in Jetta's head even after she could no longer hear their words.

"Jetta," Jaeia said, her voice barely above a whisper. "You can never do that again. Don't leave me."

Jetta dragged her knuckles across the rocks, in need of the pain. "What, and stay here and be their prisoners?"

Without waiting for her sister's reply, Jetta hurried ahead, ducking into their cavern. She jumped up onto a rock shelf and tightened the band that held back her hair, refusing to look at her sister.

"They don't treat us as prisoners," her sister said, leaning back against the cave wall. "They're protecting us. And they're not sure of us yet. You can't judge them for that. We're not sure of them either."

Jetta glared at her sister.

"I don't want to believe that everyone is out to get us," Jaeia said. "I can't live like that. I don't want to."

165

"That's ignorant, Jaeia," Jetta said. It crossed her mind to call her weak, afraid, but she bit her tongue, holding back words she knew would tear her sister apart. Jetta looked at her scraped knuckles. "Everyone tries to use us."

"Well, what about Uncle Galm and Aunt Lohien? They weren't like that."

Jetta looked away and said nothing. Even hearing their uncle and aunt's names made her stomach ache.

"Jetta, what's wrong?" Jaeia asked, her eyebrows knitting together as she pushed herself up from her perch against the cave wall.

"Nothing."

"Don't lie to me."

Jetta bit her lip and tried to rein in her emotions. She couldn't allow herself to think about Galm or Lohien.

"Jetta," Jaeia whispered, putting a hand on her foot and looking up at her. "You've only ever wanted what was best for us. There's nothing wrong with that. Galm and Lohien—they wouldn't have made it anyway. We had to leave them behind. Let it go."

Jetta flicked her foot away and concentrated on the rhythm of her breathing. She had to think about how they would get out of here, not wallow in past deeds.

If only we could have gone with Captain Reht and the dog-soldiers, Jetta thought. *We'd have gone back to Fiorah with an armed crew and killed Yahmen, saved our parents. And Jahx, Gods—he wouldn't be missing—*

"None of this is your fault," Jaeia said.

Jetta hid her face behind a stalactite as her stomach churned. *This is all my fault.*

She wanted to tear through the walls and run forever, until she reached her aunt and uncle, until she found Jahx. The only way things could ever be right was if they were a family again, even if it was back in a cruddy apartment eating stale bakken and drinking polluted water.

She didn't notice that Jaeia had climbed up next to her until she felt her sister's hand on her knee.

"Jetta," she began, a slight waver in her voice. "I'm worried about you. About us."

Jetta sat up as straight as she could without hitting her head on the rocky ceiling.

"You don't," Jetta said. She tried to sound reassuring, but it didn't come off as well she would have liked, her voice cracking. "Y-You don't have to worry about anything."

"Without Jahx, our connection feels different. Your voice is so much louder in my head."

Listening to her sister's thoughts, Jetta bristled. "You can't control me anymore. You're worried about what I'm going to do."

Jaeia's face turned red as she searched for the right words. "That wasn't the way I was going to put it."

Jetta let her head fall back against the cave wall, not minding the twinge of pain. "I could have killed that infected thing, Jaeia. And there is so much more that I can do—I can feel it."

"I don't think we should use our talents that way," Jaeia whispered.

"Even for defense?" Jetta's voice pitched higher and higher. "That is the *gorsh-shit* thinking that got us here in the first place! If we had ended Yahmen we would have never had to go through all of this!"

Jaeia looked on the verge of tears, but Jetta did nothing to assuage her distress. *I'm tired of comforting her during these fights, especially when the answer is so obvious.*

With a few deep breaths, Jaeia tried to firm up her voice. "When you use your talents like that, something ugly happens to you. I can't describe it very well. It's like all the sunshine disappears, and the world is taken over by something darker than a shadow," Jaeia said. She trailed off, her eyes disconnecting from the room.

"Well, what should I have done?" Jetta said, leaping off the stone shelf. "Try and talk that thing down as it ripped me in half?"

Trembling, Jaeia beseeched her twin. "Please, Jetta, I don't want to lose you. When you do those things... they take you someplace I can't go."

Though her voice was hardly more than a whisper, Jetta heard the sentiment behind it loud and clear.

"Are you... afraid of me?" Jetta asked, taking a step back.

Jaeia looked up at her, gray eyes wide and frightened. "I love you. You are my sister. I will always be there for you. But I can't help you if you won't let me. Promise me you won't use your talents like that again."

Jetta stripped off her dirty pants, made her way over to her bed and slipped underneath the blankets. She closed her eyes and tried to imagine being somewhere else, but she couldn't think with her sister's presence absorbing her attention.

"I promise that I will try to not make you upset like this," Jetta said, huffing all the air out of her lungs. "I will try and use our talents only to make things better."

Jaeia turned away, not reassured by Jetta's conditional promise.

Why can't she see our talents may be the only thing standing between us and another vicious enemy? Jetta thought. *What if it's the only way for us to save Jahx?*

Jetta shivered, remembering the thrill of electric strength surging through her veins when she fought the diseased creature in the forest. Somewhere within the depths of her unspoken desires, she longed for another such battle.

"We should get some rest," Jetta said, trying to get her sister to come down off the shelf—but Jaeia didn't move.

"Goodnight, Jaeia," she sighed, rolling over in her bed.

Moments later, Jaeia replied, her voice barely audible. "Goodnight, Jetta."

***

"I don't get what those things see in the boy," said an angry, insistent voice. Somebody touched her forearm, and burning pain seared her to the shoulder. Jetta tried to move away, but her limbs felt like wet sand. "They're obsessed with him when it's this one that's been carving up our senior ranks."

Another voice laughed. "Did you see her take out the Nesseri? Only took two hours. Admiral Parmoran quit that day. Old bastard had been fighting that front for years."

Everybody laughed. The burning spread into her chest, branching out into her arms and legs. She willed her eyes to open, but nothing happened.

"Yeah, but Rogman's pushing her too hard. Remember when she was bashing in the walls and hurtin' herself? That's nothing.

Just wait and see what happens next. The devil owns this one—not Rogman."

Somebody made a booming sound; laughter followed.

"I wouldn't laugh if I were you," the first voice said. The laughter came to an abrupt halt. Jetta could hear only the awkward shuffling of feet. A hand gingerly turned her head from side to side. "What happens if she wakes up?"

"No!" Jetta screamed, sitting straight up in bed. Nothing surrounded her but the dewy cavern walls and the glow of the fruit. There were no voices, only the sound of the wind whistling through the tunnels.

"What's wrong?" Jaeia asked, squirming her way out of her animal skin blankets.

"Nothing," Jetta said, clearing her throat and wiping out her eyes. "Just a dream."

Jaeia brushed away the sleepy halo of hair around her forehead. "I've been having bad dreams, too."

Pulling back the covers, Jetta discovered bandages around her legs. Someone had cleaned and dressed her wounds from the battle with the creature last night.

I didn't want the wounds to get infected, Jaeia said.

Feeling the sentiment behind her sister's words stirred up old needs. Jetta carefully made her way over to her sister's bed and crawled in behind her, resting her head on her shoulder. "Can I sleep here until morning?"

"Yeah," Jaeia whispered. She paused before adding, "As long as you don't stink me to sleep."

"Hey!" Jetta said, poking her in the ribs, "I haven't been having second helpings of that nasty plant thing Senka cooks like *some* people."

The explosion that rocked the cavern froze her heart mid-beat. Erratic gunfire and shouting followed.

A dizzy swell of nausea seized her stomach. *Am I back on the Core battleships?*

Jetta shot out of bed and ran to the entrance of their cavern, peering around the corner toward the meeting area. She couldn't see anything, but voices and gunfire echoed down the tunnel, and the stink of plasma discharge made her eyes water.

169

"What's happening?" Jaeia asked, creeping up beside her and looking over her shoulder.

"I'm not sure."

"They're in danger—the Grand Oblin, Senka—all of them. We should help."

For a guilty moment, Jetta's spirits rose. If the others were distracted by some kind of invasion, she and her twin could slip out unnoticed and try again for the Narki city.

"Jetta," Jaeia said, hearing her thoughts, "I'm not going to abandon them." Without giving her a chance to respond, Jaeia leapt and took off down the tunnel.

"Jaeia, wait!" Jetta shouted, but it was too late. Jaeia had already rounded the corner into the flashes of gunfire.

"*Skucheka*," she muttered, racing after her. *Stupid. Why does she do this?*

This wasn't the first time Jaeia had put herself in danger to help another, but Jetta never expected her sister to be so reckless. *What does she see in these people?*

Jetta came to an abrupt halt behind her sister as she rounded into the main cavern. The attack on the Exiles came from all sides. Rawyll and Dinjin exchanged fire with two assailants near the fire pit while Crissn dragged Senka out of the crossfire and behind the shelter of towering stalagmites. She clutched her stomach, blood seeping between her fingers. Once again an old man, the Grand Oblin held off a burly attacker near one of the lower tunnel entrances with his walking stick while chanting something that did not carry over the gunfire.

"Get out of the way!" Rawyll shouted. Jetta dropped behind an outcropping of rock, but Jaeia didn't listen. Picking up a stone, Jaeia threw it at one of the men firing at Rawyll and Dinjin, hitting him squarely in the temple. As he fell, the other assailant aimed his gun at her. Jaeia dove to one side, but the gunman's shot hit the wall, spraying pieces of rock everywhere. Jetta flinched as she felt the rock pummel her sister's body.

Furious, Jetta burst from her hiding spot and tackled the gunman, hitting him squarely in the chest. Even though she was half his size, the impact knocked him backward, sending his gun flying.

Rawyll took aim at the Grand Oblin's attacker and shot him in the side, toppling him into the dirt.

"Dinjin, go check the entrance for more of them. Crissn!" Rawyll shouted. Crissn peeked out from behind the heap of boulders. "Go with him and check the shields."

"But Senka is hurt—I should get her to the lab," Crissn said.

"Now!" Rawyll growled.

Crissn ducked out of hiding and scuttled along with Dinjin toward the main entrance.

Jetta ran to her twin and brushed debris from her face. "You okay?"

"Yeah, fine," Jaeia mumbled, sitting up. She spat out a mouthful of dirt and combed her hair back with her fingers. "Just bruises."

"What got into you?" Jetta asked.

Jaeia pointed toward Senka. "Come on, we should help her."

"Not so fast," Rawyll said. He pointed to the two gunman and then to Jetta. "You—help me tie them up. We can't take the chance that they'll survive."

"Jaeia, come with me," the Grand Oblin said, grimacing as he bent over. "Help me move Senka to the laboratory. You grab her legs."

Jaeia and the Grand Oblin slowly dragged Senka down one of the aft tunnels, leaving Jetta with Rawyll. Giving him a sidelong look, Jetta crouched down and held the first gunman's hands as Rawyll produced a length of cord from a storage box in the corner.

"Do you know how to tie a knot?" the tattooed man asked her. Jetta shook her head and sat back on her heels as Rawyll demonstrated several types of knots for binding prisoners. "Make sure it's tight, and if you have enough, secure the arms above the elbows, too."

Why would he teach me something I could use against him when he clearly doesn't trust me? she wondered, but decided not to waste any time pondering and imprinted his skill.

Dinjin and Crissn returned shortly after Rawyll and Jetta had secured the two men. Gasping for breath, Crissn stood with his hands on his knees while Dinjin mopped the sweat from his forehead with his uniform sleeves.

"The trail is clear," Dinjin said. "I think it was just them."

Rawyll grunted. "Just these Northies? Their numbers must be down."

"Those kids have been the only arrivals in months. No wonder their numbers are low," Dinjin replied, plopping down on a rock.

"At least it wasn't the Prigs," Crissn mumbled as he started for the same tunnel Jaeia had descended. "I'm going to check on Senka."

Rawyll cursed under his breath as Crissn tripped over a rock.

"Can't believe you and Crissn are from the same stock," Dinjin chortled. "I thought you killed your young if they showed any signs of imperfection."

"If you really think we're savages, why do you ask questions that will get you killed?" Rawyll snapped back. Jetta scooted away a bit, not trusting the tattooed man or his tenuous grasp on his temper.

Dinjin sported a lopsided grin. "Sorry. Can't help it."

Jetta knew it wasn't the greatest time to ask, but her need to know outweighed her fear of Rawyll. "Who are the Northies and the Prigs?"

Rawyll walked over to the large man he had shot and kicked him in the side. Blood gurgled from the Northies' mouth, and he made a strange sucking sound.

That Northie is human, Jetta realized. *He won't survive these kind of wounds.*

"What are those?" Jetta asked, pointing to the blemishes spread across the dying man's body and clustering underneath his eyes.

"The middle stage of infection," Rawyll replied curtly, picking up another gunman's head by his hair and showing Jetta the same blemishes circling his eyes. "The Northies are mostly Scabbers— humans from Old Earth—who were exiled here after the Dominion took over that solar system. Nothing special. They attack the caves every few months once they've amassed enough men or stupidity to try for our supplies."

"The Prigs are worse," Dinjin interjected. "They're a mix of outerworlders and rejected Core bastards."

"I can't believe the Dominion sends their own people here," Jetta said as she watched Rawyll check the fat man for supplies.

"Lower-level perpetrators, insubordinates," Rawyll grumbled, "and apparently you."

Jetta thought through what they had said, and what she had already learned, and realized the inconsistencies. "The Grand Oblin said they were after your supplies here, yes? And the Macca? That's why they raid you?"

"Yeah, so?" Rawyll looked up at her, and Dinjin's eyes narrowed.

"Well, these guys aren't that sick—you said Sentients don't last more than a day or two without the suppressant, so there are other sources of Macca or suppressant. And these caves, though a good place to hide, aren't worth attacking just for the sake of safety. So it must be your supplies. What do you have here that is so valuable that they would risk raiding you? They already have guns, so that can't be it."

As Dinjin and Rawyll exchanged glances, Jetta sensed a drastic shift in their control over their conscious thoughts. Invisible ice walls, frigid and towering, shot up around their emotions, blocking her from their psyches.

Frustrated, Jetta wanted to make physical contact to deconstruct their guard, but part of her knew that level of aggression was too much of a gamble. She wasn't sure what their reaction would be, and she feared her sister's wrath if she spilled any more blood.

"You're a smart one, kiddo," Dinjin said, no hint of sarcasm in his voice. "Bet there aren't too many who pull one over on you."

Jetta didn't tell him that wasn't true. "Tell me."

Rawyll withdrew a gun from his holster and pointed it at her head. "Don't try any of your tricks on me, little girl, or I'll have to prove Dinjin's theory that we Oriya are savages."

Jetta slowly retracted her mind's reach, but did not take her eyes off him the tattooed man. He was scared but had no intention of killing her—at least not outright.

You're lucky you have that gun, Jetta thought, temper boiling.

"Don't do anything stupid, Rawyll." Dinjin's lips compressed into a single line of concern. "We need her," he added quietly.

Rawyll looked at him indignantly but returned his weapon to its holster. "Then it's your turn to babysit. I'm taking these sacks down to the hole so I don't have to smell them all night; we can check 'em and burn 'em in the morning. You get to clean up the fat one."

As Rawyll stormed out of the meeting place, towing the prisoners behind him, Dinjin chortled again. "Ah, you can always count on the Oriya for two things: their ability in a fight and their pleasant company. Not much else, really."

Jetta ignored his jocularity. "So I guess it's your turn to not tell me what you're hiding, then."

The Kulu kicked off one of his boots and tugged off his tattered sock, wincing as he inspected his foot. Dried blood and dirt crusted around denuded skin, and gray-green streaks crept up his foot from his toes to his ankle. It reminded Jetta of the rotting foot fungus she had seen in the Fiorahian mines.

"Lots of nasty things in this place," he said. "Tralora is just a pot of disease."

"Tell me what's going on," Jetta said. "I have to know what kind of danger we're in."

Dinjin tossed his boot aside and rested against the rock wall. "Tell me something about you first then. Are you a child of the Roundup?"

Jetta reached out toward her sister to get her input, but Jaeia's mind was too caught up in helping Crissn and the Grand Oblin look after Senka.

"You do know what the Roundup is, right?" Dinjin asked. "When the Dominion went planet to planet to recruit children into their military?"

Jetta weighed her options. As a USC commander with information about the Dominion Core, he had knowledge she could use—but he would ask her questions in return. She considered stealing his knowledge, but she held herself back, sensing he was trained to detect her measures.

"So what if I was?"

Dinjin half-smiled. "Well, I would just be impressed. The Core does some intense psychological programming. Once inducted, most kids never step out of uniform. The kids that don't take to it are sent to the front lines, and the ones that do—well, they are the most ruthless. The Core drives any sense of decency out of them."

"What are you saying?"

"I'm saying you're something special."

Jetta frowned. "Stop feeding me *gorsh-shit*."

The Kulu laughed and tried to pat her arm, but she dodged his hand. "You must have been a pain in the *assino* to raise."

"Nobody raised me," Jetta said, crossing her arms. "That's probably the problem."

Dinjin reached for his boot and tugged it back on with a wince. "The only thing we're doing here, kid, is trying to protect you—and us—and maybe, dear God, find a way off this rock. There are some things about this place, the people, the circumstances—that kind of thing—that I wish *I* didn't know. You get it, right?"

Listening to the wake of emotion left over from his thoughts, Jetta decided he was definitely holding back. Rankled, Jetta's hands convulsed with the prospect of violence. *Who is he to decide what I can handle?*

"You know that if I wanted to, I could take that information from you right now."

Dinjin nodded. "But you won't. You understand that I am a USC commander, and that I fought for the rights of the telepaths, and that if you did such a thing it might make me rethink my stance on that whole issue."

"What?" Jetta whispered.

Dinjin shook his head. "Must be part of their programming. You didn't know, did you?"

Jetta said nothing.

"The USC fought to protect the telepaths after the Dissembler Scare really took flight. We tried to stop the registrations and the arrests."

Jetta shook her head in disbelief. *Why do I feel guilty?*

"I didn't know that," she said quietly. "I just thought the USC was a crappy government that tried to regulate commerce and law in the Homeworlds."

"Yes, that's true," Dinjin said. "But that was in the beginning. When the Dominion began its hatemongering against the telepaths and gaining power, the USC banded together and formed a unified military to stand up to the Sovereign's army. We were the last resistance against the Dominion Core."

"You fought to protect the telepaths," Jetta whispered, then stiffened. "But I was enrolled in the Core, and that makes me your enemy."

Dinjin got up, stretched his back, and moved over to the corpse of the fat human. He stood over it as if he was trying to plan a way to move the body, but Jetta could tell he was stalling.

"That does bring up an interesting point," Dinjin said, turning toward her. Jetta heard the shift in the tone of his voice. "Did you fight on behalf of the Core?"

Jetta was about to reply "no" when she suddenly found herself unsure.

"Well then," Dinjin grunted as he tried to drag the corpse by its arm. "Seems you don't know quite what side you're on, do you?"

To her surprise, Jetta felt a pang of shame, followed by a rush of anger. "Look, I'm tired of being screwed with. I just want to go find my brother, and if you have information that could help me, then I want it. I don't care about anything else."

Exhausted, Dinjin gave up and sat down on the belly of the fat man, pushing out the remaining air in his lungs and belly with a loud hiss. The sudden tanginess in the air made Jetta's nose wrinkle.

"Kiddo, none of us here are out to get you. Not all the world is bad, you know."

Jetta felt the fear in the shallows of his mind and sighed. "Yes, it is."

***

Jaeia couldn't believe how much lab equipment the Exiles had stolen from the Narki city. Filling the entire lower level cavern, computer housing rose to the rocky ceiling in competition with stalagmites, leaving barely enough space to move about. Most of it she didn't recognize, but some of it she figured out from the design, specifically the power source for Crissn's machinery.

"It's a 'string puller,' isn't it?" Jaeia asked, pressing a cloth against Senka's wound. The Vreaper woman moaned softly, squirming on the rock slab serving as an exam table. Crissn, kneeling by Senka's side, analyzed her with a bioscanner, worry etching lines across his forehead. "Those can generate years' worth of power on a liter of concentrated hydrocell fuel. They collect energy by disrupting the vibrations of nicentint strings, right?"

"Y-yes, theoretically. Nobody really knows why it works so well, though." Crissn pushed his spectacles up the bridge of his nose and gave a nervous laugh. "I'm impressed. D-did you read my thoughts?"

"No, I already knew that," Jaeia said, trying not to take offense. In any case, Senka needed help. Though the wound only oozed now, the burns around it worried her.

"I understand the burn marks, but I don't understand why her blood vessels are changing color," Jaeia said, taking a seat next to Senka on the rock slab while she held pressure to her wound.

"The Northies seem to have found plasma weapons that also discharge toxins, just in case the blast doesn't do the trick."

"Will she be all right?" Jaeia asked.

Crissn removed his glasses and sat back on his heels. He placed a hand on Senka's shoulder and hung his head. "Probably not. I don't know. The plague makes it hard to predict. Besides, I'm not much for Vreaper anatomy and physiology."

"You seem to know enough. What did you do before you were sent here?" Jaeia asked.

Crissn's eyes shifted nervously as he removed a roll of bandages from his medical kit. "Well, uh, I was a scientist of sorts. Did a lot of work with medical equipment for the different Houses before me and Rawyll, uh... left Oriya."

"Houses?"

"You know, warrior families? Tribes? Rawyll clearly didn't give you his lecture about the 'great warrior culture' of the Oriya," Crissn said, waving his hands. "Well, I wasn't a warrior, obviously," he snorted, "so I became something like an indentured servant to one of the Houses, just so I could stay out of the shows."

"Shows?"

"Like the fighting rings on Old Earth—I'm sure you've heard of those. I'd be the bait."

"Yeah, I've heard of those," Jaeia said, thinking back to conversations she had overhead on Fiorah. The Underground Block was the premiere venue where abducted Sentients were sold and traded for bouts in the rings. She always thought it was strange how it was mostly humans that were auctioned off and returned to their home planet to die for spectacle.

"So, I worked for Rawyll's House patching up all the warriors after their 'mighty battles' and all that *gorsh-shit*. That's why I can *furgu* my way through this stuff," Crissn said. Jaeia didn't know his native language, but she got the idea.

"What can I do to help her?" Jaeia asked as Senka moaned again.

Crissn finished bandaging her abdomen, but the wrappings were already soaked through. He shook his head and wiped his forehead with his sleeve. "You're not as bug-headed as your sister, are you?"

"No. She'll even say I'm 'the good twin.'"

"Well, in that case, just stay and watch her for a while. If she stops breathing, give her this," Crissn said, handing her a hypodermic injector, "and if her color gets worse, give her this." He handed her another. "You know how to work them?"

Jaeia turned the hypodermics over in her hand, identifying the different buttons and medication settings. It was older technology, but she understood it from one of her many gleanings years ago. "Yes—but where are you going?"

"To go check with the Grand Oblin."

"Where did he go, anyway?" Jaeia asked.

Crissn fumbled with his spectacles and looked away. "He, um, went to the lower levels to see if we have any antibiotics in storage."

From the way he avoided her eyes and staked down his thoughts, Jaeia could tell he was lying. Seeing no easy way around Crissn's mental barricade, she strained to hear the familiar frequency of the Grand Oblin's mind.

"I hear him, but he seems really far away, and there's a lot of interference."

Crissn forced a laugh. "I wouldn't know how you telepaths work your magic. You stay here, okay? I'll be back in a moment."

Muttering to himself, Crissn headed for a tunnel at the far end of the cavern where the Grand Oblin had gone earlier. Jaeia followed Crissn's thoughts as he descended deep into the mountain, but they soon grew as distant and muddled as the Oblin's.

What is that? Jaeia thought, encountering a cloud of white noise. Goosebumps popped up all over her arms and legs. *Why does that remind me of the Dominion Core?*

Senka's body shook, and Jaeia snapped to attention. She opted for the injector filled with white medicine and depressed the plunger into Senka's neck.

Senka's eyes shot open, and she sat straight up. Jaeia held her by the shoulders as Senka pawed at her face

"I can't see—I can't see!" she cried.

178

"It's okay, I'm here, it's Jaeia," she said, extending herself into Senka's mind. She tried to steady the Vreaper's thoughts with her own, but Senka's mental pattern didn't match anything she recognized.

"My God, am I blind?" she wept, touching her eyes.

"No, it's just the medication I gave you. You were having a seizure—I had to."

Senka nodded and shivered. "What happened? My stomach hurts."

"You were shot by a Northie. Crissn bandaged your stomach and is going to go find some antibiotics."

Tears rolled down Senka's cheek, and Jaeia sensed the dread in the officer's thoughts. "He went down to the lower levels?"

"Yes, he did."

"No..." Senka whispered.

"What's wrong?" Jaeia asked, gently touching the Vreaper's arm.

"I just hate those antibiotics," Senka said, keeping hold of Jaeia's hand. "They make me feel... funny."

Jaeia squeezed her hand. "You know I'm telepathic, right?"

Senka chuckled, closed her eyes and rested her other hand protectively across her stomach.

"It is not my place to tell you what goes on down there. You should ask the Grand Oblin if you really want to know, okay?"

Jaeia nodded but peered more deeply into her thoughts. *Senka believes she's right by not talking about whatever is bothering her so badly. It's worth investigating, but I won't find answers through her.*

"Is it hot in here?" Sweat stained Senka's neckline and dripped down her forehead.

"No, it's your fever," Jaeia said. "Do you want me to get you some water from the meeting place?"

"No, no—stay with me, please," Senka said, tightening her grip on her hand. "You feel good to hold onto."

Jaeia gripped her more tightly. "Nobody's ever said anything like that to me before."

"Really?" Senka said. She paused to cough up a gout of blood. "God, my ribs ache."

"Most people we meet are afraid of us," Jaeia said.

"Why?" Senka asked. "I thought you hid your telepathy."

Jaeia shrugged her shoulders. "Yeah, we always have. I guess they can just tell we're different."

"Well, truthfully, you and your sister are a bit intimidating."

"I know Jetta seems unfriendly, but she's affectionate in her own way. Sometimes she just cares too much... and things get out of hand."

Senka tried to laugh but ended up wincing.

Jaeia scooted closer to her. "You're not like the other Exiles."

Senka smiled but did not open her eyes. "The Grand Oblin and I are the only ones who like kids."

"Do you have kids?"

"I did," Senka whispered, gingerly drawing up her knees, "before the wars started."

Blood leaked through the bandage again. Jaeia added another stack of gauze pads to Senka's stomach, but the Vreaper woman took over applying pressure. "What about you? What happened to your parents? Were they smart like you?"

Jaeia shook her head. "Don't know. Rawyll was right to call us launnies—we are street rats. Our *Pao*—or uncle, in Common—took us in, but it didn't work out very well. Fiorah's no place for kids."

"You grew up on Fiorah?" Senka exclaimed. The movement made her grimace, and she lay back down. "I thought that place sold off children—in pieces. Hard to believe you lasted there."

"Then maybe you'll understand why we ended up with the Dominion. At the time, it seemed like a good choice."

"How did you survive?" Senka whispered, shivering and shaking. Jaeia wanted to get another hypodermic or at least call for Crissn, but Senka's grip was too strong.

"Well," Jaeia began, unsure. A part of her wanted to tell Senka everything. It would infuriate her sister, but it was such a relief to talk to someone who seemed to care. "If my brother and sister and I didn't have our talents, we would have been killed or sold off in the Underground. Our owner only kept us around because we were useful."

"What do your talents allow you to do? It didn't seem like Jetta really wanted to share, before."

That was the dangerous question—the one Jetta forbade her ever to answer. If anybody knew the full extent of what they could do, it would mean their death.

180

"Well, I can say we learn very quickly. When somebody is explaining something, it's not their words that reach us, but their thought patterns," she said, pointing to her head, even though Senka couldn't see it. "It was one of the ways we stayed alive on the mining ships—we could fix anything else another worker could fix."

"You're a sponge, is what you're telling me," Senka said, laughing wanly.

"Well, Jetta does always tell me I have a lot of holes in my head," Jaeia giggled.

"But you can do more, can't you?" Senka said.

Jaeia bit her lip. *Why am I so trusting?* "Yes, we can."

"Is that what the Core used you for?"

Jaeia squeezed her eyes shut and inhaled so deeply she thought her lungs would burst. "I don't really know."

For a moment she watched Senka breathe and listened to the thread of her psionic projections. Feeling the cold emptiness of death edging its way around Senka's mind, Jaeia panicked. *She's dying—I have to act now.*

"I'm going to go get Crissn," Jaeia said, trying to stand, but Senka held fast.

"No, it's okay," Senka whispered, coughing fitfully. Fresh blood dribbled down the side of her face. Jaeia looked down at the new bandage on Senka's stomach and saw that it had saturated. "I don't want any more... antibiotics."

"Senka, no, please—"

"Promise me something, okay?" Senka asked, eyes barely open. The whites were bloodshot, and her pupils dilated.

Jaeia cringed, feeling the edge of an impending sorrow. "Okay, Senka."

"Promise me you'll really give the others a chance. All of us here—we've hit on hard times. We've done things we regret. But that doesn't make us bad people. I have faith in them, just as I have faith in you, Jaeia."

"Why do you have faith in me?" Jaeia asked, voice about to crumble.

"Because it doesn't... doesn't take a telepath..." Senka said, her head rolling to one side, "to know you are... good."

Senka's hand went slack, and Jaeia carefully placed Senka's arm across her body. On Fiorah dead bodies littered the alleyways and the dumpsters—even the hallways of their old apartment—but she had never actually seen someone die. Senka's psionic presence, which had been steady and distinctive, faded into nothing. Jaeia tried to hold onto her thought patterns, but they slipped away like water through her fingers.

"Hey—what happened?" Crissn shouted, tripping over a bundle of wires as he emerged from the lower level tunnel.

Jaeia just shook her head and sat back on her heels. When she looked up, the Grand Oblin stood next to Crissn, whispering in his ear. Crissn held a container filled with a black, viscous fluid.

"Jaeia, come with me," the Grand Oblin urged, resting a hand on her shoulder. "Crissn needs to attend to Senka now."

"But Senka said she didn't want any more antibiotics," Jaeia said, holding onto the Grand Oblin's fingers. She tried to give him her memory of their conversation, but the old man was either unreceptive or unable to read her projection.

"No, no, no—we need Senka—we can't go through this again, Grand," Crissn said, clutching the container to his chest.

"Isn't she dead?" Jaeia asked.

Crissn and the Grand Oblin exchanged glances before the old man opted to speak. "Not with our resources, she's not."

Jaeia pressed her hand to her face. In his nervousness, Crissn leaked information, and for the first time, she could hear pieces of his thoughts clearly, as if he screamed them at her. What she heard choked the air right out of her.

Jaeia hunched over. "What are you hiding here?"

Crissn turned away, his hands knotting in his hair.

The Grand Oblin raised his arms and closed his eyes. "Jaeia, let us go find your sister. I will tell you what you need to know."

A sharp, acidic feeling unsettled her stomach as the Oblin led her away. She wasn't sure how Crissn was going to resuscitate Senka's lifeless body, especially given her previous injuries, but she had felt the nature of his thoughts and knew his confidence.

Jaeia braced the side of the tunnel wall as they ascended to the main cavern. "Do you know what my greatest fear is?"

The Grand Oblin didn't look at her.

"That Jetta will be right about you. About all of you."

"Jaeia, you must trust my judgment," the Grand Oblin replied softly.

Jaeia didn't respond. She didn't think she had to, really. If the Grand Oblin was a telepath, he would sense her apprehension, her faith teetering on the edge of despair.

I am alone, she realized. *I can't tell Jetta any of my concerns about the Exiles, or she'll justify the use of her talents. And then I'll—*

She stopped mid-step, grinding her fingernails into the rock wall. *—I'll lose my sister.*

"Jaeia," the Grand Oblin said, "not every Sentient means you harm."

Jaeia thought of her aunt and uncle, imagining them back in the apartment, their expressions both worried and welcoming as they greeted her at the kitchen table. The windows, not yet boarded up, cast sunlight on the table full of food. Her brother and sister, thin but happy, drank pigeon's milk and laughed at some inside joke.

A smile, tinged with sadness, touched her lips. "I know."

***

As soon as her sister walked into the main cavern, Jetta reared her head. Jaeia's swirling thoughts confirmed her doubts, and she sprang into action, sprinting toward the lower level tunnels.

"What are you doing?" Dinjin called after her.

The Grand Oblin tried to place his walking stick between her and her sister, but Jetta dodged, grabbing Jaeia by the arm and pulling her back down the tunnel.

Jaeia dug her heels into the ground, but Jetta dragged her along. "Stop!"

"We are going down there," Jetta said through gritted teeth, tightening her grip on her sister's arm.

Jaeia brought her elbow down on her wrist, breaking Jetta's hold. "Why does it always end up like this with you?"

You know we need to go down there, Jetta said silently.

"We don't need to do it like this."

But Jaeia kept pace with her. Jetta knew that deep down Jaeia shared the same reservations. The Exiles were purposely uncommunicative with them, and Jetta wasn't sure why. Part of it was their uncertainty about the twins' background with the

183

Dominion Core, but there was more to the story. The Exiles *needed* them to stay, and Jetta would not allow them to be exploited again.

"Hey—stop—where are you going?"

When they entered the first of the lower tunnels, Jetta found Crissn standing over a cold, ashen Senka. She couldn't feel anything from the Vreaper, and her sister's memories told her of Senka's death. She might have paused if she hadn't sensed the others close on their trail. Instead, Jetta picked up her pace, heading down the tunnels beyond the lab.

"Why is there so much more fruit here?" Jaeia said, nodding toward the rocky walls overgrown with Macca.

"Worry about that later. Which way?" Jetta said between breaths.

Partially covering her eyes with one hand, Jaeia pointed down the tunnel in front of them with the most Macca. "Toward whatever that—that feeling is."

Jetta knew what she meant. She had sensed the distortion when they reached the first opening, but didn't know what to make of it. Similar to the buzz of an old television tuned to a dead channel, the sensation drowned out every little sound in the room.

As the psionic white noise intensified, Jetta slowed her pace, unsure if she wanted to proceed down the next tunnel. Wind passing through the tunnels brought the sound of a curious metal clicking, like the chatter of an idling engine, to their ears.

"Ugh," Jaeia said. "What is that?"

Swallowing hard, Jetta stepped into the new cavern. A sweet, putrid stench, like fruit decaying in the sun, assaulted her sense of smell. Jetta covered her nose, but when she saw the source of the smell, her arm fell to her side.

"What is it?" Jaeia asked, running in behind her. As soon as she caught sight of it, she stumbled to a halt.

Jetta couldn't catch her breath, and her heartbeat roared in her ears.

Metal grinding on metal

(It hurts my ears)

Please don't—

184

"He disappoints me."

BURNING

My skin is—

The thing at the far side of the cave looked at her with half a face. Metal casings and circuits punctured the inflamed skin of its jaw and forehead, defiling the last remnants of its organic host.

It has no eyes— Jetta realized. Citrine pus dripped from its empty orbital sockets and collected around the metal pins driven into its neckline. *But it sees me—*

Spider-like mechanical appendages directed themselves toward her, inspecting from afar. The harsh cacophony of its mind gave no impression she could glean, only a sense of icy dread that slithered into her gut.

Gods, Jetta, look— Jaeia said, pointing. Tubes draped from its neck and sides, draining viscous black liquid into the pool of turgid water at its feet. The fruit clustered the heaviest on the walls at that end of the cave, its vines all routed into the pool. The creature's blood, taken up by the fruit, meant it was—

That metallic taste—

Dinjin and Crissn both ran into the lower cavern, breathing heavily.

"You're in a lot of trouble," Crissn huffed, resting on his knees a moment.

Rawyll barreled in after them, a firearm already drawn. "What the hell do you think you're doing?"

Jetta couldn't have responded even if she wanted to. Her feet were cemented to the spot, her breath sucked from her chest, fingers and toes tingling as her heart beat faster and faster.

"Leave them be!" the Grand Oblin shouted from further down the tunnel. After a frantic scuttling, the plump, female version of the Oblin popped out through the entryway. "Let me handle this."

"Handle this? You haven't handled this since they arrived!" Rawyll shouted.

"The Oriyan has a point," Dinjin said.

185

Jetta could not take her eyes off the creature.

That thing——I know that thing— Jetta relayed to her sister. The mechanical creature's head gyrated, and it let out a few high-pitched squeaks. Its solitary leg, long and bent the wrong way, kicked against its ties, trying to free itself.

"Get out," the Grand Oblin told the men. Her voice, calm at first, rose to a scream. "Get out!"

Crissn quickly left, but Dinjin lingered. Rawyll didn't move until the Grand Oblin lifted her walking stick.

"If you don't settle this now, *I will*," he said, turning to go.

Falling onto her knees, Jetta threw up the meager contents of her stomach. She continued to heave until the Grand Oblin came over and touched her shoulder.

"I'm sorry. I knew this would upset you. I didn't want to tell you if it wasn't necessary," she whispered.

Jetta wanted to run, but the room swooped around in a dizzy spin. She looked over at Jaeia, who knelt on the floor and wiped her mouth with a trembling hand.

"What—what is...?" Jetta managed to say.

The Oblin looked surprised. "This is a Liiker, a creation of the Motti—you might know them as the Deadwalkers."

The Motti. *I know that name.* She covered her ears as the phantom sound of gnashing metal filled her head.

"—You are an organic being that I do not despise—"

Cold blackness ate at her belly. She remembered. That thing— that *thing* with the burning red eye—

(Cornering me in my room. Nobody can see. It wants something from me—)

"He disappoints me. If only he had your desire..."

She broke apart from the inside out. Spidery metal legs crawled up her body as her brother wept.

"Kill it!" Jetta screamed. "Kill it!"

The Grand Oblin settled his hands on her shoulders and looked grimly into her eyes. "We cannot. It is what is keeping us alive."

Jaeia's broken thoughts raced in the back of Jetta's mind as starry motes burst before her eyes. Panic ate up her last ounce of reserve, and she threw herself toward the exit, but the Grand Oblin held her fast.

"Don't touch me." Jetta clawed at the Grand Oblin's face. "I'll kill you!"

"My child," she heard the Grand Oblin whisper, as two warm arms wrapped tightly around her shoulders. "What happened to you?"

***

When Jetta blinked open crusted eyelids, she found Jaeia hunched at her bedside in their cavern, looking ghostly in the phosphorescent light of the Macca.

"I don't like this place, Jetta."

Jetta pinched her forehead with her fingers, but couldn't push past the memory of the rank cavern and the mechanical beast it harbored. Fear fluttering inside her ribs, Jetta turned to her sister. "Ready to go?"

Jaeia nodded.

A frail voice interjected. "Please, don't go." The Grand Oblin, once again an old man, stood in the doorway to their cavern, hanging onto the rocks with a trembling hand. "It is not safe—for any of us—if you do."

Jetta plucked a few bundles of Macca from the wall, wrapped it in her blanket, and took her sister's hand in hers. "We don't trust you. It's time we left."

"We haven't lied to you," the Oblin said. "I've been protecting you."

"Protecting us?" Jetta scoffed. "What—by letting us drink the blood of that thing?!"

The Grand Oblin kept his voice low. "The Liikers are despised across the Starways. Your reaction is not at all unique. Unfortunately, the Liiker's augmented immune system is the only thing keeping us alive."

"Augmented immune system? What?" Jetta gaped at him. "This is so stupid. Why the hell are you still here, then, if you've found a way to survive? And why the hell do you have a Liiker here in the first place—and—"

The Grand Oblin held up his hands, but Jetta cut him off before he could speak.

187

"No—I don't want any more explanations," Jetta said, shaking her head. "My sister and I are leaving."

"Please, hear me out."

Jaeia clung to her sleeve, her thoughts a conflicted flurry in the back of Jetta's skull. A part of her sister wanted to listen to the Oblin, but Jetta refused. *That Liiker is sinister and wrong; we have to get away.*

"If you don't like what I have say, then you may go," the Oblin said.

Jetta clenched her teeth to keep herself from yelling but stayed put when she felt the break in the Grand Oblin's concentration.

He's vulnerable, Jetta thought, feeling the Oblin's self-control faltering with his emotion.

Dabbing the sweat from his forehead with the sleeve of his robe, the Oblin continued. "We siphon some of the Liiker's blood into the pool from which the Macca derives its hydration. Alone, the Liiker blood is intolerable—if it doesn't kill you, it will drive you mad— but the Macca is a very safe and effective delivery system. That is why we still aren't able to leave."

Pressing her hand over her mouth, Jetta tried to keep down the contents of her stomach. The thought was beyond revolting. She and her siblings had been forced to skin dead rats when Yahmen withdrew their rations, but nothing compared to this. When she looked into the Liiker's eyeless face, she felt a little less human.

It's a part of me, she realized, wanting to peel out of her own flesh.

"How did you... discover this?" Jaeia asked, folding her arms across her stomach as her skin took on a greenish cast.

"Before they ended up here, Rawyll and Crissn had been working in the fighting rings on Old Earth, supplying Liikers as bait to the main attractions. Crissn had already spent years experimenting on Liikers before he was exiled, and he was the one to come up with the idea of filtering their blood through sort of medium. Even with his experience, he managed to kill almost the entire lot of them before figuring out how to do it."

Jetta held up a hand. "That doesn't explain how the Northies and Prigs are still alive. Shouldn't they be monsters by know? There has to be another source of a suppressant."

The Grand Oblin nodded. "The Northies use a restasis chamber to keep themselves alive. It's not as effective since it's programmed for Narki anatomy, but it has slowed down the progress of their infection, allowing them to survive for several months."

"Restasis chamber?" Jaeia repeated.

"Like recycling themselves—but their tissue degrades after every use, and the infection gains a stronger foothold," the Grand Oblin explained.

"I saw little spots on those Northies that attacked—especially under their eyes and behind their ears," Jetta said.

"So you see the shortcomings of their method."

"Where can I find this restasis chamber?" Jetta asked, temporarily forgetting her disgust.

The Grand Oblin shook his head. "The restasis chamber is enormous and immovable, and the Northies have a hard enough time generating the energy for it in that crumbling city. Furthermore, that's where they've set up their base, and it's heavily guarded."

"Well, what do the Prigs have?" Jetta persisted.

The Grand Oblin shuddered. "There is a species known as the Heli, and one of their abilities allows them to move active sickness from one body to another. The Prigs have at least two in their group. Sometimes the Prigs will capture one of us or the Northies, and the Heli transfer all their infection to their prisoner—or in harder times, to an unlucky member of their own group."

"You said 'active sickness.' So they're still infected?" Jaeia observed.

"Yes," the Grand Oblin said, pointing to his forehead.

"But they could escape," Jetta said, voice rising to a shout. "Why don't you make a deal with them so you can get out of this hellhole?"

The Grand Oblin folded his hands on top of the walking stick. "My dear, barring the moral ramifications of sacrificing other Sentients for our own escape, and assuming we could make it past the Warden, we would spread infection. There is no cure. Every ship in this sector would hunt us down."

"The Warden?" Jaeia repeated.

"He is employed by the Dominion to make sure there are only arrivals, not departures, to Tralora. You can see his vessel at night— it's like a bright star circling the sky."

189

Jetta dropped the blanket and backed up into a rock, bracing herself against it. If she stayed here, she'd have to drink the blood of that thing, but if she and Jaeia joined the Northies, they'd die a slow and miserable death. As for the Prigs, they couldn't risk becoming sacrifices. *We're trapped.*

The walls of the cave came closing in around them. Squeezing her eyes shut, Jetta reached out to her sister, but Jaeia was just as distraught. *There's no one to balance us out.*

Hovering on the horizon of her mind, the Grand Oblin gently pushing against her anxiety, but she pulled back. *There's no difference between him and the dead machine in the recesses of the tunnels.*

Jetta wanted to rid herself of her unwanted emotions, but the other minds on Tralora were too distant, and dumping them inside any of the Exiles in the caves would be dangerous.

"Stop it," Jaeia whispered. *The consequences are too great,* she added silently, pushing the memory of Jetta's misdeed across the psionic planes. Pouring her emotions into a ship's operator aboard the mining ship resulted in a downed ship and the shooting deaths of ten deckmen.

Jetta struck the rocky wall with the back of her fist. "Why are we so important to you, huh? Why won't you just let us go?!"

The Grand Oblin's brow creased, and he chose his words very carefully. "You are under my watch now. I couldn't allow you to come to harm."

"You have no idea who I am or what I've done!" Jetta shouted.

Realizing what she said, her fury melted away. She looked down at her feet, her voice stripped down to a whisper. "Hell, I don't even know. I could be a horrible criminal, and by protecting me—whatever you're doing—keeping me alive—you could be committing a terrible crime yourself."

The Grand Oblin drew a circle in the dirt with his stick. "On Tauri-Mone, when a priest's thoughts became disordered, he took the day to meditate. Have you ever done that?"

Jetta couldn't believe his suggestion. "I want to find a way off this hellhole! I don't want to sit on my *assino* and get in touch with my 'feelings!' And I'm certainly not staying here knowing what you do with that—that *thing*!"

Anger expanding with every breath, Jetta tasted the rich and corrosive fury boiling through her chest, arms, and legs. With every heartbeat she lost sense of reason, her animal instincts hyper-tuning to the old man's movements. *I could easily overpower him. With one thought I could—*

"Fool me once, shame on you. Fool me twice..." the Grand Oblin chuckled. His eyes narrowed and he spread out his fingers.

Feelings and thoughts came to a grinding halt. She wanted to fight—didn't she? No, she didn't. Not anymore. She wanted to sit down and think, collect herself. The ungrounded energy inside her fizzled away to a dull memory, and her body's natural rhythm took over. Closing her eyes, Jetta crossed her legs and placed her arms on her knees. *Time to rest.*

The old man's voice came from very far away. "I will check on you in the morning."

Her sister's thoughts returned to her mind, in tune and balancing with every breath. *That stupid old man did something to our minds,* Jetta projected to her sister, but lost grasp of the anger behind it.

Just like how Jahx used to do, Jaeia whispered back.

The thought of her brother upset her again as she fell into the deep recesses of her own mind. As the world fell away, Jetta settled into a place she had never gone before.

***

After weeks of tracking and lost deals, Reht Jagger finally found Mantri Sebbs floundering in one of the many dingy interstellar bars of unregulated space. From a safe distance he watched with amusement and disgust as the Core officer overturned the near-dead body of a private dancer on the table in one of the exclusive sections of the bar. Her head fell back under its own weight, a frothy white substance foaming from her mouth.

Even over the screeching and howling of the musicians onstage, Reht could hear his Talian warrior snarl in revulsion.

"I know, old friend," Reht chuckled.

They watched Sebbs cover his nose with his shirtsleeve as he searched the crevices of her body for something valuable. The stench must have been horrible if the smoke from the bar hadn't smothered it.

191

"Wait for me on the ship," Reht said.

Mom crossed his massive arms over his chest and growled. The flashing red lights from the stage made his teeth appear drenched in blood.

"I promise I can take care of myself," Reht said, patting the gun holstered at his hip. "And besides, good ol' Mantri's done enough methoc these days that his heart is about one beat away from crappin' out. I think you'd put him over the edge."

When Mom didn't budge, Reht supplied him with a more persuasive reason to return to the *Wraith*.

"Someone's gotta keep an eye on Diawn and Billy Don't. I thought I saw the two of them messin' with the gravity specs again, and I know how you hate motion sickness."

Mom's eyes ballooned out of their sockets, and he took off into the crowd.

Not wanting to draw unnecessary attention toward himself or Mantri, Reht took his time approaching the booth. He had shaken the tail that had followed his crew since the Vrea sector, but he knew he couldn't get comfortable, even among his own people.

After checking over his shoulder, Reht parted the translucent curtains to the private booth and stepped inside. "Still hard up, aren't you?" Reht laughed as he lit a cigarette. He blew a curl of smoke into Sebbs's face, which sent the startled Joliak into a coughing fit.

"Who the hell—?" Sebbs drew a corroded knife from his belt.

"Come on, Sebbs, that's no way to treat an old friend."

Sebbs let loose a sigh of relief when he recognized his face, but he didn't let go of his weapon. "Jagger, what are you doing here?"

"Enjoying the atmosphere," Reht said, cocking his head at the nude dancers parading across the lower stage. The hooting and cheering only escalated as the dancers paired off and teased the crowd.

Reht returned his attention to Sebbs. The Joliak's nose twitched continuously. *The dumb chak probably burnt out his nostrils sniffing crystal.* "Be a doll and lower the knife, will ya?"

Sebbs thought about it before slowly replacing his weapon on his belt. "Don't know who to trust these days."

"Ain't that the truth." Reht nudged the prostitute draped over the table with his hip. "You had enough money to rent a booth, but now you're ripping off the girl?" Only the gurgling sounds coming from

192

her throat suggested she was still alive. Reht picked up her limp head and saw the white tinge to her tongue. Methoc overdose.

"She was just with the one of the VIPs, so she's loaded. And I didn't do this—she did. Too drunk to realize what flavors she mixed. I need the money, Jag," Sebbs said, resuming his frantic search. The Joliak mumbled to himself as he patted her down, his trembling hands not daring to descend into the dark crevice between her mountainous breasts.

Jagger sniggered and stuck his hand into her cleavage, retrieving the large wad of cash. "Same old Sebbs. You can't even have fun with the lukewarm dead ones."

Sebbs snatched the money from his hand, his eyes jittery wells of chemical need. He wondered how long his friend had gone without a hit as the ex-Dominion officer stuffed the cash down his pants.

"Sebbs, you know this ain't really my territory, so I'm risking my *assino*. You know why I'm here?"

"N-no."

Reht rolled his eyes. *It's going to be the same old routine.* The dog-soldier captain slapped him upside the head. "Because, ya dumb *penjehto*, you're not only a wanted man in the slums, you're also tagged."

Sebbs staggered into the table, looking hurt. "Don't—*don't* hit me, Reht!"

Jagger glanced over his shoulder again to make sure they were still safe. The rest of the bar, entranced by the nude dancers spreading the show onto the floor, took no interest in their conversation. His own primal need throbbed between his legs, swallowing up his senses and calling for him to ditch the Joliak, but he turned away from the scene, even as one of the girls wrapped her legs around a patron's neck and slowly gyrated. This was business, and his crew—his own life—depended on it.

"Don't you get it?" Reht repeated, his new frustration making its way into his voice. "You're *tagged*. You're dog meat. You're dead."

"Tagged?"

"Yeah. You're wanted on all sides now, partner. And if they get you, then they get to me, and I don't like that," Jagger said, stabbing his smoke out on the hooker's metal armband.

Sebbs scratched his head and looked wildly around.

193

"What kind of information are you selling, Sebbs, and to whom?" Jagger continued, taking a step closer.

"Now look," Sebbs stammered, drawing his knife. "I needed the money to pay off certain parties."

Jagger grabbed the Joliak's wrist and pried his fingers off the blade. The weapon fell to the floor, the *clink* muffled by the musician screaming on center stage.

Reht moved his hand to Sebbs's throat, slowly squeezing down. The vein on Sebbs' head bulged in the red light, on the verge of exploding.

"Awhh, Sebbs, did you make some enemies going AWOL from the old Dominion?" Sebbs fought for every word. "I was captured on the run by loyalists. I had to tell them about an old supply depot for the USC rebellion you had mentioned—it was the only way I could avoid arrest!"

Reht's squeezed down harder on the Joliak's neck. "Okay, okay!" Sebbs choked out, slamming his fists against Jagger's hands. Grinning, the dog-soldier captain loosened his hold, but only enough to allow him to talk. "I told them about the message points where they could find informants. That's all, I *swear*."

Keeping one hand on Sebbs' throat, Reht withdrew a cigarette from his front pocket and lit up. "So that's why the Alliance border patrol impounded my ship and my crew was interrogated for ninety days. It's all coming together." Jagger blew a puff of smoke into Sebbs's face before holding the burning end of the cigarette two finger-widths from Sebbs's right eye. "This is where you make a choice, Sebbs, as to which side you gonna play."

"Look, Jag—that was so long ago. And they had my fingers in a vice, my tongue in a spindle, and my—my—" the Joliak whimpered, glancing down at his crotch, "—was next in line for the chopper. I'd part with my life before I'd part with my parts."

"So you sold out your business partner. I'm crushed, really."

Jagger pushed the cigarette into Sebbs's forehead. The Joliak screamed as a wisp of smoke rose from the charred flesh. Casually, Jagger put the cigarette back in his mouth, inhaled deeply, and blew out a ring.

"Not only did you cost me my business with that Starways *ratchakker*, you killed all those chumps along the message points,"

Reht said, releasing him. "I don't care much about those *assinos*, but it reflects badly on me."

Sebbs collapsed into a chair and placed a quivering hand over the burn on his forehead. To Reht's surprise, tears welled in the Joliak's eyes.

"I'm using this money to buy more time so I can get the information I need to stop all this," he said, shivering and snuffling like a launnie.

"What do you mean, 'stop all this'?" he asked, grabbing the Joliak by his chin.

A scream tore through the bar. Reht parted the curtain just enough to see two men breaking bottles over each others' heads as a humanoid female tried in vain to push them apart.

Unaffected, Reht let the curtain fall back. "Things ain't so bad now. Business is pretty choice, the Alliance is pissing in the wind."

The Joliak pulled at a knot of his frazzled hair. "Things aren't what they seem."

"Your acting skills can't save you now, *penjehto*," Reht said, shoving the dancer off the table. Her body landed in a gurgling heap, arm bent awkwardly over her head. Casually, Reht leaned against the edge of the table. "You disrespect our trust."

"Look," Sebbs said, cautiously rising on unsteady knees, "I know who led the Dominion at the Raging Front, and I know who destroyed our frontiers and the Royal Interior—it wasn't General Volkor! There is something terrible out there, but I need time to prove it!"

Reht studied him a moment, trying to distinguish between the verbal vomit of a junkie and actual intel. The war that had raged between the Dominion and USC had ended, but the mention of Volkor pricked up his ears. The Slaythe. That piece of *gorsh-shit* the Dominion Core had force-fed the public during the war. Reht hated every last inch of him, from his cropped black hair and square-cut mustache to the booming voice that cut over every airway. Volkor was something out of a catalog, so perfectly crafted to fit the image of a battle-tested Fleet Commander that it sickened him. If it wasn't for his military prowess, he would have thought it was some kind of joke.

"This is going to sound crazy, but do you remember those launnies in the bar on Fiorah?"

195

Reht's mind rewound back to the time when he stopped off at the torrid planet at the end of the universe for the chance at a cheap arms deal. He remembered the wild little girl that spilled into the bar that night, bruised and disheveled, and then his gut kicked in. Her language, her confidence, her cunning—something unheard of in a child her age. He remembered how special she was, how much he thought he could have gotten for her.

"Yeah, so?"

"You were right about them being so valuable, Reht. You were right."

"I want explanations, you dumb *jingoga*," Reht said, slapping him across the face.

Sebbs nursed his jaw and scooted farther away. "They're Volkor, you impotent *chakker!*"

Reht chewed on the remnants of the nail on his left thumb. Even fully baked, Sebbs had always been one of his more reliable informants. He found the idea of the launnies becoming Volkor inconceivable, and yet the impression she had made that night kept him from killing Sebbs.

"Look, you junked-out piece of Dominion *yaketo*, I don't need you alive to get my reward. Give me a reason not to slit your throat. You've got four minutes."

Sebbs massaged his eyes with his fingers, his voice trembling. "I know you won't believe any of this—you'll think it's just a hallucination, a story I'm making up to get you to spare my life. But I'm not."

"Three minutes and fifty seconds. Time's a tickin', friend."

"Look, once I got stationed on Fiorah, I got in pretty deep in the scene. I started selling the new Dominion interrogation drug, Sidious White, to supply my methoc habit."

"Why would anybody want an interrogation drug?" Reht asked.

"It was a sensory enhancer cooked up right before the Dissembler Scare. It *chakked* with neurotransmitters in the brain, gave the prisoners pleasure when they did what was asked. Regulars like it because it took away any kind of anxiety, feelings of consequence—any bad feelings at all. But it was highly toxic—I never touched the stuff."

"Don't deviate, Sebbs. Get to why the kids are Volkor," Reht said, flashing his incisors.

196

"It was about a month after you came to Fiorah that I started dealing to a few superior officers, namely General Salshy. The poor bastard was always so strung out. I was really low on my own supplies, so I gave him a mixed dose of methoc and Sidious to pump him—he never knew what hit him. He started flapping his tongue like a streetwalker."

Sebbs paused, searching for something in his pockets. He produced several empty boosters and a balled-up packet of 45-nite. With an anxious sigh he tossed the cache over his shoulder and stammered on. "He talked about Fiorah, how much he hated the rock, wanted to nuke it, but he was charged with extracting as much Sapphire as possible. Salshy said that the Sovereign's new war angle was bioweaponry, and Fiorah was the only known source of Sapphire in the galaxy."

Swallowing hard and scratching nervously at his grizzled, unshaven face, Sebbs continued. "I was always curious about Sapphire—where it came from, what was so unique about it—so I did some digging on Fiorah. I figured it would make a wicked drug to sell if I could get a deal going with the head guy."

Reht glared at the Joliak, grinding his knuckles together.

"Y-yeah, so, I found out that Sapphire came from Yahmen Drachsi's mines. Turns out the bastard's business went sour and he figured out a new use for the ore—tweaked it, turned it blue and bottled it, named it Sapphire. It was pretty lethal, even in small doses, so he banned it for his own workers but sold it in the streets."

The Joliak took a drink of stale brew left over on the seat next to him. Lips puckering, he repeatedly wiped his mouth with the back of his sleeve. "But the Dominion had Drachsi's number—there was no way for me to deal through him. Frustrated, I tanked Salshy again and tried him for his keycodes. It was dangerous, stupid—but I wanted access to the mainframe, the top secret files—whatever—I wanted in. I knew that whatever they were cooking up with Sapphire was going to be top notch, enough to keep me riding forever, enough to maybe get me a ticket out of the Core. But what I found was—was..."

He didn't finish his sentence right away. Mind splintered by the gestalt pollution of drugs, Sebbs' bloodshot eyes searched the crowd behind Reht for someone with a hit. The raw need, the hunger for chemicals, was a dependency Reht loathed, but at the same time, one he had helped create.

"Focus, Sebbs," Reht said, slapping him across the jaw again.

"I told you not to hit me anymore!"

Reht crossed his arms across his chest. "I'm not playin' this time, Sebbs."

Sebbs angrily pulled at the greasy knots of hair on his head. "Look, I-I found out about a project called ICE."

"ICE?"

"Something... God, if I could only remember... it's like in some root language. 'Inhibitus cui Cerebres Excelsius, I think."

Reht thought it over. "Without conscience, the mind excels."

The Joliak made a clicking sound with his tongue.

"Don't look so surprised. I was once an educated man."

"I didn't mean that—"

"Continue, please," Reht gestured. "And make it worth it to me, Sebbs."

The Joliak's hands couldn't stay still as he talked. "ICE was some secret Dominion project underwritten by the Sovereign himself. It was where Sidious White came from. The Sovereign was worried an arms war against the USC would take too long and potentially not go in his favor, so he approved the use of a silent chemical war. The intent was to take over the USC by manipulating its commanders and politicians. Sidious was a good induction drug, but it was lacking when it came to Sentients that possessed extracerebral abilities, like telepaths. Apparently it heightened telepathic abilities."

"Let me guess," Reht said, "that is when the Dissembler Scare started. The Dominion cooked up that nonsense to eliminate those that wouldn't be susceptible to Sidious White."

Sebbs slapped his hands on the table. "Yes! Exactly! And when Drachsi started leaking Sapphire on the market, the Core took interest. The junkies liked Sapphire mainly 'cause it was like the purest speed ever—no other rush like it—but the Core investigated it for its properties as a focal core suppressant and amnesic."

"Focal core—?"

"It made a person susceptible to suggestion."

Reht made a motion like was looking at his watch.

"Okay, okay—this is the most important part: The Core did something nobody else would ever dare do—they hired *the Motti*."

"What?"

"They needed their expertise in biotechnology and chemical conversion when they were unable to process Sapphire and Sidious White together."

"The Motti," Reht muttered. His lips upturned, and he spat out the vile taste in his mouth. He had never actually seen one, but the nightmare had been described to him in sickening detail in the Underground bars: Thousand-year-old fermenting human bodies, pale and waxy like fungi, flayed and interwoven into spidery carriages, skittering around the organic innards of their biomechanical ships.

Not much more else was known. Bar rumors pegged the Motti for Smart Cell experiments gone berserk, or the failed test subjects of a military experiment to recycle dead soldiers. Others swore that they were part of a dying race of outerworlders, and the easily pliable bodies of the Old Earth humans were their only means of survival. Either way, they were the Deadwalkers—the reanimated corpses of ancient humans—and even for someone like Reht who intermingled with the dark undertow of the universe, it got under his skin.

The scene beyond the thin protection of the curtain got a lot louder, snapping Reht back from his thoughts. Listening to the ruckus, Reht deduced someone had lost a hefty bet on the other side of the bar. Sounds of breaking glass and bones forced him to raise his voice. "Alright, so? Get on with it Sebbs."

Fumbling with his hands, Sebbs continued. "The Motti came out with several different versions of the combined Sidious White and Sapphire, which the Dominion trialed on isolated populations, like Fiorah, until they perfected the drug. They named it Benign White. I saw Salshy's notes on the drug—he observed many other officers sneaking snips of it for battles because it heightened their senses and focus—but most importantly—as he put it—it was like a 'soul silencer.' Allowed them to do the things they needed to do to win the battle without any sense of consequence."

"Yeah, but what's the price on such a lady?" Reht said.

"Heavy side effects—worst withdrawal symptoms ever recorded. I saw one vid of a guy they were testing. He scratched away his skin until he hit bone, screamed like his nerves were on fire."

Reht drew a communicator from the pocket of his pilot's jacket after a chair flew past their partition.

"Mom, you there?" he called over the noise of the bar. The communicator crackled with static and Mom's grumbling.

"Prep the ship. This place is getting hot. I'll be there with the package—dead or alive—in two minutes," he said, closing the communicator and replacing it in his pocket. He cocked his head at Sebbs, encouraging him to get to the point.

"Y-you know I defected just before the USC crushed the Core. I was making enemies with my debt and I needed fast cash, so with Salshy's codes and some others I had acquired through my dealings, I hacked into the old Core mainframe again to research Benign White. I wanted my ticket out of a tight jam, and I thought the chemical base and proof that the Dominion was screwing with the Motti was enough, but I stumbled upon something much, much bigger."

Sebbs's eyes nervously darted from side to side. "The Sovereign's original deal with the Motti to perfect mind control drugs had turned into something else."

"Something else?"

Sebbs forced a laugh. "None of us has ever taken the Deadwalkers seriously, yeah?"

Reht didn't know how to respond. The Motti and their dead army of biomechanical offspring, the Liikers, had always been pariahs among the Sentients. The Motti were garbage pickers, sifting through junkyards and graves on lesser developed worlds, stealing parts to cook up some new hoard of Liikers. At best, Liikers were low-priced trade on Fiorah's flesh market, mainly fodder for fighting rings and not considered Sentient even among the Liberalist groups. But he couldn't fully dismiss the Deadwalkers, not with his youngest crewmember, the little Liiker boy that drove him crazy, saving their crew almost every mission.

"The Dominion orchestrated the Dissembler Scare, but the Motti masterminded something far more evil than arrest and detainment. The Deadwalkers convinced the Sovereign that they could strengthen his army by creating a telepathically networked chain of command."

200

"Using Benign White," Reht inferred.

"Exactly! They controlled the telepaths and linked them to key officers in the Core. Instant communication, entire units moving in complete unison without communication dead zones or real time delays."

"But not all telepaths are mind readers," Reht said, mulling it over. "What did they want with the rest of 'em?"

"They used the mind leeches to link up with their handler, but the rest of the telepaths formed the network, connecting them across the Starways."

"Leeches," Reht said, wagging his finger at Sebbs. "You know I don't like that slang."

"Y-yeah, sorry—sorry. I forgot about your woman. Sorry," the Joliak said, raising his hands in anticipation of the blow.

"Keep going, Sebbs," Reht reminded him, digging his nails into the Joliak's shoulder. Sebbs bent over and winced. "How do the launnies fit into all this?"

"Remember that test I gave them?"

"Yeah," Reht said. "They're freaky smart—so what?"

"That wasn't exactly it. It wasn't so much that they were smart—it was their ability to learn that made them so special. Something about them being able to imprint the brain patterns of other Sentients."

"What the hell kind of telepath is that?"

"Nobody knows. They were orphaned, sold on Fiorah. Nobody'd seen anything like 'em. The Dominion never could crack their DNA. Kept coming up human. Impossible, right? No Deadskin could do those things."

"Okay, they're freak jobs." Reht said, taking a step closer to Sebbs. "Give me more than that."

"Don't you see?" Mantri said, gesturing wildly. "The Motti must have realized their potential. They convinced the Core to have them exposed to every single bit of military knowledge they could, through games, simulators, teachers—whatever—to turn them into—"

"General Volkor!" Reht exaggerated with a booming voice.

"Yes! The Deadwalkers made them into the commanding 'hub' of the other telepaths."

"Let's pretend I'm buying this *gorsh-shit*," Reht said, rolling his finger in the air. "So what's the catch?"

Sebbs rocked back and forth, his eyes unblinking as his gaze fell to the floor. "I—I think the Motti set up the Core. Think about it—the Dominion was poised to destroy the USC at the Raging Front and then—*poof*—they stopped fighting and the USC claims some fantastic victory. Something must have happened to those launnies. Something must have triggered them to turn against their handlers, and I know those Deadwalkers had to be in on it."

"Then what happened to the Motti?" Reht said, flicking away the nub of his spent cigarette.

"I-I'm not really sure," Sebbs stammered. "Things got really screwy after the Raging Front. There weren't many logs about the events after that. I know the Dominion ordered the execution of the two girls, but the records were inconsistent."

"What do you mean?" Reht asked, scanning the brawling crowd for signs of trouble coming their way. The crowd had now become violent, and even the dancers and musicians were beginning to clear the floor. Needing a fast escape, Reht eyed the narrow corridor leading to the rear exit as beer bottles shattered against the center stage.

"I couldn't find a report about the disposal of the girls' bodies. It's not protocol, but it's not something the Dominion would forget to document. It wasn't a glitch, I checked, and no files were deleted. I don't think they were killed, but my codes wouldn't get me any farther. That's why I needed to buy some time and some allies so I could just think—get this thing figured out."

"Why, Sebbs—tell me why," Reht said, taking him by the collar.

"Because the USC didn't really defeat the Core," the Joliak screamed. "It was the Deadwalkers. They probably took the boy, the other telepaths and somehow converted the Core military into Liikers—I don't know how, but with all their drug experimentation they must've come up with somethin'. This new massive crop of Deadwalkers could attack the borders at any second! My Gods, think of it, Reht—no one could defeat that army!"

"Holy Mukal," Reht mumbled, confliction pinching his brows together.

The Joliak scraped at Reht's fingers. "Those two girls were once part of 'General Volkor' with their brother, and are the only Sentients that will understand how to fight the Deadwalkers. If I had more time, I could prove all of this, but I've made too many enemies, and I've had to hide—"

Reht let go of Sebbs as police alert sirens wailed across the bar. The two of them dropped to their knees, pressing hands to their ears against the blast of sound. As troops stormed the premises, the emergency floodlights activated, and the bar lit up like midday on Fiorah.

"Attention. Attention," a voice intoned through a bullhorn.

Reht peered out through the curtain. The light stung his eyes, but he could see well enough to make out the white and gold uniforms of the Interfederational Guards.

"We are here to arrest the defector known as Mantrilius Sebbs," the announcer said. "Present him and you can go about your business."

"You're even hotter than I thought, Sebbs," Reht said, grabbing the Joliak's wrist. "But I need you to buy back my rights into the USC's good graces."

With the cops still combing through the maze of broken beer bottles and bloodied drunks near the stage, Reht made his move, shoving the Joliak toward the rear exit. As they turned the corner into the narrow corridor, they collided with a tall, buxom waitress emerging from a private room.

"You alright?" Reht said, helping the waitress back up. She looked down at him, her face lighting up, and he bit back a curse, bracing himself.

The large woman pressed him into the wall and licking his earlobe. "You never call, you never stop by. I wonder why I still love you, Reht Jagger," she said, puffing out her lower lip and teasing his hair with her red plastic nails.

"Hey, new fancy?" she asked, noticing Sebbs and smirking.

"Not quite." Reht half-frowned and tried to buy himself a little room by putting his hands against her shoulders, but she just leaned into his touch. "I need a favor, Janey, and quick. Where's the emergency exit?"

Janey leaned back against the opposite wall, folded arms pushing up her breasts. "What's in it for me?" she asked, batting fake eyelashes.

Shrill screams and protests followed the electric zap of shockwands. The smell of burnt flesh wafted down the corridor, somehow registering above the miasma of piss and smoke.

"The cops are sweeping the booth," Sebbs muttered anxiously.

Reht suppressed a grimace and bent forward to place a quick peck on Janey's painted lips. Before he could pull away she pressed into him so hard that he fell back against the wall. He nearly choked on her slippery tongue and the sour taste of fried meat and chewing tobacco.

When she finally released him, he gasped for breath and fought the urge to spit out the contents of his mouth. Out of the corner of his eye he caught Sebbs's mixed look of horror and amusement.

The waitress sighed and flipped back a panel cover on the wall. "Not a better kisser in the whole galaxy."

"The exit, Janey?" Reht repeated, wiping his mouth with his sleeve. The walls quaked with the sound of gunfire. Lurid flashes from the plasma rifles lit up the corridor, illuminating the plastic coated imperfections of the waitress' face.

"You're standing on it," Janey said.

Reht looked down. Amidst the chipped linoleum and bare floor was a single, glossy black tile.

"Hold onto your jewels." Her gaze dipped below Reht's waistline, and she winked.

"Get ready, Sebbs," Jagger muttered, yanking Sebbs onto the same black tile. "She really means it."

Janey blew him a kiss and hit the switch. Blue, liquid coolness shot up from the floor, dissolving his skin in an icy blink. A confusion of light and sound wiped past. Heat brought Reht back together, refusing cells in a burst of starlight on a receiving box near the loading dock.

"What a rush..." Sebbs mumbled, his eyes circling wildly in their sockets.

As soon as he regained feeling in his limbs, Reht grabbed the Joliak and ran for his ship, holding his gun against the Sebbs' neck. The *Wraith* hovered a few meters off the dock, engine cells glowing fire-orange, ramp lowered. Reht hauled Sebbs up by the collar, scrambling aboard right behind him.

"What took you so long?" Ro asked, shoving Sebbs into one of the empty passenger chairs.

"This place is crawling. We need a fast exit out. Where's Diawn?"

"Right here," she said, dropping from the deck above onto the bridge.

"Take the helm. Ro and Cray—to the weapons pit. Mom, Tech—set up Billy Don't. Where's Vaughn?"

"On the terminals," Tech yelled as he disappeared down the hatch to the engine room.

Reht strapped into the command chair just in time as Diawn floored the ship's engines, slamming him back in his seat.

"We've got company. Not even Billy heard 'em coming. Must be using those new subspace silencers to mask their signals," Diawn muttered as she hurtled toward the glittering arc of Interfederational Guard ships surrounding the city.

"We can jump to Crest Point near Phaleon V if you can make it past their perimeter," Reht said, sending calculations through his command terminal to the navigation system.

"*If* I can?" Diawn cranked the ship hard to port and spiraled out of a scout ship's range. A brief transmission to lower arms echoed through the ship, and Reht silenced it with a fist against the speaker.

"Hold on!" Diawn laughed, banking starboard, then port, dipping the *Wraith's* nose down into a dive before adjusting hard-front. Plasma beams sliced past their ship as she evaded the flagship's targetmen. Ro and Cray returned fire, temporarily deterring the fighters tailing their ship. In the back Sebbs paled and clutched his stomach.

"Jump calculations ready. At your mark, Diawn," Reht said.

The dog-soldier captain white-knuckled his armrests as Diawn sailed smoothly alongside the Interfederational Guard, taunting the enemy before engaging the engines. Sebbs had already slumped to the floor.

Light flashed throughout the bridge. Invisible forces pulled Reht in two different directions before snapping him back together.

"Gods, I hate jumping," Reht muttered as new stars appeared on the viewscreen.

"Why didn't you kill him, Jagger?" Diawn said, eyeing the Joliak as she engaged the autopilot. "Growing soft in your old age?"

Diawn smiled devilishly as she unstrapped herself from the pilot's chair, tugging at the chest lashes on her bodice. Lately she had been trying to get his attention even more than usual, and he wasn't sure why, but he certainly didn't mind.

Reht rubbed the scruff of his chin and thought about what Sebbs had told him. "I might be crazy, but I think the old junkie just might be worth something," he muttered.

Diawn frowned as she lifted up the unconscious Joliak's head. His tongue drooped from his mouth, and spittle slicked his chin. Shaking her head, she dropped him to the floor with a thud. "He won't fetch more than twenty thousand on the bounty boards or the flesh markets."

"No, he won't," Reht said, rising from his seat. "But he'll be worth something to the Alliance."

Diawn passed by, her fingers grazing the top of his pants. "That sounds dangerous, Captain."

The glint in her eye, the smell of her; the way she moved her hips. Despite everything that had just happened, he couldn't help himself. Then again, he could never resist her. Very few men or women could.

"Pilot—come see me in my den right away."

"Of course, Captain," she whispered, her lips tickling his ear.

As he and Diawn headed for his den, he eyed his crew. Sidelong glances and silent hand motions indicated the uncertainty of their captain's decision. Most of them were true dog-soldiers, in it for the payoff and the rush, not parleying with any government or organized military. Taking Sebbs to the Alliance was a stupid risk, even for a hefty payout.

As he hopped out of his chair and made his way to his den, Mom caught his arm. The Talian's expression warned of danger. *The Alliance couldn't be trusted.*

"Don't worry, old friend," Reht whispered, patting his first mate on the shoulder with an exaggerated grin. "You know we gotta do this."

Mom's baritone growl rumbled in his chest. Silver eyes lowered to the ratty bandages around Reht's hands, hiding secrets etched in flesh.

"Yeah," Reht whispered, grin faltering. "That's why."

***

Jahx did not want to open his eyes. Restraints held him down at the wrists and waist. The air, hot and humid with decay, made it hard to breathe without gagging.

Who are they? Heart thudding inside his chest, Jahx sensed the beings all around him, watching, waiting. *Am I still on the Core warship? How much time had gone by?*

Frenzied chatter came at him for all directions. Voices overlapping, deliquesced with mechanical clicks, made his skull hum. *Oh Gods—*

Calm down, he told himself, but his racing heart made it hard not to give in to panic. *You have to stay calm or—*

(Don't think about that)

(Trust yourself)

Relaxing his muscles and stretching out his mind, Jahx tried to orient himself in the din. There were many voices in this place, but one rose, throbbing and angry, above all the others. It sounded familiar, but he wasn't certain if it was his own memory or one of his sisters'.

With eyes open—

With eyes open—

With eyes open—

The thought repeated endlessly, rooted in a rage that beat at his consciousness, driving him back into the prison of his body. Even there it cut at him, brutal and unrelenting like one of Yahmen's games. His nerves threatened to unhinge, but he lay still, trying not to alert his captors.

Mechanical chatter escalated. The air current changed; something large moved toward him, scraping along the ground. Labored, raspy breathing came down above his head just before a sharp object pierced his right ear. Jahx screamed, bucking against his restraints, trying to get away from the pain as it drilled into his head.

Someone—something—hissed. The restraints released, his arms and legs freed. Jahx clutched at his ear, feeling around the canal until his fingertip found the edge of a metal chip. After a few seconds, the clicking and chattering organized into a language he could understand.

"Awakening, yes."

Jahx dared to open his eyes. Faceless humanoid heads hunkered around him on spiny legs. Towering above them all was the monster from his nightmares, a half-faced corpse perforated by circuits and wires, fused on a spidery carriage. A single red eye burned inside the remains of its right socket as it inspected him with devices protruding from its palp.

The creature bent over him, its multi-jointed mechanical legs groaning and squeaking. "Can you hear me, Jahx?"

He could, and with more than the translator crammed into his ear. What he heard in the creature's tangled, caustic thoughts made him break out in a sweat.

Death. Destruction. Torment without end—

"I am M'ah Pae. I am the Motti Overlord," the creature hissed, and at the gesture of one mechanical leg, the hoard of faceless heads moved aside. "Follow me."

Not knowing any other recourse, Jahx complied. He tried to get off of the platform, swaying forward and nearly falling over on legs that felt like blocks of wood. When he looked down he saw that his arms and legs, swollen and discolored, ranging in hue from green to blue and black.

"What is happening to me?"

"You are evolving," the Overlord replied, walking away from him.

Jahx closed his eyes and took slow, deep breaths. What colors, he wondered, were his lungs? His face? The panic bubbling inside him gnawed at his resolve. Why hadn't he chosen the escape pod?

(No—this is the way it's supposed to be,) some inner logic told him.

With tentative, clumsy movements, Jahx limped along pulsating passageways slicked with a clear film. Luciferin globes, stapled into the ceiling in four meter intervals, illuminated the spiny creatures imitating his graceless movements.

As he ducked under dull, yellow support structures reminiscent of cartilage, and ceilings dripping with ichor, Jahx shuddered. "Oh Gods..." Jahx realized. *It's like a body cavity...*

One of the walking heads came up behind him and thumped him on the back with its forehead, nudging him forward. He nearly toppled over.

"Follow me," the Overlord demanded.

Trembling, Jahx could barely keep himself upright. The psionic projections in this place were a tempest of misery and hatred, beyond anything he had ever known or thought he would know.

"Insufferable humanoid," M'ah Pae growled, snatching Jahx up beneath the arms with the sharp grips at the end of one of his mechanical legs, cutting into his ribcage. Jahx cried out, but the Motti did not relent. "Do you know why I let you awaken now?"

"No," Jahx said, struggling to free himself as the Overlord carried him toward a flexed passageway that looked much too small for them to pass through. Holding Jahx low in front of him, M'ah Pae hunkered down, squeezing through the ring. The band of tissue relaxed around the Motti's hard mechanical parts, gleaming wetly, and closed tight behind them as they slid through to the other side.

M'ah Pae vocalized something that sounded like tortured metal. "I will show you."

In the Overlord's thoughts Jahx sensed something he had long been familiar with after dwelling within Yahmen: the thrill of anticipation.

As the Overlord carried him along, Jahx looked around, his terror congealing into a numb dread. Things built from machine and flesh scampered in and out of holes in the walls. Some of them were as big as the mounted heads, but others were smaller, more complicated creatures wreathed with mechanical prostheses.

"What are those?"

"Liikers. They are part of the Motti. They are our children."

Jahx focused on M'ah Pae's thoughts and instantly regretted it. He witnessed humans and humanoids dug out of graves or abducted from unprotected passenger cargo ships, reduced to essential parts and fused with their new mechanical bodies.

With his heart threatening to pound its way out of his chest, Jahx didn't know if he would pass out or vomit. He focused again on his breathing, and on the voice that led him here.

(This is the way it's supposed to be. Trust yourself.)

They squeezed through another passageway, and the smell of rotting flesh assaulted his senses. M'ah Pae extended his limbs so Jahx could get a better view of the chamber.

"Why?" Jahx whispered. Bodies piled upon bodies well into the thousands. Adults, children, and the elderly of every gender from a wide range of Sentient races created obscene mountains. Only a few remained untouched, the rest missing limbs or having the beginnings of mechanical devices fused into their decaying flesh.

"These are the ones that have failed," M'ah Pae said.

"What did you do to them?"

"They were unsuitable, unusable in the confines of their flesh. I have made them useful. I have made them necessary. Even if they cannot survive to become a Liiker, they will be purified into usable proteins, into fuel, and they will have a purpose."

This time Jahx was sure the screeching sounds were laughter.

"I will purge and perfect you, too, Jahx," M'ah Pae said, smiling. Black gums oozed yellow fluid. "I will show you a life without the disease of the flesh."

Jahx threw up, his stomach cramping until it emptied completely. "You defile life," he said, tears streaming down his face. A dark satisfaction spread through M'ah Pae's thoughts, seeping into Jahx's mind and making his insides feel cold and lifeless. Gritting his teeth, Jahx's mind burned with impulses he had never felt before, even on Fiorah.

"The Motti do not defile life—we purify it. This universe is polluted by excess, by the stink of immoderation. We destroy what is useless and purge the flaws of the flesh."

Jahx noted the subtle falter in his voice, the change in the consistency of the vocalizations, and realized his opportunity. But it meant delving beyond the corrosive exterior of the Overlord's mind and contending with whatever malignancy lay beneath. He would have to push further then, risking more than he had ever risked before for his one and only chance.

Every nerve fiber lit up in his scope of awareness, as if to protest the idea. *It's madness, an empty sacrifice. You can easily save yourself.*

After all, M'ah Pae was just like Yahmen. He fed off of pain and thrived in the face of suffering, hiding his true desires beneath his twisted philosophy. The last time Jahx had entered Yahmen's head it had nearly killed him, and he would have lost himself in the tangle of his owner's shadow if it hadn't been for Jaeia. Besides, maybe he was wrong and Jetta was right; maybe he wouldn't be able to connect with M'ah Pae any more than he had been able to with Yahmen.

Jahx closed his eyes. He could hear Jetta whispering in his ear, telling him to kill the monster.

No, he countered. *That's the easy way out.*

He couldn't shake his belief—the same one that kept him from killing the Dominion officers, the cadets, the laborminders, the child laborers—any Sentient that had hurt him. He believed that even in a beast like M'ah Pae a seed of hope existed.

My faith with kill me...

Even if you're right, Jetta once told him, *that doesn't mean everybody's worth saving.*

No, Jahx thought, the blood rushing in his ears, *this is the one Sentient I absolutely have to save, or there will be nothing left for my sisters, for anybody.*

He couldn't explain the thought, even to himself, as the terror choked his bowels. But his inner determination would not yield.

I am a coward for not acting sooner, he thought. *Jetta would never have hesitated to act on her beliefs.*

Holding the memory of his sisters as an anchor, Jahx delved past the Motti Overlord's mottled skin, past the synthetic blood pumping through his veins. He strained through the clicking and buzzing of machinery to find what was left of his decrepit organic brain. Almost immediately the icy consciousness of M'ah Pae engulfed him, suffusing him with the Motti Overlord's vision for the future of the Starways—the replacement of corrupt, untidy neurons and gray matter with the beauty and precision of circuit boards and central processors.

Bone-splintering cold dulled his senses and dimmed his sight, but there was no pulling out now. If he did not find what he was looking for, he would break apart.

"There are evil people, Jahx; why can't you just accept that? We can kill Yahmen and be done with this—we can save our aunt and uncle and be free! You're the one that's keeping us back."

Jetta's words cut through him, spurring him forward as semi-optic shadows dragged at the edges of his consciousness, making it harder for him to differentiate between himself and the half-dead machine. Dizziness and nausea had faded along with any other recognizable sensations, replaced by line codes and subprograms that sent little vibrations through his six spiny legs. The same obsessive thought repeated over and over again in his head: With eyes open, they burn—

(No!) *Jahx screamed, trying to keep hold of himself.* (Please,) *he pleaded,* (give me the reason...)

Voices assailed him from the depths of the dead machine, whispering in a language long forgotten as macabre scenes played out across his cortex. He felt his legs, transformed into pincers, selecting torsos from an overcrowded bin of discarded carcasses. He analyzed metal alloys and transducers before selecting which ones to introduce into a live specimen. He saw his own reflection, bereft of humanity, in a discarded sheet of metal left in the junkyard as he searched for new parts for his creations.

If he couldn't find it, then he confirmed his sister's accusations—he was weak, cowardly, a waste of undiscovered talent. Everything he had done—or hadn't—would amount to nothing. All those times he could have stopped Yahmen, all those times he could have saved Jetta and Jaeia, his aunt and uncle...

He felt himself calving like an iceberg, splinters disintegrating into the darkness as he descended into the fetid depths of the Overlord. He saw a man with obsidian eyes and a glittering, savage smile. The man's nettling voice made his skin crawl with desires he knew were not his own.

His mind jerked away, and Jahx found himself standing in the middle of a smoldering city, hovering over the broken body of a blonde woman he had killed. Her blood seeped out of her ears and nose as she whispered a name: Josef...

(Please,) *Jahx pleaded,* (please be there!)

Trusting his intuition, Jahx held fast to the name the woman whispered, focusing on it, bleeding the last of himself into its fragile existence. Just as M'ah Pae's shadow eclipsed the last of Jahx's consciousness, he found something unexpected buried under the ruin of malice and disillusion.

The rush of hope brought revitalizing warmth to his awareness, driving back the shadow long enough for it to lose its hold on him.

He remembered himself and resurfaced with a new understanding of his purpose.

Jahx's eyes blinked open. "You cannot lie to me," he whispered. "And you cannot hide anymore. I see you."

M'ah Pae's face contorted and his grip slackened just enough for Jahx to draw in a real breath. "Why did you awaken me?" Jahx said, voice changing pitch and intensity, surprising both of them. "Did you want me to tell you of your own undoing?"

A mechanical leg sliced upward, and his face exploded in pain. Jahx's tried to hold together what was left of his nose as blood spurted down his neck and chest.

"No," the Overlord hissed, his eye seething in its socket. "I will tell you of your undoing. You are the most powerful telepath in this galaxy. You could destroy me, this ship—the entire enclave—with a mere thought. You know you have this power, yes?"

Jahx alternated between swallowing and spitting out the coppery blood that filled his mouth and throat. If he could have answered the Overlord, he would have told him that he had always known he had such power. Even back on Fiorah he could have killed Yahmen with a single thought, but that wasn't what he believed his powers were for, despite everything that had happened to him and his sisters.

"And yet you do nothing. Your senseless compassion is your undoing," M'ah Pae said.

"I know who you are," Jahx choked out, "and I know why you chose me. I will help you even if you kill me."

M'ah Pae spat in his face, corrosive saliva eating through Jahx's skin and exposing the white of his bone. "I have no intention of killing you, Jahx. But I will destroy your soul."

***

Black fire traced every nerve in Jahx's body as bioelectric wires burrowed underneath his skin. As mechanical probes dislocated one arm, then the other, and fed wires into the joints, he struggled to stay conscious through the pain. This wouldn't be for nothing, he told himself again and again. When cold steel pierced the back of his neck and his head filled with thousands of wriggling worms, Jahx realized this would be his last moment owning all of himself.

213

The smell of charred flesh reached his nostrils as his vision faded to black. "Welcome to oblivion, number 00052983," a voice hissed in the dark.

Please don't let me be wrong...

Emptiness whistled past him as he fell, offering no resistance. He fell and fell, away from the pain he was already forgetting, when something collided with him, pinning him down like a living insect to a specimen board.

Other minds, gifted like his, fluttered around him like frenzied moths, trapped alongside him in some nether existence on the brink of life. They tore at him, and their pain became his pain until he hardly knew where he ended and they began. Part of him wanted to let them devour him, to simply allow his light to dissolve into the scatter of restless wings, but he knew he couldn't—not after all he had gone through—and he fought with every last ounce of strength to maintain what little was left.

Reaching out and away from the tangle of tortured minds, Jahx stretched farther and thinner until there was nothing left of him to stretch—and with one final thought, connected.

***

Number 00052983 took its place on the buzzing walls of the comb. While only a single entity in the maze of rows forming the ship colony, it connected physically and psionically with rest of the Liiker enclave, forming the massive networked mind.

Hearing and seeing all of the Liikers, speaking to and for them, Number 00052983's purpose illuminated in the bioelectric lattice of inner space:

Purge and purify.

With eyes open, we burn.

The humidity in the living ship brought beads of sweat across its one remaining brow. Fleshy portions of skin still exposed to the air, red and swollen with the newly installed wires and circuits protruding from its orifices, wept sanguineous fluid. Accessory Liikers smeared organic stabilization goo over its body as Number 00052983 inserted a feeder into the network and integrated into the central intelligence.

CHAPTER IV

Jetta opened her eyes, but it was too dark to see. She thought she had gone blind until the shadows shifted, and she could discern the layers of dark matter swirling and pooling around her feet.

(Hello?) she cried, trying to make sense of her surroundings. She couldn't feel anything of substance, not even beneath her, as if she floated in midair.

(Hello?!) she cried again. She didn't want to be alone—not in this place. The cold confinement of emptiness was more terrifying than any enemy she had ever faced.

Something stirred within the shadows. Someone else was there. Someone familiar. (Hello!)

She tried to find her arms and legs, but her body, appearing and reappearing, was no more tangible than smoke.

A voice, concealed by darkness, whispered ever so softly into her ear: (Please, oh please, find me, find me—kill him.)

(That voice—I know that voice!) Jetta thought excitedly, trying in vain to turn around.

The dark world shuddered, and the shadows drew in around her like a circling predator. A low rumbling gave way to footfalls that grew louder and faster with each step. She thought of Yahmen and all those nights he would come charging down their hallway in one of his drunken rages, but these footsteps were made by someone— something—much bigger and meaner.

Panic fired into her heart as the footsteps neared. She couldn't move, and she couldn't see into the darkness beyond herself. She was four years old again, hiding in the closet, knowing that it was only a matter of time before Yahmen found her.

Something brushed past her essence, sending her senses reeling. (Jahx!)

She breathed in his scent, his aura, and it filled her with joy. But as soon as she thought to cry out his name, something bit into her, sending spasms of pain down phantom limbs. Jetta screamed, commanding her body away from the agony that gnashed its way deeper and deeper into her core, but she remained hovering above the groundless plane.

A behemoth roar reverberated all around, drowning out her cries as the shadow world changed. Serpentine tendrils unfurled from the pitch, slithering toward her as she writhed and wriggled in midair, trying desperately to gain purchase.

216

Then someone—something—latched on to her and yanked her from the encroaching menace, sending her spiraling away from any sense of body and self.

(*Please—oh please—find me, find me—kill him.*)

Jetta snapped forward, grabbing a handful of rocks. Breathing heavily, she took aim at every rock formation in the cavern until the memory of the dream crept back into the shadows. Slowly, she put the rocks back down.

"*Skucheka...*" Taking deep, calming breaths, she told her pounding heart that she was safe.

Wait—what is—? Jetta thought, touching her aching left side. She lifted her shirt and gasped at the ugly scratch marks that twined their way across her stomach and bloodied her clothes. Looking at her own hands, she saw the blood caked underneath her fingernails.

"Jaeia," she whispered. Her sister had fallen asleep propped up against the wall of the cave, just as she had last seen her before their encounter with the Grand Oblin. When she didn't wake, Jetta sent her a silent message. *Jaeia!*

Jaeia's eyes popped open. "No!" she cried, throwing her arms out to prevent herself from tipping over. It took her a moment to get her bearings. "I had a terrible dream..." she whispered, pulling her knees against her chest. When she saw Jetta's wounds, she uncurled.

"Who did that to you?" Jaeia asked, crawling over to her, eyes wide with concern.

Jetta bit her tongue, trying to hold Jaeia's mind at bay as she struggled to make sense of what had happened as she slept. *I can't remember.*

Her mind felt clouded, like it did back on the Core ships. She wanted to just ignore what was happening, but her left side got worse with every breath.

Closing her eyes, Jetta searched her memory.

"Oh Gods," she said as a headache split her concentration. Spotting some of the Oblin's leftover sleeping root in a bowl near their bedding, Jetta realized what she needed to do.

Jaeia crept closer and tentatively took hold of her arm. "Jetta, after all of this—I'm scared. We should go."

It pulled at Jetta's heart to see her sister like this, but she couldn't leave without knowing more. "I agree—and we will—but this first."

"Jetta, no!" Jaeia said as Jetta grabbed a root and milked the orange gel from its tip. "That—that thing down there—my dream—please Jetta, *please*—"

When she closed her mind to Jaeia, she heard a muffled sob.

"I saw Jahx," Jetta whispered. "I have to go back."

Jetta smeared the orange gel on her chest, closed her eyes and willed herself back to sleep.

***

At first she saw nothing but the bloodlit darkness behind her eyes. Jaeia's pleading and the pain of her bones grinding into the rocky floor receded as she focused on how she had felt in her dream. If it was something more, her only hope of recapturing it was following its psionic vibration.

Nothing happened.

Her heartbeat pounded in her ears. Jaeia's hands gripped her arms, shaking her. Even with the sleeping root she could never fall asleep with this much distraction.

Concentrate.

Focusing all of her thoughts on Jahx, Jetta remembered the calm blue of his eyes, the soft curves of his face. His shy half-smile lit up her heart as she imagined him twirling the hair at the base of his neck around his finger, his other hand reaching out to her.

Reaching back to him, Jetta's awareness drifted away from the cave, her connection to her body narrowing to a pinpoint of light. Her sister's cries, once in her ear and in her mind, disappeared.

Jetta opened her eyes to pitch black nothingness. (I've returned.)

(Where are you?) she called out repeatedly, meeting only a stillness both infinite and lonely.

Still without a body she could recognize, Jetta fought for one, as if inside a lucid dream. She stared into the abyss until her grasp resolved into hands, and her footing found an invisible surface to anchor her consciousness.

Satisfied, she tried moving forward. The air, soupy and frigid, smelled like ashes. With each step she took, the legs she could not see became colder and harder to move.

(Where are you?) *her voice echoed into the nothingness. The sound had all but faded when it intensified and came rushing back at her with renewed force.*

She covered her ears as her own words split into a thousand screaming voices, sharpening into the shriek of metal on metal. As she curled up into a ball, trying to shut out the noise, she remembered. (I know that sound—)

Raw fear surged through her phantom body, dissolving her limbs. I have to concentrate—

Heavy footfall sounded in the darkness, breaking through the shrieks in a discordant symphony. Her heart lodged in her throat, and she shut her eyes. The footsteps rushed at her, cutting across leagues of endless darkness in the giant, pounding steps of a hungering animal.

Suddenly, a familiar smell settled over her, triggering her earliest memories in a sweep of supercharged emotion.

(Jahx!) *she sobbed, reaching out blindly into the shadow.*

Concentrating as hard as she could on the memories of her brother, she opened her eyes. Two blue eyes stared back at her, distant and pale.

(*You have to find me*)

(*And kill him.*)

"Jetta!"

Gulping for air, she pawed at the hands that shook her by the shoulders. "Stop—" she cried. When her eyes finally came into focus, she saw her sister kneeling in front of her.

"What is happening to you?" Jaeia asked, not letting go. "You were acting crazy!"

Jetta swallowed hard and wiped the sweat from her eyes with trembling hands. "What do you mean?"

Before Jaeia could respond, Jetta dove into her sister's memories only to see herself flailing about.

"I don't know why he would do it, but the Grand Oblin did something to change our dreams," Jaeia said, wiping tears from her eyes.

"Did you have a nightmare about Jahx too?"

Jaeia sat back on her heels. "I tried to tell you that before you went to sleep again. It was terrible..."

As Jaeia's words trailed off, Jetta saw the reflection of her sister's dream glinting off her thoughts. Embroiled in her own urgency, Jetta glossed over her sister's experience.

"Look," Jetta said excitedly, "I thought I was just having a nightmare—but it was too real. Jahx found me—he called to me!" Jetta said. "He's somewhere far away, but he's still alive. We have to go find him!"

Jaeia sucked in her lips. "Jetta, you aren't listening to me."

Jetta's mind screeched to a halt as she sensed the depth of her sister's fear. "What?"

Jaeia's voice cracked and tears reformed anew. "I don't know if it's true or not, but..."

Jetta grabbed her sister by the shoulders, pressing her forehead to hers, plunging headfirst into the fray.

(I hope you'll understand.)

Grainy and distant, the memories laid before her came from someone other than her sister.

(Who is this?)

The gunfire ceased. Bullet-riddled soldiers lay dead all around her. Overhead light panels dangled from blast holes, some flickering, others sparking, most of them completely dark. Smoke filled the debris-littered room, making her choke.

She crawled out of her hiding place and listened. At first she heard nothing. She knew it was a mistake, but she called out. Even though these were bad men, she wanted very desperately for one of them to be alive. (I don't want to be alone—not when the monster comes for me.)

Her voice echoed in the hallway but quickly died out. She expanded her mind, even though she didn't want to. Just around the corner she found it, along with many others. It had been watching her, waiting.

It repeated back what she had called out, as did the rest of them. In a panic she ran down the corridor, her stomach going cold as she realized she couldn't possibly get away. There were hundreds of footsteps—no, not footsteps. It sounded more like thousands of pointed feet skittering across a metal floor.

(I hope you'll understand.)

220

Sadness mixed with a peculiar understanding. "Everything will be all right..." Jahx whispered.

She sees the auxiliary computer console where the image of a jump-ship flashes like a beacon of hope. Her hands, which she now knows are his, work desperately on an alternate escape plan—but not for him.

(No, no,) *she cried softly.* (Take it, go, please, for me!)

The feeling of sadness and understanding returns. He knows something she does not.

(Jahx, no,) *she whispered.*

(I hope you'll understand.)

Now she is in another place, another time. A body hangs before her in a room that is a wet, intestinal red. Slick yellow and white support structures arch overhead, punctured by routing wires and flashing terminal interfaces. Fuel and gristle insult her nose, making her gag.

Hell—

Tasting the raw edge of vomit in the back of her throat, Jetta dares to step closer to inspect the body, feet sloshing through pink exudate.

No, no, NO—

She can barely make out the outline, but she knows it's his by the soft curve of his face. Reaching out, Jetta touches her brother's cold and lifeless skin.

Impossible! *she shrieked across the psionic planes, tearing at the seams of her sister's reality.*

"No!" she screamed, slamming back into the present.

"Now you see," Jaeia whispered, scrubbing tears away with the back of her hand. "Those were his memories. I think he's—"

Jetta didn't hear what Jaeia said next, but her sister's grief hit her like a sledgehammer to the chest.

"I don't believe it," Jetta said between sobs. "I won't. What I saw—"

"Wasn't real. It was what you wanted to see, what you wanted to believe," Jaeia whispered, her head cradled against her knees.

Jetta stood up, cold anger rising like a carrier wave. "Then if Jahx is dead, what's the point of leaving now?"

221

"Jetta, I can't be here anymore," Jaeia said, voice teetering on the edge of a sob. "I can't drink the monster's blood—I just can't. You feel the same way."

"No, I don't," Jetta said. Apart from anger, she felt dead inside. Not even the psionic pull of her sister held the same clout.

What is happening to me?

"I don't even know what to feel right now," Jetta whispered, pressing the knuckles of her thumbs into her eyes.

"If I were in you," a feminine voice observed, "I would be afraid, too."

A stout body waddled in from the tunnel connecting to the other cavern. Jetta glared at the Oblin.

"What did you do to us, old man?" Jetta said, rushing toward her, but she came to an abrupt halt. Behind her, Jaeia gasped. Trailing behind the fat woman was Senka.

"But—but," Jaeia stammered, "You're—"

Senka's eyes, dark and sunken in a face that had gone eerily gray, barely met her gaze. Dried blood and something slick and black caked her clothing and bandages. Her face contorted oddly in what Jetta realized was an attempt at a smile.

"The Liiker," Senka said quietly as she moved stiffly toward them.

"The 'antibiotics'?" Jaeia asked. "That's what you call the Liiker blood?"

"It has very powerful healing properties," Senka said, no longer making eye contact.

"Something happened," the Oblin interjected, fumbling with her walking stick. "I lost my connection to the two of you."

"I thought I made it clear that you shouldn't be digging around in our heads!" Jetta shouted.

"Look at your injuries," the Grand Oblin said, pointing at her.

Jetta did not look, but her cheeks went hot as the others scrutinized her wounds.

"Telepaths are different from other Sentients. Very powerful dreams can affect your body as well as your mind. That is why I was helping you—I didn't want something like this to happen. But I can't anymore; something is stopping me," the Grand Oblin replied. Her amethyst eyes went solemn. "Even though I don't know what it will do to you, I will show you what's left. I would rather your conscious mind sees it before your subconscious ravages your body. Then maybe we can sort all this out."

"So, those dreams we had—those are our memories?" Jaeia asked, her voice trembling again. "The ones we can't remember?"

"Yes, trying to surface." The Grand Oblin nodded. "I experienced some of them with you—or at least with one of you—a short while ago. That is why I came here."

Jaeia tried to catch Jetta's eye, but Jetta refused to look at her and shoved out her thoughts.

Gathering up her robes, the Grand Oblin clumsily hopped up onto a rock. She motioned for them to sit next to her, but Jetta stayed where she was. Jaeia moved toward the Oblin but did not join her on her perch.

The Oblin sighed and looked at her shoeless feet. "I know you think what I did was wrong, but I did what I did to protect you, to help you through what you have experienced. I could never let harm come to any Sentient, especially a child."

"We're *not* children," Jetta said adamantly. "We may be seven, but I've never felt like a child, and I've certainly never had the opportunity."

"I suppose in some ways you're right," the Oblin said, smiling sadly.

"But still," Senka added. "You wouldn't have stayed if you remembered everything—if you didn't have a chance to see things differently."

"She knows too?" Jetta asked. "Does everybody else in this place know our business but us?"

"I only learned about certain events over the last few hours, as one of you was dreaming," the Grand Oblin said. "Jaeia, I think it was yours. I seem to be completely cut off from you, Jetta."

"But you've already showed us what the Core has done to us. Are you saying there's more?" Jaeia asked.

The Oblin looked at her hands and nodded. "Yes, there is."

Afraid, Jetta wrapped one arm around her sister. Jaeia's fear compounded her own, sending waves of acid up her throat.

"It will take a great amount of trust on your part, but I want you to take my hand and see the past, remember what really happened."

"We are your friends, we would never want to hurt you," Senka added, hugging her arms to her chest. "You have to believe that."

Jetta ground her teeth together. No adult could be trusted. Still, the Grand Oblin might be hiding something that would prove Jahx was still alive, and for that reason alone she had to extend her hand.

"You know I could kill you. All of you," Jetta said, her eyes flicking back and forth between the Oblin and Senka.

Neither the Grand Oblin's outstretched arm nor Senka's gaze faltered.

Jaeia's head tilted to one side as she listened to the Oblin's thoughts. *It's time to learn the truth, Jetta.*

Heartbeat roaring in her ears, Jetta lifted her hand to the Oblin's, and remembered.

***

Captain Reht Jagger watched with amusement as Tidas Razar, Military Minister of the Starways Alliance, stroked his chin with two fingers. If they had been in an outerworlder bar, that kind of hand motion would have landed him a male escort. Razar had done it as long as he'd known him, probably to make it look like he gave a *chak*.

Mantri Sebbs, on minute fifty-two of his rant about the launnies of Fiorah, the abducted telepaths, project ICE, and the Deadwalkers, tested even Reht's patience. The Jittery Joliak always had a problem getting to the point when he was short on methoc, and unfortunately for all of them, Sebbs was dry as a bone.

Finally, after Reht had kicked up his feet on Razar's desk and studied the wall decor, the Minister raised his hand for Sebbs to stop. The old military bastard shot a look of resentment Reht's way before speaking.

"I'll have you know that our military strength has increased exponentially since the defeat of the Eeclian Dominion. The United Starways Coalition is finished. Now we are the Starways Alliance—fully funded, supported by the public and universally recognized. Never again will there be a threat to democracy and peace."

"B-but—the launnies—those Deadwalkers—" Sebbs stuttered.

Reht laughed and slouched further into his chair. Tight as the situation was, he couldn't remember feeling so comfortable. Looking around the room, he realized just how fancy the Starways Alliance had gotten since its days as the USC. None of the usual stuffy military-issue furniture and equipment—the warship was outfitted more like a hotel. Even the air was scented like something out of a modern home catalog: "Summer's Breeze #141," or something like that. Reht wanted to make a joke about putting the taxpayers' money to good use, but he didn't have a chance.

Tidas Razar lifted his fingers off his desk. He looked bored. "Certainly you read the net posts. Do you not know about our new chief commanding officer, Urusous Li? Only twenty years old, but has already graduated command school and beaten all our top commanders, including our former chief, Admiral Unipoesa, in the Endgame. Unheard of—simply unheard of. He's also lead one of the most successful post-war cleanup campaigns in the history of the Starways."

Razar grunted. "So tell me, Sebbs, why do we need your help?"

Sebbs squirmed nervously in his seat, looking to Reht for backup. Unfortunately for him, Reht enjoyed his discomfort too much to intervene just yet.

"I know about Li—I do—but I'm telling you it won't be enough. At least hack into the old Dominion databases—surely they can't all be corrupted. I gave you those codes—you can confirm that I'm not making this up!"

The Minister chuckled. "Why Captain Sebbs, I've never known you or your escort to be such generous men. I can hardly believe you'd give up so much information without asking for something in return. Maybe a pinch of methoc? Some Bearnigi smokes, hmmm? What is it to you, Reht? Maybe a night at La Raja with the ladies of Neeis?"

Reht shrugged his shoulders. The statement wasn't as much about him as it was about Sebbs. He might be a dog-soldier, but Sebbs was a hardened criminal in their eyes.

"This isn't about that!" Sebbs pleaded. "Don't you think it's strange that even the Sovereign has disappeared? Doesn't that hint at more than just a victory for the Alliance?"

The Minister suppressed a smile. "It's not that uncommon for a tyrannical leader to cower in the face of defeat, go into hiding, and wait until he makes new allegiances before reemerging. Our Special Missions Team will find him, and he will stand trial for his crimes. Speaking of which," the Minister said, tapping his fingers together, "you are a wanted man, Sebbs—a very wanted man—and I think I'll enjoy your trial more than chasing your *ideas*."

Tidas Razar picked up a report on his desk and rattled off a few of the intergalactic charges Sebbs faced, even including the fines and debts he had incurred on the streets.

Sebbs shot another desperate glance at Reht. The dog-soldier captain smirked and tipped back in his chair. At Sebbs's furious glare, Reht groaned and took pity on the poor junkie.

"Minister, I saw one of the launnies Sebbs is jabberin' about in the Underground bars of Fiorah. She wasn't your average kiddo, I can tell you that. If she wasn't a telepath, she must've been smarter than the lot of us. Even without all this I 'spect the Core could've used her for something nasty. Besides, Tidas, old friend—Sebbs isn't stupid enough to waltz right in here, not even if I doped him. You gotta consider that he means what he says to risk all this."

"It will take time to investigate these *claims*. Meanwhile, I appreciate you bringing Mantri Sebbs into our custody, Captain Jagger. I will be happy to provide your crew with an escort to the interior," the Minister said, pressing a button on the top of his desk and ending the meeting.

"You don't understand!" Sebbs cried, rising from his seat as two guards entered the room. "Jahx and the other networked telepaths are still alive! This half-*assino* operation will be crushed when those Dominion soldiers become fully integrated Liikers!"

Jagger didn't move from his seat as the guards closed in with stun guns. He kinda felt sorry for Sebbs when he hit the floor, eyes frozen open like a crazed animal.

"Captain, my respects to you and your crew," the Minister said as the guards dragged Sebbs away by the collar. "However, some of the other council members are still unsure of your loyalties. Beginning today, your passage through federated space will be strictly regulated."

A retort perched on the tip of his tongue, but Reht stopped himself when the alarm strapped to his thigh vibrated. *Something's happened; the crew is in danger.*

He should have gone right then, but he couldn't stand to be cheated, especially by a tight-collared old military fart. "Minister, ouch—I can't accept that. You know I've always backed the USC, and that hasn't changed since the formation of the Alliance. He might not have made good choices, but Mantri did what he had to do to survive. My crew can't be held responsible for that."

"That's where you're wrong, Reht. Someone has to take the blame in the eyes of the military council. You are the most convenient target. That's politics." The Minister's mouth twisted in a humorless smile as he showed the dog-soldier captain the door.

"You lose me, Tidas old pal, and you lose your best bet in surviving what's to come," Reht said, folding his arms across his chest, refusing to budge from his seat.

"We have Sebbs, Captain—the one you claim will be our invaluable informant—so why would we need your scrap crew?"

Reht snorted. "Because I'm the only one that kid knew and trusted before she was sent away to be brainwashed. If she don't see a familiar face, then she ain't gonna help you. Don't they teach you anything in your fancy command schools?"

"You overestimate your importance, Jagger. You always have," Tidas replied.

Reht leaned in toward Tidas, revealing his incisors. His urge to deck the Minister grew stronger by the second. "When you sit on your *assino* in *gorsh-shit* meetings instead of actually being out there," Reht said, stabbing a finger at the observatory window, "you lose perspective on how things really work. When it comes down to that, the rules of politics don't apply. You know how to find me, Razar. I'll be waiting—but with a much heftier price tag."

Reht left before the Minister could answer and before he did something stupid. Mom, forced to wait outside the Minister's office during the meeting, matched his gait as he strode down the hall, a low growl rumbling in the Talian's chest.

Something up, Reht thought, concern bristling the hair on the back of his neck. He tried to play off his worry, walking with his hands in his pockets and head held high, grinning at the Alliance guards escorting him back to his vessel, but as soon as they arrived at the dock, he hurried to the *Wraith*.

Once on board the ship, Diawn grabbed him by the collar and threw him against the wall, licking her lips.

"Happy to see me?" Reht chuckled.

Diawn sensuously pressed her face against his, her lips grazing his ear. "Billy did something," she whispered. The two Alliance guards lingered for a moment, gaping at the enthusiasm of his pilot.

"My lady missed me, so I'd best be getting on." Reht nodded to the guards, wrapping his arm around Diawn and tickling her chin with his finger. One of the guards shook his head, the other tripping over himself as they descended the ramp.

"Goodbye, gentlemen," Reht waved as he sealed the door. When the locks clicked over, he turned to Diawn as she squeezed her breasts back into her top. "What did he do?"

Before she could answer, Reht tore his way down to the engine room. As soon as he spotted Billy Don't, he wrenched him away from the terminal, shaking the little Liiker by the shoulders.

"What have you done?"

Billy Don't emitted a shattering scream, and Reht dropped him in favor of protecting his ears. "Remind me why the *chak* Tech gave that thing a voicebox?"

Diawn wrapped her arms protectively around the little Liiker boy. "He tapped into their mainframe. We could be traced."

Grinning and blowing bubbles with his digestive lubricant, the Liiker boy with only half a face spun around on his back wheels, babbling and squealing in delight, oblivious to Reht's anger.

"Mom, take the helm and get us out of here *now*," Reht yelled into the intercom. The ship beneath their feet vibrated as the engines fired, and they lifted off.

"Diawn," Reht gritted out, "This time he's gone too far. I've had it with that psychotic tin can." The dog-soldier captain drew a knife from his sleeve and turned toward Billy Don't.

"No!" Diawn shouted, lunging for Billy. "Don't you touch him!"

Tears ruined the dark makeup around Diawn's eyes as she cradled Billy Don't against her triple breasts. What she saw in the demented Liiker, Reht didn't know. The little bastard could talk directly to the *Wraith's* computer, and fix internal problems faster than his engineer, Tech, but that was the limit of his use. The Motti had discarded Billy for a reason—his brain didn't fully take to the implanted neuro-network, resulting in impulsive behavior that landed him the nickname, "Billy *Don't*."

"Don't take him away from me," Diawn said, smoothing back the few remaining blonde locks of hair on Billy's head.

"I thought you didn't get attached to people," Reht said, kicking the Liiker's front wheel. "Or things."

Billy yelped and tried to spin away, but Diawn held him fast, staring down Reht.

In the back of his mind stirred a vague recollection, perhaps an off-handed remark, or rumor Reht had chanced upon over the years about his pilot. Something about Diawn's abandonment as a child, her despoiling at a young age by one of the circuit pimps that turned orphans into intergalactic sex slaves. Maybe Diawn related to Billy Don't on some twisted level, seeing the ugly, mirrored truth of her own brutal world.

Billy Don't craned his neck to the left and as Reht reared back the knife. "Cooohh—duuds. Coooh—duds."

Reht froze mid-strike. "Am I crazy or did he just talk?"

Over the last few months, Tech had been working on a program to help Billy Don't speak again, but nobody, not even Diawn, had expected much to come of it. It was too much for anyone to hope for, especially for a discarded Liiker.

"He's saying 'codes,'" Diawn whispered, looking directly into Billy's real eye. She gripped the Liiker by his shoulders and used her sweetest tone. "What codes, Billy? What are you trying to tell us?"

Billy Don't inserted his interface module into the computer, and the monitor flickered. A long string of codes appeared on the screen. Billy Don't integrated them with the files and unlocked all of them.

"Holy Mukal," Reht said, leaning on the bulkhead as he skimmed through one of the first files. The little Liiker had integrated Sebbs's codes with the remaining fragments of information the Alliance had recovered and organized it into something concrete.

He tucked the knife back into his sleeve—at least for now.

After scanning through the compiled information, Reht thought he had pieced it together. "Sebbs isn't that crazy." Reht traced his finger along several paragraphs and shook his head. "Something *must* have happened internally to the Dominion."

"You can't call on the devil and then expect to control him," Diawn muttered, standing at Reht's side and reading over the information with him.

"Look at this—the Sovereign signed this mass execution order right before the Raging Front."

"Alliance said it was for the leeches," Diawn read.

Reht ignored the slur. "Naw, I'm betting not. That was their meal ticket. Bet that was for the Deadwalkers. Must've pissed 'em off something fierce," Reht said, scrolling through the text. "Gods, I'm not sure who to root for here."

"This is some hot stuff, Reht." Diawn looked anxiously across the room at Billy, who rocked back and forth and smacking his real hand against the metal plating of his chest. "They're going to be on our backs for this."

"Not if we flip it on them. Make them deal."

"What could we possibly have that they would want?"

Reht grinned, his incisors gleaming. *Time for the big payout.* Diawn wouldn't be happy, but this was too good an opportunity to miss.

"Sebbs figured out that the twin girls were exiled, not terminated, and before he left our company, he graciously told me their location," he said, pulling up a star chart on the nearby display. He pointed to a tiny star cluster, zoomed in closer, and then stabbed his forefinger at the second of five planets circling the red dwarf star. "Crazy things that boy will remember when a pack of smokes—and his balls—are on the line."

Tech popped his head out of a conduit and dropped from the ceiling. "You want us to rescue those kids off Tralora?" Tech said, nosing his way over to the display. "You're crazy, Jag. It's diseased. There's no cure."

Jumping up and catching the railing above his head, Reht swung up to the command deck. With a smirk on his face he stuck his head back down and winked at Diawn. "Pilot, I need you set a course to Polaris, now. We don't have much time."

Her expression soured. Diawn had never been his most stable crewmember, and his plan would certainly test what little sanity she possessed. Unfortunately, he didn't have time to charm her now. Time to play stupid. "What is it, babe?"

"Nothing," she replied curtly before disappearing up the navigational ladder.

"You're in for it, you know," Tech commented before scuttling down to the engineering terminals.

Reht returned to the bridge. It was still too hot for Triel of Algardrien, Prodgy Healer, to resurface, but this payoff depended on it. And, after all these years, he would have been okay with any excuse to bring home his Starfox.

***

Fiorah had only one picture house in the slums, and the only time it didn't show adult films was midweek during the hottest part of the day when nobody would be out anyway. During happier times, Galm and Lohien took the triplets to see an antiquated flat-projection pictures on the evolution of spaceflight. Even though it was a lazily crafted commercial for one of the starship dealers in town, Jetta didn't care. She liked learning about transportation across the Starways and new developments in space flight, but more importantly, it was something her family did together. All five of them sat in the front row, even though nobody else was there except a few stragglers escaping the heat.

The picture house smelled like a strange mixture of concession food, mold, and body odor, and whatever lay buried in the ankle-deep garbage on the floor. None of that bothered her. Strangely fascinated by the weird sound of Galm's shoes sticking to the floor, Jetta also enjoyed the occasional treat when they found a discarded box of candy with a few remaining pieces.

Wedged between her siblings, with Galm and Lohien a seat away on either side, Jetta relaxed in the presence of her family. But here, alone in the heart of her worst nightmare, Jetta couldn't turn away from the terrible reel of memories the Oblin had been keeping at bay.

Rogman appeared before her, closely trailed by a man who looked more dead than alive. Veins wound their way over his gray skin like tiny snakes. Avoiding eye contact, the grey man's wide-eyed gaze looked beyond any object in the room. She couldn't access his mind, but she tasted something familiar in the echo of his thoughts. She asked Rogman who the man was, but he only ever answered, "Another leech."

Leech—a word frequently whispered among the Core personnel. Fear attached to that name, and envy, but she couldn't glean more information from anybody.

(Jaeia, Jahx—where are you? I don't understand why I'm having such a hard time reading other people's thoughts...)

Something sharp pierced her neck. "This will make you stronger, quicker."

"This will evolve your flesh." Fire poured into her veins and worms crawled into her belly.

"This will make you mine."

Everything changed. The cold sterility of the Core ships dissolved, replaced by the stink of old meat and the wet, pulsating walls of a body cavity. Unfamiliar machinery wound its way through the glistening slickness.

(Where am I?)

The thing with the burning red eye stood over her, inspecting her with one of its many ocular devices. Before she could move or speak, the view changed. She couldn't see; she could only hear the sound of an argument pitched just below a scream.

"This is not in our agreement. We will not authorize any of them to be 'integrated.' Their behavior problems will be addressed with the White."

(Rogman?)

Shrill noises and metal scraping against metal.

"No, and that is final. You have only one job—don't chak *it up!"*

Jetta tried to look away from the memory as it reformed, but as she resisted it swelled in her mind's eye. She saw Rogman and the other decorated officers standing on the observation deck while men in lab coats huddled around their datafiles and chattered excitedly. Anticipation and expectation hung in the air.

"Get your secondary fleet out faster today," Rogman ordered. "I want a quick victory, not a pretty one. Their forces will surrender once you cross the Front."

(Why did they care so much about the game? What is it about the Endgame that is so important to them?)

Jetta looked away from the Endgame display and saw her uniform sleeve threaded into her body. (What are we doing? This is all wrong.)

Resist, *she commanded her siblings, and in the stillness of her sudden lucidity, she heard her words go further than their three minds, rippling out across the psionic plane like a stone dropped in water. Other minds, like hers, carried her voice, their collective presence reaching into her, extending her consciousness across a distance she couldn't begin to measure. As her psionic awareness sharpened, she saw herself become the central axis in a constellation of the brightest stars in the galaxy.*

Everything finally made sense. Without drugs disrupting her train of thought, she pieced together the truth. The leeches. The collective presence—her heightened intuition. Lessons with a new high commander every day. Separating them, controlling the intensity of her connection to her siblings' minds. The thing with the burning red eye...

... And General Volkor. Terrible, soulless eyes that followed her everywhere, around every corner, through every newsreel, banner and poster that lined the walls and decorated each room of the ship. Soldiers greeted each other by hailing him, praising him and his glorious victories to unite the fractured Starways.

Rogman's thrown me against all the top commanders—so why haven't I played Volkor? *It was an old thought, one that she hadn't been able to answer at the time. But even then, through the chemical haze, she had felt the connection, though she couldn't hold onto the thought long enough to draw the inevitable conclusion.*

She did now.

Volkor the Slaythe, the Usher of Death, the destroyer of worlds.
We are Volkor.

Jetta awoke slowly, pressing her palm against her forehead as a relentless hammer pounded the insides of her skull. Perched atop a series of stalagmites, the Oblin, morphed back into an old man, smoked his favorite pipe stuffed with black leaves and thistle. Purple smoke unfurled from his lips as he contemplated her.

Jaeia, Jetta thought, reaching out to her sister across their bond.

Sitting next to her in a daze, Jaeia did not look up, caught in the terrible revelation they shared. *We killed millions of innocent people.*

It's not our fault, Jetta tried, tears pricking her sinuses. *The Core tricked us.*

What we did—unforgivable—

I can't do this, Jetta realized, shoving away her sister's guilt, and her own, and turned to rage.

"Is this what you wanted?" Jetta shouted at the Grand Oblin, throwing a handful of rocks across the room. Jaeia began to cry. "Did you want to break us down only to build us back up as you see

233

fit? What exactly are your plans for us? Because I have news for you—it doesn't change anything. I'm still going after my brother and there's nothing anybody can do to stop me!"

"Jetta," Jaeia choked out between sobs. "Please, don't. Please—"

Clutching her head in her hands, Jetta fought against the onslaught of emotions threatening to unhinge her sanity.

(What have I done?)

Sadness, guilt and shame beyond anything she had ever experienced gutted her from the inside out, leaving an aching canker that drained her anger.

(I am unforgivable.)

When she saw the look on Jaeia's face, she realized that the feelings came from beyond her consciousness.

"Stop it, Jaeia!" she screamed, scraping up another handful of rocks and whipping it at her twin. The Grand Oblin leapt down from his perch and swatted the rocks away with his robe.

"Control yourself, Jetta—"

No.

Jetta struck the Oblin, sending him staggering backward. Running up the tunnel, past Rawyll and Dinjin, she kept her eyes on the cavern exit. When Crissn tried to stop her from deactivating the bioshield, she punched him in the gut and kneed him in the groin.

Running hard and fast down the mountain, Jetta stumbled and slid down most of the trail until she reached the valley floor, unaware of anything but the urgency wailing inside of her chest. Her lungs ached as she ran through the brush, branches catching at her skin.

I don't know how, but I will escape, she thought as she fought her way through a tangle of tree limbs, *even if I have to kill all the Northies and all the Prigs or battle the infected along the way.* And it didn't matter that she would do it alone. *Jaeia is weak. If I'm going to find Jahx, I can't let that weakness get in the way.*

The sun, sinking behind the mountains, made the treetops glow orange and red in its dying light. In the back of her mind Jaeia struggled to be heard, but Jetta shut her out.

"Don't worry, Jahx," she whispered as the last sliver of sun disappeared behind the peaks. "I'll make things right."

Reht instructed his crew to dock on Spacey's Port in the Polaris system. A dingy bar and fuel station located on an asteroid circling the giant planet of Ploto, Spacey's was a hotspot for those traveling in and out of the system and a safehouse for those who knew somebody in the business. Some time ago, Reht had acquired some pricey Old Earth artifacts for the owner, Guli Varocassi, who had subsequently granted him an unusual degree of access to the bar's facilities.

When he entered the bar, Mom, whose head grazed the ceiling, got him the attention he needed.

"Reht Jagger, old friend, what brings you here?" Guli asked. The short, portly man wormed his way out from behind the bar, his eyes trained on the giant Talian at Reht's side.

Guli was completely human, a rarity in this region. Most humans who had any sense stayed away from the outerworlds, but Guli was different. Ruthless and violent, he possessed a keen sense for running an outerworld crime ring and never went without half a dozen weapons inconspicuously strapped to his body. Tokens of those who had dared to call him a Deadskin or question his authority—a combat belt, fingers and teeth, a length of dried skin— hung above the bar as a fair warning.

"Come to the bar! Let me serve you your favorite." Guli smiled and revealed a row of crooked yellow teeth. Mom, still at Reht's side, turned away in disgust as Guli scratched at the bare belly hanging over his waistband. Reht smirked. He never knew how his first mate survived as a dog-soldier with such an extreme aversion to uncleanliness.

Reht slid into one of the barstools as Guli poured a steaming green fluid that bubbled and splattered everywhere. Into Mom's larger mug he decanted a single drop of red liquid. He then lit a match and placed it carefully over the top of the mug. When the smoke finally settled and the fireworks subsided, Mom slammed back the brew that had risen to the brim.

"Always a scene," Reht said before taking a swig of his own drink. The instant the liquid touched the back of his tongue he gagged, his cheeks puffing out and his throat tightening. Mom slapped him on the back, and Reht let loose a wheezy cough.

"*Chak*, Guli, what did you put in this thing?"

Guli laughed, spraying the giant Talian. Mom growled and wiped his cheek with the back of his hand.

"A little Bassi ale, Hiji tonic, and some ingredients you might not want to know about. Spices it up, eh?"

Reht shook his head and placed his hand over his drink to avoid a refill.

"Business seems to be looking up," Reht said, nodding to the crowd of people standing shoulder to shoulder in the bar.

"Yes." Guli took their glasses away and set two glasses of Tequeken brew in front of them. "The Alliance is too jacked squabbling over fragments of territory left over from the Dominion Wars to really concern themselves over our operations."

"Here's to that." Reht tipped back his glass and downed the beer.

As he set down his drink, he rallied his confidence. With Guli there could be no hesitation, no hint of fear, or he'd end up tacked up on the wall.

"So, enough chit-chat." Guli donned a sinister smile. His index finger twitched as if to fire an invisible gun. "What brings you here, Captain Jagger?"

The bar owner's voice was a little too relaxed, a little too smug. *He knows.*

Body tensing, Reht readied for assault. He scratched his left ear to signal his Talian warrior.

"I came for the package I asked you to keep safe for me six months ago."

Guli leaned back and crossed his arms over his jiggly belly. "Is that right?" He looked over his shoulder and then immediately back to Reht and Mom, clearly signaling someone in the crowd.

Dropping his hand below the bar, Reht clicked off the safety to his gun. As his hand returned to the bar's surface, he sported a casual smile. "You didn't think I wouldn't come back for it, did you?"

"Her kind's still not welcome, Jagger. It would be unwise to make a move now."

Something told Reht that Guli wasn't advising him on the political state of the Starways. When Mom brushed his shoulder, Reht knew he'd picked up on it, too.

236

"I brought you some sweet and dirty hard cash as a token of my sincerest appreciation," Reht said, opening the flap of his jacket to show Guli the stack of money tucked away inside. With uncommonly quick reflexes, Guli plucked the money from his pocket. He brought the cash to his nose and inhaled deeply.

"Come with me," Guli said, motioning for them to follow him behind the curtain separating the main bar from the kitchen.

Passing by the cooks attending to their bubbling pots and pans, Reht tried to ignore the molding spills or worms hatching out of steaks left out overnight. He had eaten at Guli's before, and while it wasn't the dirtiest joint in the outerworlds, he didn't want to know exactly had been spicing up his meals.

Long stairwells winding through a maze of basements and subbasements revealed the true nature of Guli's world. Sentients laying down working girls or sleeping off benders on broken slabs of furniture didn't bother Reht as much as the interrogators pumping their victims for information.

"Please—Gods—I don't know anything!" a bloodied humanoid wailed as two thugs held him down.

The interrogator approached, bat resting on his shoulder, taking his time. "Oh, you're gonna remember something for me, boy!"

"Quite the system you got going, Guli," Reht said as he stepped over a drunken Toork crying to himself on the stairwell. "I'm impressed."

Guli shrugged. "I get by."

They finally came to a door guarded by two of the largest henchman Reht had seen in Guli's establishment. "These are guests of mine, Chezi, Mari. Let us pass, please."

Reht eyed Mom, who emitted a low growl. They followed Guli through a hallway lit by old fluorescent tubes and into a boiler room littered with broken bricks and tiles. Mom crouched to avoid hitting his head on the pipes as all of their attention went to the dusty trap door in the center of the room.

"For your inspection." Guli handed Reht a key. The guards followed their boss closely, trading steely looks with Reht's warrior.

"Hope you don't mind them," Guli said. "I always have my associates present when I close a transaction."

"Whatever." Reht shrugged.

Mom stepped between his captain and Guli's men, flaring out the tips of his claws. The henchman grinned like feral animals.

Key in hand, Reht found himself hesitating. Not all the fear behind the Dissembler Scare was unwarranted. Then again, he reasoned, if anything was the least bit out of sorts, none of them would be standing there now. At least not with their guts intact.

Keeping Guli and his men in his peripheries, Reht dropped to his knees and unlocked the door. It swung open easily, affronting them with the smell of mold and mildew. Covering his nose with his hand, Reht peered inside. A single candle barely illuminated the room below, enough for him to see his dirt-floor landing. Reht nodded to Mom to stay on top as he dropped down.

Even by his standards, the hideaway wasn't fit for habitation. His stomach churned as his eyes passed over the room's contents. A mattress crammed with wheatgrass, crawling with bugs. Empty food cartons, stacked neatly in the corner, buzzing with little black flies. Corkboard shelving, sagging beneath the weight of an old television, ready to collapse.

"Starfox," Reht whispered when he spotted the dark-haired woman curled up in the corner of the room by a crude latrine. She turned her head, the blue of her eyes catching the candlelight, but her gaze slid past his. He recognized the behavior; he had seen enough of it in the war camps as a child.

"I came to get you," he said, kneeling down next to her. "It's still not safe, but we need you."

She shivered and drew her legs against her chest when he reached out to touch her.

"I am so sorry, Triel. I never meant..." He couldn't finish the sentence. *What have I done?*

Desperate to shelter her after the Dominion massacred her people, Reht had miscalculated just how bad Guli's could get.

"I couldn't come back before—it was too risky," he whispered, brushing a lock of hair away from her face. He gently touched her cheek, but the coldness of her skin made him retract his hand. Reht had seen her in bad conditions, but nothing like this.

I should never have left her. What if Guli had—

Triel turned her head, this time locking eyes. "Behind you!"

He drew his weapon and spun around, firing blindly at the opening of the trap door, not worrying about his aim. Whenever she

238

was around it seemed like his instincts were keener, as if her telepathic gifts amplified his intuition.

Mom roared, and after a brief scuffle, something heavy collapsed to the floor.

"What was that?" Reht asked as Mom stuck his blood-splattered head down through the trapdoor opening.

Mom pushed the charred remains of a guard down through the hole so Reht could see that his shot had found its mark.

"I see and smell," Reht said, covering his nose. "What about Guli?"

Mom grunted and made a slicing motion across his neckline.

"Oh. Well, he wasn't my favorite customer anyway. Let's go," Reht said as he typed in the commands on his comlink to alert the rest of the crew of their immediate departure.

Grabbing his Starfox's hand, he tried to pull her to her feet, but her legs wouldn't support her weight. Mom grumbled as he jumped down, but tenderly picked her up and cradled her with one arm.

As they exited the stairwell, a band of Guli's men burst out of the kitchen, guns charged and poised. Reht opened fire, taking out several before they had a chance to aim. Mom dropped his claws and laid into the men closest to him with his free hand, shredding any weapons or appendages that got in his way, blood and sinew splattering the walls. Two of Guli's men managed to fire off a few shots, grazing the Talian's thigh and shoulder, but it didn't faze Reht's warrior.

After the men retreated into the bar, Mom gingerly set down Triel next to some storage boxes by the sinks. Ripping the industrial freezer from the wall, Mom jammed it into the kitchen door, barricading the entrance.

"We need a new exit," Reht yelled over the commotion, keeping his back to sinks. The two remaining cooks, initially frightened, signaled each other with hand motions. One of them gripped a frying pan a little too tightly, and the other, moving around the kitchen island toward the sinks, wiped his butcher knife on his apron with quick, nervous movements. "Can you make me one?"

With a bellow that shook the walls, Mom charged toward gap between the sinks.

"Holy—" Reht said, grabbing Triel and rolling out of the way of his warrior. A watery mix of bricks, concrete and broken pipes rained down from above as Mom rammed through the exterior wall.

"That works," Reht said, assisting Triel through the resulting hole.

The dog-soldier captain breathed a tentative sigh of relief as he spotted the *Wraith* hovering over the bar, ramp down with Vaughn guarding the deck.

Scooping up the Healer in his arms, Mom ascended the ramp first, Reht covering his back as guards poured out of the front entrance of the bar.

"*Chak,*" Reht cursed, his right arm catching rebound shocks from the gunfire. Hunkering down behind the ramp, Reht waited until Ro and Cray fired off several plasma rounds from the ship's weapon pits to draw away the attack.

With a grunt, Reht hurled himself up the ramp. Vaughn caught him by the jacket and helped him the rest of the way into the ship as Diawn pulled the nose of the ship up and away from the assault.

"Well, that was—" Reht didn't have the chance to finish his sentence. Diawn floored the engines, sending them all careening backward.

"Hey, can't argue with the results," Reht chuckled as Mom growled and picked himself off the floor.

"Triel... it's good... to see you," Vaughn mumbled while strapping himself back into the navigational terminals. It was the most Reht had heard the ex-con say in months.

She smiled and spoke with a shaky voice. "Good to see you again. All of you. I didn't know if you were going to be able to come back."

Using his teeth, Reht tightened the bandages on his left hand, trying not to let her words dig into him. "Come on," he said, wrapping his arm gently around her waist. "Let's get you to the infirmary."

Diawn's piloting made the short trip exceptionally difficult. The ship rocked side to side, plummeting hard and then jackknifing upward at a nauseating velocity.

When they finally reached Bacthar's infirmary, Triel collapsed into the exam chair.

"Sorry—Diawn still enjoys testing our upchuck reflex." Reht shot her a lopsided smile as he removed a med kit from the shelf.

"Need some help?" Bacthar asked, ducking his head in. He grinned when he saw the patient in his chair. "Well, well—Triel of Algardrien—so good to have you back."

"Doc," she smiled, reaching out to take his hand. The Orcsin gave her a big hug, wrapping his thick black arms and wings around her entire body.

Reht tapped the surgeon on the shoulder. "I got this one. Maybe in ten, okay?"

"Okay—I'll just get some grub for the lady." Bacthar winked at the Healer and disappeared toward the galley.

It took him a few moments to work up the nerve as he prepared the dressings, but he finally found his voice. "What happened?" He watched her closely as he soaked a cloth and began cleaning her face.

"Guli took an interest in me. He never tried to hurt me—he was too afraid. But he was making plans. He started to deprive me of food, sleep. He thought maybe then he could convince me to..."

Even with tears brimming her lids, Triel didn't cry. His Starfox rarely broke down, even in the worst of circumstances.

Reht bit down and tore another strip off his thumbnail, infuriated not only at Guli but at himself. "I'm sorry, Starfox. If Guli hadn't taken you in, the Core would've found you, and you'd probably be a Deadwalker."

"A Liiker?"

"It's a long story," Reht said, passing her the cup of warm Mugghra soup Bacthar laid on the counter.

"You said it still wasn't safe," Triel said. Despite what Reht had instructed earlier, Bacthar began to quietly inspect the Healer as she sipped the steaming Mugghra.

"No, it's not. But this is important."

Triel looked him up and down. "This isn't regular crew business, is it?"

Gently, she took his hand, probing his mind. He closed his eyes, allowing her through, remembering just how good she felt. He hadn't realized how much he missed the electrifying feeling of her essence, or the way his body and mind instantly relaxed when he felt her presence intertwine with his. He had almost forgotten himself and their circumstances, lost in her psionic rhythm, until she squeezed his hand.

"The things Sebbs said... You're not joking, are you?"

"I'm not the joking type, am I, Starfox?" he said, cocking his head and smiling.

"Reht Jagger," Triel whispered, "What exactly do you think you're doing?"

"I'm doing what I do best," he said, brushing the wayward strands of her dark brown hair from her face. Her eyes narrowed, and he could see the uncertainty.

"Well, besides the malnourishment you look healthy enough, Triel of Algardrien. I'm sad to say I've seen you worse," Bacthar reported as he shut off his bioscanner.

Reht sensed a heavy presence overcast the infirmary and turned to find Diawn leaning against entryway with a sour look on her face. The Healer pulled her hand out of Reht's, her posture stiffening.

"We're safe. I put us on a course for a star cluster where we can take shelter for a while," the pilot said.

"Good," Reht replied. "With Guli gone they'll be fightin' over his scraps before they come after us, anyway."

Diawn stared down Triel. "We shouldn't get too comfortable."

"Right, yeah, yeah. Di, go check on Billy and make sure he's not picking up any Alliance signals."

Diawn said nothing, but she made a point of locking eyes with Triel once more before she left.

"She hates me," Triel said.

"Nah," Reht muttered, running a hand through his hair and avoiding her eyes.

"Don't lie to a Prodgy, Reht Jagger. She's hated me since I first came on board. She's a starky."

"A what?" Bacthar laughed, scratching his head with his left wing.

"Starky. It's an animal on the planet Marsubeoux known for its strange mating patterns. One female will dominate an entire tribe of males, and any female that enters her territory is killed. I invaded her territory when you took me aboard years ago. She feels threatened."

Bacthar grinned. "What kind of books did you have down there?"

"Odds and ends that Guli didn't use to roll into smokes, but there were two volumes of an encyclopedia that I liked to read before I ran out of...um, bathroom supplies."

"It's good to have you back," Reht said, trying to avoid a fight. "There are a lot of things I need to get you up to date on."

Since he made no attempts to negotiate peace, Triel sighed. With one slender finger she traced the familiar scar running down his left cheek.

"All this time you didn't forget about me," she whispered.

He bent over and kissed her—softly at first, then more vigorously when she pressed back. The rest of the world forgotten, Reht took the Prodgy Healer in his arms, and fell into her touch.

***

"Are you okay?" Jaeia asked, touching the Oblin's sleeve.

The old man massaged his chest where Jetta had struck him but managed to come up with a smile. "Child, I may look old, but I'm as spry as the next fellow."

Jaeia tried to apologize, but the Oblin interrupted her.

"Don't," the Grand Oblin whispered, resting a hand on her shoulder.

Wiping her eyes, Jaeia breathed a sigh of relief that it was just her and the priest in the cavern. After sensing the impressions of the other Exiles' thoughts, she couldn't bear to face them.

"Here," the Grand Oblin whispered, plucking a faded square of cloth from the folds of his robes. "This handkerchief is the finest Sali silk, a gift from someone very special to me. The humidity in this place hasn't been very kind to the material."

Jaeia indicated her thanks but did not use it to wipe her face; she didn't feel like she should.

"My sister wasn't always like this," she said. "Well, not this bad. But then, Jahx was always there to help me."

Tears came steadily now, as did all the feelings she had assiduously kept to herself. Losing their parents, then Jahx, and now her sister's increasingly volatile behavior—

The Grand Oblin leaned heavily on his walking stick. "You don't think it's your fault, do you?"

Jaeia shivered, though she didn't feel cold, and wrapped her jacket more tightly around her body. "I didn't do what I was supposed to."

"And what was that?"

Jaeia chewed on her lip. *Another secret I'm not supposed to share.*

"You don't have to tell me if you don't want to," the Grand Oblin said, standing back a little.

With a sigh, Jaeia brought her knees up to her chest. "You already know so much about us."

"On the contrary," the Grand Oblin said, pointing his stick at her. "I know the things you've seen, but that doesn't tell me much about you. We are how we interpret the world around us, and how we choose to act on those interpretations."

Jaeia rested her head on her knees. "I don't know why I want to tell you. Maybe Jetta is right about me."

The Grand Oblin smiled. "I think Jetta does not choose to see the same potential you do, Jaeia."

"But what if I'm wrong?"

"What if you're right?"

Jaeia regarded him solemnly. "I made a promise to my brother a long time ago, before things got really messed up. I promised him I would always look after Jetta, but I didn't. Now I don't know where she is, what she's feeling—and I can't stop her if she decides to..."

Wait—what am I doing? This was their biggest secret, the one that even Jahx feared would bring them harm if it ever got out.

"Go on," the Oblin whispered, his eyes growing wide as his body expanded, retracted, and then swelled again.

"W—what's wrong?" Jaeia asked.

Pressing his fingers into his sternum, the Grand Oblin muttered a few words under his breath. His form stabilized, and he exhaled a long, slow breath. "It is one of the disadvantages of my age, child. My shape betrays me. Please, continue."

Jaeia heard past his words. "You're afraid of me, too."

As the Grand Oblin melted into the form of the middle-aged woman, his beard reabsorbed into his face and the silver hair on top of his head receded, replaced by kinky brown strands sprouting from the same roots. Wrinkles filled out until they were merely the creases of middle age, and his frame, once thin and frail, blew out like a balloon as he shrank in height.

"Well, you know I'm incapable of lying to you," she chuckled, voice losing its raspy baritone.

Breast flopping back and forth as she readjusted her robes, the Oblin sighed. "I am not afraid of you, child, but I am afraid for you. It is not safe for a telepath to grow up without guidance, discipline— and it sounds like you and your sister had none. I can't imagine what it was like to grow up hearing the voices, desires, and thoughts of others and not knowing how to handle them."

"Especially on Fiorah," Jaeia said.

"Gods!" the Oblin exclaimed. "That world is a telepathic nightmare, especially for a child."

Jaeia shrugged. "We did okay. We helped each other."

"So that's how you survived. You have a special connection with each other?"

"Yes," Jaeia said. "We watched out for each other. But now that Jahx is gone, it's harder. It's just Jetta and me."

"And what is this thing in Jetta you fear so much?" the Oblin asked.

Shrinking away from him, Jaeia squeezed her eyes shut. *Maybe I can just disappear.*

"Jaeia, if you tell me, I can help you. Then we can bring Jetta back."

When Jaeia opened her eyes she realized she was crying again. "You know what I am—and you want to help me?"

The Grand Oblin nodded.

"I was... I *am* the Slaythe. I am General Volkor. I am a killer."

"I know what happened, Jaeia. I saw all of it."

"Then why do you want to help me?" she asked. Trembling all over, she backed against the rock as far as she could.

The Grand Oblin smiled. "Because of who you are, Jaeia, not what you have done."

"What do you see in me?" Jaeia whispered.

"I see opportunity drawn from misfortune. I see hope," the Grand Oblin whispered back. "Now, tell me. What is this thing you fear?"

Jaeia saw sincerity in her amethyst eyes. For a brief moment she saw her uncle too, as he was in her earliest memories.

"Before I tell you anything more, I want you to understand how much I love my sister."

"Of course," the Grand Oblin said.

"She has always wanted what was best for my brother and me, and I know she would lay down her life for us," Jaeia said, rubbing her knuckles against the rock wall, trying to keep her words from sounding so defensive.

Although there was no urgency in the Oblin's voice, she held her breath, clutching her walking stick to her chest as she waited for Jaeia to continue. "Go on."

"I know my sister would never hurt another Sentient without reason, but this love she has for us—because of it, it's a constant battle to prevent her from harming others. She thinks that's the only way to protect us."

"How would she harm them?" the Oblin asked.

This is it; our secret. Jaeia opened her eyes and looked at her squarely.

"I don't know what it is. I've never heard of any Sentient with powers like this except a—a Dissembler."

Deep lines of concern etched into the Oblin's face. "No, I don't believe it. You are not Dissemblers."

Jaeia shook her head. "No, I know that. I don't think that this ability necessarily has to harm someone. It's just the way Jetta uses it."

"Tell me more," the Oblin said, taking her hands. "Please."

Warm, wrinkled hands made her relax, if only for a second. "Jetta told you that she has a way of finding out your worst fears," Jaeia said, "but it's more than that. Even if it's just a seed of a bad feeling or something that you had forgotten a long time ago, she'll find it—and make it grow. You become conflicted, confused—or worse. She makes your nightmares real."

"So she's used this power before?"

Jaeia nodded grimly. "Jetta was the first to discover the full extent of her talent. We were fighting for the Endgame championship in the Dominion Core Academy against a former student with an undefeated record. Jahx was losing, and Rogman had already threatened to send us back to Fiorah, so Jetta got in this kid's head and... made him hallucinate his dead brother. She broke him." She winced, knowing how that sounded.

246

"It sounds like she used it as a last resort."

"I guess. But Jahx didn't like it, and I agreed with him. Whatever is inside us—it's too powerful. Things always turns out badly."

"There's more, isn't there?" the Oblin said.

Jaeia froze, voice locked in her throat. *Why am I so scared?*

Maybe she didn't want the Oblin to know just how terrible things had been—and how much worse they could get. Or perhaps she didn't want the priest to see her weakness, her inability to control her sister—or herself. All of her pride, her purpose in life revolved around maintaining the balance, but her shortcomings had resulted in disaster for their family.

And then the words came in a sudden rush, her voice catapulted from the deeps of her. "When Jetta uses that talent that way, it pulls her away from me, makes her change. I don't know how else to explain it. That's why I don't like it, and that's why Jahx didn't like it either."

"But you said it could be used for good, Jaeia."

"I don't know. Maybe if she had more control. Maybe if she didn't use it against people. Maybe if she found a way to help them instead."

"Well, what about you?"

All the air disappeared from the room. Jaeia's mouth opened, but no sound or breath could escape. She saw the dead eyes of the boy in the coolant room accusing her, his lips, slightly parted, whispering her name.

"My talent?" Jaeia laughed nervously. She remembered the boy's face, the way his pink cheeks had turned a stone-cold blue, the way his eyes had dilated and fixed on something she couldn't see—

It was just an accident.

"My talent doesn't work on everybody, at least it didn't when I was younger and needed it the most," she said, thinking of Yahmen and all the times she tried to use it on him. "But I have this thing..."

It was just an accident!

Jaeia gulped for air as her breath hitched in her chest. No, she couldn't feel guilty about that now. It was an accident—a horrible accident—she hadn't meant for him to die. "I-I call it a second voice. People have to listen to it."

"What do you mean?"

She had just been so tired, so hungry. She'd had to make him do it—

Jaeia squeezed her eyes shut, trying to make the memory go away. "I can control somebody's behaviors by speaking to them a certain way. But it's always backfired..."

Dead—he's dead—I killed him—

"...so I use just a little of it, sometimes to help Jetta calm down or before she starts a fight."

"The Moro do something similar," the Oblin said. "Maybe you are a mixture of Moro and something else, yes?"

"Maybe," Jaeia shrugged, looking down at her feet.

"It's remarkable, Jaeia, it truly is. For you to discover your talents on your own and learn how to use them—that is truly exceptional. But I would like to be able to help you further, and maybe the two of us can get a handle on how to use this greater talent you speak of for something good."

"I would like that," Jaeia said. She pressed her thumbs into her eyes, forcing away the images of the dead boy.

But nothing will ever bring him back—

She cleared her throat, redirecting her thoughts to her sister, away from her guilt. "So you can understand what's going on with Jetta?"

"I do," the Oblin said. "She is a very spirited individual. I don't think mere reasoning will do for her. I think she is one that will have to discover the truth on her own."

"But I can't just let her do what she wants."

"I'm not saying to abandon her. I'm advising you to let her see what she needs to see, feel what she needs to feel, but be a helping hand when she needs it."

Jaeia looked doubtfully at her hands. If only the Oblin knew.

"Do you think she's dangerous?" she whispered.

The Grand Oblin didn't respond immediately. "I think she carries with her things that are very dangerous. Fear and guilt for starters. That will lead a person down a dangerous path. But you can influence her, and help her. Just as she will help you."

"I've heard something like that before," Jaeia whispered.

The Grand Oblin knelt down in front of her. "What about you, Jaeia? How do you feel about your brother—about all of this?"

248

Jaeia drew in a long breath and slowly let it go, trying to keep herself from crying again. In the past she avoided dealing with her own emotions by attempting to control her sister's, but without Jetta, Jaeia faced the truth alone.

"I understand what my sister wants to do. And truthfully, part of me wants to do exactly what she's doing now—running, trying to find him. But I know—*I know*—that's not what we need to do. Jahx just isn't..."

She couldn't say it. From what little she remembered, her brother had been killed. Still, Jetta's adamancy about her dreams burdened her with doubt. But if any part of her even considered her sister's argument, it would only feed Jetta's drive.

"How can I make all of this right?" she finally said, crying again. "How can I help Jetta when I can barely make sense of anything myself? I feel like a monster for the things I've done, and I'm worried with Jetta gone and alone and angry. I just don't know."

"Jaeia," the Grand Oblin said, changing shape again. His elderly male form returned, beard thickening, hair spinning silver, teeth disappearing. Even though the skin around his eyes sagged, the empathy remained. "What happened to you—what you did—was not your fault."

Jaeia exhaled a breath she hadn't realized she'd been harboring all this time and wiped her face with his handkerchief.

The Oblin rested a hand on her shoulder. "There are those who care about you deeply. Always remember their love, and listen carefully to the voice inside you. If you do this, then you will find the answers—and absolution—you seek."

Jaeia closed her eyes and listened.

***

Mantri Sebbs held his head in his hands as he banged his knees together, trying to keep himself from falling apart. The lack of stimulus—the low light, the gray walls, the absence of sound—drove him mad. And this was only his first hour in his new accommodations.

This is it. I've finally managed to piss it all away. I'm going to spend my last days rotting in an Alliance holding cell until the

Liikers come and turn me into another Deadwalker. And I can't even take one last chakking *hit before it all goes down.*

"I'm a *chakking* waste!" he screamed.

At first he thought the voices were in his head. After all, he hadn't given himself a boost since the Alliance confiscated his stash. He held his breath and concentrated on the sounds coming from just beyond the prison door. Seconds later the door slid smoothly away, and blinding light flooded the tiny cell. Two broad-shouldered figures entered, grabbed him by his armpits, and yanked him to his feet. Another man entered, slowly, and got very close to Sebbs. Though he couldn't make out the man's face in the intense light, the shape seemed oddly familiar.

A stinging slap bit his cheek, and a trickle of blood crept down Sebbs's chin. One of the guards wrenched him forward into a painfully awkward position.

"Leave him with me. Go!" the man shouted.

That voice—so familiar.

After the guards shut the cell door behind them, Mantri could finally see his assailant's face.

"Damon?" Sebbs exclaimed.

"The one and only."

The Alliance officer drew a smoke from the inside pocket of his uniform and, with one swift motion, lit it and took a long drag, sighing with relief as he blew a ring into the air vents. He caught Sebbs's eye with a conspiratorial grin before he pounded his fist against the wall and muffled a moan with his hands.

"You could at least try not to make me sound like such a woman," Sebbs said.

"We could make it more realistic if you want."

Sebbs huffed and crossed his arms. As relieved as he was to avoid being reduced to a sport for the Alliance guards, it stung to have to take charity from Damon Unipoesa, of all people.

"Mantri Sebbs, I warned you when you signed up for the Core."

"Damon Unipoesa, I thought we weren't friends anymore after I beat the crap out of you in grade school."

"Why do you think I hit you just now?"

"It's a little late to get even, don't you think?" Sebbs snatched the smoke from the officer's hand. Unipoesa struck the wall again and yelled into his forearm.

"Look, I don't have much time. I told the council members that I would interrogate you personally since I hate Dominion rubbish. There are rumors that you're crazy, and I can substantiate that, but I don't think you're *that* crazy. So, before they ship you off to a nuthouse, tell me something that makes it worth saving your worthless hide."

Sebbs puffed out a cloud of smoke, coughed raggedly, and wiped his tired eyes. Unipoesa took the smoke back before he could take another drag.

"You were lucky, Damon, catching that Diapherenza flu. Getting rejected by the Core was the best thing that ever happened to you. Can't believe your sorry *assino* ended up the big hero of the Starways."

"Still playing the victim, huh, Sebbs? You should have gotten out the second the Sovereign took over the military. Was it really worth it to sell information to dog-soldiers?"

"It paid the bills," Sebbs muttered, stealing back the smoke from Unipoesa's hand.

"You mean for your little chemical romances, right? Ah, Mantri. Everyone had such high hopes for you."

"It's been lovely talking to you, Damon, really. Just like old times. Reminds me of why we weren't friends anymore. Maybe you should come back tomorrow and we can rehash some of your past *indiscretions*, unveil some of those skeletons in *your* closet."

Sebbs turned away and slumped against the wall. He wanted to make it all go away, but Damon, twice his size and stature, wouldn't hesitate to send him to the Labor Locks if he did anything stupid. *What I wouldn't give for a real smoke, or a boost.*

His hands started to shake. Soon he'd be withdrawing hard, puking and pissing himself like a launnie. Stuffing his hands under his armpits, Sebbs banged his head against the wall.

"I'm sorry, Mantri. I'm sorry I wasn't a better friend. I should have tried harder to get you out."

Sebbs turned and looked at the Alliance officer more carefully. Time did not treat Damon well. Deep wrinkles furrowed his forehead and his hair had prematurely grayed. *Something happened to him.*

"I may be a bit strung out, but I swear you just apologized to me. What the hell? Did I warp into an alternate universe or what?"

251

Damon forced a smile. "Things are different now, to put it mildly."

"What do you mean?"

Unipoesa mashed the end of the smoke on his boot. "Let's just say that I'm one of a handful of Alliance officers that sees straight through all this political *gorsh-shit*. I read your files, and I know what you said to the Minister."

"How'd you get your hands on that?"

"I'm the admiral who won the Raging Front," Unipoesa said quietly. "I'm privy to most everything an 'advisory' battle commander can get their hands on."

"You know about the Deadwalkers—and the leeches—and those launnies?"

"I know that I wasn't responsible for the win at the Raging Front. The Core ships—they just froze up, lost their coordinated attacks. Their communication network must have been down, or something happened internally. It was like shooting fish in a barrel. And I got the credit for it."

"And when you mounted the final attack at their base—?"

The admiral's eyes fell hard on him. "There weren't any battleships defending their base. All their starposts and command centers were abandoned. We thought it was a trap at first, but six months later and no contact, the reports were changed to read that they had fled in defeat."

"Didn't you say something when this happened?"

"I didn't want to rest on my laurels. Neither did some of the other commanders," Unipoesa said. "But the politicians—the public—they didn't want to hear that. We won; we had defeated Volkor the Slaythe. There were deals, allegiances—lots of funding. So it doesn't matter what I believe now, does it? They'll just say I've got war stress."

"Well, what about those launnies? And the other telepaths? Project ICE?" Sebbs asked. Unipoesa pounded his fist against the wall again, making the Joliak jump back.

"It would certainly explain why the Core created the Dissembler Scare, why they had a sudden rise in military power. And if what you say is true about the Motti, and Jahx—then yes, it fits with my story."

"I'm not crazy, Damon, you know that. I'm done a lot of methoc and Yarrni smokes in my day, but I could never up make something up that wild."

"Yes, I know."

Unipoesa leaned back against the prison wall. He smoothed his hair back over his bald spot. "The trouble with your story, Mantri, is that we've captured several officers, and even with advanced interrogation techniques we never pulled anything out of them like this," the admiral said, pounding his feet against the floor.

"Only a select few officers in special military ops knew about their dealings with the Motti and ICE," Sebbs said, nervously pulling at the hair on his head. "Don't you think the Motti would take them first?"

Unipoesa looked pensively at Sebbs. "Let's say I believe you. What about the two girls? Where are they and why did you think they're the only chance for the Alliance—or rather, for charted space?"

"Look at the records. Jahx has never been defeated in battle. You're going to need someone close to him to take him down. You need his sisters."

A shadow fell over his friend's face. Admiral Damon Unipoesa stepped back from him and forced a laugh. "Maybe you're crazier than I thought, Sebbs."

Mantri shook his head. *Am I going toxic from withdrawal? Why is Damon turning on me?*

"Damon, wait—" Sebbs grabbed his arm. The admiral shoved him back and pinned him against the wall by his neck.

"Find them," Sebbs pleaded, hands shaking violently as he tried to pry the admiral's fingers off his throat. "Use the codes I gave to the Minister—find the missing pieces. I don't want to be a Deadwalker."

Unipoesa slapped him hard again across the jaw. He leaned forward, his lips next to his left ear, and whispered: "I'm sorry, Mantri, about everything. Please forgive me."

The admiral pressed a vial into his hand and turned to leave. As the prison door shut with a loud clank, Sebbs looked at what the admiral had given him.

"*Gorsh-shit* eating..."

Unipoesa had left him with a dose of the Prude Lady, a painful but fast-acting detox booster. He hated Damon for his pity.

Sebbs crammed himself into the corner and cradled his head in his arms. For a moment he wished he had never taken action. At least then he would still be on the spice ships, sucking down Beurethal ale and forgetting about the world around him. It would have been easier.

Then he remembered what the Moro priest had told him, and he closed his eyes and injected the booster.

***

Jaeia huddled miserably under her blanket, wracked by shivers. Tracing the swelling flesh that ran from beneath her jaw all the way to her collarbone with her fingers, she realized the terrible truth. *The sickness is getting worse.*

After their dreadful discovery the day before, she hadn't been able to bring herself to eat any more Macca. The thought of eating something that came from that eyeless, soulless *thing* had repulsed her beyond her ability to comprehend.

(I was almost one of them.)

But soon, nothing could reverse the infection spreading through her body.

Come back, Jetta, Jaeia projected across their bond, *I know you're sick too—you can't be out there—you can't leave me here—*

Jaeia's words bounced back, echoing off the brick wall Jetta erected between their minds.

Jetta's not going to come back, she thought, tugging fretfully at her jacket sleeves. *It's up to me to get us out of this.*

(It's always up to me.)

Wiping the fever sweat from her forehead, Jaeia thought through her only option. The anger and fear swirling in the Exiles' thoughts scared her, but it was time to emerge from her cavern. No matter how much the Grand Oblin tried to assuage their concerns, it wouldn't be enough. They all knew who General Volkor was.

The Exiles still need me for something, Jaeia thought, *and I'm going to need them to find Jetta.*

Taking a deep breath, Jaeia stepped out into the low light of the tunnel that led to the meeting area.

What if they don't listen? Jaeia thought. The temptation to use her talent rose up in animal hunger pains, but fear knotted down her stomach.

(I am no better than Jetta,) whispered a dark voice from within. *(What if I kill someone else?)*

Jaeia stopped in her tracks, unexpectedly faced with her darkest secret.

(Gods, Verk, I am so, so sorry—)

Guilt thrust her back to the scene of the crime. Jaeia was four again, skeletal and starving, trying to decompress a coolant reactor on the target mining ship while Jetta, Jahx and Galm fixed another massive leakage in the engine core. Verk, a twelve-year-old Cerran-humanoid, crouched over his meal of bakken in the adjacent storage closet, confident that Jaeia would not try him for his prize. After beating out all the other kids that day in the food scramble, his prize amounted to more than she had seen in days.

(So hungry.)

Survival instincts outmatched any rational thought. I just need a moment's rest—the remainder of his bakken, *she thought to herself, licking her lips.* What is one meal and an hour's work? Then I can rejoin my family.

"Give me your bakken," Jaeia whispered, second voice pulling apart the seams of the boy's mind. "Watch the reactor for any pressure changes."

Wide-eyed, Verk scooted away from his meal, leaving her a half-eaten loaf she devoured in seconds.

It was easy to forget that Verk had never been around a coolant reactor, or that monitoring the reactor for pressure changes was too much to ask of any child laborer. A full belly, a chance to rest, made for heavy eyelids, even crammed in the storage closest. (I just want to sleep.)

Noxious smells of sublexane woke her from her slumber. Jaeia bolted to the coolant reactor, but it was too late. Verk, cold and lifeless, with his eyes fixed open, slumped against the monitors.

He didn't release the pressure in the main chamber, *Jaeia thought, pulling the manual override levers to pump out the deadly gas from the room. (I killed him!)*

255

The laborminders didn't pay it a second thought as they tossed Verk's body in one of the carts routed to the furnace, but she couldn't get the look in his eyes out of her head or forget the way his brother wailed upon hearing of his death.

Jaeia leaned against the tunnel wall, breathing hard. "Oh Jahx... I wish you were here," she whispered, wiping her eyes. "You'd understand; you'd keep us together."

Keeping her brother's strength in mind, Jaeia resumed her course to the meeting area, letting her fingers brush along the rocky wall. The textures on her fingertips soothed her anxieties, keeping her locked in the present. It was an old trick, one that she picked up on Fiorah. Sliding her fingers over the tiny holes and bubbles in the warm cement walls of their apartment lent a strange calm as Jetta raged and stormed and threw things around, or when Galm sat catatonic in front of the television and refused to talk—and especially on the terrible day when Yahmen forcibly removed Aunt Lohien from their home.

Voices grew louder as she approached the meeting area. Stray words caught her ear, and the intensity of Exiles' emotions beset her heart.

Liikers. Telepaths. Volkor.

Jaeia leaned back on her heels, ready to turn around, when Senka's voice rose above all the others. "Then why didn't you let me die? If you really believe they're not to be trusted, then my life isn't worth it, is it? Be realistic—they are the only chance we have. If you don't believe they're good kids, then *let me die.*"

Senka's words made her cringe, but thinking of her sister, Jaeia willed herself to step into the cavern. The rest of the group turned and looked at her. Rawyll, in the midst of cleaning one of his blades, stood up, his thoughts almost as menacing as his glare. Jaeia tried not to let her fear register as she approached them.

"I know there are things that you want to ask me. The Grand Oblin has tried to guard us from our memories, and from your fears, but it's not..." Jaeia glanced over to see which form the Grand Oblin had taken. "...*his* responsibility to look after my sister and me, and, I know you need to protect yourselves, too. So... I'm here. I'll tell you what you want to know."

"What are you?" Rawyll's eyes refined into slits as he firmed up his grip on his weapon.

256

Jaeia stood her ground. "I am Jaeia Drachsi of Fiorah. I am one of three triplets, and Jetta is my identical twin. My mother was a streetwalker, and we were adopted by Galm Drachsi and his wife, Lohien Chen, seven years ago."

There were low murmurs and doubtful thoughts.

Rawyll shook his head. "But what the hell are you? You look human, but it's not possible that you are. You're telepathic, but you're not like any other leech. You claim to be seven years old, but you haven't the body or a brain that matches."

Jaeia shrugged her shoulders and looked nervously to the Oblin. "I can't answer those questions. This is the way I've always been."

"Have you always used your talents?" Dinjin asked.

Jaeia hesitated. "It's helped us survive."

"How?" Rawyll demanded.

Jaeia saw that Senka's eyes were downcast, and her feelings were a guarded mixture of empathy and trepidation. For some reason this made Jaeia more nervous, but she knew she had to keep going.

Dragging her fingertips along the studded top of a stalagmite, she spoke as calmly as she could. "We have a weird way of learning; we imprint what we need off of an open mind. It takes us seconds to understand a lifetime of knowledge."

She shifted her weight from foot to foot as they talked heatedly amongst each other.

"What kind of telepath is that?" Dinjin asked.

"Gods, jeez," Crissn mumbled. "Don't want someone knowing my business. That's violating!"

"It's a dangerous power—" Rawyll said, pointing his knife at Jaeia. "Can't be trusted with a kid."

"Just calm down," Senka tried, stepping in between Rawyll and Jaeia.

"They're not like other kids, Rawyll," the Oblin said, raising his hands.

Jaeia closed her eyes and cleared her throat. "Look—this is about General Volkor, isn't it?"

The adults fell silent and turned all of their attention to her.

"We never wanted to kill anybody," Jaeia said, fumbling with her shirtsleeves. "Somehow the Core found out about our ability to learn, and we were exposed to hundreds of battle commanders and military specialists and forced to play them in simulations. If we

257

didn't, we were punished, and because of the drugs, we weren't even aware of the real consequences of participating. If I had known I was being molded into—into—"

That's when she stopped. She didn't think she needed to go on anyway. If any of them were at all perceptive, they would see just how deep her wounds went.

"They made you into the Slaythe, and they drugged you so that you didn't even know what you were doing," Dinjin said. "that's brilliant."

"Dinjin!" Senka snapped.

"No, no—it's perfect, is all I'm saying. Those kids were the amalgamation of the entire Dominion Core military."

"It's *gorsh-shit*," Rawyll said, pointing a finger at her. "You said you can copy people's minds? Then why the hell didn't you figure out what was going to happen to you? Didn't you see it coming?"

"We can't glean from an unwilling mind—" Jaeia tried, but gave up when Rawyll began cursing.

Crissn fiddled with his spectacles and whispered to the Oblin. "C-could the Core have used Rai Shar too?"

Jaeia overheard the nervous Oriyan. "What is Rai Shar? I've heard it mentioned before."

Nobody wanted to answer her question, and Jaeia drew the obvious conclusion: They had used it to protect themselves against her and Jetta.

"Mental conditioning. The Dominion Core and the USC put their top officers through the training to protect their secrets from interrogation techniques and telepaths. Highly effective," Dinjin finally answered.

The Oblin cleared his throat and relented. "It is part of the ancient psionic traditions of the Taurian priests of my Order. We used it during meditations and to prepare those coming of age for the dangers of telepathy. I studied it extensively and taught many students."

"Rai Shar came from telepaths?" Jaeia exclaimed.

"Who better to develop the technique than those who possess the power?"

"I'm sorry to interrupt, but I have a very important question," Senka said, walking toward her. "Jaeia—what happened to the other telepaths?"

Jaeia sucked in her lower lip. "I-I don't know. I just remember... they were like my voices. No, that's not right—they were my intuition. I can't say concretely that I know they were there, but one day I became aware of them. I believe they were in the battles with us, but we never actually talked to them. I don't know what happened to them."

"Kind of like your brother, right? You don't know what happened to him?" Rawyll said. "Sounds suspicious to me. Those Dominion bastards are probably still using her brother in battle. I'll bet they sent her and her sister down here as bait for us so they can get the final piece of their puzzle. They're probably thinking exactly what we're thinking!"

"Wait—what?" Jaeia said.

"No, I don't think that's how it is," the Grand Oblin replied calmly.

"But the device—" Crissn interjected. "I see where Rawyll is going with this—I do. We're fools to think they were sent here by 'accident.'"

"But that's just it," the Grand Oblin said, laying his palm on Crissn's heaving chest. "Tell them, Jaeia."

"The Motti—the Deadwalkers, as you all call them. They're in my memories, too," Jaeia said. "I know they were behind the Core drug development, and possibly more. One day everything became so clear—the day we resisted. It can't be coincidence. I honestly don't know anything else. All I know is that my brother saved us by sending us here. We were supposed to be executed."

"I don't believe it. It's just a clever means of getting the device," Rawyll said, throwing down a cleaning rag and pointing his finger at the Oblin. "You honestly think that this is plausible?"

"What is this device you're talking about?" Jaeia asked. All of them looked at her out of the corners of their eyes, but none answered her question.

"Rawyll, look at that child and tell me that you do not believe her," the Oblin said.

The Oriyan weaponsmaster slung his weapon, approached her and placed two fingers underneath her chin, tilting her head upwards.

His eyes narrowed and his lips curled. Jaeia could feel the strain in the back of his mind as he searched for something.

"This one is not lying," he concluded. "But that doesn't mean it's the truth."

"I agree," Dinjin said. "No offense to you, Jaeia."

Jaeia listened to their thoughts, all of them lingering on the importance of "the device."

"Is this device what you wanted me for?"

Still, nobody answered her. The tension of the group felt like a lump of hot iron in her belly as she silently watched Rawyll and Dinjin grab supplies and weapons.

"Where are you going?" Senka asked, stepping in front of the exit to block Rawyll and Dinjin as they strapped the weapons to their hips and gear to their backs.

"To fetch that pest of a launnie before she gets herself killed. You get to babysit that one. Make sure she eats some Macca or I'm force-feeding her when I return."

"It's no use," Jaeia said quietly, stopping them in their tracks. Dark memories of the past formed her words. "She won't come back until she's ready. This isn't the first time she's done something like this."

Rawyll buckled a hunting knife to his thigh and continued preparing for their departure.

"Please don't go. Not like that, at least," Jaeia said. "Jetta doesn't exactly respond well to aggression."

"Don't worry, that's why I'm going along," Dinjin said, smiling and readjusting the straps on his pack.

Jaeia's heart sank. "Please, don't do this. She's not thinking straight. I don't know what she might do."

"It's all right, Jaeia," the Grand Oblin said, touching her shoulder. "They can manage themselves."

Jaeia didn't bother to disagree with him, knowing that he wouldn't have minded her arguments anyway. *He's a different kind of telepath; maybe he knows something I don't,* she thought, sensing the Oblin filled with a strange levity. Still, she was afraid—for Dinjin and Rawyll as well as for her sister.

Both Senka and the Grand Oblin stood behind her as they watched Rawyll and Dinjin make their way toward the waxen glow of moonlight that marked the tunnel's exit. Crissn paced back and forth as their footsteps faded, talking to himself.

"Well," Crissn said, "I guess I'd better go check on our harvest." He glanced at Jaeia, his face blotching red. "Not that you couldn't figure out what that meant, but that's the term we use for when we milk the Liiker blood and infuse it into the fruit for—"

"Thank you, Crissn," the Grand Oblin said, waving him away. "I'll join you shortly, all right?"

Resuming his conversation with himself, the Oriyan scurried down the tunnel toward the lab.

Jaeia sat down on a nearby rock and faced her remaining audience. "I've been honest with you. I'd appreciate if you'd level with me."

"You have to understand, Jaeia," the Grand Oblin said gently. "You were unknown to us, and from what I could discern, it wouldn't have been safe to immediately expose you to our problems with the device, the Northies and the Prigs, the suppressant we use... For that, I apologize."

"Is that why you taught the Exiles Rai Shar? Are you blocking their thoughts from us?"

The Oblin dabbed his watery eyes with the sleeve of his robe. "I've helped them control their thoughts just as I helped you."

Jaeia closed her eyes. "I guess I can understand why you did those things. But please, can you tell me about this device you keep talking about? And Senka—why do you want to die so badly?"

Senka brushed the hair from her face, her eyes distant and unreadable. "The device is actually the flash transport system the Narki invented. It wasn't a rumor. The Prigs and the Northies know we stole some highly classified technology from the labs when we were getting some equipment for Crissn, but they don't know what exactly it is. If they did, they would gang up on us in a heartbeat."

"It's worth a fortune, isn't it?"

"Yes, it is."

"Then why are you still here?" Jaeia asked. "I'm sure it's worth your freedom."

"It is, but we'd have to alert the right people, and that's not possible with the Warden monitoring and filtering all incoming and outgoing com traffic. We'd be limited to an old broadcast signal that could take months or even years to reach anyone—assuming, of course, that the Warden let it out. That or we'd be limited to a single datastream into the wave network."

"What's the closest planet?" Jaeia asked.

"Plaly IV," Senka sighed.

"The Labor Locks," Jaeia said. She had heard people speak of them, back in the mines. It was the only place she'd ever heard of that sounded worse than Fiorah.

"So you see our predicament. We have something valuable enough to turn the tide of the war for the USC, but we have no means of alerting them."

"But how do you know it even works?"

Senka hung her head. "That's why they've kept me alive. I'm a quantum engineering specialist, so I'm the only one who understands how to use it. I spent months deciphering Narki technical code to properly assemble and use the *dich* thing. I know how to dematerialize objects, but bringing them back—well, that's something I have a theory about, but I don't have the necessary equipment."

"So why do you want to die so badly?" Jaeia asked.

Senka laughed mirthlessly. "You spend enough time on this planet, you watch enough of your friends die—it wears on you. I had always held out hope that my husband and children survived the Scare. But when you said those things about the other telepaths..." Senka hid her face in her hands. "I know they're gone."

Jaeia wrung her hands, wishing she could help. Extending herself into Senka's mind, Jaeia sifted through to the woman's last memories of her family—the frantic phone call from her husband as a Dominion tracer squad beat down his office door, her children's cries as black-masked soldiers carried them away in the middle of the night.

"There is always something to hope for," Jaeia said as she pulled away from Senka's consciousness. "I will help you escape Tralora however I can. Then we can all find new beginnings."

The Grand Oblin smiled, and for a brief moment, his body contracted—not into the short roundness of his female form, but something much smaller. Form rebounding, he pulled out his pipe. "Why don't you tell her what our plans are, Senka?"

Senka nodded. "You and your sister are special, which makes you valuable. If it's true that you were covertly sent here, then we can contact the Warden. With all your military knowledge about the Dominion, he'll see a price tag on your head so high that he'll be blinded to the fact you're telepaths and infected, and he'll seek out a paying party."

Jaeia's brow furrowed. "That doesn't make much sense. What about you? What about who we'd be sold to? What about the infection?"

"You'll use the flash transport device and take us with you so we can get past the Warden. That's the easy part. Everything else is going to be tricky."

After a pause, Jaeia finally asked the question she had been holding back for days. "Why hasn't the USC come for you? Has any government tried to cure this?"

Senka shook her head. "Tralora is a death sentence, remember? Besides, with everything going on up there, who has time to worry about curing a few POWs? Still, if we can convince the Warden to send our message, and the USC realizes it's from the Commander or myself, then they'll risk traversing in Dominion territory and the disease to get here. That device—and you—could mean the end to the war. Hopefully, in the process, the rest of us could be saved, too."

"The fact that Crissn has helped us survive this long means there's a chance, Jaeia," the Oblin said. "I'm sure with others pursuing his avenue of research, we could find a cure."

"You mean using that—that—" Jaeia's voice faltered. She collected herself and tried again. "You mean by using the Liiker."

Senka and the Grand Oblin nodded.

"I don't know. You're betting that we can get the Warden to sell the idea of us to the USC and hopefully not to someone else, like his Dominion employer. Then you're chancing that the USC can cross enemy lines to get here and somehow figure out a way to get us off this planet. *Then*, somehow, someway, they'll be able to further Crissn's work with the Liiker to find a cure. And finally, the USC will have to decode the work you've done with the flash transport to retrieve you from the wave network. Right?"

Senka and the Grand Oblin exchanged glances before nodding again.

Jaeia laughed, but suspended her doubt for a moment. "Okay, well, I guess I have some pretty good negotiation skills. Convincing the Warden would probably be the easiest part."

The Grand Oblin gave her a salute with his pipe.

Jaeia looked to Senka. "So then, what does the transport device look like?"

Senka reached into the front flap of her uniform and withdrew a shining silver wand and what looked like a golden key. The wand unfolded from its five-centimeter length to about a meter.

"I don't recognize all the components," Jaeia said, surprised at how light and cold the key felt in her hand, "but from what's exposed in that chamber there, this looks like a tracking device."

"That's what will draw back our signal. This antenna will transport our 'material' into the wave network, and then the key, which you are holding, will pick up our signal once you're ready to transport us out. All you'll have to do is relay my instructions to the USC development teams so that they can retrieve us intact. We don't want to come back missing any limbs!" Senka said, laughing uncomfortably. "The technology is pretty advanced, but I think I've done enough decoding that they'll know what to do."

If this works, it with change space travel, Jaeia thought. The modern method of transportation utilized energy-consuming jump drives, which enabled a ship to create a small wormhole and travel up to a hundred million light years at a time. However, only military grade vessels and expensive civilian ships could afford the fuel, maintenance and upkeep. Using the wave network linked the entire Starways by folding space-time to allow for live communications. If the Narki had invented a way to transport material into it and then retrieve it anywhere the wave network could reach, it would give the USC a considerable military advantage.

"A single scout ship could move an entire legion of warships. Talk about surprise attack," Jaeia said, handing the key back to her. "Please—show me how it works."

Senka pointed out the dial on the bottom of the antenna and showed her how to operate the switches controlling the power. "It doesn't have spare energy for more demonstrations, but I can tell you that when I press this button," she said, pointing to a black depression in the middle of the dial, "the transport field illuminates, and you can widen or decrease the field with this dial. You have to point and hold with this button to designate exactly what you're transporting into the wave network—otherwise you'd take the whole cave floor and rocks along with the people."

"Okay, got it," Jaeia said.

"I'll show you my research and instructions later, and we can go over what you'll need to know, all right?"

"No, really," Jaeia said, face flushing. "I mean I already got it all."

"What?" Senka exclaimed.

Jaeia averted her eyes and rubbed her hand across the top of a stalagmite.

"Oh. Well, I was thinking pretty openly on the matter. That saves a lot of time, huh?" Senka said, conjuring up an unsure half-smile. "I'm going to get some rest. Rawyll had us up all night arguing."

"Why is it that he's so afraid of us but still wants to help us?" Jaeia asked the Oblin as Senka ascended up the passage to her own cavern.

The Oblin filled his pipe again and relit the contents, in no particular hurry. After a few quick purple puffs he answered her question. "Rawyll is an Oriyan weaponsmaster. Even disgraced and barred from ever returning to his home, he still adheres to his former discipline. Therefore he will always help those in need, especially to better those he serves."

"You're implying he serves you," Jaeia said.

"Our group has survived much, child. There is quite the history here, but now is not the time."

His eyes glittered, an opaque sheen covering the irises.

"What is it?" Jaeia asked, feeling the circle of his thoughts throb and fall into disorder.

The Grand Oblin touched his forehead with shaky hands. "She's doing it again," he whispered, falling to his knees and dropping his pipe on the ground. Jaeia grabbed hold of him before he careened headfirst into a stalagmite. "Jetta's leaving this world. I can't stop her. Someone—something is taking her."

Jaeia immediately steeled herself against the vacuum of his psionic energy. "What's happening? Jetta cut me off a while ago; I don't know what's going on!" Jaeia shouted, holding him by the shoulders. The Oblin's eyes bulged, and his irises turned a ghostly white.

"What is this place?" he whispered as his eyes rolled to the back of his head. Jaeia called desperately for Senka as the Grand Oblin went limp in her arms.

Senka raced down the tunnel, catching herself on a rock.

"What's wrong with him?" she asked, feeling his neck for a pulse.

"I don't know! He just passed out. I think he was trying to keep track of my sister."

"Well, he's alive," Senka said, helping Jaeia lay him gently to the ground. "And we've got bigger problems."

Jaeia read her mind and looked toward the main tunnel. Gunfire and shouts reverberated off the rocky walls.

"We're under attack."

***

Number 00052983 supervised the raid just as it had countless others. This attack, however, held particular importance to the enclave. This would be the strike that would awaken the Starways.

After ordering all regional units to zero in on a lowly starpost on the border of regulated space, Number 00052983 deferred primary functional command to one of the subordinate hubs. Initial assessments from the sensor pods confirmed only a watchman and handful of scientists occupying the post; no threats detected. However, because of the greater importance of the mission, Number 00052983 kept the operation running in the foreground of its central processor.

Watching behind innumerable sets of monitors and organic eyes, Number 00052983 witnessed the clutch ships ramming into the post, driving their feeders into the hull and ripping through the superstructure. Flashtraps buzzed to life, jamming the distress signal sent out by the frightened watchman trying to make sense of the sudden attack.

Through the gaping holes made by the clutch ships dropped the soldier Liikers, pouring in and over each other like a swarm of insects. The stampede echoed throughout the entire Liiker network, overcharging the receptors with feedback and eliciting an organic

266

response. A wave of *something* flooded what was left of Number 00052983's neuroreceptors, but it identified as a residual emotion and deemed irrelevant.

Alphanumerics ran down the center screen of Number 0052983's stalk. The soldier Liikers required approval for the organic pod selection. Number 0052983 approved the watchman. The humanoid was in good physical shape to endure the transformation without proper biomechanical conversion.

One of the soldiers held down the shrieking watchman between two pincers. Number 00052983 didn't immediately recognize the language and accessed the shared database to translate his cries.

"Please, I'm not a threat! Don't kill me, please! I've never harmed a Deadwalker!"

Sensory equipment mounted on the soldiers' chest guided the placement of the bioclip. Olfactory input registered as an alphanumeric blip as the watchman's bowels unclenched. The bioclip bored into his skin and routed itself neatly into his neuroreceptors.

"You will speak," commanded the lead Liiker soldier.

The watchman's eyes swam in his sockets until two of the drones zapped him with resuscitation electrodes.

His jaw dropped open. "I am your voice."

Soldiers carried him away by his feet, allowing his head to smack against the corners of walls and bounce down the stairways. After all, his flesh was almost useless; they had elicited the functions they needed.

After securing an emergency shuttle, they tossed him in. A Breaker Liiker, designed to hack into computer programs, burrowed into the command panel and lay in the coordinates for the shuttle.

Trigos. The central Homeworld of the Alliance.

The ghostly thought linked with an undesired emotion that Number 00052983's safeguards filtered before it could reach the rest of the network. Number 00052983 logged the improper input, sending an alert to the higher commands that it might need a neural network cleanse. Even though the threat of bioelectric reintegration was nullified with Benign White, an organic emotion, especially an intense one, could attract other stray bioelectric activity to the network, potentially overloading the stalk domain safeguards.

A command flashed across Number 00052983's viewscreen—
shut down tertiary drive for full scan. The stalk released its tertiary
controls, allowing its superiors to deconstruct parts of its random
access memory.

As Number 00052983 waited for the signal to reassume total
control, it analyzed the risk of bioelectric interference from its
original host. It tried to run a comparative analysis to assess the
importance of its function relative to other stalks within the enclave,
but it encountered strict firewalls, just as it had before when it tried
to single itself out. However, after careful determination, Number
00052983 concluded that the possibility of strong bioelectric
interference was too remote a concern, and it shut down any further
queries into the matter.

CHAPTER V

After less than an hour of trekking through the dense underbrush of Tralora's forest, Jetta was spent. Scratches and abrasions crisscrossed her shins and forearms, and bits of leaves and sticks covered her clothing.

"*Gorsh-shit*," she muttered, pulling a twig out of her hair as she reached the clearing at the top of a hill.

Despite the aid of the moonlight and the break in the trees, she could no longer see the wall to the Narki city. Only a flickering firelight, far to the north where the trees thinned and remnants of old buildings cluttered the hillside, gave any sense of direction.

Another encampment, she thought. From what little knowledge she managed to glean off of Rawyll, she guessed it was likely the Prigs. Thinking of the sickness transferring Heli, she veered a little south on her western course.

Cold and exhausted, Jetta's focus faltered as she picked her way through the brush. Feelings and thoughts she didn't want crept into her conscious: *(I shouldn't have left Jaeia behind—)*

"No," she said, batting aside a tree branch. *I can't start second-guessing myself.*

Snagging her toe on a vine, she tripped and slammed into the soft ground, narrowly missing the stump of a fallen tree. Infuriated, Jetta grabbed a handful of grass and ripped it from the ground.

"*Skucheka!*" she swore in Fiorahian.

"Watch your step, little girl," someone snickered.

Jetta froze in place, sensing the multiple presences surrounding her. A peal of laughter echoed through the forest.

How could I be so blind? I ran right into them.

"Danni—where did this one come from? Is she a Prig or a Caver?"

"Musta be a stray 'therwise she'd not be out."

She caught a glimpse of one of them in the moonlight. He appeared to be human, but discolored patches dotted his pale skin. More alert now, she also detected the slight odor of perspiration and disease that carried in the breeze.

"Come on, we don't have time for this—the Prigs are going to beat us to it."

"Get off, Fender—that Oriyan will kill 'alf of 'em off before they gets to the entrance. But 'em Prigs 'll soften 'em up for us, yeah? Patience, yeah?"

Judging from the voices she heard, Jetta guessed that there were six of them, all male.

They're not going to just capture me, Jetta realized, sensing their intent. She brought her knees underneath her, keeping in a low crouch. *They want more.*

"See—see—this one's a lively one. Much better than the last pearly."

Jetta moved the hair from her eyes. "What the hell is a 'pearly'?"

Several of them laughed. A pair of eyes flashed in and out of the trees. "Pearly—pretty and white—like a brand new."

One of them came out from behind her, breathing heavily.

I can't take on this many, she thought, turning and facing him. Hungry eyes gazed longingly upon her flesh.

A million thoughts sluiced through her head at once, and she tipped forward, catching herself on her forearms.

"*Hei meitka,*" she muttered.

"What's wrong with that one? Is she turning?"

"Nahhh, she's good—no spots, no nothing. Pro'lly faking it."

The men stepped in closer, excitement and anticipation electrifying the air.

Why can't I run? Jetta thought, the hairs on the back of her neck and arms standing on end. She wanted to flee, but something kept her grounded.

"Oh my Gods..." Jetta looked up, seeing more than the starlit sky.

"Fire all weapons"

"Strip them down"

"They will starve"

"There is no place for mercy in battle"

Stolen memories from the Dominion officers, ones she thought she had buried deep, leaked into her consciousness.

This can't be happening right now. I don't need battlefield tactics, she thought, knuckling into her temples. *Get out of my head!*

As she tried to suppress the foreign memories, their emotion came through in a fiery concussion that washed away all other

271

thought. Jetta heaved for breath, stunned at first, then reanimated with savage needs.

The Core officers were never afraid, she realized. They were so sure of their superiority, hungry to exert their dominance. A venomous smile cut through her face.

Killing the Northies is too easy, she laughed to herself. *I will frighten these men. I will make them submit.*

Jetta stood up slowly, reveling in the power that charged through her body.

"You want to hurt me?" she said with such cold intensity that she didn't recognize her own voice.

Two of the men stopped in their tracks, while the other four took a defensive posture.

"What the hell is she spouting off? Fender—"

"Shut up. Wally, get the rope. We'll tie her down and come back for her once we finish business with the Cavers."

Yes, Jetta thought, *come at me. COME AT ME.*

"Already, little one, play nice," one from behind sniggered.

Jetta spun around on her heels. Moonlight revealed the skin peeling off the man's chin and forehead, and the deep ulcerations carving out his cheeks.

This man licked his lips and smiled at her like a feral animal readying to attack. For a moment she delighted in his wickedness.

"You're going to be the first one," she whispered.

"Oooohhh," the others guffawed, egging him on.

As the man closed the distance between them, Jetta absorbed his presence, wanting to sense his every emotion, every thought, as she took him down. *I want to feel your last breath as I bleed your heart dry.*

Sensing he would strike out with his right hand, Jetta side-stepped and parried the blow, rendering the attacker off balance. She threw herself at him, tackling him to the ground.

"Come on, Wally, stop messin' 'round."

In the darkness of their struggle, she found his face and pressed her thumbs into his soft eyes until she felt them pop, spraying warm goo on her fingers. He screamed, bucking wildly, breaking her hold.

"My *chakking* eyes—my eyes!"

Keeping her attackers in sight, Jetta rolled off the injured man and kept low, readying for the next assault.

"Now we ain't playin', kid. You're dead," one of them snarled as they continued to close in on her.

Adrenaline pumped through her veins, spreading liquid fire throughout her body. She wanted more than to physically harm the Northies—she wanted to use her forbidden power. And without Jaeia there to interfere, she knew she could take it farther than she had ever taken it before.

"This is your last chance," she said, though she wasn't trying to deter them.

They came at her from all sides. She didn't struggle; she let them grab hold of her limbs and allowed the fifth to place her in a chokehold.

"Pearly, you hurt Wally pretty fierce. I think the only things' fair would be for him to borrow 'em pretty eyes of yours."

"You want to borrow my eyes?" she squeaked out from her constricted airway. "Fine. I'll let you see."

Closing her eyes and submerging in the borrowed emotions of the Dominion, Jetta allowed her forbidden power to break from captivity and surface to the forefront of her mind.

(Finally,) a voice within her whispered. *(I am free.)*

All five of them let go of her, and she fell to the ground. Her perceptions changed; everything in the physical world seemed to come to a crawl, as if time itself had been affected.

In the low light Jetta watched their shadowed figures seizing on the ground, bending into impossible shapes. Guttural noises, like strangulated screams, sang from their lips.

Jetta picked herself up off the ground and stood over them, transfixed. As her talent burrowed into their minds, their pain leaked into her, bringing her visions of their terror. One of them feared fire after being burned as a child—

Skin charring black, body aflame, nothing to extinguish this pain—

(MY GODS, SAVE ME)

—Another feared dogs after being attacked in a junkyard.

Long, sharp teeth
Hot panting

Sinking into my throat, tearing away

So much blood dripping—

(DON'T HURT ME)

—One of them had been beaten by an angry mob—

Teeth splintering against the asphalt
Angry shouts deafening, ribs breaking
against steel-toed boots—
(PLEASE STOP, *OH PLEASE STOP!)*
She closed her eyes, stumbling backward, wrenching herself away from their nightmares. "Now you see..."

Something warm hit her cheek, and she dabbed it with the fingers of her right hand. The liquid felt slippery between her fingers, and stained her clothes. She traced the source to the split skull of one of the men still writhing on the ground. Captivated, Jetta leaned in, holding up her hands to shield her eyes from the hot spray.

Jetta—

The voice came from nowhere, bringing her to her knees.

"Jahx, I—I—" she stuttered.

Her hold on the men fractured, and the intensity of her emotion faded away. A tide of sickness washed over her as she looked over her work. *This isn't me—why would I do this?*

(I didn't defend myself—I used my powers to cause suffering.)

"W—who are you?" one of the men said as he clawed at his throat.

None of them will live, she realized. She felt the precursor of death, *the empty numbness* as she and Jaeia had named it back on Fiorah, eating its way through the core of their psyches.

Jetta knelt next to the closest one and bent down close enough to see his face in the moonlight. His eyes were open but unseeing, his body arched in pain. In his contorted face she saw her own reflection, and she knew what she had become.

A frothy mix of blood bubbled from his mouth as he drew his last breath. "I am General Volkor," she whispered into his ear.

Jetta sat back on her heels, gutted and alienated from her own conscience. In the back of her mind she imagined the icy, inhuman Motti Overlord standing next to her.

"You are a humanoid I do not despise. You are different from the others. You share my disgust for the infectious impurity of the Sentients."

At the time she didn't understand what he meant. Now she did. He saw the stubborn brutality of her inner animal and how it could not be tamed, how she could barely keep it at bay. With growing shame, she realized why her sister was afraid, and why Jahx had always kept a watchful eye on her.

I am no different than—

Slurping sounds and labored breathing. Unrecognizable thought patterns. Something else lurked in the forest shadows. She stood up, nearly tripping over one of the dead bodies as she backed away from the thing slinking out of the trees.

A tentacle curled and uncurled in the moonlight. Jetta heard a hissing sound, followed by the sound of snapping bones.

"No, please..."

Red feelers tapped the ground, and a hairy appendage stepped near one of the bodies of the Northies. She held her breath. A pink and purple tentacle wrapped around the neck of one of the men. Distant sensations of pain radiated from his being as the tentacle squeezed tight. *He's not dead—*

At first she thought to attack the infected creature feeding on the man she had hurt, but her survival instincts pulled her in the opposite direction. *Besides,* the little voice inside her said, *you wanted to kill him anyway.*

"No," Jetta whispered, "I'm not a monster..."

His head bobbled back and forth, and then his eyes shot open. He initially struggled against the squeeze of the tentacle, managing to choke out:

"Please... help..."

A cold sweat broke out across her forehead, and a painful lump lodged in her throat. With shaky hands she felt her way backward, not taking her eyes off the feeding creature as she slowly edged her way out of the clearing. She knew she should make her break for the forest while the infected was distracted by the Northies, but no matter how she justified it, the guilt dragged tears out of her.

"I'm sorry."

She took off toward the city, rocks cracking against her shins and tree branches slapping her face.

I have to make things right, she thought, running faster. *I have to find Jahx.*

Blinding pain made her forget the world as she struck her head against a low branch. She fell backward, but instead of hitting the ground, she kept falling—

Her body disappeared, but her ears, eyes, and voice remained.
(This can't be possible—how did I get here?)

Immersed in inky blackness, Jetta's nose filled with the smell of ashes, depriving her of air. The feeling of suffocation overpowered her nerves, but when she sensed him near, she cried out with all the breath left in her.
(Jahx!)

A voice called back with frightening urgency: (Please, oh please, find me, find me—kill him.)

(Jahx!) *she tried again, trying to find him in the soupy darkness as she gulped for air.* (Where are you?)

Other voices emerged, distant but distinctive in their pain, crying out in a thousand different languages.

(Who's there?) *Jetta called out to the chorus of tortured souls.*

Footsteps rose above the din, marred with the sounds of mechanical parts rubbing together, like the discordant symphony of a corroded engine. When she tried to extend herself, the frenetic mass of psionic energy repelled her backward.

(You must find me and kill him.)

Without hands to protect her ears against the deafening noise or the means to run away from the bestial thing headed her way, Jetta panicked. Throat stuffed with the bitter taste of ash, her attempts to call out again came out in garbled confusion.

(Jahx! Help me PLEASE!) *she thought.*

Something latched onto her and dragged her away from the monstrosity bounding toward her. She smelled his scent and felt the familiar rhythm of his being.

(Jahx! Jahx—I found you! Where are we? How do I get you out of here?) *she managed to choke out.*

But he said nothing. She could barely make out his outline and the soft white of his skin as he pulled her along.

276

(You must kill him. You must KILL HIM.)

Jetta tried to will the formation of a body like she had done before, but her strength and focus faltered. She spun away, like water swirling down a drain.

(Jahx, please—how do I find you? Who do I have to kill?)
Two blue eyes frantic with fear replied:

(You must find me)

Jetta came to sprawled out in the bushes, a sliver of moonlight peeking down at her from the thick tangle of trees. Her heart pounded mercilessly in her temples as she tried to steady her breathing.

What just happened?
(That was no dream.)
No, she thought, *it was too real.*
Maybe I hit my head hard enough to cause a hallucination, she argued with herself. *But wait—I know I heard Jahx before that. He broke my concentration when I was fighting the Northies.*
(Or is it all in my head?)
I did lose control of myself, she conceded. *Anything is possible.*

As she wiggled her way out of the bushes, Jetta realized that needed her sister's perspective on the issue. And probably the Grand Oblin's, too.

I don't want to go back and waste valuable time, she told herself, but her conscience whispered through: *(I don't want to face them after what I did.)*

Finally free, she patted around in the shadows until she found a tree to lean against.

"*Demei Uo,*" she muttered in Fiorahian.

For the first time in years, she allowed herself to cry. The last time she could remember doing so was when Yahmen took Aunt Lohien away. After that she had vowed to never let anybody make her feel that way again, even if it meant dumping her feelings on others, or release through physical pain.

But this was different.

277

She kicked the tree and raked her hands along the bark, feeling the wood splinter underneath her nails. The pain felt good, but the relief was temporary.

"Jaeia," she whispered between sobs. "Help me, Jaeia."

With that she opened her mind, reaching out to find her sister across the uncharted leagues of timeless space. *Jaeia?*

Nobody answered. Normally her brother or sister waited on the outside of her psionic barricade, ready to dive in and reprimand her as soon as she relented. *Gods—I don't sense her at all!*

Jetta searched for her sister's psionic tune as she barreled her way back the way she came. When she came to a clearing, she looked to the eastern mountains. In the distance she could hear explosions, and gunfire flashed in the open mouth of the mountainside.

Without hesitation she ran back toward the caves. Concentrating on the location, she fell in tune with Jaeia's thoughts and felt her sister's panic like a hot ball of lead in her stomach. Taking little comfort that her sister was alive, Jetta commanded her legs and arms to pump faster through the biting underbrush and thick growth of the forest, ignoring the pain and rubbery fatigue in her muscles.

"I may be a monster," she muttered as she leapt from the grass onto the rocks. "But I will protect you with everything I have left."

***

Even without her telepathic powers, Triel of Algardrien knew the situation was much worse than Reht had been willing to admit. Instead of fighting, Ro and Cray spent their time taking inventory and running diagnostics on the weapons system. When she passed by the engine core, she found Mom braving the dirty washout, growling as he scrubbed the conduits to a sparkle. Tech and Billy Don't huddled over the jump sequencer, reconfiguring the autodriver for the third time, oblivious to the Healer.

"This can't be good," she mumbled, walking through the empty galley.

"There you are," Diawn said, coming up from behind her.

Triel jumped, but tried to pass it off with a smile. "Diawn—sorry—I didn't see you there."

The *Wraith's* pilot scowled as she stepped in a little too close for Triel's comfort. "You'd better watch yourself, leech," Diawn said, running one of her lacquered nails down Triel's jawline. "And don't get too comfortable."

Allow her hatred to pass through you, the Healer told herself as the pilot shouldered her way past Triel toward the bridge. Diawn's anger simmered beneath the Healer's flesh, making her feel feverish and tense. *Fear and hatred will make you Fall. Let go of poisoned emotions.*

Slowing her breathing, Triel focused on the truth behind her volatile relationship with Diawn.

Reht Jagger, Triel thought, half-frowning as she hugged her arms close to her chest. *Why do you have to be such a heartbreaker?*

Memories of their chance meeting replayed across her mind's eye:

On the run after a terrible fight with her father, Triel endured the rancid conditions of a waste management transport freighter, hiding in one of the sludge cylinders for a week. The toxins from the sludge suffused her system, making it impossible to heal herself.

"Oh, father," she whispered, swallowing hard to keep from vomiting. "I don't know why I rebel."

After being dumped in a landfill, it took Triel two days to pick her way out of the garbage heap. The entire ordeal caused such significant weight loss that some of her people's markings faded, but it allowed her to pass unnoticed onto a refugee vessel.

Disembarking onto the frigid docks of Saelis, Triel made her way to the nearest trash barrel and vomited up her recent meal of Tader worms. That's when she saw Reht getting into an argument with a local merchant. The merchant had been giving him a hard time until the Talian warrior joined him on the docking platform.

A fabled blue warrior of Tali, *Triel marveled. There weren't many Talians left after the Blood Dawn Massacre, but those that remained were the fiercest.*

Mom's immense size struck her; he easily towered over every other Sentient at the docks. Despite his massive, muscular frame, he moved with the same stealth and grace as the elusive mountain wolves of Algar.

The warrior's eyes, two discs of shining silver, tracked every movement the merchant made. When the merchant tried to reach for

Reht, the tips of his claws protruded through the skin of his hands and arms to give fair warning of what would happen next.

Finally, when the Talian did not agree with how the business transaction was progressing, he dropped his claws. The merchant shoved a package into Reht's chest before taking off into the crowd.

Reht caught her staring at him.

Run and hide, *Triel told herself, but she couldn't. There was something very strange about the dog-soldier captain. He was handsome yet grizzled; his face was scarred and unshaven, and his hair was a mess of shocking white.*

The bandages covering his hands caught her eye as he squared himself to her. Old and frayed, it looked like he had been wrapping and rewrapping them for ages. Even from afar she sensed he was hiding something beneath those rags, and the mystery only drew her in deeper.

Triel sensed the mutual attraction as he slowly made his way through the crowd with an overconfident swagger. Nothing deterred him, not her sickly appearance or that she wore the tattered remains of a man's travel suit. He never lowered his gaze, never lost his smile as he wound his way to her.

Lost in the mixed coloring of his eyes, Triel eased her way into his mind. She detected his arrogance, his rebellious nature, but beneath it all, a chink in his armor she wasn't accustomed to finding in his type.

"Captain Reht Jagger," he introduced himself, offering a hand bound in bandages. She took it lightly, not yet sure of what she was feeling.

"Raina," she lied, using one of her many aliases.

Reht smiled slyly. "This here is Mom," he said jabbing his thumb at the Talian warrior. "He and I were in a bit of a tiff with a local retailer, but that's all straightened out now. Looks like you're not feeling so well," he had said, pointing to the trash barrel. "May I offer some medical assistance on board my luxury cruiser, the Wraith?*"*

A luxury cruiser it was not. Triel couldn't decide whether to laugh or be concerned when she spotted the clunky-looking vessel. With mismatched parts and welding tape to hold down the communications dish, she wondered how it could possibly achieve liftoff, let alone execute a jump. But as she boarded, she spotted the custom upgrades that gave the starship its formidable reputation, even with all the abuse from its dog soldier passengers.

Triel didn't know why she trusted him so immediately. Normally she traveled alone and in large crowds. By joining Reht on board his vessel, she had singled herself out and limited her resources. But luck, for a change, favored her.

The dog-soldier captain took her in, introduced her to the crew, and had Bacthar tend to her sickness. It took a little while for her to warm up to some of the more unusual personalities of the crew, especially the wild duo of Ro and Cray, but they grew on her over time. All of them except for Billy Don't and Diawn.

She did everything she could to avoid Billy Don't. His Liiker mind, a hive of disjointed emotions and white noise, caused her deep-seated headaches when she got too close. Tech explained to her that it was "technopsychosis," the result of faulty neural-mechanical integration, but this did little to ease the psionic battering.

"And this is Diawn, the best pilot in the Starways," Reht said, trying to get them to shake. Triel extended her hand, but Diawn avoided contact, greeting her with a venomous sneer.

Keeping a low profile didn't stop Diawn's from trashing her few personal belongings and stealing her food. After her first night in Reht's den, things got out of control.

"Baby, you got to understand, she's really the best pilot in the galaxy," Reht said, trying to calm the Healer down. "And she's a killer negotiator."

"She's going to kill me, Reht!" Triel said, swinging her legs off his bed and picking her clothes up off the floor. "She wrote my name in blood across the lavatory mirror!"

Reht chuckled and stretched out his arms, trying to bring her back in bed. "Let me tell you about little miss Diawn Arkiam…"

Frustration and fright turned into pity as Triel listened to the pilot's history. Brought up on the streets, Diawn became a victim of back alley investors wanting to make her more saleable. None of Diawn's physical enhancements had been voluntary, nor had she been willing to take in her first hundred clients. It wasn't until she had met Reht that she had elected to use her assets. When Reht described the details of their relationship, Triel finally understood the true nature of the problem.

"She tried to sell herself to me on Ularu, her homeworld," Reht
said, playing with the ends of Triel's hair. *"But I seen her action in
the bars and streets. She could seduce anyone—gender, race,
sexuality doesn't matter—into overpaying for a favor. So I made her
an offer. Do the same thing, just as part of my crew."*

"You took her off the streets. You gave her a family," Triel said,
leaning against the headboard of Reht's bed. *"You're not just her
captain—you're her savior."*

Reht shrugged, playing with the bandages on his hands. "I
wouldn't go that far."

*Triel pieced together the rest. Reht's insatiable desire for female
companionship blurred the lines of his relationship with Diawn.*

"Maybe we shouldn't do this," Triel said, trying to leave again.

Reht caught her by the wrist and pulled her back onto the bed.
"Stay here, with me. Be part of this crew. I'll talk to Diawn."

"Why? What could I offer?"

"You'll assist Bacthar, the ship's surgeon," he said, touching
her palm and then brushing his fingers up her arm.

Her attempts at covering her markings had failed. He knows
I'm Prodgy!

"I know you're name isn't Raina," he whispered, drawing her
closer. *"But I can understand the need to keep secrets. I'll just call
you Starfox."*

"Starfox?" she said, not resisting him.

"Because you shine like a star," he said, playfully nibbling at
her neck. *"And bite like a fox."*

Triel laughed. *"Don't act like you didn't enjoy that."*

*Reht stopped what he was doing and looked her straight in the
eye.* *"No. I love it."*

The way he said love, *the way his expression softened when he
looked at her, Triel couldn't help but say yes. Besides, she could
easily justify it by telling herself it was far safer to join the crew than
to be on her own.*

(I think I love him.)

Breaking from her reflection, the blue-eyed Healer worked up
the nerve to walk onto the bridge. She found Reht slouched in the
commander's chair, his head propped on his elbow as he chewed on
the butt of a smoke.

"Level with me, Reht," she said, seating herself next to him on one of the nearby terminals. Diawn shot her a nasty look, but Triel pretended she didn't see it.

"I already told you what I could, Starfox," he muttered, leaning back and stretching.

The Healer could hear his thumping heart rate and feel the roar of his rising blood pressure. *He's not telling me the full truth.*

She played with the webbing between her fingers, not quite knowing how to begin without revealing the extent of her upper hand. "Reht, the crew is on edge. You don't need telepathy to sense that."

"Uh-huh," he said, distracting himself with a minor report on his armrest monitor.

She crossed her arms, unfazed.

"Join me in my office," he finally said, surrendering.

He indicated for her to follow him as he lifted up the trap below his feet and jumped down to the cramped half-deck below. It was merely a small electrical and plumbing station, but it was the only area of the ship not serviced by the video cameras, and the thick layers of rusty pipework made for sufficient sound-proofing.

Reht closed the hatch above them, forcing them both to crouch in the guttering light of a single light bulb. "Triel, I told you the reason I brought you out of hiding was because of a new threat of the Liikers."

"Yes, and that the Alliance is not taking the information Mantri Sebbs gave them about the converted telepaths seriously. So, what are you trying to avoid telling me?" she asked, touching his knee. She briefly connected to him, feeling the sting of acid in his stomach and the anxiety that cinched his bowels.

Reht yanked his knee away and frowned. "Don't."

"Sorry," she replied, pulling back her hand.

"Look, I'm going to have to ask you to help me. And what I have to ask you to do might not only be dangerous," he began, avoiding her eyes and patting down his pockets for a smoke, "but might also be a bit of a moral stretch for you."

"Oh?" She felt the nature of thoughts by the way his biorhythm shifted. Her eyes glazed over, and she held her breath.

Reht found the crushed remains of a cigarette in his back pocket and lit it anyway. "I need you to save the commanding officer that led the Core."

"You mean?" she said, trailing off. *Impossible—*

He took a long drag from his smoke before continuing. "Yeah, well, kind of. General Volkor wasn't real—just a publicity stunt. It was a cover up for three little kids, one boy and two girls, that the Core was juicing."

Triel reflexively shook her head. "I—I can't believe that."

"It gets worse. The boy was taken away by the Deadwalkers, and the girls were sent to Tralora after the Core meltdown. According to Mantri, the boy is like this superprocessor of the new Liikers the Deadwalkers cooked up using Core soldiers and telepaths—crazy, eh?"

Triel couldn't breathe.

"No chance the Alliance can toss with these new Deadwalkers. So Sebbs is hell bent on bringing back the two girls 'cause he's convinced they're the only ones that might know how to defeat him."

"So all that time," Triel whispered, "General Volkor—the one the holy men on Jue Hexron prophesied as the Slaythe, the destroyer of worlds—was just a pinch of *launnies*?" Triel couldn't believe the absurdity. "*They* caused the annihilation of Polaris Prime and Algar?"

The dog-soldier captain nodded as he extinguished his smoke on his boot.

"You're the only one who can get them off that planet, Triel, 'cause you're the last Prodgy. Regular docs and meds can't cure any of those on that planet. You're the only chance we have."

"I-I don't know what to say, Reht." She gripped the pipework behind her, certain she'd topple over if she let go. *I promised to make Volkor pay—*

"I met one of them kids a long time ago, on Fiorah. They ain't bad, Starfox, just messed up."

Triel thought of her father, his gentle baritone voice whispering for her to let go of her anger, her fear, but all she felt was the pain and loss of her people, her home and everything she had ever known. She didn't understand how Reht could ask her to do this—unless, of course, it was because he had a sizeable investment in the matter.

284

Seeing her reaction, he backed off a bit. "You have a while to think it over. Tralora is on the opposite side of the universe, and even though I'm riding Tech and Mom to push our jumps, it'll take a while."

A loud scraping sound came from above as someone removed the deck plating. Diawn peered down, her eyes narrowing when she saw the two of them together.

"Captain," she said sharply, "we have a problem."

"We'll talk about this later," he said to Triel as he hoisted himself back up to the main bridge. Triel slowly followed but seated herself in the back near the navigations terminals.

Reht's face lit up with a giant grin when he saw Minister Tidas Razar, seething with fury, on the communications display.

"Surrender your vessel now, Captain Jagger," the Minister said. "We traced you skulking around in our mainframe. You are now a federative offender."

"Ah, come on, Tidas, the nearest ship you've got is the *Gallegos,* and it's still pushing through the Vareiopolos system."

Triel sighed. Reht was clearly enjoying himself, much to the displeasure of the Alliance Minister.

"You and your pack of *ratchakkers* are going to the Labor Locks, Jagger," the Minister growled.

"Tidas," Reht said seriously, as if he was done amusing himself. "I have what you need."

"Oh, please, humor me," Razar scoffed.

"I have a Prodgy. I have a Healer."

The Minister's face turned ashen through the spectrum of blue filters. "Impossible. There are none left."

Reht waved for Triel to come down into the telecommunication field. She reluctantly descended to the platform and turned her head just enough so that the Alliance official could see her markings. She didn't like being part of Reht's scheme for another "big deal," especially now.

"Look, Tidas," Reht said, "let's focus on the issue that matters. Sebbs is right, and you're just beginning to get your heads out of your *assinos* and put the pieces together. By now you've discovered the truth about Volkor, the triplets, and where they're located. You know that you can't just nab 'em off Tralora without killing them except with a Prodgy—and it just so happens that I have one Prodgy."

"You're assuming that those kids are still alive. Tralora is an extremely dangerous planet. Besides, it's old Dominion territory. There are still loyalists lurking around."

"I know those launnies are alive—they were raised on Fiorah. They know how to survive. And Dominion territory? Come on, Minister—just the Warden is guarding it these days. Don't pull that."

"You don't know that a Prodgy—a Solitary, nonetheless—can save them."

"It's the best chance you have."

"We'll see," the Minister snarled. "In the meantime, you will surrender your vessel to the *Gallegos* when she intercepts you at Tralora. If you resist, I have authorized the commander to use whatever means necessary to bring you back—dead or alive."

Reht sported a dented grin as he made a motion across his neck to have Vaughn cut the comlink. The dog-soldier captain strode over to Triel and attempted to place an arm around her shoulder, but she shrugged it away. In no way did she want to be part of something like this. She wasn't interested in making a huge profit, and she certainly wasn't interested in saving the Slaythe, even if they were just little kids. Nobody—young or old—with a mind capable of that kind of destructive power should be allowed to live.

"Sorry," she whispered.

Triel had wanted him to follow her, to tell her it was okay, but instead he let her walk off alone. In the back of her mind she could feel Diawn delighting in her disappointment.

***

Jahx found a way to hide himself, though he knew it wouldn't last much longer. Trapped with the others in the lost space between life and death, he maintained enough of himself in the transition to have some awareness of the corporeality he had been forced to leave. With every last ounce of strength he concentrated on this awareness and tried to retrace his steps.

M'ah Pae cannot find out what I'm capable of, he worried. But the only way to keep the Motti Overlord from fully exploiting his mind was to stay attached to what little the Deadwalkers kept alive

286

by the pulse of artificial life. Jahx cringed. Staying linked to his body meant a whole new kind of suffering. As he concentrated his energies on maintaining that link, he faced the awful truth.

Awareness came through in jumbled pieces that gradually assembled themselves. Hearing came first, then recognition of shapes and movement. Buzzing noises filled his ears, and the steady clicking of something nearby, perhaps even within him.

Looking down and saw little more than a flap of flesh across a mechanical torso. He didn't recognize himself. Nothing felt real. Heat was no longer something that made him sweat; it was merely a temperature reading running across the screen that had replaced one of his eyes. The stink of the oil and organic decomposition registered as "within programmed parameters," completely absent of emotional or physical response.

Strapped or fused upright, Jahx could only turn his head by a few degrees, enough to see that he was one of thousands of stalks in a field of half-flesh corpses.

(What have I been reduced to?)

His innards, dug out and filled with twisted machine, spun and hummed in response. Sensory data scrolled down his new visual field, but he couldn't understand it. Right then he didn't care what he felt, even if it was pain.

(My body is not my own anymore.)

Shutting himself down seemed a viable option until he encountered the programs specially installed within his matrix to safeguard against self-destruction.

(I can't go on like this,) *he thought.*

Voices from beyond cried out.

Don't leave—

Help me—

The others wouldn't allow him to self-destruct. They needed him. Since they didn't understand that they were trapped, they were unable to reconcile the breadth of their predicament. Jahx was their only hope, a shining beacon in the dark pandemonium of limbo.

Despite it all, he had to try. He couldn't allow M'ah Pae to turn him into the unthinkable. He would shut down system by system, starting with the metronomic clicking in his chest. Slow it down until it stopped. Even though M'ah Pae had stripped him of almost all his essence, he still retained limited control of his talent.

You can't leave me—

How can you abandon me—

—I'm so afraid—

The cries escalated in the back of Jahx's mind as he focused on slowing the beating in his artificial chest. As the interval between clicks grew longer, their pleas became more desperate.

I need you!

—can't go on—

So alone

His conscience arrested his reasoning. (If I end this way, the others will be lost forever in limbo...)
But before he could even reevaluate his choice, he *appeared.*
Mucosal lips parted wetly. An elongated jaw chomped down on the remaining black stumps of teeth. Grinding gears screeched as the towering Overlord bent down to Jahx's level, flashing a prideful smile.

M'ah Pae plucked out his own eyepiece and placed one of his pincers in Jahx's head, digging out the portal latch. From what little sensation he had left, it felt like a tickling inside his skull, but when the Overlord placed his eyepiece inside him, a tidal wave of nausea swept over him. The slimy eye rolled around his head until it settled in a compatible input/output port.

"I am always watching."

Jahx felt his hold on his physical self slip. He couldn't let go—not now. He had to stop himself from becoming what M'ah Pae wanted.

"I am always listening."

M'ah Pae removed a syringe full of a viscous white substance. The Motti Overlord flipped open Jahx's abdominal hatch, revealing pink intestines punctured by tubing and wires, and twisted in the syringe.

"I know you're still in there," *M'ah Pae whispered into what was left of his ear.* "I can feel the defiant stink still leaking from your pores."

He depressed the plunger, slowly infusing the narcotizing cocktail. "Whatever you are holding onto is futile."

M'ah Pae's lips grazed the side of his ear. Jahx knew that it shouldn't be more than a proximity readout that registered in his newly designed matrix, but somehow a chill made its way down his synthetic spine and into the threads of his awareness.

"Do you not know what you have become? You are mine now."

Jahx felt M'ah Pae's slippery eye roll around in the head portal where his ear canal should have been. Somehow the foreign eye connected with his matrix, downloading images and sound bytes into his central processor. And in the bloodlit dark where his eyes should have been played a nightmarish reconstruction of what the Overlord wanted him to see.

Symbols, figures, faces—a blurred amalgamation of visual information jerked past like a film compiled of random frames. The thousands of eyes behind his own filtered the datastream, enabling him to interpret the dizzy swarm of information.

He remembered.

(Organic life identified)

He heard his voice, commanding, unifying and destroying in logical and precise patterns of deduction and inference.

(Disrupt communications)

(Eliminate all subspecies)

(Disseminate virus to neutralize Sentient reactants)

(Reserve enough for feed)

Compliance is simple, and so rewarding. Annihilate a warship, and there is satiety. Obliterate a star system and the exhilaration is divine.

(I am Yahmen hurting Jetta), Jahx thought.

He couldn't imagine himself conceiving let alone enacting of any of it, and yet his stalk executed entire worlds without hesitation. Even after absorbing all of the knowledge of the Core, the Voices, the fallen soldiers, and the Motti—it did not equate to what that part of him had become.

The Motti Overlord whispered, "I have destroyed your body and stolen your mind. Surely there is nothing else. Give in to me and save yourself the suffering. Let go, Jahx. Let go."

***

289

The hammering in her head worsened with every heartbeat. Jetta touched her forehead just above her hairline and felt warm clumps of clotted blood. Eyesight blurring, she wobbled to her feet, trying not to think about how bad the injury might be.

With a mixed feeling of relief and urgency, she reached the edge of the forest where trees and rocks came together at the base of the mountain.

"*Skucheka!*"

Too late. About a hundred meters above her she spotted Rawyll, severely injured, struggling with a Prig. Dinjin was behind him, slumped against the mountainside, his abdomen a gaping wound glistening with purple organs. From the sound of gunfire, she knew that the other Prigs had successfully breached the entrance.

"No!" she cried as her vision telescoped, and she lost her footing. *I can't lose consciousness now—*

Thrust back in the nightmare world, Jetta lashed out at the soupy darkness, trying in vain to return to the physical world.

(*I have to go back—Jaeia needs me!*)

The footsteps, the voices, the grinding metal came after her much more quickly this time. She curled in on herself, readying for the attack. When she sensed her brother's presence, she dared opened her eyes, and the clamor faded to a whisper.

(Jahx? Oh, Gods—)

Jahx stood directly in front of her, his head hung low and shoulders slumped. Disheveled and wearing dirty rags, her brother wouldn't look at her, but she could see his lips moving.

She tried to reach out, but she didn't have the means to bring herself to him.

(Look at me!) *she shouted.*

(*You have to find me*)

(*Why won't you speak to me directly?*) *she projected across their bond, but he did not answer. Instead, the frightening thing in the darkness roared to life, creaking and groaning like a worn-out machine as it lumbered toward her. A splintering cacophony of suffering and psionic dissonance bellowed across the dark plane, forcing her to retreat into herself.*

(What is that?) Jetta couldn't make out its shape, only distortions in the shadows and odd shimmers of light. As it approached, she saw tiny embers poking through the darkness, like thousands of glowing red eyes.

Jetta remembered seeing pictures of demons in the leaflets that the missionaries of Fiorah handed out, but those diabolical creatures were cartoonish and laughable. This was something much different, much more evolved. The smell of sulfur and decay filled her nose, and it made her wish back the stink of ashes.

(Jahx, run!) she screamed as it opened up its black maw. Spiny fingers grew out of the shimmering distortion of shadows and reached for him. Jahx's head arched back as it touched the base of his calf and his face turned ghostly gray in an instant.
(You have to FIND ME!)

***

Jetta came to choking a man wearing the threadbare uniform of a Core soldier. Chunky yellow mucus oozed from his eyes, and his tongue waggled from his mouth, but she kept squeezing until she heard the telltale crunch.

I have to rescue Jaeia! she realized, letting go of the man.

Out of the corner of her eye she saw Rawyll reach to her and shout some sort of warning as she sped up the mountainside. She didn't hear it, nor did she need to; she knew she had the power to kill any enemy that would stand in her way.

Jetta skidded to a halt at the mouth of the cave. Three Prigs fired plasma weapons at Crissn, who had taken shelter behind a rock slab. The Oriyan repelled most of their attacks with a reconfigured energy shield, but it wouldn't hold up much longer.

"Hey!" one of the Prigs shouted. The others, alerted to her presence, turned their fire on her. She dodged the first few rounds, but as she slammed the nearest Prig against the rock wall, she was hit by the rebound shot off of the energy shield.

Pain exploded through her side as she was knocked off her feet and rolled to the edge of the cliff. Catching herself on the lip of the precipice, she looked down into the darkness of the forest below and held back a scream.

"Shield is down—go, Teag!" one of the attackers shouted.

Fear overcame pain as Jetta frantically pulled herself up. As she flopped onto solid ground, she managed to see the two remaining Prigs take off into the cave entrance. Someone screamed, and the gunfire faded as they descended into the tunnels.

"*Skucheka*," Jetta cursed. It hurt to breathe. Looking at the gushing wound in her side, she realized she didn't stand a chance at catching up to them.

Fuming in pain and frustration, she let go of her control and allowed her mind to expand. She didn't want to resort to using her talent again, but like before, she didn't have a choice.

Frisson washed over her with such exhilarating energy that she forgot what she was worried about. Tasting the carnage and the blood in the air only furthered her desires.

I want more, she thought, shivering with anticipation. *I will go even farther than before.*

(They will suffer.)

In her rage she didn't understand the length of her range, nor did she sense those minds that were ensnared in her wake. Delighting in her own power, she was blind to the difference between friend and foe as she reached back into the darkest fathoms of her mind.

***

Tidas Razar loosened his collar as he searched around his office for his private keycodes. It was too hot, and the air seemed considerably thinner than he could tolerate.

"Environmental controls, increase oxygen limit by ten percent and decrease temperature by five degrees," he ordered into the voice command unit. The central computer made a series of clicking noises as it processed his request.

"Oxygen saturation already at ideal maximum. Temperature at Starways regulatory levels. Override?"

After finding the keycodes in the safe behind the bookshelf, the Military Minister scrambled back to his desk.

"Override, *dichu*! And call up Admiral Unipoesa now!"

The keycodes and Unipoesa were all he had now. The codes would allow him to reactivate border bases and military units without the authorization of Chief Commanding Officer Urusous Li. Li had already denied his previous requests to arm the fleet, and the

General Assembly had backed the CCO's order. Their CCO had assured them that the Eeclian Dominion had been destroyed and General Volkor defeated. Nobody wanted to believe that an army could be assembled that quickly, especially one that could rival the strength of the allied Homeworlds. War fatigue dominated not only the Starways citizens and the General Assembly, but even the Alliance Senior Council.

Tidas knew the truth.

As he waited for Unipoesa's callback, he watched the composite reel pieced together by his intelligence agents, making sure it wasn't just a bad dream. The reel contained surveillance tapes, personal video logs and shaky marine video-cams, starting with the video log of a pilot and the scanner records of his ship in deep space near the boundaries of the unregulated territories. A tiny blip on the radar from the orbit of the fourth moon of Oriathos barely got the pilot's attention until he picked up the federation signal.

Through surveillance cameras on an Alliance outpost, Tidas watched as the inspection team boarded the battered shuttle. As reported through personal video logs, the inspection leader noted that the onboard computer was barely functional, life support had failed, and the lone occupant appeared dead.

The video that followed made Razar shift uncomfortably in his seat. Marines joked as they dragged the dead watchman from the shuttle, but stopped laughing when they saw the terrifying artifact imbedded in his chest. One of them screamed when the dead body started to twitch.

Tidas blinked several times as he watched the grainy black-and-white footage. The corpse's head bobbled back and forth as his torso and buttocks bucked off the floor. Finally, the watchman bent at the waist and sat straight up, his head hanging limply to one side. He spoke through some unidentified internal source as his jaw hung awry.

"In four days you will be purified," the dead body choked in some guttural and grossly inhuman voice. One of the marines shot it fifteen times, but the bullets did nothing to faze the corpse.

Tidas stopped the reel with a fist slam, holding his head with his other hand. Li had laughed at it, called it a cheap trick. But the young commander's eyes had not seen Razar's years of battle. Nor

293

had Li and the other officers or councilmen been there when he questioned Sebbs.

Now he sat at his desk, his nervous habit taking hold as he arranged and rearranged some of the newer secured files. Finally, the wire came through to connect him to Admiral Unipoesa.

Unipoesa read him correctly and skipped the usual formalities. "How bad is it?"

"Admiral, what is your position?"

"I'm pushing her jumps, but we're still about two hours away."

"At all costs, Damon, retrieve that Prodgy Healer and get those launnies off that *godich* planet. Do you have the pods ready?"

"Yes, my SMT has already swept and checked twice now; we've got the whole rescue process laid out."

"Do it again."

"Sir, with all due respect, I am aware of the importance of this mission."

"Let's get one thing clear between you and me, Damon," the Minister said through clenched teeth. "I know that you are one of the more *informed* officers of the Alliance—I have been personally watching your activity for some time now."

"You know that everything I've ever done has been for the Alliance and the Starways," the Admiral replied calmly.

"That remains to be seen," Tidas said gruffly, drumming his fingers on his desk. "For now, I will overlook your indiscretions in light of your report. If the Deadwalkers do have some kind of bioweapon to mass-convert Sentients into their puppets, then I require your faculties."

With a grim expression, the Admiral nodded. "I know. You need my help to convince the Assembly to override Li."

"Ah, Damon," the Minister laughed mirthlessly, "you did your job well back in the day—you made him an attractive hero. The General Assembly will follow him to the grave."

Unipoesa removed himself from the viewscreen for a moment, only to return with a knotted forehead and a face turned scarlet.

The Minister knew he had struck a sensitive chord. Unipoesa had trained Li from near infancy under the secretly instituted Command Development Program, molding him into one of the deadliest officers ever to take helm of an Alliance fleet. Damon posted his reservations about Li's psychological stability after some unexplained incidents during training, but when his flawless Endgame record was leaked to the Homeworlds media circuit, he earned an indisputable position not only in the fleet, but in the public's heart.

Things only got worse after it became public that the young prodigy defeated the great commander Unipoesa of the Raging Front—his own trainer—in the Endgame. It wasn't long after that Damon was forced to take an advisory position by a unanimous vote in the General Assembly. Li's youthful attractiveness and media savvy brought in more funds for the Alliance military and government than Damon's battle-worn image ever could.

"Sir, I must be frank," the Admiral said. "Our efforts mean nothing if Li remains in command. He would not share the helm, least of all with pair of launnies, and with his political powers, it would take more than a miracle to remove him from his post."

"That is why you're going to have Pancar convince the council to put you back in command."

"You know—?"

"Never underestimate me again."

"Noted, Sir. But what about the launnies?"

"They've commanded under the mask of Volkor," Tidas stated as he rechecked the security of their channel.

Unipoesa's face turned to stone. "You couldn't be suggesting..."

"Wouldn't you like another set of medals, Admiral? Assuming, of course, that they are victorious. You and I know that Li can never find out about those launnies. He would make their past—how shall I say this—'indiscretions'—public. And if the public found out that the same bloody leeches that persecuted them were at the helm of their military, it would be a political firestorm. So you see why you must be reinstated as chief commander," Tidas said.

The admiral hesitated. "We're asking something tremendous of them considering their history with organized military. I don't know if they would agree to such extreme terms, especially given what is at stake for them."

"Come now," Tidas said, waving him off. "You turned that sorry pissant of a kid into the jackal he is today. I'm not worried about your powers of persuasion."

Damon ran his fingers through his hair. "This is beyond anything I've ever asked a child to do."

"Don't do this, Damon, not now—this is our only choice, and you know it. If you, even for a moment, have any reservations, you'll compromise this mission. Are you keeping up on your Rai Shar?"

"Yes," Damon said, fingers pinching the bridge of his nose. "I've done all that. I'm ready to face them."

"Good," Tidas said. "Just make sure that you get them—with or without Jagger's help. I'll send an encrypted message for Pancar to persuade the council to reinstate you. I'll tell him we've spoken"

With that the Minister of the Alliance military forces signed off, leaving Admiral Unipoesa the task of retrieving Jetta and Jaeia Kyron.

***

For the first time in his life, Jahx was angry with himself. He had always had faith in his intuition, in the gifts that had given him insight into the unspoken languages of the universe. But this was wrong. He was wrong. Now everyone would pay for his mistakes—those who were alive and even those who were not quite dead.

(Jetta was right about me...)

He tried not to let the thought through, but he could feel himself caving under the weight of the truth. With patience, pain and isolation, the Motti Overlord achieved complete control of Jahx's body. Soon, the systematic extermination of the Sentients of the Starways would be realized. *I have become what I fear most.*

If the others had been united in wanting to end their enslavement, it would have been easy for Jahx to lead them all away peacefully. But a collective memory had been created in the neuroelectric void, an angry one, by the fragments of experience of those that once lived. All of them had suffered through the Dissembler Scare and had lost everything, and from this memory arose a yearning for vindication so powerful that it took everything he had to avoid its toxic effects.

We need to battle the Motti—not the Sentients of the Starways! he projected, but the others couldn't hear him. With their awareness limited to raw desire, his will alone would not be able to steer the other telepaths in the right direction. They could only comprehend the power at their fingertips, and the enemies the Motti targeted.

Jahx couldn't help but question all that he ever believed. *How can I justify my actions when I'm murdering innocent people?*

But he knew the truth. He had always been afraid of his power, afraid of the possibility that he might have to hurt someone to help someone else. He didn't want to make that choice, but he couldn't go against the call of his instincts.

Jahx entered his body again to grant himself temporary relief from the distortion of limbo. The voices of the others constantly tore at his mind, seeking answers that he couldn't provide, but his body was no longer a refuge. Only emptiness, and a strange feeling of nakedness remained.

(I can't do this much longer,) *he thought. He concentrated on his fragile grip on reality as he extended himself into the physical world again.*

(*Don't leave us*)

(*They must be stopped—*)

(*They are the enemy*)

(*Finish them*)

(*You can't leave*)

(*Afraid*)

(*You are the only one*)

(*Take this pain away*)

Thousands of minds wrapped around his, pulling him back, drawing him away from his body. They knew what he wanted to do, and for all of their different reasons, they wouldn't let him.

Jahx fought back with all the strength he had left. He didn't consider, however, that the Motti had been watching the stress levels of his stalk and identified a lingering presence—and that his enemy was waiting for him.

With his head fixed to the stalk, Jahx could not look away. The Motti leader, patiently standing by, lifted his undercarriage with two of his pincers and removed part of a humanoid hand. After slipping it on the end of one of his spidery legs, the grayish hand displayed movement in all five fingers.

297

The dead hand turned purple as it caressed Jahx's cheek and pulled at the few remaining strands of hair on his head. A part of him felt relief that he couldn't really feel it.

"The most powerful telepath in the galaxy, useless until I made you useful. That is my gift to you."

Jahx could barely hold on. The Motti Overlord removed his eye again and set it in the portal in Jahx's head. He didn't want to see any more death, and he didn't want to know any more about the weapon he had become. But where could he go? He didn't want to return to the pandemonium where the other voices leeched from his essence.

The movie reel in his head began to play. He witnessed the Motti Overlord and his underlings standing over the controls to the stalks, programming him and the others with new priorities. Not long after, he saw a mucus-like white substance pumping into his veins after he gave an order to attack an unarmed civilian outpost.

(This is not what I am meant to do.)

Jahx's vision faded. He had to act now.

M'ah Pae chuckled, emitting a sound like grinding glass. "There is nothing for you Jahx—why remain? I have only begun to show you the true power of your mind," *he said, digging his dead hand into his cheek. An electronic warning signal went off in his head that the external pressure exceeded safe limits.* "Leave my construct or I will destroy your soul."

***

At first Jaeia thought she would black out. The fever from the sickness used up her last reserves, and the flashfire hits she had taken in the arm and thigh seared through her like no pain she had ever felt before, robbing her of what little control she had left.

But as one of the Prigs stood over her, preparing to deal her death, the faintness turned into something else. Something much worse.

"What the hell?" the Prig said, sticking a finger in his ear. His face twisted with pain, and he dropped his rifle on the ground to clutch his head.

Time slowed to a crawl as she became aware of every nerve fiber, every cell throughout her body. The incredible sensation grew worse until she felt a fire spread through the branches of her awareness.

Then the burning stopped. She wasn't in the caves anymore. Looking around, she realized she was back on Fiorah, in their old apartment, standing alone in the entryway where she slept.

The single bulb in the living room flickered as she timidly peeked around the corner. There he was, sitting in his usual spot in the ratty armchair. Tendrils of smoke rose from his hand where a cigarette burned red in the shadows. In the other hand tipped an almost-empty bottle of Half and Half, 20-20, *his favorite drink.*

His speak was slurred, but she was used to deciphering his inebriated words. "So, you're alone again."

No, *she thought. She didn't want to relive this memory.*

He chuckled and took a swig. "There's always one in the family. Always one."

His mind wandered, and Jaeia followed his thoughts as she had several years ago: Left behind. Unnoticed. Discounted. Forgotten.

"Where are the other rats? Why are you always left behind?"

Galm had taken Jetta and Jahx with him to the market to try and sell some of their clothing for food rations. He didn't have enough transport fares for the four of them, so he asked one of them to stay behind. Maybe it was because Jetta and Jahx had already readied themselves to go, or maybe it was the way Jetta looked at her from the corner of her eye, but she sensed that Jetta wanted her to stay so she could go with Jahx.

Jaeia swallowed the aching lump in her throat. Being thrust back into the memory made her come face to face with the question that had quietly festered inside of her for her entire life. She knew it was irrational and stupid, probably only paranoia and jealousy, but she had always secretly felt like she was the odd one out. Jetta and Jahx were fiercely close, and even though they all shared the same bond, Jaeia knew Jetta and Jahx shared something very special between them. Maybe it was because they were so polarized, or maybe it was because they felt the need to watch over each other so closely. Whatever it was, Jaeia wasn't a part of it.

(No,) *she whispered.*

Yahmen cackled again. "You know what I say? Those gorsh-shit *eating bastards deserve to pay for what they've done. You should make 'em pay!"*

299

(No!), *she cried. The vicious yearnings of his heart flooded her mind: He wanted her to act on her anger, to destroy their apartment and what few possessions they had left, and then take it even further. He wanted her to hurt her brother and sister.*

Yahmen seethed with the idea of revenge. "You're pathetic and useless. You're just gonna sit there and cry like a little launnie."

He whipped his bottle of booze at the wall, bits of glass and alcohol spraying everywhere. Pointing a finger at her, he stumbled over in her direction. "I was never weak. I always—ALWAYS—got what I deserved!"

He grabbed her by the collar. Jaeia gagged at his breath and turned her head to avoid the flying spittle. "They will look at you and laugh if you don't take them. Take them!"

Jaeia cupped her face in her hands. Yahmen was right. She was the odd one out. The one who looked after everybody else but who seldom got noticed—at least not in that way.

(I am alone.)

Her heart ached like never before. She no longer considered that she was being irrational, or that she was in the caves about to be shot by a Prig, or that perhaps this was all an illusion. Loneliness and jealousy burned its way into every corner of her being. She didn't want to exist like this anymore. She wanted any escape for her torment—

Death, lurking in the shadows, whispered promises of sweet release.

(Take my pain away,) she projected. Something cold and invasive wrapped around her skin, and the world faded to gray. Her heartbeat became erratic as she slowly detached from her body.

As her last ties to the mortal world unraveled, another part of her, one that she never knew existed with such fervency, called out from within. (I have to live... for my sister.)

***

Admiral Unipoesa couldn't remember the last time he had slept as he lay in his bed on top of the covers, still dressed in his battle uniform. When the image of Tidas Razar formed on his desk, he wasn't sure if it was the real Minister or just a projection. He

300

stumbled to attention, but the Minister was more concerned with other matters to notice.

"There's a silent movement in the works; the people are talking. I would hate to think that there is a traitor among us leaking classified material to the public."

Unipoesa sighed. "If I hadn't given those representatives enough information, they wouldn't have a voice against the General Assembly. If I could sway the General Assembly, then you'd have a chance to take down Li for me."

Razar popped his jaw forward and reset it with a click. "You're a clever man, Damon, but you're taking a huge risk for the Alliance... and for yourself."

The admiral slumped into the nearby chair and covered his face with one hand. "I know the old adage. Don't burn down your house to stay warm for one night. But it won't matter if we can't beat the Deadwalkers."

Razar's back straightened. His hologram image was only half of his size, but his presence filled the room. "If there is anything left of us, then we are going to finish the job the Deadwalkers started. This is going to lead to a civil war. Li won't sit back; he'll take up arms."

Damon squeezed his eyes shut and tried to imagine something calming, like his last shore leave, but when he opened them there was only the cold weight in his chest. "You were the one who wanted me to take the helm again."

The Minister didn't blink. "I won't go down with you, Damon. I wouldn't have secured your reappointment like this."

"This was the only way to do it and you know it. This is not the first thing you and I have disagreed about, Tidas, and it's not the first time you've set yourself apart from me so I could take the fall."

The Minister leaned forward, his image fluctuating as he projected through the corner of the desk.

"Mind your words, Admiral. One day I might take offense to them."

Damon stared at the Minister. He was tired of fighting, but to end all this, he knew it was going to cost his life.

The image of the Minister readjusted itself on the floor in front of him, resizing to his actual proportions. "Get some sleep, Admiral. I will get the council to back your reinstatement. And when this is through, you and I will settle our personal matters once and for all."

Rising from his chair, the admiral brushed down his uniform in front of the mirror, and decided he didn't like the man looking back at him.

"You old bastard," he muttered, "I know what you're up to—I know what you're trying to do. You can't win Maria back, and you'll never see Tarsha again. You're going to pay for your crimes."

The man in the mirror gazed back at him with quiet indignation.

Before he could reach for his bottle of Old Earth vodka, the admiral exited his quarters and headed to the bridge.

**

Reht Jagger expected more of a challenge on their journey to the Narki homeworld. The Warden of Tralora, a beastly fellow who cut deals with anyone who wanted to dump their enemies on the planet, should have given them a hell of a fight. Reht even ordered Ro and Cray set up the stock weapons for the brawl, but the orbiting watchtower had been long abandoned.

"Whatcha think did it?" Reht said, tossing his pack of cigarettes from hand to hand.

"Bastard took off when the Dominion caked," Diawn muttered.

Reht's gut instinct told him that the Warden would have never skipped off just because the Dominion had folded. The job was a pretty sweet one, and surely profitable. He suspected that something had scared him pretty bad to make him want to run.

He leaned over and whispered into Mom's ear, "Is it possible the Deadwalkers passed through here?"

Mom typed some commands into his console and looked back at Reht. It confirmed his suspicions. To avoid alarming the rest of his crew, he played it off casually.

"Whatever," Reht said, stretching out his arms and leaning back in his captain's chair, "I ain't questioning."

An encrypted signal brought their transmission receivers to life, and Reht nearly jumped out of his seat.

"Where are they?" Reht asked, looking at Vaughn. The ex-con rubbed the shiny dome of his head as he traced his finger along the display of the planet.

"South pole," he answered in his usual monotone drawl.

"Ahhh, good ol' Damon's feeling dangerous, jumping underneath a planet like that, thinking I wouldn't see 'em. They must have upped his meds. Put them on screen!" Reht chuckled.

Diawn, who manned the helm, downloaded the signal from the Alliance ship.

"Captain Jagger," Admiral Unipoesa said wearily, "I believe you have something I need."

Reht couldn't believe the admiral's appearance. His eyes, dark-ringed and bloodshot, made it look like he hadn't slept in days. Listening to the admiral rush his words, Reht heard a strain that went beyond typical military stress. *This is a man who's run out of options.*

With a smirk on his face, Reht slouched deeper into his chair and waved his hand for Admiral Unipoesa to continue.

"The terms of your proposal cannot be met; the Alliance will not negotiate with a criminal. However, given the situation, I have proposed to the council that, upon your delivery of the Prodgy and the subsequent rescue of the two girls, your recent crimes against the Alliance be dismissed. There will, of course, be strict stipulations that follow regarding your future conduct and liability with this operation."

Reht read between the lines. The admiral would not provide any reward, or an apology. Like every other criminal the Alliance couldn't afford to try in court, they'd be forced to flop around in a caged area of federated space where it would be impossible to make deals, make money, or even piss without an Alliance official breathing down their necks, just waiting for an excuse to ship them all to the Labor Locks.

Mom, who stood out of visual range of the Alliance officer, looked at the captain and shook his head, coming to the same conclusion. He typed a quick message into his terminal and sent it to Reht.

"You've got to be kidding me," Reht muttered when he read his first mate's warning on the armrest display. *That* chakker *raised his shields and is charging weapons.*

Reht scratched his right ear, alerting his crew to ready for battle. Ro and Cray left their posts at the secondary terminals and ducked back toward the weapons pit.

Admiral Unipoesa looked sharply to his left and then returned to the hologram axis with a cheaply forged smile. "Come now, Jagger. Your scrap-metal tugboat is no match for a starclass warship. Lower your defenses and transport the Healer to us."

"Can't do that, Damon," Reht chuckled, pulling at the bandages on his right hand. "That would be bad business. I brought you a considerable gift in such a time of need. I would expect some kind of show of appreciation."

The admiral did something that Reht hadn't expected. He sighed heavily, his shoulders slouching forward. "Captain, let's forget the *gorsh-shit* for a moment and talk straight about this. All the things you value—your ship, crew, money, drugs, women—whatever—are not going to matter in less than a month. Maybe even a week. Even during the Dominion occupation, you were able to run your business, but Reht—this is different. The Motti don't want to rule us—they want to eradicate us. Now, I will ask you not as your enemy, but as a fellow Sentient, to give us your Prodgy so we may carry out this mission."

Reht had not been expecting that at all. Usually during a deal there was considerable banter, a lot of adrenaline, and perhaps even a battle, but *never* a plea from a hardened admiral who considerably outgunned him. Part of him was disappointed by this change in procedure, and for a moment he suspected an ulterior motive. But when he saw the admiral waiting for his response, eyes unblinking and lips pinched at the sides, he knew it was no trick.

Reht shook his head. "How am I supposed to buy into a deal with no guarantee?"

The admiral choked out a laugh. "Look, Captain—you have my word, if we're still around after this mess is over, I will stake my own career on winning your crew's freedom. Hell, if you're that short-sighted, I'll send you over the access codes to my account on Trigos. There's 50,000 credits in there. Drain it for all it's worth."

Reht frowned, tightening up the bandages on his hand. He wasn't sure if he wanted to know the truth. Clearing his voice he asked what they all wanted to know. "So, those puppets got your snarllies in a bind, yeah?"

"They're pushing the interior; they've obliterated over thirty worlds in less than twenty-four hours."

Reht rolled his eyes. "Come on, man, I ain't that gullible—that's a little extreme."

The admiral scowled but maintained his tone. "They have bioweapons... and nukes."

"Nukes?

Then Reht got it. The old Dominion warships.

Sebbs was right. *That junkie* assino...

"There isn't much time. I need that Healer, Reht," the admiral said.

Reht didn't need any further explanation. He heard the tension and the fear behind Unipoesa's words and knew that it was no exaggeration.

Diawn kicked him in the back of the leg and whispered: "*Chak*, Reht, hand her over already."

The dog-soldier glanced at the rest of his bridge crew, all of whom looked right back at him apprehensively. *They know it's serious, too.*

Reht tugged on the ends of the bandages on his hands. He never let any deal go raw on him. 50,000 Starways Alliance credits was a decent take, but not for a job this size. He'd lose the respect of his crew, perhaps even jeopardize their loyalties.

Besides, he couldn't let his woman be taken aboard an Alliance starship. That's not how he planned things to go down. *What if they take her away?*

(I don't want to lose her again.)

"Let me go," Triel whispered, coming out from behind the structural pillar. "He's right, Reht. No more games."

"Starfox," Reht started, grasping the Healer's hand as she walked into the visual field of the admiral. "Wait—"

"There isn't much time," she said, softly but adamantly as she withdrew her hand from his. Her eyes glistened with tears, lips trembling as she tried to convey her insights. "You have to—for all of us."

"Seriously," Diawn said. "Give her over. She ain't worth it. *Chak* everything else—let's just get the hell out of here."

Reht ran his hand through his hair. The rest of the crew, save Diawn who just wanted the Healer gone, all thought the same thing: As soon as they handed Triel over, they'd be sent to the clink or the Labor Locks.

(I don't want to lose her again.)

For a moment all Reht could see were the bloated faces of his mother and father, slumped over the breakfast table, murder weapons buried in their backs. He remembered the sweet coppery smell of blood and the way his home, once a happy place, had been instantly transformed into something ominous and foreign.

His hands ached, just as they had so many years ago when they were scarred with acid. Even the pain, incredible and consuming, never erased the guilt of what he had done.

That bastard Unipoesa must know about the death of my parents and the genocide on Elia to chak *with my head like this,* Reht thought.

(I would rather face the Labor Locks or mutiny. I can't bear another Elia.)

"You *etaho benieho,* Damon." Reht slammed his fist against the armrest. "Send over your bank codes first. Once we get the money, we'll dock aboard your vessel—but we get our weapons."

Diawn smiled and turned back to the helm.

"Fine," the admiral said, "but please, with haste. Our scanners have located them, but the readings are fluctuating."

"What?" Reht said.

"Someone or something is killing them."

***

It took Jetta a moment to realize where she was. When she opened her eyes, she saw the fresh yellow light of dawn creeping over the mountaintops, and the stars fading in the sky. The wet smell of morning dew and trees touched her nose, and she inhaled sharply.

Slowly she propped herself up on her right elbow and then forced herself to sit up straight. The terrible pain in her side didn't bother her as much as the sight of the two Prigs near the entrance of the cave.

Hugging her injured side, she hobbled over to them only to quickly turn away. The sight of their faces, ugly and malformed, their bodies twisted into impossible shapes, made her cringe.

"I did this?" she whispered, feeling *Plethaæð*, the Fiorahian term for the morning after binge drinking, drugs, and things she wished she didn't know about. Most of the miners joked about their

306

moral depravity, and Jetta had always looked down on them for it, but now, in her time of revelation, she understood why they choose not to acknowledge the gravity of their behaviors.

Coughing made her side scream in pain, but she couldn't stop herself. A feeling of helplessness wracked her stomach when she saw the veins bulging in her hands and felt the swelling in neck and chest.

The sickness—it won't be long now. Oh Gods, Jaeia! she thought. *She probably hasn't eaten any Macca, either.*

But then something more terrifying dawned on her. *Jaeia called out to me when I used my talent against the Prigs. She wasn't trying to stop me—she was begging me to let her go!*

She stifled a cry when she saw Crissn face-down behind the energy shield generator and tumbled her way down into the meeting chamber. There she saw what she feared most.

"Jaeia!" she screamed, coming upon her sister's body lying motionless in a pool of blood. When Jetta touched her face and felt her cold and waxy skin, she knew with utter certainty and despair that her sister was dead.

"I can't—I can't—" Jetta started, retracting her hand. She looked for a weapon. *If I killed my sister, my twin, then—*

"Jetta..."

Jetta gasped. Jaeia's eyes opened, and her hand moved on top of hers. "You came back."

"Oh my Gods, I am so sorry, Jaeia," Jetta said, scooping her into her arms. She kissed her cheek and took her face in her hands. "Are you okay? What happened?"

Jaeia urged her to set her back down, and Jetta did so as gently as she could.

"The Prigs attacked. I was about to be killed when something awful happened. My worst fears... too real..." Jaeia saw the look on her face and her gray eyes widened in revelation. "No... You didn't..."

"They were attacking you. They killed Dinjin, and I had to protect you. It just—it just was... too much to control..."

Listening to herself try to explain her actions only made her feel worse. *Why do I always end up hurting the ones I love?* Jetta hung her head and dug her nails into her thighs. *Because I am a monster.*

307

"I know you didn't mean to hurt me or the others, Jetta," Jaeia said, reading her thoughts. "Don't."

Digging her nails in ever deeper, Jetta closed herself off to her sister, suddenly angry.

"We need to help the Exiles, Jetta," Jaeia said, pointing over to the bodies of the Grand Oblin and Senka a few meters away. "They're hurt badly and—"

A coughing fit seized the rest of her sister's words. She covered her mouth with her hands, but blood trickled out between her fingers.

"We're not going to last much longer ourselves, Jaeia," Jetta said, removing her sister's hand from her face. Looking over at Senka and the Grand Oblin, Jetta sensed thready pulses of life in their crumpled bodies. *They're going to be dead in minutes. If only I had medical knowledge—*

(Hopeless.)

(I am so sorry—I didn't mean to hurt any of you!)
"What are you doing?" Jaeia said.
I can't help Jaeia or the Exiles.
(There is nothing left.)
"Wait—Jetta—no!"

With an unexpected burst of energy, Jetta stumbled down to the lab and through the winding tunnels toward the white noise. The pool of murky water smelled rank with the Liiker's blood, but her nausea quickly turned to rage.

She slowed as she approached it. The fleshy machine screeched and clicked as she neared, kicking wildly with its backwards leg.

(Kill the monster)

After hacking up a wad of blood and mucus, she grabbed the Liiker's head in her hands. The flesh felt like rubber, the metal exoskeleton cold and slimy. It lashed out its serrated tongue at her and squirted its digestive lubricant, but she held its head away from her face.

"Even if I die today," she said, arms trembling with anger and sickness, "I will end all those who have taken from me."

With a quick twist of her arms and upper body, she snapped its neck. Jetta dropped the Liiker into the water, blood and water splashing her face. "I'm more than Volkor."

CHAPTER VI

"Do you have *any* medical training?" asked the medical chief.

Triel of Algardrien squeezed the webbing between her fingers to calm herself. The chief reeked of his loathing, and even when she closed off her mind, the bitter aftertaste of his physical presence remained.

"Yes, but I'm not up to date with some of your technology. I haven't formally practiced the interarts in a few years."

"The interarts—is that what your people call it? The mixing of sorcery with medicine? I thought your tribe cut ties with the modern world when that *gorsh-shit* was finally outlawed by the Core."

Triel fought to keep from showing her discomfort. She hated this type of confrontation; it infuriated and frightened her at the same time. "I was different. I didn't follow the path of my tribe."

The chief medical officer swaggered toward her. Despite measuring a quarter-meter shorter, he still got up in her face. "This is *my* ship, and *my* staff. If you so much as look the wrong way, I'll have the guards take you down. I don't trust leeches, and I certainly don't trust one that associates with dog-soldiers," he hissed.

Triel held his gaze unflinchingly, though she trembled inside.

"Doctor," Triel said as the chief turned to go back to his office. "Won't you be attending during the rescue?"

He reeled around and shot her a cold glare. "I'll watch you from the monitors. You couldn't pay me to be in the same room as a Prodgy during one of your 'episodes.'"

Inside the medical bay, Triel looked at her support staff—two trauma surgeons, two technicians, three infectious disease doctors, and two critical care nurses. They did not feel the same disdain for her as their supervisor, but the old fears stirred up during the Dissembler Scare still lingered. Their anxious faces reawakened all the disgust and isolation she had felt during the beginnings of the Dominion Wars, making her stomach lurch.

I have to concentrate, she told herself. *For the greater good. (For Reht.)*

"I'm Triel of Algardrien, a Prodgy Healer."

She took a deep breath, trying to mute the sound of their racing hearts in the back of her mind. "When I integrate with the Kyron sisters and begin the healing process, I'll need you to also monitor my status. We only have one shot at this, so we have to work together."

310

Some team members exchanged sidelong glances, while others looked down at their feet and shifted their weight.

The staff doubts me. They worry that I'm not strong enough alone, that I'll Fall.

Old feelings stirred, threatening her equilibrium. After all, how could she sacrifice herself for Volkor the Slaythe?

(He—no, the twins—murdered my family.)

Triel pinched the webbing between her fingers as hard as she could, trying to keep her thoughts peaceful, but years of suppressed indignation broke through.

(I want those girls to suffer for their crimes.)

No, Triel told herself. *That will solve nothing.*

Anger turned to grief as she thought of her tribe. The Dominion gave no warning when they set down on her homeworld, Algar, abducting her people and destroying her world. *(Do not help the ones hiding behind Volkor's mask. You will only be helping murderers.)*

Another wave of emotion surged through her. Guilt, fresh and unrelenting, carved into her like a dull blade. *(I should have never abandoned my people.)*

Triel closed her eyes. She had to keep calm. If she was to succeed at this, she couldn't afford to let her darker feelings even brush her mind. If they took hold, she really would become what they all feared.

One of the surgeons cleared his throat and stepped forward. "What are we going to do if there are other life forms with them?"

Triel wished they hadn't asked, but they had to know. "Traditionally, Prodgies never heal alone." *Never used to,* she thought bitterly. "It's dangerous. Additional tribe members are always present to help balance out physical, mental, or spiritual impurities harbored by the one the Healer means to restore. To do otherwise leaves the Healer at risk of involuntarily taking on the subject's pollutants and becoming a Dissembler. To minimize that risk, I can only attempt to rescue the two girls."

"What guarantee do we have that you won't turn on us?" the other surgeon asked, eyeing the guards at the infirmary entrance.

Triel shook her head. "It depends on their different states of health, and mine too. That's why you're going to be watching me closely. If anything happens—if anything starts to look suspicious—you have clearance to..."

Pausing, Triel looked each of them in the eye, searching for something. Not knowing what it was, nor finding it, she swallowed hard and finished the sentence: "You have clearance to terminate me."

The medical team talked among themselves, their voices low. Triel turned away and pretended to review a file as she pushed their fear from her mind.

I must be strong. For my friends, for Reht. They're all I have left.

Getting a hold of herself, Triel turned back to them. "We have approximately ten minutes until the ship is in alignment with the drop site. Everybody should be fitted in their biosuits."

As soon as her team exited to the lockers, she hurried into one of the private exam rooms and silently wept. She didn't know if she could save the Kyron twins, but worse, she couldn't decide if she wanted to.

***

Jetta collapsed halfway up the tunnel, leaving behind her a mangled trail of Liiker parts.

What was I thinking? she lamented, clutching her wounded side. She tried to prop up on her left elbow and crawl, but her nerve endings screamed, and she fell back down. *I shouldn't have left Jaeia.*

Without the fiery pulse of anger, the satisfaction she felt destroying the Liiker evaporated, leaving her exhausted and in pain.

I have to fight this, she thought, refusing to accept the truth. She had always been able to push herself beyond her limits. On Fiorah she had gone a week without food, days without water or sleep—

(My body is dying.)

Jetta tried once more to lift herself by the arms and pull herself up the tunnel, but her muscles spasmed, and she flopped back down.

(I can't reach Jaeia or save Jahx. I will never save Galm and Lohien. I will never keep any of my promises.)

"Come on," she whispered, not ready to give up. "Think of something. You can do this. Think..."

Jaeia... Jahx... I'm so sorry.

And then the memory hit her. An old one—one of her earliest. Something happy. Something unexpected.

"Oh, sweet girl," Lohien said, voice sweet, almost melodic as she kneeled down and took Jetta in her arms. "What have you done this time?"

"Nothing," Jetta said, trying to wiggle away.

"Let me see," her aunt said, prying her hand open.

Jetta hid her face as her aunt inspected her wound. Lohien's voice turned firm, but not angry. "Jetta, you need to show me this when you get hurt. These splinters are making your skin swell up— you don't want it to get worse, do you?"

Jetta wrinkled her nose and hid her hand behind her back. She had been playing with her siblings in the shade of the apartment rooftop by the discarded pigeon boxes when she tripped and fell on a pile of broken pieces. Not wanting to stop their game, Jetta kept the injury to herself. But that had been two days ago. Now her hand was red and hot, and she had a hard time concealing the discomfort from her siblings.

"You always have to be the tough one, don't you?" her aunt said, sitting her on top of her lap as she cleaned her hand with rubbing alcohol.

It stung, but Jetta bit down on her lip, trying to keep from crying.

"You can squeeze my arm if you need to, okay? Let me know if you want me to stop." Her aunt picked out the splinters as carefully as she could, but the tears came anyway. Maybe it was the pain, maybe it was the stress that had been building inside her ever since Yahmen had told Galm that they would have to move into the community housing projects. Maybe it was knowing then that no matter what she did, Yahmen was going to take everything away from them.

"All done!"

Jetta looked at her hand, neatly bandaged and less painful. But it didn't seem right. Somehow there didn't seem to be a point for her aunt to go through all of that. Not for her. Not for the street rat, the reason her parents were made to suffer Yahmen's anger.

"Come here, my little warrior," her aunt said, hugging her tightly. "You're so tough sometimes that I worry about you. You

313

*have to remember that everybody needs help sometimes—even
warriors. That's why there's me, your* Pao*, your brother and sister.
We all love you so much."*

Jolts of pain kept her drifting in and out of consciousness. She
heard shouts and boots marching in the tunnels, but she wasn't sure
if it was real.

"We all love you so much..."

(*I'm so sorry, Jaeia, Jahx—this is all my fault.*)

Someone touched her hand. *Aunt Lohien?*

She opened her eyes, but what she saw only caused her more
confusion. Yellow and orange creatures with bright eyes and
flashing sensors crouched over her, talking in voices distorted with
static.

"We have the second target," a male voice announced.

The cavern ceiling swooped all around her as the rocky floor
buckled into crashing waves. She wasn't sure if she was falling or
flying away as she flailed about, trying to gain some kind of
purchase as several arms picked her up off the floor.

Something sharp pierced her thigh, and her eyelids drooped.
Jetta tried to grab one of the creatures, but her limbs were
uncooperative.

Through the haze of a half-dream, she floated through the main
chamber of the caves, spotting body bags arranged neatly in a row
and more yellow and orange creatures milling around the fire pit.
She tried to find her sister, but her entire body seemed frozen in
place.

One of the creatures bent over, and she saw a man staring at her
through a clear protective face shield. "This is Volkor? You've got
to be kidding me. Looks like a Deadskin."

Others laughed. Someone shouted orders.

Jaeia—Jahx, she called out silently, *where are you?*

The man stared at her as her body floated toward the light in the
distance. Her eyelids became heavier, and the rocky walls faded
from view. Jetta looked back at him, but this time his face changed.
She wanted to scream, but her body had detached. She watched in
horror as his nose and mouth sucked backward into his face and
metal plating drove down over decaying white skin. The yellow and
orange spoiled into a slimy carbon black. Spiny legs erupted from

314

the torso, and his right eye bulged impossibly, turning red and oozing pus.

Jetta, the monster hissed, *you are mine!*

***

Triel waited anxiously in the infirmary for the rescue team to return, pacing between the exam tables. Because her technique required skin-to-skin contact, she couldn't wear the yellow and orange protective biosuit.

I feel vulnerable enough as is, she fretted.

The rest of the medical team stood around the receiving tables, unmoving and silent. She wished they would strike up a conversation, even about something trivial, just so the worry in their hearts didn't fill her mind. They feared the mission would fail, but equally worried about Triel descending from Healer to Dissembler.

(Me too.)

Before she lost her nerve, a hologram of the admiral materialized in the center of the room. Everybody turned in attention.

"We're ready to receive," Triel said, assuming he was going to announce the arrival of the team.

Admiral Unipoesa raised his hands. "There has been a serious change in plans. The biosuits are ineffectual against the plague. All of the soldiers are already infected. They were able to load the girls onto the dropship, and the automated pilot is returning them back to port. Triel, because of how serious this is, we're going to have to evacuate your medical team and then rematerialize the girls directly into the infirmary once the dropship is close enough. You'll have exactly one hour to cure them both and protect yourself before your air runs out. Afterward, we'll have to charge the room with pharon particles. With a little luck, we'll be able to bring all three of you back."

"Are you sure you can revive the three of us?" Triel asked. "I thought pharon particles were only used in engine decontamination. Even minimal exposure is lethal to most species."

"No, I'm not sure," the admiral said frankly. "But it's the only plan our hazard team came up with. It explains why the Dominion never used the Prodgy to heal their own infected men."

315

Triel looked up to see the medical team already filtering out of the contamination room, and gripped the sides of the exam table to keep herself from succumbing to panic. *I have to save Volkor—and then I have to entrust my health and recovery to those who fear me? (I can't do this.)*

"Admiral," she said. "One condition. I want Bacthar, Reht's surgeon, to be in on this team."

"Triel—"

"I can't do this without knowing he's there."

"Fine, fine. Just get it done, Triel," he said as he terminated the transmission.

Triel sat down on one of the stools and rested her head in her hands, pushing away thoughts of the medical team members observing her from behind the protective glass.

Something between a sigh and a laugh escaped her lips as she realized the irony. She had always fought her father over Prodgy tradition, but now she upheld one of its most sacred tenets: helping others, unconditionally, in spite of what they had done. And she couldn't think of two worse Sentients to face, especially as a Solitary. Regardless of the severity of the disease, the twins couldn't be psychologically balanced. They were Volkor—the mass murderer, the tyrant—the Slaythe. They were exposed to unconscionable evil at a formative age, and they were telepaths, so their minds were already unpredictable to a Healer's touch. Triel realized it would be their emotional turbulence that would destroy her, not their disease.

I have to try. For Reht.

The receiving alarm buzzed above her head, and she snapped to attention.

"Rematerializing in ten seconds," the computer announced.

The blue teleportation fields lit up above each exam bed.

She held her breath.

When the afterglow died away, she took a moment for a visual exam. Immediately she noticed peculiarities. They were listed as identical twins in a triplet set, but minor differences in their height and weight, and in the color of their hair, set them apart. They also appeared physically advanced beyond their ages, especially their lean muscle mass, making her double-check her datapad.

"How old are they supposed to be?" she asked to her medical team through the com system.

"Seven standard years."

"That's impossible," she said under her breath. They looked no younger than their early teens.

"Is there any record of growth manipulation?" she asked the team.

"Inconclusive per report."

"I'd say this is conclusive," she mumbled to herself.

Triel let the scanner finish reading their biosigns. The girl on her left had severe flashfire burns to her thigh and arm, but the one on her right had taken a close proximity blast to the upper right quadrant of her abdomen and sustained a significant head injury. Most importantly, the infection, widespread in both of them, had yet to do any major damage to their systems.

How could their immune system be so developed at their age— and with human lineage? she wondered.

As Triel concluded her initial assessment, she found that her mind couldn't reconcile the twin girls as the dreaded Volkor. *They're so ordinary,* she thought, her mind comparing their peach-smooth faces to the domineering images of the General from the newreels. Without a collection of shiny medals or a towering, authoritative stature, they seemed powerless.

How could they be the ones that masterminded the destruction of my people?

Refocusing herself, Triel sensed that the injuries sustained by the one on her left were more serious and made her way to her bedside.

"I'm starting my internal assessment," she said, checking the biofeed on her arm that relayed her vital signs to the medical team watching safely behind the observation window. With shaky fingers, she tapped the screen. *Is my heart rate really 118?*

Triel hesitated at the bedside of her unconsciousness patient. The steady beeping of her patients' synchronous heart rates and her rapid breathing filled in the silence.

"Hey, Starfox," a jovial voice said over the com. "I got some more soup made up for you, just in case."

Hearing Bacthar's voice, Triel smiled. She picked up a pair of laser scissors and hovered over the patient. "I can do this..."

317

With a deep breath, she cut the clothing off the patient's chest and poised her hands over her sternum and abdomen. Doubt crept into her head: *Gods—I haven't healed anyone in years.*

Thinking back, she realized the last time she performed a full restoration had been on Algar, with her father's aide. *Before I rebelled—before the Scare. Back when my father believed I could be the next Great Mother.*

Triel scorned the idea. *Me, the Great Mother—the spiritual leader of all the Prodgies of Algar. No, I'm the girl who ran away.*

"No," Triel whispered, fighting her uncertainties. "I can do this."

Her breath hitched in her chest as she laid her hands on her patient's bare skin. The warmth surprised her. As she sank deeper into the patient's body, Triel lost sight of the medical bay and gained a better view of the extent of her wounds. The virus was everywhere, crawling through her like an infestation of mites, but as she had noted before, the patient's immune system had definitely slowed its advancement. She needed to know more.

The Healer aligned her mind and body with the host's to begin the restoration. When she dipped farther inside the patient, past the barriers of her physical being, she realized how unprepared she was.

"Triel, your heart rate has doubled. Are you alright?" she heard someone say, but she had gone too deep to respond.

My Gods...

Healing a fellow telepath was always a different experience, as her father had once told her. Non-telepathic minds presented as flat signatures in the psionic spectrum, much like antiquated television screens, making it easy to differentiate host from Healer. But telepathic minds were different. They reacted to the Prodgy mind, creating a new reality, making it almost impossible for the Healer to distinguish between their own identity and that of their host. Whatever afflicted the host, whatever brought them joy or sorrow, affected the Healer as well.

They're just kids—how could they have such complex emotions? she thought as she gazed within the girl's mind. Her patient's life, compounded by the thousands of years of experience absorbed in seven years, aged her beyond any being Triel had ever restored. *I underestimated them...*

Not many of the disjointed memories made sense, giving the Healer only fleeting glimpses of the girl's life. Triel found herself running from a hulking Cerran-humanoid that chased her with a belt, and then dodging the fists of an older child in a Core uniform. She felt afraid and desperate as she entered a Core officer's mind and copied the knowledge she would need to win the games they made her play, and dirty and violated when it was over.

I don't want any of this! the girl cried out.

Being left behind on a market outing left her feeling not only jealous and lonely, but angry at herself. She wept in guilt and rage at the condition of her dirty apartment. Cold, hungry and alone, she sat in the corner of a Dominion cell, ready for death to grant her relief.

The foreign emotions threatened to submerge Triel as she delved deeper, blurring the lines between Healer and patient. Terrible shame and guilt walled her in, entrenching her in its emotional drag as she watched herself force another child laborer into doing her work in the antechamber of the coolant room. *It was only a mistake,* the girl's voice echoed in the back of Triel's mind. She saw the boy's rigid, lifeless body and shuddered. *I never meant to hurt him!*

Another emotion, even stronger than the death of the child laborer, pulled Triel down through the deepest layers of the girl's psyche.

Who is that? Triel wondered, seeing a boy with black hair and blue eyes that lit up his face when he smiled. The girl's bond with him felt warm, safe, and understanding, not unlike the unspoken connection Triel had once shared with her siblings. Conversely, the sense of loss associated with him wrenched her gut, enough to stir up Triel's own memories of her last moments on Algar.

The girl's identical image, her sister, glided in and out of her awareness, a persistent and intense presence throughout the girl's life. She had known other telepathic twins, but she had never encountered such a brilliant connection. Their suffering and the constant battle for survival shaped their relationship, as well as the love that both pulled them together and pushed them apart.

This girl loves and admires her sister, Triel realized, *but there's something more—a carefully guarded fear...*

(What is she so afraid of?)

319

The more Triel experienced this girl, the less she could justify her grudge. She was no worse than any other Sentients she had known—flawed, fallible, culpable—but other qualities shone like a star at the center of her being.

Triel swallowed hard, her heart thudding in her chest, and extended herself. The patient was receptive to her, almost inviting, like a soul reaching for its other half. As she connected, a barrage of images coalesced into a yearning she found all too familiar.

Acceptance and belonging, Triel realized. *And forgiveness.*

Pulling back to a more comfortable distance, the Healer reminded herself of her purpose: *I'm supposed to heal her, not empathize with her.* Strangely, though, she felt less anxious than before, even though she now felt the illness saturating not just her patient, but herself.

Monitors alerted in the distance. *I can't wait any longer—I have to quarantine the virus.*

With considerable exertion she managed to isolate the disease, and as she navigated through the girl's immune system, she discovered the artificial enhancements that had evolved not only her defenses, but her growth pattern. Comparing the two, she realized something peculiar: *The way the virus attacks the body is not unlike the way the patient's immune system marshals the body's defense, as if the same program basics that steer the virus are driving the patient's immune system. This can't be coincidental that the two are so alike. What if they were manufactured by the same designer?*

Triel finished her sweep as quickly as she could. She purged the virus from the girl's body but did not heal her remaining injuries. *Her body will heal itself in no time. I have to move on.*

Triel's vision returned, and she withdrew from the patient's body.

"We've identified the patients," one of the surgeons announced over the intercom. "The one you just treated is Jaeia. The other one is Jetta."

"That's the little stinker, Starfox," Bacthar chimed in.

Triel pinched the webbing between her fingers and turned to her next patient. She guessed that this one—Jetta—must be the driving force behind Volkor.

Even before she laid her hands on the girl, Triel intuited that this would be different from the first healing. Jetta radiated a distinct second shadow, or telepathic aura, and she wasn't sure why.

Maybe she's holding on to a destructive memory or idea, Triel considered. *Or she's maintaining subconscious contact with a dangerous being.*

Her father's teachings came to mind: *"Telepaths sustaining abnormal connections over a long period of time suffer from hallucinations, disorientation, paranoia, and eventually psychosis. You must be centered when you heal these patients, or you could easily Fall."*

I have to protect myself from her, Triel concluded.

Triel cut away the top of her patient's clothing but kept an eye on her unconscious form. Placing her hands in the same position, the Healer expected the warm sensation of gradually sliding inside, but fell straight through.

Oh Gods, Triel exclaimed, preparing for an assault. Instead, she found herself intact with her full faculties.

I have to stay alert—the attack may still come.

After making her initial assessment, noting the patient's wounds and viral invasion, the Healer braced herself for the deeper connection.

This is Volkor, she reminded herself. The potential to commit his atrocities had to have come from somewhere, and she hadn't found that kind of malice in Jaeia's mind.

Triel did not want to touch minds with this one. *I don't want to turn into a Dissembler, not now, after all I've survived.*

(But if I don't help these sisters, who will save us against the Deadwalker army?)

Keeping her essence tightly furled, Triel waded deeper. Without barriers, the Healer spiraled downward to Jetta's core.

That's why, Triel realized, seeing all of the girl's energies directed at a single objective. All else—her memories, emotions, and personality—were ensnared within it.

Triel knew she should simply proceed and heal her patient, but curiosity gave her pause.

Did her essence give rise to Volkor?

If that was the case, the Alliance would have to make do with Jaeia; she couldn't bring herself to heal such a monster.

In the shifting light of her psionic plane, Triel reached out to touch the static sphere that encapsulated Jetta's being. The black surface felt smooth and hard beneath her fingers, stirring up images, sights, and sounds—

Triel screamed as the same hulking humanoid she had seen in Jaeia's mind leapt at her, his belt raising stinging welts on her skin. The Healer pulled back from the horror of the memory, but the sensations continued to resonate in her nerve endings.

Taking a deep breath, she sank back in.

"Jahx, if only you would let me. This could all be over with..." Jetta said as the memory shifted forward. She hurt everywhere, and one of her eyes had swelled shut. Triel could barely lift her head to make out the blurry images. Two children hovered over her, their deep though strained connection pulling the three of them closer than physical contact ever could.

As he held her hand, the dark-haired boy whispered, "No, Jetta, we can't. We can't let ourselves become monsters like him."

Jetta's rage became palpable in Triel's mind, unmitigated by time and completely resolute. Her telepathic abilities flexed with anger, barely kept in check by her siblings.

The old memory dissolved, and a new one wrenched Triel in another direction. Predatory minds surrounded her in a dark forest, closing in on her, their twisted desires creeping into her head, making her skin crawl.

"Pearly—pretty and white—like a brand new," she heard one of them say.

Jetta's reacted instinctively, and caught up in the memory, Triel understood her response all too well. But the things the girl felt—the pleasure in making her assailants suffer the horrors of their own demons, the pure ecstasy of finally letting go of her own anger— horrified the Healer.

This is Volkor. This is the potential the Dominion Core harnessed.

Uprooted again, Triel spun downward into another memory. Broken images of screaming men in Core uniforms flashed past, followed by jarring images of a crash-landing. She saw glimpses of a mutated monster staggering toward her and a Liiker clicking away in a pool of black blood, but they passed too quickly to let her extrapolate any meaning from them. She continued to fall, faster and faster, until she suddenly stopped.

Jetta sat before her, curled up tightly and rocking back and forth, the only thing visible in a world of endless shadow.

(Jahx, where are you Jahx? Please!) *she cried to herself, seemingly unaware of Triel.*

(I must find you—)

(Forgive me, Jahx—)
(I never meant to hurt you)

(To hurt anyone...)

Overcome by emotion, Triel flung herself away, fearing what could result if she stayed too long in a mind as powerful as Jetta's.

With the medical bay bright and solid around her again, Triel took a deep breath to steady herself, trying to understand what she just experienced.

Jahx.

She had seen him in Jaeia's head too. The boy who had become the Liikers' telepathic hub. He was everything to his sisters, but especially to Jetta. There was something very special between Jetta and Jahx, she realized, something so important that Jetta suffered immeasurably from it.

I can't believe it.

And she almost didn't want to. She had convinced herself that the sisters were cold-blooded killers, sociopaths, but her glimpses of their lives, the good and the ugly alike, bespoke something very different.

Jetta is conflicted, Triel recognized. *Her rage is just as strong as her self-hatred for the things she has done.*

Reflecting further, the Healer couldn't ignore the fact that war criminal or not, Jetta wasn't without empathy or love for her family.

Jetta's mind is capable of Volkor's atrocities, Triel thought, *but she is not Volkor.*

The Healer couldn't stop the tears from running down her cheeks. She had spent too many years running and hiding, subsisting on the dwindling hope that she would find an answer for all her

323

suffering. As her convictions dissolved into uncertainty, she realized that she had never really wanted to find peace or forgiveness, or even an answer.

My father would be so ashamed.

When Triel had finished the final purge of the virus, she opened her eyes. Her throat felt scratchy and swollen, and fatigue weighed down on her body, but something deep inside her felt invigorated, though she couldn't pinpoint why.

"You have fifteen minutes left, Triel. Better work on clearing the virus out of your own body before your air runs out," one of the infectious disease doctors reminded her.

Triel stumbled over to an empty bed and lay down. Looking within herself, the Healer concentrated her energies from head to toe, gradually forcing the infection from her body in a foul-smelling sweat that discharged from her pores. When she was through, she signaled the team to release the pharon particles. The overhead lights dimmed, and she closed her eyes. She wasn't as worried now about what would happen next, even though she knew her chances of survival were slim.

I wasn't expecting any of that, she thought. Tears fell from her eyes as conflicting feelings of disappointment and relief took away her control.

***

Admiral Unipoesa ordered the medical team to revive Triel prematurely so he could get a full report. Sitting on the end of her infirmary bed, pale and shaky, the Healer tried to field all of his questions about the Kyron sisters.

"Why do they look like they're young adults? I thought they were kids."

"I think the Motti tampered with the twins' hormone regulation and immune system in order to convert them into Liikers," she said, concentrating on every word. "But more disturbing is its link to the plague on Tralora—the plasmids have identical signature sequences. It's the same designer DNA."

The admiral stared at her blankly.

"Look," she said, "a plasmid is a little loop of DNA that the engineers use to insert new genes into a host. They build a certain sequence into the DNA that's like the designer's trademark. Not hard to find if you're looking for it."

"So the twins' 'alterations' and the plague were manufactured by the same designer?"

"I believe so."

"What does this mean?" The admiral said. Triel sensed his trouble hiding his emotions from her. *His Rai Shar is not as practiced as the others.*

"Given what happened to the girls and what I saw coded into the virus, I'm guessing that the Motti were testing a mass conversion method on the Narki, though they sold it to the Dominion under a different pretense. If the Motti betrayed the Core, they would need a fast means for converting all those soldiers. I think the plague on Tralora is the key."

"I thought that plague was sent to destroy the Narki," the admiral said.

Triel shook her head. "If the Narki hadn't tried to treat it, I think it would have solely affected the neural pathways in their nucleus accumbens and the anterior insula, the parts of the brain responsible for decision making, putting them in a type of state of susceptibility, almost like a stupor. Reht would say they would have turned into zombies."

"He can't know of this, of course. This is strictly classified information," the admiral reminded her.

Triel sighed and pulled her blanket more tightly around her shoulders. "I know you're going to imprison me after all this is done. And you'll tell me it's for 'my safety.'"

The admiral tried not to break eye contact. "That's not at all what I want, Triel. You're too young to be so cynical."

"I'm nineteen, but don't let my age fool you. I'm almost as old as those girls I treated today."

The admiral lifted an eyebrow.

"It's a telepath thing. It's termed 'cumulative age,' at least for Healers. We take on certain elements of the host when we restore them, and it adds to our mental age. Something similar has happened to Jetta and Jaeia. All those foreign memories, and the knowledge they've taken—it really adds up. They certainly aren't seven years old."

The admiral sighed. "I can agree with you there."

"My advice," she said, leaning forward. "Don't treat them like launnies."

The admiral chuckled. "Don't worry, I don't intend to."

"One more thing," Triel said as the admiral got up to leave. "Don't lie or tell them half-truths, okay?"

The admiral paused at the treatment room door. "Why do you think I would do such a thing?"

"Because that's what you think you have to do sometimes, isn't it?"

The admiral didn't respond.

"Lying is the worst thing you could do to them," Triel said. "You have no idea what you're dealing with."

"Triel," the admiral said, typing a code into the door keypad. "Get some rest. You're not done yet."

***

Jetta could barely open her eyes. The intense light from above made them burn. Voices exchanged relieved sentiments as she stirred more vigorously.

"One milligram of epidyaphrine," said a weary female voice.

Something pricked her arm, and a powerful rushing sensation filled her chest. Her blood pounded in her fingers and toes and roared in her ears.

"Good, good, not too much though—yes, there. Keep her systolic pressure at 165 for now. I know it's a little high, but I don't want her crashing below fifty again. I'm going to make one more pass at that abdominal wound again. Monitor my vitals."

A warm presence encased her body. It wasn't intrusive, but it was still somewhat unnerving as it intently searched her viscera.

(I have to, for Reht, for my friends,)

(Father—)

(My family is dead.)

(They do not deserve my help)

(I know what Volkor is…)

It hovered over the upper quadrant of her abdomen for a moment and then dissolved. The presence was gone.

"I think it's finally closing."

"Triel, are you alright?"

Jetta heard the unspoken words: *I am so tired...*

"I'm fine. I just wasn't expecting the admiral to want a total restoration. Look, can you finish patching the job?"

Something cool was laid over her forehead. For the first time in a long while, she felt completely relaxed. She stopped struggling to open her eyes.

***

When Jetta woke again, her eyes adjusted more quickly. Despite the halos around the overhead lights, she made out a man in a lab coat exchanging dataclips with someone dressed in a sterile gown. Panic flared in her chest as she realized she was no longer on Tralora but in some sort of hospital or medical bay.

"You're alright, you're alright," an attendant said, rushing to her side.

She ignored him and propped herself up on her elbow to take a better look at her surroundings. Head still swimming, Jetta discerned gray and white walls lined with medical equipment. She could see the end of another table to her right, but a divider curtain obstructed her view. A humanoid man stood next to her, still trying to make her lay back down, but he didn't seem threatening, so she continued to disregard him.

Jaeia, where are you? she projected. Reaching into their bond, Jetta felt her sister near, but her thoughts looping in the sinuous patterns of sleep.

Wake up, she called to her sister. *We're in danger!*

"Gods," Jetta said, rubbing her forehead. Her head felt like it was splitting in two.

A tall, slender woman entered the room. Dark hair spilled over broad shoulders. The indigo markings winding their way down the fair skin of her neck and forearms terminated on the palms of her hands. "Please, lie back down."

The woman's piercing blue eyes immediately connected with Jetta's, and her heart leapt into her throat. Jetta bit back the strange wave of emotion, reminding herself that she and her sister weren't safe.

"Who are you?"

"My name is Triel. I'm a Prodgy Healer from Algar."

Jetta looked at her skeptically while inner shadows stirred up frenetic whispers. She knew without wanting to know that every last Prodgy had been captured or killed by the Dominion. Even so, the woman bore the marks and possessed a strong enough psionic signature to upset her concentration.

"I'm part of the rescue team that helped get you off of Tralora. You've made a remarkable recovery, but you'll still need more treatment. The extent of your injuries has slowed down your recovery process. I'd like to continue to treat you, but I'll need your cooperation."

Jetta scrunched up the bed sheets in her hands. She didn't like that the echo of the woman's thoughts felt so familiar.

(She's been inside me!)

"What do you want? Where is Jaeia?" Jetta asked, feeling the site of her injury with her free hand. The wound had closed, but it was still hot to touch.

"We only want to help. Jaeia's fine. I expect her to be up and about in less than an hour."

"What about the others? Did you help the others?"

The blue-eyed woman looked confused, and there was no sense of deception in her thoughts. "There were no others, Jetta."

Jetta lay back down and tried to think, but her head still ached. *What had happened to the Exiles?*

"Are you in any pain?" Triel asked, walking alongside her bed and picking up a bioscanner. The sight triggered an immediate terror that seized her mind.

"Hail Volkor"—

Yellow hands,

"—There's too much resistance—we need more—"

(If I win, the pain will go away)

"—long live the sovereignty"

Jetta slapped the instrument out of the woman's hand and rolled off the table.

"I need some help in here," Triel shouted. Jetta staggered backward, lashing out at anybody that approached.

It took only seconds for several guards to charge in and tackle her, holding her down by the arms and legs. A booster jammed into her side, and she bucked away from the pain, but the fast-acting medication rendered her muscles useless. She struggled until everything went black.

***

Triel was working on closing the wound on Jaeia's thigh when a hand touched hers. She broke contact and looked around, but the other staff members were milling around the terminals, downloading the data they had collected about the twins.

The Healer looked down at her patient, and two feather-gray eyes stared back at her. Triel felt her trepidation, but also her outreach.

"You're okay," Triel whispered, trying not to alert the other staff members. "My name is Triel. I'm a Prodgy Healer."

Jaeia's eyes darted back and forth, and the question seemed obvious to her even without her telepathy.

"She's fine, and so are you. I managed to purge the virus from your body."

Even though Jaeia seemed to relax a little, her voice remained shaky and strained. "Where are we?"

"This is an Alliance ship. You're safe."

"Please..." she began, but her eyes rolled to the back of her head. Feeling her pulse, Triel sensed that the girl was still too weak to have recovered all of her faculties yet, but she admired her persistence. "Please... my back pocket... friends..."

Triel bit her lip, but in the end she placed her hand on Jaeia's forehead and saw the meaning behind her words. Fortunately the staff was so caught up in analyzing the twins' unusual physiological readings that they had yet to search their clothes and personal possessions. Whatever Jaeia thought was so critical, Triel would have a chance to see first. If the object was as important as Jaeia's thoughts suggested, possessing it would give her tremendous leverage with both the Alliance and the two girls.

329

Triel slid her hand cautiously underneath Jaeia's injured thigh and felt around until she found a small cylinder and an oblong object of about the same size wrapped carefully in the folds of her clothes. Triel transferred the two pieces into her shirtsleeve and slowly withdrew her arm.

"Your progress, Triel?"

The doctor caught her unawares, but a brief brush with his mind confirmed that he did not detect her theft.

"Jetta is fine, just under heavy sedation. She's ready to be revived at your discretion. Jaeia needs some minor dermabonding, but your technology can take care of that. I'd like to rest now and restore myself."

Not seeming especially interested in her well-being, the doctor dismissed her.

Triel sighed, falling in step with her escorts as she made her way back to her assigned quarters. To her surprise, they let Bacthar catch up and walk with her.

"Hey—you doing okay?"

She smiled weakly and nodded. "Yes, just really tired. Could you stop by later and bring me some soup? Nothing works better than a home remedy."

Bacthar flicked his ears in response. He might not have been telepathic, but he'd gotten the message. "Sure thing, Starfox. That okay with you, boys?"

The guards didn't break their gaze. "You'll need security clearance from the admiral."

"Of course," chirped Bacthar. He wrapped his wing around her and touched his forehead to hers. "I'll see you later, alright?"

After Bacthar walked away, one of the guards snickered. "We want to know something."

Triel didn't bother to turn around, but they continued on anyway.

"Do you consider yourself a hero or a traitor?"

Triel palmed the keypad to her quarters but didn't step through when the doors slid open. "Why do you care?"

The guard smirked. "It's a philosophical—"

"No, ethical, *dumbchak*," the other muttered.

"*Ethical* question. Does saving the last remaining telepaths, even though they murdered Prodgies, make you a hero—or a traitor?"

In the back of her mind she saw the blackened sky as the Core ships entered Algar's atmosphere.

We are unarmed—why are they attacking? she wondered. She remembered her father's words: *"Stay, Triel. Be patient. We have survived this long. We are a peaceful people. There will be no need for bloodshed."*

"*Oh, father—we have to run!*"

"*Triel, you must obey!*"

Her father fell first, then her mother. The crush of soldiers prevented her from seeing what happened to her siblings, but she could feel their anguish in her mind. Someone tried to take her, to put her in a freezer case, but she fought just as she always had.

As she ran toward the hills, she turned to see Volkor's face already infecting their village. The Slaythe, painted on each of the Core flags, proclaimed another conquest. She watched helplessly as the Dominion ships took off with a cargo bay full of freezer cases—her village, her family, her life.

It didn't stopped there. Volkor followed her everywhere, mocking her with his martial gaze and perverse slogans of peace on every banner, flag, and newsreel as she fled across the galaxy, trying to escape his reach.

Triel started to hyperventilate. Those girls massacred her family, stolen everything she loved, and she saved their lives.

How could I have saved them? she thought. *No matter what else they are, they are still capable of genocide.*

(They could easily murder again.)

"No," she whispered, her fingers curling into fists. She remembered her father's words, though they were equally as painful: *It is not our place to judge.*

(I promised to make Volkor pay!)

"No," she repeated.

"No, what?"

"I don't consider myself either. I am just a Healer."

"Just another leech," one of them mumbled.

Inside her room, she fell to her knees.

I was wrong, she realized. *Inside of them is all the wickedness of the Dominion Core.*

(How can I forgive them?)

Pain throbbed inside her skull as she crawled over to her bed and laid a hand across her forehead.

What have I done?

***

One look at the nurse checking over her vitals and Jetta saw her chance.

A Sandscrat. I remember them from street fights on Fiorah.

The three-legged desert walkers had hardened skin and spiny tentacles, but their weakness lay in natural split in the dermal armor by their neck. With the edge of her hand she chopped at the sensitive opening of jugular venous junction. She caught the nurse by his armpits as he blacked out, easing him down while she slipped over the medical table to the ground. The guards by the door stood with their backs to the scene, distracted by their own conversation, allowing Jetta enough time to silently communicate to her sister.

Get ready.

Creeping toward the two guards, Jetta stayed low as they laughed at a dirty joke. Behind the exam curtain, Jaeia cried out, drawing their attention. As the guards moved toward her sister, she leapt out from behind and cracked their heads together.

Jetta briefly regarded the two unconscious guards before undressing them. *(I'm making the same mistakes all over again.)*

"Hey," Jaeia said, jumping off the table and joining her side. Her sister frowned as Jetta put her legs through the soldier's long pant-leg and cinched the belt tightly above her hips. "This isn't a great cover."

"It's better than nothing."

"Jetta," Jaeia said, looking around nervously, "I'm missing my clothes—I need my clothes."

Jetta shook her head. "What? Who cares? Come on, we don't have much time."

"I had... I swear I put the device..." Jaeia mumbled to herself.

"Jaeia, get it together! Get on that terminal and draw up some maps of this place."

"What are we going to do, Jetta?" Jaeia said, pressing her palms to her eyes. "Capture their commander and hold him hostage?"

Jetta grinned. "Wow—didn't think you had it in you."

Jaeia crossed her arms across her chest. "Are you seriously considering that? We don't know anything about our situation."

Haven't you learned anything? Jetta thought, shoving her aside.

Using the codes she gleaned off the guards, Jetta unlocked the computer. "From what the guards said, I'm thinking that we're on deck nine, and judging by the layout and size, I would guess the senior quarters are on deck fourteen, in forward wing. I would bet anything that the commander of this ship is here," Jetta said, pointing to the blue screen. "Searching for a com signal... Yeah, someone's there."

"Wait—let's consider our situation. Someone went through a lot of trouble to save us," Jaeia said, putting a hand on her shoulder.

Jetta petulantly jerked away from her sister's touch. "We're two against a warship right now. If we don't take charge now we'll be screwed."

The concept silently processed between them, but despite Jaeia's reservations, she didn't have the nerve to oppose Jetta.

She's weak, Jetta thought to herself. She hated herself for thinking it, but she couldn't deny the truth. "Get that soldier's uniform on, Jae. Hurry."

Jetta and Jaeia exited the medical bay in the oversized uniforms and helmets, marching in sync. They caught the eye of several passing auxiliary crewmen, but when they tried to access the lift, the guard stationed in the corridor ordered them to halt.

"You two—stop right there! Show some identification!"

Ignoring the guard, Jetta hurried her sister into the lift and flipped the switch to shut the doors.

"He's altered the mechanics of the lift," Jaeia pointed out as the lights on the control panel blinked out.

Anticipating this, Jetta jumped on her sister's shoulders to unscrew the top hatch.

"Hold still!" Jetta snapped at her sister.

With the hatch unscrewed, they swung onto the top of the lift, and Jetta sealed the hatch shut with the multiphasic handgun on her uniform belt.

333

Jetta looked up and cringed. The metal-plated lift shaft reminded her of the old air ducts on Fiorah, right down to the smell of oil and rust that carried in the circulated breeze. The memory made her stomach knot, but she pushed it aside to focus on the objective.

She jumped onto the nearest maintenance ladder, the yellow glow of the emergency lights guiding her ascent.

This is it. It's the second door on the right, and I think I saw two biosignals outside the commander's door. Ready? Jetta asked as they clung to the walls outside deck fourteen's access door.

Without waiting for her sister's response, Jetta hit the sensor of the access door. The locks released, and as soon as the doors parted, Jetta shot the two guards from their vantage point inside the lift shaft. When she saw the look on Jaeia's face, she rolled her eyes.

"They're fine, they're gonna make it. I didn't kill them," Jetta said, trying to coax her sister out of the shaft.

(I am doing it again. I am acting out of aggression.)

(Why can't I stop?)

Jetta ran down the corridor and turned her attention to the keypad on the commander's door.

"This is a Forrey keypad, like the ones to the supply closets on the mining ships. I can't believe they would use this cheap *meitka* on a warship," Jetta said, chuckling to herself.

Galm taught them how to bypass a Forrey when they were only three years old. Yahmen would order them to do work that required the use of certain tools but wouldn't permit them access to the closets where the tools were stored. The only way they could complete their tasks on time was to break in, use the tools, and then discreetly return them.

Jetta struck the plate of the keypad with the butt of her gun. The metal border bent out of shape, and she pried the rest of it away to expose the internal wiring. Pinching the orange, red, and indigo lines with her thumb and forefinger, Jetta cut the black and beige wires with the metal border from the keypad and cross-wired them. The commander's door slowly slid open.

"Still got it," Jetta grinned.

After pushing Jaeia inside, Jetta fired at the keypad and jumped into the room. The doors clanked shut behind them, the sensor relay fizzling as it shorted out.

Frying the lock will give us some time, Jetta relayed to her twin. In the distance, alert sirens wailed. *But soldiers will be here soon to pry open the door.*

Spotting the officer waking in his bed, Jetta rushed over and pounced on top of him, holding him at gunpoint.

"Please," the officer asked, putting up his hands in surrender. Jetta pushed him back down on the bed and clicked the gun's safety setting off.

"You've got one chance. We want answers, now—and no *chakking* around," Jetta demanded, pressing the gun into his sternum.

To Jetta's surprise, an almost imperceptible smile curled the corners of the officer's lips. It wasn't an expression of cheap overconfidence, nor was it a preamble to a lie.

"I should have put up more guards."

Jetta ripped off her helmet and got in his face. "Now, who the hell are you and where are the Exiles? If you don't answer fast enough, I'll start by vaporizing your digits," Jetta said, slowly pulling back her gun to point at his feet.

Please, Jaeia called out silently as she approached the bedside. Holding her gun in her hand, but not taking aim, her sister tried to reason with her. *We don't have to use violence, Jetta.*

The officer shifted uncomfortably as he carefully worded his response. "I am first-class Admiral Damon Unipoesa of the Starways Alliance Fleet, formerly known as the United Starways Coalition. I am here because the Motti are poisoning our planets and our people. They're moving their Liikers into our Homeworld territories, where eighty percent of the Sentient population resides. Our commanders can do nothing to slow the attack. We need your help. As for any other survivors—there was no one else to rescue."

Jetta's stomach dropped. *Did I kill all the Exiles?*

Jaeia tried to tell her something, but Jetta pushed her sister and her own guilt from her mind.

"Why us?" Jetta persisted, pressing her knee into the admiral's stomach.

"Jetta—" Jaeia started, but couldn't find the voice to finish.

Jetta didn't move her knee or change the pressure. Unipoesa's face contorted, and he grunted in pain. "Because I know—*I know* how good you are," he said, voice barely above a whisper. "I studied your tactics during the Dominion Wars and commanded the fleet at the Raging Front."

Unipoesa's stomach spasmed, and Jetta felt her sister's hand on her shoulder.

"Jetta, enough," Jaeia said, this time more insistently. "At least let him breathe."

With her sister's presence easing her mind, Jetta let up on the pressure just enough to let Unipoesa catch his breath.

Calmer, Jetta tilted her head to the side, allowing herself to see the situation through Jaeia's eyes. He was telling the truth, or at least he thought he was, but his mind was carefully organized, tightly sealed. *He's trained in talking to telepaths.*

"Hey," Jaeia whispered, tilting her head at the door. The security team cracked the door open a few centimeters. Someone shouted commands to cut through the lock mechanism. *We're running out of time.*

Jetta grabbed Unipoesa by the collar. "Don't you know who I am?"

"Yes, I do," the admiral replied calmly.

"Doesn't that make you nervous?"

"You're not General Volkor. Your talents were exploited and you were abused. What happened to you on the Dominion starships was not your fault."

Jetta let go of him. "I never wanted to hurt anyone—and I never wanted to kill—but I find myself doing it over and over again. Tell me I'm not a monster. Tell me that I won't destroy you like I can."

There it is... she heard Jaeia think.

Fragments of Jaeia's memory flashed through Jetta's mind: A conversation with Jahx where he issued her a warning. A shaky reassurance from the Grand Oblin. Jaeia was worried about her, afraid of confronting her, but it went farther than that.

My own sister...

A shot fired past Jetta's shoulder and blasted away a chunk of the far wall.

"Cease fire!" Admiral Unipoesa shouted. Guards burst into the room, rifles pointed in their direction. Jetta kept her gun trained on the admiral as the guards shouted for her to back down.

"Jetta," Jaeia whispered, "give them your weapon."

The words cut through Jetta with icy betrayal. *Why are you always taking our captors' side?*

(I should use my talent...)

"Give them your weapon."

This time when Jaeia said it, Jetta felt it. The urge was unmistakable, unthinkable. Jetta relinquished her weapon, but it was not of her own will.

How could you use your second voice on me? Jetta projected, letting her sister feel all of her rage as she held up her hands. *That is unforgivable.*

Jaeia didn't say anything, nor did she look her in the eye as the guards patted them down

"I'm sorry it has to be this way," the admiral said, bracing his stomach. "I wanted this to go peacefully. I just hope we can talk again soon."

Jetta did not reply, but she cast him a warning look as the guards escorted them out.

You never listen to me, Jaeia thought as the soldiers led them away.

Jetta could barely contain herself. *You betrayed me. You betray us. I'm trying to get us out of here, and you're groveling at their feet. They're just going to use us like everybody else!*

You left me no choice, Jetta. Stop being unreasonable and think. We don't know everything—maybe by helping them, we can help ourselves.

Jetta clenched her fists. Angry as she was, she couldn't help but consider her sister's viewpoint. However, if the Alliance needed their help badly enough to risk rescuing them off of Tralora, then they must be in dire straits—and therefore at her mercy.

That's not what I meant, Jaeia commented after hearing her sister's train of thought.

"Always the idealist," Jetta muttered, trying to block her out.

As they boarded a lift, Jetta thought back to the way she felt in the Admiral's quarters with her emotions running high. *Invincible. I could do anything.*

(I should use my talent again—)

Despite her efforts to keep her sister at bay, Jaeia overheard her, or at least sensed the direction of her thoughts. *Jetta—please, I need you. Giving in to your talent means giving up. Don't give up. Not on me, and not on yourself.*

Jetta bit her lip hard enough that she tasted blood. *No,* she resolved. *I will not keep making the same mistakes. I won't lose control of myself.*

The dark underpinnings of her talent shuddered and stirred. The blood in her veins turned to fire, her fears forgotten.

No, she promised herself with new confidence. *I will fight for my brother and sister, no matter what the cost.*

Nothing in the Starways would stop her. Even if it meant her own life.

***

The Alliance thinks they can imprison us in here? Jetta mused as she surveyed the holding cells in the detention center, each filled with cozy furnishings and environmental controls. *We'll dismantle the furniture for weapons and tools, and access the electrical paneling for—*

Jaeia nixed her stream of thought before it evolved too far. *You've gotten us into enough trouble as it is.*

Before she could retort, the lewd jeers and whistles from the nearest cell diverted her attention.

"Hey, sweets, why don't you and me take that private cell over there?"

The familiar voice stopped Jetta in her tracks.

"Keep moving," the escort said behind her, pushing the muzzle of his gun into her back. Jetta shot the guard a sidelong glare but continued to the cell directly across from the obnoxious duo that continued to harass them.

"I know you," Jetta said as she came closer to the twosome. The one with black and gold hair stuck out his tongue in a vulgar fashion, and the other let out a shrill laugh. "You were in the underground bar on Fiorah."

A few of their cellmates also triggered her memory, especially the massive Talian whose wary silver eyes fixed on her.

"Pardon my crew."

A scraggly dog-soldier swaggered out from behind the others. Jetta remembered the captain immediately, and a strange mix of

338

feelings stirred in her stomach. When she saw him she remembered Fiorah and all they had left behind. The terrible heat, the choke of the mines. The child laborers, the laborminders—Yahmen. And then her breath caught in her chest: *Galm and Lohien.* She wasn't prepared for the rush of guilt, and she dug her nails into her palms to keep herself from breaking her step.

The dog-soldier captain seemed surprised at their appearance, eyeing their abnormal musculature with suspicion. "Little Jetta— when I met you, you were barely waist high. Now look at you—and your sister."

Jetta paused before joining her twin in the opposing compartment. One of the guards shoved her inside and activated the cell shield.

"Hey, be kind to the ladies, chump."

"Eat it, Jagger," the guard replied. Reht waved him off.

"We waited over two hours for you, you know," the dog-soldier captain said, cleaning his teeth with his nails.

"We didn't have a chance," Jetta said.

Reht nodded, as if he understood.

"Want off this *yaketo*?" he asked. Jetta didn't know the foreign word, but she guessed the meaning. "You're not their prisoners, you know."

His voice escalated as he eyed the nearest guard. "Even though they're interrogating my crew for no *chakking* reason!"

The guard ignored him.

"What are you suggesting?" Jaeia replied cautiously.

His statements are too calculated, Jetta thought. *He's planning something.*

Reht spread his arms and looked around at his crew. "I happen to have a ship, and a rather fine crew. Besides, your sister joined you all up on Fiorah, and a deal's a deal. Do you know what happens when someone cheats me? Ro, Cray—show 'em."

The pair pretended to gut each other and pull out their entrails. Jaeia turned away, sickened, but Jetta grinned.

"Well, what'll it be?" Reht asked, slouching down onto a bench.

Jetta listened to her sister's thoughts; despite everything she said earlier about listening and being patient, she felt nervous too. Being aboard a military warship made them feel like captives again, and the prospect of fighting another war for a foreign government was all too similar to their experience with the Dominion Core.

Still, the idea of leaving didn't sit any better. The risk of traveling with dog-soldiers didn't scare her—they survived alongside worse types on Fiorah.

The dog-soldiers might not have the resources to help us find Jahx.

Jaeia's sorrow touched her mind. *He's gone, Jetta. You have to start thinking about our survival.*

Gods, what if she's right? Jetta thought, squeezing her hands together as her sister's conviction subjugated her reason. *What if Jahx is dead? Then I'm just putting us in danger yet again.*

Confliction tearing her in two, Jetta finally acknowledged the ugly truth of her situation: *I can't keep hurting my sister.*

(I have to let go of Jahx.)

"Please, Jetta," Jaeia whispered. "I need you."

As she turned to her sister and reached for her hand, something terrible pierced her mind's eye.

A serpentine shadow uncoiled at the edges of her awareness, strangling her from the inside out, drawing her down, blotting out everything around her until she was swallowed by complete darkness. Frenzied voices cried out around her, clawing at her mind and shutting out all outside thought.

Only pain existed in this place. Jetta's body transmuted into a cavernous wound filled with poisonous rage, numb to herself, blinded, captive in the swell of the shadow. Her reach, her powers, became infinite, her desires insatiable, as a deep throb inside her drove her to see out the weak and malleable.

(I am the monster—)

***

Mantri Sebbs talked to himself to keep from going mad. Without the comfort of his hourly methoc or the familiarity of his usual haunts, the doom that awaited stared him in the face.

"You'll be okay, Mantri," he mumbled to himself. "You'll go crazy before the Deadwalkers storm the prison and render you down for parts. Then everything will be just fine."

"Sebbs, on your feet."

His cell door slid open, and blinding light from the hall flooded his compartment. He shielded his eyes, but the guards grabbed him by the arms and dragged him out of his cell.

"Please—I—whatever you want—" he begged.

"Mantri, we need your help."

He rubbed the sting out of his eyes and gaped. *Minister Tidas Razar?*

"W-what could you possibly need from me?" he asked.

The Minister appeared bleary-eyed and unshaven. His hands shook, and he tried to mask it by clasping them behind his back. "You are the only one who had direct access to the Dominion database before it was corrupted. I want all of your intel on the Kyron twins—we have to convince them to take command of the legions or we're as good as Liiker feed."

"Yeah, I know things," Mantri said, "but what difference does it make? You told me that you didn't need help from a junkie."

The grim look in Razar's eyes gave Sebbs reason enough even before the Minister handed him a datapad with a loaded video recording.

"What's this?

"This is from yesterday," Razar said, hitting the play button.

A league of battleships smoldered in the background as a hardened Alliance General pled with the Military Minister on the holosims. "My men are abandoning their posts. Li can't keep control—the Deadwalkers are everywhere!"

The general's image faded in and out as the Liiker-controlled Dominion ships crossed over into regulated territories.

"Come again, Command? We need orders—we can't hold the borders much longer—"

The Liiker scramblers garbled the rest of the message, but Sebbs heard his scream just before the transmission ended.

"I don't have time for games, Sebbs," the Minister said, zooming in over a photograph of a converted Dominion ship attacking a satellite station. Black veins branched out over the warship's hull, and pulsating tumors bulged out of broken windows. "You either help us or not."

Mantri almost pissed himself thinking of the nightmare creatures crawling around within the rotting womb of the ship, severing limbs from their living captives, draining their blood—

341

The Deadwalkers are coming—they'll skin me alive and eat my soul—

(There isn't enough methoc in the world to save me—)

"Alright, I'll help you!"

"Lieutenant," Razar shouted to the nearest soldier. "Get this man on the fastest cruiser we have to intercept the *Gallegos.*"

***

Jetta awoke in the medical bay again, this time with a score of guards lining the room. The blue-eyed Healer stood in the far corner reviewing a file, but when Jetta lifted her head she looked up.

"How are you feeling?" the Healer asked, approaching cautiously.

"Fine," Jetta muttered, rubbing her temples. *What happened?* she thought.

It slowly came back to her. She chose survival over Jahx. That's when the nightmare completely took over her consciousness, this time thrusting her into the heart of the malicious evil that pervaded that realm.

I became suffering, she remembered, gripping the ends of the exam table.

Confusion mixed with fear, bringing tears to her eyes. *Was that Jahx? What was he trying to tell me?*

(He's in danger—something is hurting him.)

(I was wrong. I can't give up on my brother.)

"You blacked out in the detention quarters," the Healer said as she ran a bioscanner over her head. "The medical team ran a scan on you but couldn't find anything wrong. However," the Healer said, trailing off and biting her lip, "since it was obvious something happened, they wanted me to evaluate you, but I'm in no condition for that now. So, I'm hoping you'll share your experience with me."

Jetta looked at her, and into her. During their first encounter she had been too weak to get much of an impression of the Healer, but now the emotions the Healer tried to mask were blatantly evident.

She's afraid of me, Jetta felt. Worse yet, the Healer's anxieties laced into strongly guarded contempt. *Why does she want to help me?*

342

"I'm fine," Jetta repeated. "I want to rejoin my sister."

"Very well," Triel sighed, returning to her study station. "Take her back to the detention cell."

Jetta held up a hand to halt the guard. Something about the Healer kept her from going—a mix of curiosity, sorrow, and an attraction she didn't understand.

"Why do you want to help us, Healer?" she asked.

The Healer stopped what she was doing. She did not look at Jetta, but concentrated on her words as she spoke.

"There are those who believe that you and your sister are the only ones who can save in the Starways. It's in everyone's best interests to keep you as healthy as possible."

"You're not telling me the whole truth."

"And you're not telling *me* the whole truth," Triel retorted, whirling around to face her. As silence passed between them, Jetta listened as closely as she could to the Healer's protected thoughts.

"Do you... want to hurt me?" Jetta asked.

To her surprise, the woman looked away. She traced the blue markings on her hands for a moment before responding. "Do you want the truth?"

Jetta wasn't sure, but the Healer didn't give her a chance to decide.

"I'm not sure of you yet. There are things about you—what you know, what you've done—that make it hard to tell..."

"Hard to tell what?" Jetta interrupted.

Triel sighed. "What you did before wasn't your fault, I suppose. But what you can do now... that's up to you. And I'm not sure what you're capable of."

Jetta flushed. She wrestled with her emotions, trying to hide them, but the Healer tore open an old wound. "You have no idea what I'm capable of," Jetta whispered, lowering her eyes.

After a long silence, Triel cleared her throat. "I do want to help you. I know you won't believe me, but I do. But right now I only know what you did, not who you are. If you would just share with me—"

Jetta cut her off. "Just let me go."

"Take her away," Triel sighed.

Before she could respond, the Healer gathered her things and walked out of the medical bay, leaving only a lingering trail of sadness and disappointment. With a heavy heart, Jetta slid off the table and quietly followed the guards back to the detention quarters.

***

To Jetta's surprise, Admiral Unipoesa invited them to a formal dinner in his quarters. He had painstakingly arranged for authentic Fiorahian foods to be served, hoping that they would relax with familiarity.

I can't remember eating anything other than food rations and welfare handouts, Jaeia remarked as they took their seats at the table.

Jetta silently agreed. If Yahmen hadn't tortured them by eating extravagant dinners while they nursed empty bellies, they wouldn't have recognized the dishes at all.

Inwardly, Jetta delighted in how uncomfortable the fare made Admiral Unipoesa. Fiorahian cuisine was created to please the palates of crime lords and junkies, which were anything but delicate. The spread consisted mainly of meat, some of it raw, accompanied by overly sweetened deserts that pleased only those whose tastes were dulled by years of habitual smoking.

"Oh Gods," the admiral said, pushing himself away from the table. He looked a little green after trying to cut through the stuffed yamb's heart and nicking an artery. Coagulated blood and squirming yellow heartworms spilled onto the table.

"You're supposed to shave the heart with the edge of your knife," Jetta said, flicking away some of the worms with her knife.

"I see," the Admiral said, taking a big swallow of water. "Clearly my knowledge of Fiorahian cuisine is undernourished."

"Technically, so is ours," Jaeia said.

"I was hoping that we could discuss your stay," Unipoesa said, regaining his composure.

"We want off this ship," Jetta said.

Jaeia's disapproving thoughts rang in the back of her mind. *You'd trust a pack of criminals over the Alliance?*

I don't see the difference. They both have their own agendas, but it'll be a lot easier to handle a few mercenaries over a Fleet. Besides, I'm sure Jahx is still alive, Jetta reminded her sister. *There is no argument.*

"It's not advisable. You're needed here," the Admiral said.

344

"What makes you think we want to fight your wars?"

Admiral Unipoesa straightened his uniform and nodded toward the entryway. "I invited a guest to join us."

When the guards opened the doors, a haggard man stumbled inside. Despite his sunken eyes and sickly yellow skin, they recognized him immediately. The cocky attitude and pretense from his days in service of the Dominion Core had vanished, and he stood before them twitching nervously.

"Mantri, please join us," the admiral said as a guard brought another seat to the table.

The old methoc junkie sat between Jetta and the admiral, fumbling with his hands, unable to decide whether to put them in his lap or on the table. Finally, he reached into his pocket and withdrew a pack of illegal cigarettes. Digging into the carton, he offered them around.

"How the hell did you manage to get those things? I can't let you smoke here," the admiral exclaimed.

Sebbs looked at him with pathetic desperation until Unipoesa finally rolled his eyes and waved a hand in permission.

"Why did you bring him here?" Jetta demanded. The sight of him disgusted her, and she shoved her seat back from the table to avoid the smoke that rolled toward her as he lit up.

"He knows a lot about the two of you. He was the one that alerted us to where you were located and the true nature of your imprisonment on the Dominion ships."

The corner of Sebbs's lips turned up in an unsure half-smile.

"Sebbs," Unipoesa said, motioning for him to speak. Jetta and Jaeia stared at the disheveled man until the narcotizing effects of the laced cigarette took hold, and he found his voice.

In half-mumbled words he told them about his side job selling insider information to Reht, and Reht's loose connection with the growing rebellion on Trigos. He described the dangerous discovery he made after getting an officer high and hacking into the Dominion database.

He paused, nervously patting himself down for something he could not find. Running his hand through his hair, Sebbs cursed under his breath and continued, telling them how he figured out they were supposed to have been terminated, but that the orders had been tampered with, resulting in their exile.

345

Jetta pressed the tips of her fingers into the prongs of a fork, but anger blotted out the pain. "You believe this junkie?" Jaeia glanced her way but didn't challenge her. "Did he sell you this *meitka* so he could buy his next pinch? What else is he hiding?"

"You little—" Sebbs started, but Unipoesa interceded.

"Captain Sebbs underwent considerable risk to bring us this information. Here is something else he acquired that I'm sure you'll be interested in."

The admiral cleared his throat and slid a datapad across the table. Jaeia stared straight ahead, listening to Jetta's internal voice as she read the translated letter:

My dearest children—

With this letter comes a thousand apologies. I know I've let you down right from the very beginning. Yahmen's kept me alive all these years to shield himself from harm's way, and because I took you in, you were forced to share my burden.

The most important part of this letter is the truth which I have kept from you. I feared that if Yahmen were to discover your true beginnings, he would sell or kill you. Despite what I told him, your mother was not a streetwalker. After many months and many unmentionable deals, I bought you from a drifter who picked up your escape pod in deep space. Somebody went to a lot of trouble to save you. There were items aboard the ship, artifacts from another world, and the writings looked similar to the marks on your arms. Are they something to do with your family line? Your true names? A destination? I can't say. But somebody cared enough to make those marks on you, so they must have a purpose.

Jetta, Jaeia, and Jahx, I hope this letter finds you in a better situation. Know that my selfish reason for seeking you in the Underground changed the moment I held you in my arms. I have no right to ask for your forgiveness, so I will leave you with this: Never look back and never think of Fiorah again.

Galm

"This letter," Jetta said, closing her eyes and recalling the sensation of Galm pressing the paper into her palm as they said goodbye. "The Core soldiers took it away during decontamination. I never knew what it said."

346

"I'm glad we could share this with you," Unipoesa said.

"Not good enough!" Jetta said, stabbing the fork into the table. "What else do you know about us? What else was in that pod?"

Sebbs nursed the last of his cigarette. "Very little. The Dominion somehow figured out your true family name is Kyron, but I'm not sure how."

"That's not really helpful," Jetta said.

"You're here, aren't you?" Sebbs said, grinding out the butt on the admiral's plate.

A long silence followed. The Joliak hadn't lied, and the letter from Galm seemed authentic. Still, she didn't trust what she had read. If she believed in the letter, she would have to embrace a whole new realm of possibilities. *A real mother and father—and they could still be alive! Maybe they didn't abandon us; maybe they were forced to make a terrible decision?*

Sliding her hand under her shirtsleeve, Jetta rubbed the tattooed symbol on the inside of her right upper arm. The inked skin felt hot, like it would burn through her clothing. *It could be our family name—or a clue about our real home.*

Jetta glanced over at Jaeia and tapped into her thoughts. Holding her right arm, her sister struggled to absorb the shock of Sebbs' information.

Galm was never going to make it on Fiorah once we left. This is probably the last we'll ever know of him, Jaeia thought. *He's gone.*

Jetta gritted her teeth against Jaeia's guilt and withdrew from their shared connection as much as she could. *I can't afford those feelings right now.*

"I'm sorry for what happened to you, really, I am," Sebbs said, his tone softening. His shoulders sagged forward, and he cupped the admiral's wine glass, which Unipoesa quickly took out of his hands. "Before it was just a slack job spreading Dominion propaganda. This was different," he said, frantically pawing for another cigarette in the empty package.

Unipoesa rested a hand on the Joliak's shoulder, but Sebbs shrugged it off and gnawed the back of his fist. "I didn't want this, you know? This responsibility. It was just a slack job, just a way to fly. I'm not Reht. I don't even have half a soul. I never wanted to go out and save the galaxy. But this *gorsh-shit* happens, and I—I can't take it. How could that leech priest be right about me? I'm not *chakking* worthy of anything!"

"What priest?" Jaeia asked, but both of them knew before he even answered, seeing the familiar face of the Grand Oblin in the memories that leaked from the Joliak's mind.

Jetta—if Sebbs confessed to the Grand Oblin, it would explain why he knew so much about us.

Sebbs? I don't believe it.

"Did you speak to the Grand Oblin?" Jaeia asked. Jetta sensed her sister's opinion of the man shift dramatically.

"*Chakking* leeches," Sebbs said, holding his head in his hands. "What good did it do? That priest said I would bring about 'the Awakening' in this big prophetic voice, made me feel real important. But it's all a bunch of *gorsh-shit*—"

"—Sebbs," Unipoesa interrupted. "Tell them what they need to hear—why we need them to help us."

Sebbs mumbled and looked away.

"Sebbs!" the admiral barked.

Sebbs wiped his nose with his sleeve and looked at them fiercely through bloodshot eyes. "Your brother is a Deadwalker."

"He is a Liiker," the admiral corrected.

"He's a *chakking* mechanical corpse."

Jetta didn't hear whatever Sebbs said next. An empty stillness took hold of her mind, and she feared breathing or even moving. The true meaning of her dreams clicked into place, and the fragile hope that Jahx had somehow escaped unharmed crumbled away. Frantic, she reached out to Jaeia for support, but crashed into a wall of pain.

Tell me he's lying, Jaeia, Jetta called to her sister, but Jaeia curled into herself, unable to give her sister any emotional support. Their brother, a third of their telepathic connection, was dead but still alive, suffering under the will of the Motti.

Jaeia—

I can't— her sister silently sobbed.

Jetta never felt anything like the seismic emotion building in Jaeia's mind, the grief and guilt shredding her rationalizations. *No, no, no,* Jetta told herself, pitching forward. *It isn't true. It can't be.* Rage boiled inside her, pouring hot fire into her arms and legs.

348

"It's all *gorsh-shit*!" Jetta screamed, standing up and throwing her plate at the wall. It shattered, sending bits of food every which way. The admiral didn't move, but Sebbs took cover under the table.

"It's all bloody *gorsh-shit*!" she repeated, taking the table by the sides, ready to throw it aside, ready to throttle the admiral until he took it all back. Jaeia laid a hand on her shoulder, her eyes pleading with her to stop.

"It's not only your brother. The other telepaths—the ones the Core commanders used for their communication system—have all been converted to Liikers," the admiral said calmly. "I thought you'd need proof of all this, so I compiled a dataset for you."

Jetta tore the datafile from the admiral's outstretched hand and whipped it at his head, but the admiral was quicker than he appeared, dodging it before it connected.

"Calm down!" the admiral shouted, retrieving the datafile as Jetta looked for something else to throw, "or I'll call in the guards and have you sedated."

Look at it already! Jaeia said.

"Give it to me," Jetta said, taking it from him, this time scrolling through. Through her tears she could barely take in all of the field data, the interviews, the intelligence reports, the mission logs and video cams.

"I won't believe it," Jetta said, her hands trembling as she laid the datafile on the table. "I won't. It's not possible."

"Something terrible happened to Jahx, Jetta—something terrible happened to all of you, and to many others. I have no simple explanation for any of this."

Jetta turned her back to them, leaning against one of the support beams that arched over the dinner table. She closed her eyes, wanting to dump her emotions into somebody else, wanting to escape the life she failed.

The admiral straightened his uniform again. "With a potent bioweapon, your brother commanding the telepaths, and the telepaths commanding their newly integrated Dominion army, the Motti have a power we couldn't possibly rival."

Jaeia wiped the tears from her eyes. "This bioweapon—do you have a way to stop it?"

"No, we don't. And it doesn't matter. If our forces try to counteract the virus, the Motti nuke the planet and move on. With the Dominion's warships, weapons, and a growing number of conquests, the Sentients of the Starways face genocide."

The admiral opened his arms in supplication. "Please, I implore you, help us. You are the only two that understand the way Jahx thinks, what he could do with an army like that."

"Why are they doing this? What do the Motti want?" Jetta barely heard the words escape her sister's lips. Jaeia needed an explanation, but Jetta didn't see the point. *I will kill all the Deadwalkers—*

"Their origins and motives are both unknown," the Admiral said. "Until all this they were merely reclusive, hostile on contact but not a threat. Now they are abducting Sentients and scorching planets with disease and nukes, leaving them entirely uninhabitable. They want to make sure none of us could possibly survive."

"Maybe they're just jealous of our skin," Sebbs laughed. Nobody else saw the humor.

Jetta felt like she should remember something about the Motti. *M'ah Pae...*

The twisted half-man with a burning red eye smiling at her with metallic gums. She remembered her intense revulsion and dread as the monster promised her power and revenge. His sinister words rang in her ears: *You are a humanoid I do not despise. You are different from the others. You share my disgust for the infectious impurity of the Sentients.*

"No. It's much more than that," Jetta said. "Much more."

She froze in place, overcome by the same nauseous feeling that had seized her years ago. *This is about Fiorah—about Yahmen.* The Motti Overlord recognized the brutal animal within her, the one she had come to rely on for survival even as it sought to destroy her. *M'ah Pae saw his evil reflected in me.*

"This is about an old hatred that cannot be reasoned with," Jetta whispered. "This is about someone, something that was once weak and wounded, and has come to depend on its anger just to stay alive. This is not something you can understand."

Complete silence. This time Unipoesa didn't stop Mantri as he snatched the admiral's wine glass and took a giant gulp.

Where did that come from? Jaeia asked. Jetta didn't answer.

The admiral shifted uncomfortably in his seat and cleared his throat before speaking. "Then you understand our predicament."

"I know what you want," Jetta laughed mirthlessly. "You want us to fight him. You have a lot of *penjehtos* to ask me to do something like that."

Jaeia tried to say something, but Jetta didn't give her a chance. "I don't care who you are or what you represent. There is nothing you could say to convince me to turn against my brother. We have no business with you."

"I can't spare you any starcraft," Unipoesa said, running a hand through his hair.

"Then we'll go with the dog-soldiers."

Admiral Unipoesa sighed. "This is so much more complicated than fighting your brother, Jetta. I wish you could see that."

"No," Jetta replied, standing. "It's not."

Jaeia joined her sister at her side, tears streaming from her face. *Please, Jetta—I'm so confused. Let's just wait—*

No! Jetta said. *We're not going to listen to his lies.*

"Well then," the admiral said, turning to face the window. "Go safely—for the short while that you still can."

The light of the nearby star cast an eerie glow across his face. Jetta couldn't tell what he was feeling, not that she tried very hard. All she knew was her own determination and the lengths she was going to have to go to save her brother.

***

Reht spit a mouthful of steaming, oily liquid across the floor of the bridge. "What the hell is this?"

Ro snickered. "Ah, Cappy, it's just ale from Talisse, some snips from Mom's stash, and a little engine grease."

"Bastard Farrocoon," Reht muttered, throwing the mug at Ro's head. He ducked in time to miss the mug, but the steaming contents splashed his neck and shoulders.

"*Ratchakkers!*" he howled as he scampered down the bridge hatch, Cray running after him, laughing uncontrollably.

"Diawn, where are those *chakking* launnies?" Reht yelled. "And are you keeping that crazy tin can away from them? Don't want to be getting their panties in a bind. I have a feeling they won't warm up to our wee little Deadwalker."

351

She spun around in her seat with a scowl on her face, once again taking his pissiness personally. "*Yes.* Tech put Billy in a sleep cycle and locked him in storage closet. Not very nice if you ask me."

Reht chuckled. "Come on, Di. It's just temporary. Anyway, Billy Don't ain't complaining."

Diawn's eyes burned. "The girls are in nav/ops with Mom going over the ship's schematics."

"Not the real schematics, right?"

His pilot continued to glare at him. "No, the jimmied ones. Nothing critical."

"Good. Vaughn, keep your eyes on the scopes," he barked as he headed to the back deck.

Leaning against the doorframe to nav/ops, Reht took a moment to let Mom cycle through the blue schematics of the *Wraith*, studying the twins. Mom grunted every time the twins asked him to go faster, but the Talian obliged.

Gods, I could make a fortune off of them in Underground, he thought, watching their eyes zig-zag across the schematics. His hands ached at the thought. *(Elia, my homeworld—I can't forget.)*

Focus, he told himself. This wasn't the time to get greedy or sappy.

"Hey Mom, we got a little problem. Looks like Billy Don't got into the freezer again and made the food canisters explode," Reht whispered in his ear, jabbing his thumb back toward the galley.

Mom shot up and bolted toward the galley with his claws fully exposed.

"I love messing with him," the captain chortled.

Reht moved to sit between the twins as Jetta rotated the view of the outer hull. "Beauty of a ship, ain't she?"

"A beta class cruiser equipped with highly illegal weaponry, a shield capacity that maxes out the reflux port—something like that is meant for a star-class warship, not a standard cruiser—an outdated emergency life support system and sanitation management, and an engine that belongs on an intergalactic starrunner," Jaeia said with a raised brow. "It doesn't make sense. If I had to guess, I'd say you left out a few select details."

"Look, most of it is in Tech's head. And the bottom line is, I fix never to be in a fix." Reht smiled, revealing his long incisors.

"All of the ship's resources are tapped out by the engine and weapons systems. At least that explains why the temp is sub-arctic in here. And your sanitation management is completely useless. What do you do, piss out the window?" Jetta asked, wrapping the civvy coat she had borrowed more tightly around her chest.

Reht just chuckled and slapped her on the shoulder. "Come on, little lady, you gotta see the beauty of this Betty. She flies faster than any other ship in the galaxy, and *no one* can outgun her. We've never needed advanced life support in the decade I've been in the business, and in terms of the temps and sanitation—well, this ain't a luxury cruiser. You gotta do your business in the jackbox," Reht said.

"I'd rather piss out the window," Jetta muttered.

"So what are our jobs on this ship?" Jaeia asked quietly as she shut down the projector.

The room darkened when the hologram terminated, making it so Reht could barely see the whites of their eyes. "You don't sound too enthused about our little operation," he said, scratching the scruff on his chin as he leaned back against the wall.

Jaeia shrugged her shoulders, looking away from her sister. "I feel like we're running away."

Reht snorted. *This is going to be easier than I thought.* He didn't know Rai Shar like the Alliance chumps, but he knew plenty about the art of *gorsh-shit*, and believing in it enough to fool even himself. "Well, of course you are. I thought you were smart, launnie."

Jetta's hands turned to fists. "Watch your mouth."

"Hey, I'm the captain!" Reht said, slamming his hand down on the console. Jetta didn't move, but Jaeia jumped a little bit.

"Now, where were we?" he said, drawing a smoke from his pocket and lighting it with the same hand. "You," Jagger said, pointing to Jaeia and blowing out his smoke. "Do you always do what your sister wants? This was her idea, wasn't it?"

Seeing the flicker of frustration in her eyes, he knew he'd struck a chord. It was obvious to anyone that Jetta was the leader, the pushy one, but a sharp eye like his could spot the mounting friction between them. Jaeia was strong in her own right, and with a little support she would push back against her sister's will.

Jaeia's my ticket, he thought greedily.

353

"What the hell, Jagger?" Jetta said. "We're both here, aren't we?"

"She ain't," Jagger said, pointing his smoke at Jaeia. "She don't believe in this."

Jetta took a hard look at her sister. Reht didn't know how telepathy worked, but by the way their eyes locked and their bodies swayed in unison, he knew they were exchanging thoughts.

"Hey, keep it here, ladies."

Jetta looked back at him. "You don't care about us. This is all about your payout."

"Pretty much. I lost my Healer saving your *assinos*. She suited up with the other side. Seems to think there's something worth fighting for. So you owe me everything."

Jetta looked surprised. "Why would she do that?"

"Because she knows that this isn't something you can run from, Jetta," Jaeia said. Jetta looked like she was going to hit her sister.

This is too easy—

"It's a bunch of *gorsh-shit*," Reht said. "The military will do anything to spin a tale, keep their best players in check, and believe me, Triel's one of their best players. A Healer in these times? She's the only one. She can save all their pruny old asses from bruises, bullets, venereal disease—whatever. Even you two—you're their best commanders. Hell, you're the greatest commanders in the history of this galaxy. Your medals are bigger than my *chakking* balls. So yeah, they'd try anything to keep you, too. My Starfox, Gods love her, is a sucker for sob stories. Believed all their *gorsh-shit* about them Deadwalkers."

"It's not *gorsh-shit*," Jaeia said, voice quivering. "None of it is. It's just really hard to—"

"Shut up!" Jetta said, standing abruptly. "Don't say it. Don't!"

Jaeia looked at her. "I can't fight you, Jetta. You're stronger than me. You're so much louder in my head. But the Deadwalkers are real, and what happened to us is real. We can't run from it."

"Then why the hell did you follow me? If you're so sure of it, why don't you go fight him then? Better yet, why don't you get inside my head and make me do it?" Jetta screamed.

Jaeia looked like she wanted to say something, but instead broke into tears. She got up and left, slamming the door behind her.

"She ain't gonna last a minute in this suit," Jagger chuckled. "She doesn't have balls like you. It's kill or be killed out here. You can't have mercy, can't have a heart."

Mumbling to herself, Jetta absently wiped the cold sweat breaking out across her brow.

Stay cool, he reminded himself. *You're not quite there yet.*

"Look, kid, in this crew we all got something. You're gonna have to tell your sister that. There ain't one of us that don't have a past. There's booze, there's *assino,* there's drugs—they take some of the pain away, but not all of it. She's gonna have to put it behind her."

"You can't put something like this behind you," Jetta said, looking at him contemptuously.

"Come on," Jagger said, blowing smoke into her face. "I risked a lot to save your *assinos.* If you tell me it was wrong, I'll slit your throat right now and be done with it. But I lost my Healer to the Alliance because of you. You'd better make something of yourself and set things straight with your sister, because I expect high returns."

She could have killed him—easily—but he knew that she was smart enough to respect his sacrifice.

Arms hanging limply at her sides, Jetta plopped back down. "Set my sister straight," she said, laughing weakly. Any other words she meant to say died at her lips.

"I'm getting some chow. Get your *assino* in gear in an hour. You're gonna have your first shift."

Playing the sister card played off. When he glanced back and saw her staring out into the starlit blackness of space with tears streaking her face, he knew he had gotten to her—or, at least, he hoped he had.

***

How am I ever going to confront Jetta?

The question weighed heavily on Jaeia's heart. Her whole life she had succumbed to her sister's will, acting as her passive moral compass, but this time she had to find a way to stand her ground.

355

Wiping the tears from her eyes, Jaeia slunk out of the steamy sump room. She jumped back and yelped when she saw the engineer hanging from the pipes along the ceiling.

"Sorry, didn't mean to scare you," Tech said, swinging down and landing on the catwalk. "Hey—you okay?"

"Y-yeah. Sumps check out," Jaeia said, and picked up her pace so he wouldn't see her tears.

"Thanks!" the mechanic shouted proudly as she hurried away.

Swallowing her fear, she reached out to find Jetta. Her sister's mind was closed up tight, just like it normally was when she wrestled with her emotions. But even though Jetta had cut her off from her thoughts, Jaeia could still sense her presence, and using that connection, navigated through the ship to one of the aft storage rooms.

When she opened the door she shuddered at the smell; apparently this was where the dog-soldiers had crammed all their useless garbage. Jaeia waded through the piles of junk toward a group of unlabeled barrels. She wavered a moment, thinking about the potential toxicity of whatever simmered inside, but she finally slid behind them and joined her sister, who had wedged herself in the corner.

"What are you doing in here?" Jaeia asked.

"You're right. We're running away. We can't run away. We'll never be fast enough."

Jaeia put an arm around her sister and hugged her tightly. Surprisingly, Jetta let her.

"There aren't too many people I love in this world. Jaeia, if the Deadwalkers got you, too—I'd—I'd—" Sharp, racking sobs broke off Jetta's words. Jaeia hugged her more tightly as tears squeezed from her own eyes.

"We have to go back," Jetta finally whispered, using the back of her sleeve to wipe her nose and eyes.

"What made you change your mind?"

Jetta shivered. "You. I have to do something right, don't I? I mean, everything and anyone I've ever tried to help—even you— I've always ended up hurting. And maybe that's because I've been wrong. Maybe this whole time, I should have been listening to you."

After staring at her sister for a moment, Jaeia found herself blinking back grateful tears. She had despaired of Jetta ever having

356

that kind of trust in her. "So you'll go back to the Alliance with me?"

"If you think that's right. I mean, we can't do much of anything in this box of *meitka*," Jetta said, looking at her squarely. "But you have to promise me something."

"Okay," Jaeia whispered, suddenly frightened.

"Don't ever use your talents on me again. What you did to me in the admiral's quarters—what you've done to me in the past to make me do what you want—just don't. I'll never trust you again."

Given that Jetta's behavior had only been getting worse, and that her second voice was her only recourse against her much stronger sister, Jaeia didn't think she could make that promise, but the intensity in Jetta's eyes left her no other choice. "Okay, Jetta."

Jaeia rested her head on her sister's knees and tried to change the subject to something more positive. "Hey, I have to tell you something. It's a secret."

Jetta tilted her head. "Oh yeah?"

"The other Exiles—Senka, the Grand Oblin, Rawyll, and Crissn—they're okay."

"What?! What do you mean? How did you...?"

Jaeia fiddled with her sleeves and sported an uncertain smile. "The flash transport device—I used it to store them just before we left. I tried to take Dinjin even though he'd been killed, but I passed out before I could store his biomemory."

"Flash transport?" Jetta repeated. Jaeia opened her mind to her, and Jetta retrieved the information. "My Gods—that's what they were fighting about. That's why they needed us. That's why..."

Jetta's eyes went glassy, and Jaeia felt her pang of shame. "They really weren't that bad, were they?"

Jaeia cupped her sister's cheek in her hand. "Jetta, you're okay. You saved us from the Prigs, and I stowed away the Exiles."

"Well, where's the device?"

Jaeia leaned back a little. "Hopefully safe. I think the Healer took it; I can kind of remember telling her about it when I was waking up. I'm not sure what she did with it, but I don't want to rat her out to the Alliance."

"Why not?"

Jaeia crossed her arms across her chest. "Just a feeling, really." To herself, she wondered: *Why am I so trusting?*

357

"Jaeia—"

"Let me deal with it, okay? It's not like with all this going on anybody will be able to help get them out right now anyway."

Jetta nodded absently, locked in some internal struggle. "Jaeia," she began, but couldn't seem to find words.

"Can you show me?" Jaeia said, pointing to her forehead.

"No..." She opened her mouth, shut it, and shook her head. "No."

Jaeia bit her tongue and let it go for now. *Maybe she'll open up to me later.*

(She would have told Jahx.)

The thought was fleeting, but the bitterness that lingered was hard to swallow. Jaeia closed her eyes. Ever since Jetta's psionic attack in the caves she had been having a harder time keeping herself in check.

"Well, we should tell Reht, right?" she said, sliding out.

"He's gonna be pissed."

"Nah. We can deal with the Alliance, tell them we won't negotiate with them unless they pay off the dog-soldiers. I think Reht will be okay if there's money exchanged."

"Wow," Jetta said, laughing. "When did you become such a diplomat?"

"Let's just say I've gained plenty of experience dealing with your crap."

"Very funny, Jae," Jetta said, crossing her arms.

Jaeia grinned and scooted her way out from behind the protection of the barrels.

"Jaeia, wait," Jetta called. Her green eyes pled with her silently, but Jaeia couldn't tell what she wanted. "Never mind."

Jaeia walked out, unsure of what just happened and less sure of what she was feeling.

When the next battle comes, can I trust Jetta to do the right thing?

Fear gripped her heart. The more important question burned brightly in her mind: *Can I trust myself to handle us both?*

***

"I got you two commanders," Reht chuckled. "So I figure you owe me a million in hard cash and one Healer."

"That wasn't the agreement."

"You thought I'd just let your fat *assinos* walk all over me?"

The admiral's eyes narrowed. "Just whose side are you on, Jagger?"

Reht played with the bandages on his hands, a wide grin cutting across his face. He always believed in "insurance policies" against his employers, so a few years back he paid Sebbs a year's supply of methoc to learn about his former schoolmate's activity with the USC. He had been saving his ace in the hole for quite some time now, and the sweet moment had arrived to lay down his hand.

"Awh, Damon—it hurts me that you'd think so poorly of my motives. But, on that note—if you try and stiff me, I'll make sure the twins find out about your personal history mind-*chakking* little kiddos. I wouldn't want to be there when they find out your dirty little secret."

Outside interference made Unipoesa's image fluctuate for a moment, but Reht could have sworn it was his temper.

"You think this is a game, Jagger, even now?"

"Awww, Damon—nothin's free in this universe. 'Sides, we both get what we want—I get some play money, my darling Starfox, and you get your elite commanders. Fair trade and everybody's happy."

"Get them back here, Jagger—*now*," the Admiral said, voice strident and tight.

"And my payment?"

"Oh, you'll get yours, believe me."

***

Over a four-way interconference, Damon Unipoesa watched his former protégé throw a fit.

"Stand down? You want that washout to take the helm?" Li screamed, throwing a datapad across the battle bridge. "The Deadwalkers are slowing their advance. In another eight hours we'll—"

"—lose all of Xeith. Urusous, you are on temporary hold from duty," Minister Razar said.

"This is insanity!" Li jabbed his finger at the blue and black image of the chancellor on the holosim conference display. "Have the Deadwalkers rewired your brain, Reamon? Unipoesa is a burnout!"

"Stand down, Li, you're embarrassing yourself," Unipoesa replied calmly. He ran a hand across his mouth to stifle what he really wanted to say. "You don't want to have the guards take you down to your own brig, would you?"

Chancellor Reamon looked around at them nervously. Unipoesa's heart sank. Li was not stupid; he would pick up on the lack of synchrony and realize that it was not a decision supported by the General Assembly. A bitter taste filled his mouth as Li signaled his camera crews to resume filming.

"You're going to divide the Alliance at a time like this? You would really ask your best commander to stand down in the middle of the greatest war in the history of the Starways?"

Old anxieties fluttered to life beneath his rib cage. *Hold it together*, he chided himself, glancing at the bottle of vodka by the edge of his desk. "You're losing that war, Li. Now is not the time for pride."

Li's face flushed. "Funny thing you should mention that to me, Damon. But let's go with that. Pride. How about another round of the Endgame? I'll put my Vice in charge for the ten minutes it'll take to destroy your worthless *assino*. And while I'm playing you, I hope you keep an eye on the body count—those are the lives you're spending on your wounded pride."

Out of the corner of his eye, Unipoesa caught the Minister moving restlessly in his chair. He hated Li for being right about his abilities, but he despised himself more for creating the situation.

"We don't have time for that," the Minister said. "I order you to stand down, Li."

"No—wait," Chancellor Reamon squeaked out. "I-I can't condone this without some sort of assurance."

"Assurance?" the Minister exclaimed.

"Yes—after all, with the admiral's history—we shouldn't be so rash."

The chancellor's words felt like hot coals in his gut. "Fine. I'll patch into Li's simulator on deck five for an Endgame match.

Countdown is set for twenty minutes, Li. Now, do I have your word that you'll stand down after your defeat?"

Li's eyes widened with rage, but his voice turned cold and strangely emotionless. "After I beat you, I'll make sure you spend the rest of your days in a geriatric lockdown."

Damon Unipoesa smiled humorlessly and terminated the link to Li and Chancellor Reamon. "Maybe we'll keep warm for just one night," he sighed, reaching for the bottle of vodka. Fear, anxiety, and regret had strung him out for too long to care what he said anymore.

The Minister shook his head and with a tone of solemnity replied, "Good luck, Admiral. You'll need it."

***

Jaeia felt something nagging at the admiral's thoughts. She watched him closely as they followed him to the simulator that would connect them to Urusous Li's terminal. Even though the admiral carefully controlled his feelings around them, a very strong emotion bubbled just under the surface of his psyche.

For it to be this noticeable, it must be really upsetting, she realized. As the admiral began instructing them on the Endgame, she promised to revisit the observation later.

"I know you two were exposed to the Endgame at the Dominion Core Academy."

"You could say that," Jetta said.

The admiral ignored her sarcasm. "It actually has a fascinating history. About 1,100 years ago, a brilliant but troubled young man from Old Earth named Martin Stein constructed the Endgame as part of his graduate school thesis. Even though Stein claimed to create the game for anti-war purposes, the U.S. military used his programming to centralize its forces during the Last Great War."

"Thereby contributing to the fall of Earth," Jetta interjected.

Frustration appeared only briefly across the admiral's brow before he continued. "Despite the holocaust, the schematics survived with those making the Exodus. What happened after that is still a mystery. The game reemerged during the formation of the United Starways Coalition and quickly became the final for military school graduates. Those wanting to gain higher rank played each other for prestige."

361

Jaeia's eyebrows rose. "I had no idea it had terrestrial origins."

The admiral smiled politely. "Unfortunately, it's not too hard to believe, coming from one of the Stein brothers. The human race has always been divided, but those two gave humanity the means to destroy themselves."

Without elaborating on the other Stein brother, Unipoesa turned their attention to the simulator. "In this match you'll have a standard sample of game pieces which you can control through projected keystroke or voice command. I will go through that with you after I show you your console here," he said, pointing to the terminal out of range of the camera that would televise the showdown. "It is connected to mine by short-link. My terminal is dead, so anything I type in is inconsequential."

Unipoesa reviewed the keyboard and keystrokes with them, but neither of them needed any reminders.

I wish I could forget, Jetta relayed silently to her.

"I'm sorry there isn't more time to let you practice. Do you have that, then?"

"Yes," Jaeia said quietly.

"Which one of you will be playing?" he asked, wiping the sweat off of his forehead.

Jetta withdrew from the conversation, leaving Jaeia to answer for them. "We both will."

Jaeia put on her best smile and tried to draw attention away from her anxious twin. In the back of her mind, she could sense Jetta's conflict as the contest stirred dysphoric memories.

"Don't worry," Jaeia said, seeing the look on the admiral's face. "We're used to playing together."

The admiral gave them a terse nod and moved to the inactive terminal on display. Jaeia moved to the active simulator outside the cameras' range and readied herself at the keyboard.

Come by me, she thought, coaxing her twin over with a subtle motion of her hand. Jetta was slow to respond, her eyes losing focus as an invisible force drew her inward. When Jetta took her place next to her, Jaeia could feel her sister's turmoil without any extrasensory perception.

"Now I will prove to the Starways that I am, without a doubt, the rightful fleet commander by defeating you once again. I'll even grant you the advantage of initiating the game," Li proclaimed on the

362

monitors, flashing an arrogant smile in full view of the cameras. Unipoesa sighed and indicated with a raise of his finger for the twins to start the game.

Jaeia extended herself into Jetta's mind, trying to calm her thoughts. *Jetta,* she called, *please, I need you.*

Li cut into their territory right away, sending three of his battleships directly into their front lines. Jaeia retreated her fighters and formed a new perimeter around the targeted ground troops.

Jetta, I can't do this without you, she begged.

Jetta stared at the display. "A classic defense would be the four point Hart-Morrei. I think I used it when we... invaded..."

Jetta stopped short. Jaeia saw charred swaths of land and scattered remains of dead bodies. Ruined buildings still burned in the blood-tinged sky.

"Jetta, stop," Jaeia whispered, squeezing her eyes shut to push out her sister's imagination.

"It was real... it was all real..." Jetta mumbled.

Jaeia commanded several land-to-air units to draw fire away from the main warship. It would distract Li for a few moments, but not for long. Jetta had to fully engage with her or they would lose.

Unipoesa looked up at her, frustration and fear creasing his face. He saw their hesitation.

"Jetta—you don't think I remember?" Jaeia whispered. She loosened her grip on her thoughts, letting Jetta feel the betrayal and violation that had been her whole world back on the Core ships. "I know what we learned and what happened to us is all the same to you right now, but you have to focus on playing this game."

When Jaeia closed her eyes and tapped into her sister's memories, a vortex of pain and confusion assaulted her senses. Core soldiers laughing at them, calling them leeches, launnies, Deadskins, Fiorahian rats. Stealing knowledge from Dominion officers, but imprinting their essence, too. That thing with the burning red eye. The strange elation of victory. Losing time. Losing perspective. Losing themselves. *Where's Jahx?*

"*Stop.*" Jaeia's arms dropped to her sides as she pulled out of Jetta's mind. Several game pieces disintegrated on the screen as she clutched her head, trying to make sense of it all. Li's forces advanced again, tipping the score; they were unquestionably losing now.

Is it all a lie? Are we killing real soldiers—real people—again?
she asked herself.

Jaeia looked around, sensing the desperation behind the hard
faces of the Alliance officers. *This is not the same. They're anxious,
not eager. It's the difference between survival and reward.*

Jaeia took a deep breath. "We can do this, Jetta."

Jetta tugged at the neck of sweat-soaked shirt, struggling to
breathe.

*She's the strategist; her instincts for battle are much better than
mine. If we're going to win this, I have to calm my sister down.*

"It's not real," Jaeia whispered into her Jetta's ear.

Jetta wiped her forehead and whispered, "I feel angry. And
empty."

Jaeia stomach knotted. "Please, Jetta. If we win this, we'll have
the chance to redeem ourselves."

Jetta bowed her head. "I'm sorry, Jaeia. You're right. I'm just..."

Jaeia reached over and took her sister's hand in hers. *You don't
have to say it, Jetta. I understand. Just remember—there's nothing
you and I can't do together. Trust me.*

To Jaeia's relief, she felt her twin's tension ease a little, enough
that she took control of the game pieces, rejoining her sister for the
counterattack.

Jaeia smiled as Jetta took down Li's pieces one by one. Even in
the worst conditions her sister saw new offensive angles better than
anybody she had ever encountered. She didn't know whether it was
the commanders and specialists Jetta had absorbed from, or
something unique to her, but either way, combined with Jaeia's
intuition and defensive capabilities, the game turned.

He's been fighting as if he's already won, Jaeia silently told her
sister as she rallied another complement of their forces to a different
location. The tiny blue pieces marched back across the spherical
playing field toward a greater complement of soldiers hiding behind
a natural obstacle.

*You can tell he's used to winning. He's sloppy, and he
underestimates us. This is actually sort of fun!* Jetta responded. Jaeia
took her eyes off the game for a moment to enjoy the devilish smile
spreading across her sister's face.

As she briefly delighted in the old Jetta, Li commanded his green pieces swiftly and fluidly toward their test targets along the border of their territory.

I can see why he advanced so quickly, Jaeia said as several green pieces enveloped one of their decoys.

He's fast and he talks pretty, but he doesn't pay attention to his back lines or his secondary defenses. Do you see that?

Immediately Jaeia spied the opening. Listening to each other's thoughts and exchanging jocular commentary, they formulated their battle plan.

Ten years from now, he'll still be wondering where it came from, Jetta joked as she typed in the command for their hidden pieces to resurface.

Li's army approached another one of their decoys. Thinking he could simply overpower their small group of visible blue pieces with an all-out assault, he spread himself too thin among their scattering pieces. Their fleet's deceptive retreat drew him deep within their trap, and with one keystroke, Jetta commanded the hidden pieces to resurface and fold in around him, destroying his unsuspecting army in seconds. As their blue pieces drowned out his green, the scoreboard above the sphere racked up a record number of points.

We beat Li in less than ten minutes, Jaeia thought, glancing over to Unipoesa. *Why isn't the admiral happy?*

Unipoesa, playing the front man in the game, did not look the part of a commander who had just outwitted his greatest rival.

He looks tired and defeated, Jaeia observed. *As if he lost the game, not Li.*

Overcome by rage and confusion, Li slammed his fist against the com panel. "You cheating bastard. You can't beat me!"

"Cool down, Li," Unipoesa said.

"No Sentient can achieve victory that quickly, especially with the odds stacked against him. You used a computer program or a processor. You stinking *ratchakker!*"

"You've lost, Li. Now you must stand down," the Minister announced over the interlink.

Chancellor Reamon, who had overseen the game, still gaped at the scoreboard. "No Sentient has ever scored this high. *Dichit,* Damon, if this is true, why didn't you say something sooner?" Reamon bumbled. "Get Li out of there!"

Several armed guards dragged the screaming Urusous Li from the terminal projection to the brig with the cameras still rolling. Reamon and the Minister faced the admiral squarely on the conference link.

"Admiral Unipoesa, the General Assembly hereby reinstates you as CCO of the Alliance Fleet. Now what in the name of the Gods was your ship doing so far out in unregulated space in the first place?" Reamon asked.

"Retrieving a federative offender."

The veins on Reamon's forehead throbbed. "Couldn't it have waited?!"

"Just securing the homeland, Sir."

Minister Razar leaned into the cameras. "Central Command is preparing for your arrival and will be equipped to make the broadcast for the Fleet."

"Let's hope that these numbers aren't falsified and that you have better luck than Li," Reamon said before cutting his communication link. The Minister favored the admiral with a salute before terminating his own link.

The admiral lingered a moment before approaching them. "Good work. Now, please, get some rest. There isn't much time left."

Jetta, looking utterly spent, started to follow the escorts to the exit, but stopped when she realized Jaeia was lagging behind.

Jaeia's eyes fixed on the Admiral. "Go on, Jetta," Jaeia said. "I'll catch up with you later."

For a moment Jetta looked like she would protest, but fatigue silenced her, and the guards showed her out.

When her sister had departed, Jaeia approached the admiral. "May I have a word with you?"

Unipoesa nodded, and the two were left alone in the simulator.

"Does our presence bother you?" Jaeia asked, hiding her trembling hands behind her back.

The admiral's eyes shifted away as if he was searching for a prepared response. "Why would you think that?"

"You already know I'm a telepath," Jaeia said, trying to engage him. He nodded but didn't speak.

"I know you're not afraid of us like the others are. It's something else."

He smiled weakly. "I'm an old man with old regrets. Nothing you can do about that."

Jaeia knew she should let him walk away and forget about it—that's what he wanted—but she couldn't. His negative emotions felt like her fault, or at least her responsibility, and she eyed him worriedly.

Noting her gaze, the admiral patted her on the shoulder. "Jaeia Kyron, the reports did say that you were the empathetic one."

"Yeah, but I'm just as stubborn as my sister."

The admiral smiled for her. "Please don't concern yourself with me now. Concentrate on what you and your sister need to do to win this thing. Then maybe we can talk about less important things, okay?"

"All right. As long as you tell me one thing, Sir."

"Yes?"

Jaeia took a deep breath. "We're not just abject killers to you, right?"

The admiral's brows pinched in confusion, but then his face relaxed and he rested a hand on her shoulder. "No, my young friend. Even so, it's time to get you ready for your war."

***

She didn't know how long it had been since she last slept, but alone in their assigned quarters with a soft bed to lie upon, Jetta still couldn't sleep. The silence was terrible, transforming into a tangible thing that pressed down upon her from every side. In silence and solitude she couldn't hide. The darkest thoughts and emotions she kept bottled up suddenly broke free, splitting her at the seams.

Lying atop the sheets, Jetta curled into a ball, tucking her face behind her knees. Battling Li had reawakened old wounds, none of which she would acknowledge, but they ravaged her nonetheless. As much as she tried to distance herself from the destruction she had caused during her time with the Dominion Core, she couldn't ignore the ache in her stomach and tightness in her chest.

Jetta reached over to the nightstand where she had left a datapad. She didn't know why, but she had to see.

"Show me the aftermath of the war with the Eeclian Dominion," she instructed the interface.

367

The datapad scrolled through the death tolls and video reels of the various battles. Subconscious remembrance raised the hairs on her arms and legs as she saw Dominion Core warships crushing the feeble USC rebellion. She scrolled through the newscasts from countless worlds with a numbed expression as refugees gave tearful testimonies of their ordeals. She saw beautiful landscapes transformed into graveyards, and men, women, and children, young and old, thrown into mass burial sites by exhausted salvage teams.

Jetta tucked the datapad under her pillow and curled back into a ball. *I can't let that get to me,* she reminded herself. But when she tried to refocus her energies on finding Jahx, her mind began to slip.

"*Skucheka,*" she muttered, massaging her temples. *If I'm not careful, I'll fall back into that nightmare.*

A cold shiver shook her to the core as she thought about her most recent experience: *I went inside the monster.*

No—I was the monster.

Jetta arched her head back and gritted her teeth, nails digging into her legs, trying to find release in physical pain.

"Hey—you okay?"

Jetta turned to see her sister framed by the doorway. Jaeia moved to sit next to her on the bed, but Jetta rolled away. She couldn't tell her sister about her feelings or her nightmares; Jaeia would just try to talk her out of what she wanted to do.

"I'm fine," she lied. "What did you say to the admiral?"

"I just thought—"

"That he thought we were just natural born killers, right? Kind of like everybody else thinks?"

"What do you mean?" Jaeia asked.

Jetta pulled the sheets up from under her body, wrapping them haphazardly around her shoulder. "You can't tell me you don't feel it—and this is supposed to be a safe haven for us. The ones who know who we are fear us. It makes me sick. If it wasn't for you, Jaeia, I wouldn't want to be me."

Concern creased her sister's brows as she searched for the right words. "You don't mean that."

"Yes, I do."

"You're not a bad person, Jetta, and neither am I. We just happen to be telepathic during a really bad time, and we've had

368

some rotten luck. But we're older now and have the ability to change things."

"You're so funny, Jaeia. You try to act as if you don't have the same fears as me, but you do."

"Maybe you're right," Jaeia said, sighing and turning away. "But I still believe in giving people a chance. And believing that things could be okay."

"We can't win this war, Jaeia," Jetta whispered.

Jaeia rested her head on her knees and looked off into the distance. "Jetta, I love him too, you know. This isn't easy for me either. We have to rely on each other now more than ever if we're going to get through this okay."

Jetta massaged her stomach, hoping the pain would go away. She didn't want to tell Jaeia, but if she was going to face her brother she had to. Closing her eyes, Jetta let the words come out without thinking.

"I used my—my hidden talent on Tralora, and I killed the Northies. I made them suffer, too. I didn't want to, but once I started, it felt good—very good." She pressed her hands into her stomach, hard enough to make her grimace. "I liked making them pay."

Jaeia's eyes widened.

"But as soon as I realized what I had done, I just felt empty." Jetta hid her face. "I don't want to be a monster. I want to be a good person. I want to help you and I want to help Jahx. But I don't know how to do it."

Jaeia protected her thoughts too closely for Jetta to read them. Seconds of silence passed like days as she waited for her sister's reaction.

"The best thing you could do right now," Jaeia said evenly, "is take command with me when the time comes to face Jahx."

"Well, I haven't given up on him like you have," Jetta said angrily, shoving the sheets aside and tumbling out of bed. "I still believe there's something we can do."

"What are you talking about?" Jaeia asked, standing pressed to the wall as her twin paced the floor.

"I think you've been wrong about my nightmares. I think Jahx has been trying to contact me because he wants me—us—to save him. And it's getting worse. I told you that I blacked out in the

369

detention quarters because I was still recovering from the transition off of Tralora—"

"Yes—"

"—but it was another nightmare, and this time it wasn't Jahx that I felt—it was the monster that's hunting him. We *have* to help him."

Jaeia looked away, pain leaking from her thoughts, taking Jetta aback.

"Okay, Jetta—let me see."

Jetta squared her shoulders. "Good—then maybe you'll stop thinking I'm crazy."

Jaeia approached her with the same trepidation she had seen the first time she proposed murdering Yahmen. Jetta felt the urge to run, but held her ground. *I have to show my sister—she has to believe.*

The coolness of Jaeia's hands on her skin made her jump back a little. She took deep breaths, forcing her heart rate to slow. It frightened her to conjure up the memories of that dark place, but she tipped her head back, and the darkness submerged them both.

Transferring her experience took only a matter of seconds, but in those short moments, Jaeia's body went rigid as Jetta showed her everything, from the first nightmare to the most recent. They poured out of Jetta without restraint and seared Jaeia from the inside out like undiluted fire.

Jetta held on tight to her sister as her knees buckled, slowly easing her to the ground. Jaeia lay in a crumpled heap on the floor, weeping softly. "Jahx..."

Jetta sat down next to her. "Do you believe me now?"

Eyes open but unseeing, Jaeia could give her no response. Her body shivered violently as tears spilled down her cheeks.

There was no other way, Jetta told herself, feeling guilty for assaulting her sister which so much sensory information all at once. *Now she knows why I can't face Jahx—at least not the way everybody wants me to.*

Jetta crouched down next to her. "They should have taken me."

"What?" Jaeia said, emerging from her daze.

"Because," Jetta whispered, "in that place, Jahx is surrounded by nothing but evil. Even on Fiorah he always looked past that kind of ugliness, down to whatever speck of good was left in a Sentient. He always found something—or at least said he did—and that kept

370

him going. I never did. I was able to thrive in the face of the worst souls the Starways has to offer. He's suffering because the place he's in—there's nothing good there. It's pure viciousness."

Terror-stricken, Jaeia could barely speak. "Jetta—"

"I know I'm not as strong as Jahx. I don't have the same telepathic reach as he does. I just wish they would have taken me. At least I would have been able to keep myself together there."

Turning away from her twin, Jetta closed her eyes and dipped back into the dark undercurrent that fed her desires. "And I would have destroyed them."

***

Jaeia wasn't sure of her own intentions when she asked Admiral Unipoesa if she could visit the Healer. She needed to ask her about the flash transport device, but that wasn't all.

Old fears made her think the admiral would refuse an unauthorized, unsupervised visit between two telepaths, but to her surprise, he allowed it. She didn't even have to stretch the truth or use her second voice.

He trusts me more than I thought, Jaeia thought as she walked to the Healer's quarters. *Or maybe he's desperate to keep me trusting him.*

Jaeia stood outside the Healer's door, waiting for the guards to allow her access. As one turned to the keypad, the other scrutinized her, his eyes traveling up and down her body. She stepped backward as if to slide out from beneath his gaze, but he had turned the full wattage of his attention toward her.

Jaeia sensed that he wanted to say something, but instead he switched the safety off his weapon.

Why are you so afraid? Jaeia wondered, stepping inside hurriedly as the door opened.

The Healer sat cross-legged in the middle of her quarters with her hands pressed together in front of her face, appearing to be meditating. Jaeia noticed that she had ripped the mattress off the bed and thrown it on the ground, leaving the pillows on the bed frame. Packages of food were cached in the corner nearest the mattress, and every light turned on.

371

"May I come in?" Jaeia asked, hovering just inside the room. The guards shut the door behind her, and she heard a faint *click* as the security locks reactivated.

Triel opened her eyes but did not deviate from her posture. "Are you feeling sick?"

Jaeia shook her head. "I just came to see if you still had..."

Triel relaxed her arms and extended one of her legs. "The crew."

The echo of Triel's thoughts told Jaeia that one of the crew members of the *Wraith* had obtained the device.

"I'd like it back."

"What is it?"

Jaeia shook her head. "I don't know enough about it, honestly. One of the Exiles instructed me to hand it over to the Alliance."

Triel crossed her arms, not buying her ignorance. "I don't have to tell you that we're not exactly in an ideal situation, do I? That device is an insurance policy, and the crew of the *Wraith*, including myself, are now on that plan. If things get dicey, we'll figure out a way to use it, whatever it is—and by your attitude, I can tell it's valuable."

Jaeia chose her words cautiously. "That device is not meant as an insurance policy, or whatever you want to call it. People's lives are at stake. If you were to sell it or destroy it—"

Triel angled her head to her shoulder. The woman's psionic presence brushed up against Jaeia's mind, trying to inconspicuously sift through her thoughts. "Jaeia, I'm sorry how this worked out; it wasn't intended to be against you. I'm actually surprised you don't see it my way."

Jaeia considered using her second voice, but then she stopped herself. Triel was a Prodgy Healer, and the last thing she wanted to do was unintentionally cause her to Fall into a Dissembler state.

"Look," the Healer said, "it's hard to make promises right now, but if things work out, I'll give it back. If they don't—if the Alliance or anyone else tries to hurt or manipulate me or any of my crewmates—then I'm truly sorry."

Jaeia's first impulse was to go straight to the admiral, but a moment's thought made her hesitate. First of all, the Alliance couldn't possibly use the device for the upcoming battle. Back on Tralora she'd barely had enough time to absorb Senka's knowledge of its operation, and even then, regenerating the flashed matter was theoretical. Secondly, she knew better than to think that she and Jetta were free people; it would be prudent to have allies like the dog-soldiers.

Most importantly, she didn't have time to argue with Triel over what was rightfully hers; there were other more pressing issues at hand. As much as it pained her, she'd have to wait for a better opportunity to secure the safety of her friends.

She stood near the couch that took up an entire wall of Triel's room, brushing her fingers over the fabric on the nearest arm. She didn't like the way the thread felt against her fingers, but the distraction of it eased her tension.

Softly, Triel added: "You might not believe me, but I do feel badly about taking what was yours."

(Can I trust her?)

Although Jaeia couldn't entirely remember being restored by the Healer, she remembered the aftereffects: a sense of calm, even when it should have been impossible. *Just like how Jahx used to temper situations when I couldn't.*

"Make it up to me then."

Triel looked at her curiously. "How so?"

"The battle coming up—it's something I don't think I can prepare for."

"Facing your brother?"

Jaeia sat down on the couch and brought her knees to her chest. "Worse—facing my sister."

"You two have very different outlooks," Triel said, tilting her head to the side.

"That's an understatement," Jaeia said, laughing weakly. "Since our brother isn't with us anymore, our connection isn't right. Imbalanced, I guess, is the best word. But the worst part is that even though Jetta knows she's out of control sometimes, she doesn't really want my help. In the end, she thinks she can do it all herself."

Jaeia thought back to what Jetta had said: *"I was able to thrive in the face of the worst souls the Starways had to offer... At least I would have been able to keep myself together there..."*

It was more than just Jetta's overconfidence—she was angry that Jahx was chosen over her. Deep down Jetta believed that *she* was the most powerful telepath, not Jahx. Jaeia had never seen her

373

sister act or think the way she had lately, and her growing unpredictability scared her.

"I—I don't know what exactly I'm asking for, other than your help."

"Because I'm a telepath?" Triel asked.

"Yes, but also because..." Jaeia said, trailing off. She couldn't find the right words, maybe because she really didn't understand her own trust in the Healer. She hardly knew Triel at all. She tugged at the ends of her sleeves. *Jetta would certainly disapprove.*

But Jahx would be—

"Jaeia," Triel said, interrupting her thought. "I don't know how much help I can be to you, honestly. I'm having a hard time dealing with things myself these days, and you know how dangerous that is for my kind."

Normally Jaeia would have never taken rejection personally, but in this case, she did, and she couldn't help her resentment.

"Well, I hope you feel better."

As Jaeia walked back to their quarters, each step she took seemed heavier and heavier. She didn't really want to be there, alone with her sister and her temper, but she didn't want to be anywhere else either.

"Jahx," she whispered. "If you're really out there, help me."

***

Triel came upon the dog soldier captain as he usually was: naked. Except for the bandages that covered his hands, Reht preferred to wear as little as possible. Not that Triel minded, really. Reht had a slender, muscular build, and though he bathed infrequently at best, she found his natural smell intoxicating.

Since Mom considered nakedness unclean, Reht typically avoided nudity in the common areas of the ship, but his den was fair game. As she stepped inside his private quarters, she saw him reading a newsreel with one leg on the bed and the other on the floor. Finding him spread out like that made her blush, but she didn't turn away.

"You still have the package I gave Bacthar, right?"

Reht put down his smoke and gave her his best impression of being hurt. "Starfox, please."

374

Triel wished she was a more attuned telepath right then; she needed to know exactly what he was thinking.

"What do you intend to do with it?" she asked outright.

Reht feigned interest in the newsreel as he took a long drag. "We'll see. I'm not sure what it is or what it does, but if those launnies nabbed this thing off Tralora, then it's most likely Narki. Tech nearly pissed himself when I had him take a look, so I'm sure it'll fetch a good price. In other words, I'm keepin' it. You know the Alliance is gonna screw us the minute this thing is over. We need a ticket out."

"I know, Reht, but you can't sell what isn't yours."

"Well, maybe I'll do it to get you back. I can't believe you're still servin' those Alliance chumps," Reht said.

"I'm tired of fighting about this. You know it's important that I see this thing through."

"Of all the—" Reht started.

A call from the overhead com interrupted him. "Cappy, you expecting a launnie?"

Reht grumbled and threw the newsreel on his bed. "What the hell? Did you set this up?"

Triel shook her head.

"I ain't putting pants on, so no, send her *assino* away."

After a pause, Ro got back on the com. "You wanna see her, Cappy. Sorry."

The smoke dropped from Reht's fingers, and he nearly jumped out of his seat as the burning end singed the hairs on his thigh.

"That little rat bastard—why the hell did he let you in here? I'm busy!" Reht yelled as Jaeia walked through the door with Cray at her heels.

What is she doing here? Triel thought. Jaeia appeared composed, but the Healer sensed her nervousness through her body's stress responses.

"I came about the device that Triel took for me. It's very important. The lives of my friends depend on it."

Reht smiled, and Triel knew that she had just confirmed his suspicions about its importance.

"Cray, it's alright," the captain said, shooing him away.

"But Cappy, Ro said—" he protested.

"Now!" Reht shouted. He then turned to Jaeia. "Look little miss, your sister was pretty smart, so I'm assuming you are too. That's a good thing, 'cause I'd hate to have to explain to you what a *chakked* situation this is for me and my crew, and that I don't do rescue missions for free."

Jaeia stood her ground. "You don't know what it is, or how to work it, Captain Jagger."

"Yeah, but you do," Reht said, slouching back in his chair. "And you're gonna tell me."

"Why do you think that?" Jaeia asked.

Triel looked back and forth between them. Reht had a devilish grin on his face and Jaeia seemed calm, but both of them were faking it.

"Because you owe me and you owe her," Reht said, pointing at the Healer. "I pulled her out of hiding and risked my crew to bail your *assino* out of that rabbit hole. Hell, you *know* you owe it to her."

Keeping the surprise off her face proved difficult. *Reht's never employed this kind of tactic before.*

Jaeia gave a slight twist to the sleeves of her jacket, but otherwise her face and body betrayed no emotion. Triel could tell she had trained herself to be like this, and it piqued her curiosity.

"Right now I don't know what to think of you, Captain Jagger. Part of me is encouraged, really; I guess this means that you think Jetta and I can pull this thing off. But another part of me is disappointed. I guess I was wrong when I assumed that the reason you risked your crew and your Healer in the first place was because you saw the bigger picture. It was never about you or me, really."

Triel covered up her smile. *This girl is good.* She saw right through all of Reht's *gorsh-shit*, straight to what made him a bad dog-soldier, but a decent man.

Reht chuckled and stood up, readjusting himself in the process. Jaeia swallowed hard and jerked her eyes back up to Reht's face as he strode forward.

"Launnie, I can't decide if I want to kill you or induct you into the crew. Reminds me of a young Starfox, yeah?" the captain said, wrapping his arms around the Healer. His touch distracted her for a moment, and she melted into him. She'd forgotten how much she liked the simplest things from him. "Well, what do you think, Starfox? Should I give the launnie's toy back?"

Without warning, Diawn burst into the room. Her jaw dropped when she saw Reht, in the nude, embracing Triel. "What are you doing?!"

"Whoa, darlin'—who put your panties in a bind?"

Diawn snarled at him. "Ro told me what this was all about. You'd better not be giving the package back to her! And you—"

Triel backed away from Reht as Diawn stormed toward him. "Cover your eyes—don't look at him. You shouldn't even be here, leech. Don't they have a cage for you on that Alliance ship?"

"That's not very ladylike, Diawn," Reht said, tapping his lip. "Don't make me put my pants back on."

"You never take anything seriously, do you?" Diawn hissed, turning on him. She grabbed him by his nether regions, and his eyes burst out of their sockets. "You're going to sell us out just like always—just for her. But I'm not going to let that happen. Someone has to teach you how to be a good dog-soldier—a good man!"

Triel didn't even see the weapon Diawn carried until it was too late. She plunged the hunting knife into Reht's side and withdrew it before he hit the ground. When Jaeia tried to duck out of the way, Diawn kicked her upside the face, sending her flying into the wall, her head cracking against a support beam.

Shocked, Triel didn't move as Diawn came for her, even when the blade's edge sliced across her chest. *Diawn's going to kill me.*

"I hope you rot in hell, leech."

The knife rose to her throat. *This can't be how it ends for me—*

"Leave her alone."

The words were like nothing Triel had ever heard. They perforated her mind, inundated every fiber of her being. It was as if she had never heard anything or anyone else before that moment.

"Leave her. Put the weapon down."

Triel strained to move her head toward the sound. Jaeia stood near the wall, holding the back of her bloodied head. The look in her eyes paralyzed Triel's heart. *That's not the girl I healed.*

Triel turned back to Diawn, whose hands shook wildly. The knife clattered to the floor.

"I—I—I," she stuttered.

Diawn's eyes rolled back in her head as the color drained from her face.

What is she doing to her? Triel wondered. *It's just like the controlling act of a Dissembler—*

The thought of the Fallen broke her from her trance, and she dove to Jaeia's side. She placed her hands on Jaeia's cheeks, touching their foreheads together. *This isn't the pure malice of a Dissembler,* she thought. Triel felt the edge of something ferocious and predatory that would stop at nothing until satisfied. *But it's close.*

Not knowing what else to do, Triel prayed the ancient peace chant used on the Fallen: *Peaceum alas leju.*

Jaeia held onto her wrists and pushed her away. Two gray eyes met hers. "It's okay."

Triel gulped for air. "What was that?"

Jaeia shivered. "I'll explain later."

Just as the words left her mouth, Mom tore through the captain's door, knocking it off its hinges. He let loose a deafening roar, and even Reht, barely conscious, covered his ears. Ro trailed behind, rifle in hand, teeth bared.

The Talian grabbed Diawn up by the ankles. When she tried to free herself, he snapped at her face, and she immediately froze. With the situation well in hand, the Healer went to Reht's side.

"I'm alright, I'm alright," Reht said, clutching the wound in his abdomen.

"We need to get you treated," Triel said, touching his clammy skin.

Reht scoffed, bracing the wound. "I'll be fine."

Mom dangled Diawn near the captain's face so he could inspect her.

"Set her down. We need to have a chitty-chat."

Mom dropped her, letting her hit the plated floor with an audible crack, and moved to Triel. Glowering, he pointed to the slash mark across her chest.

"I'll live," she said, touching his shoulder.

"Launnie, get out of here. This is private soldier business now," Reht said to Jaeia.

"Reht, please. She's not right—" Jaeia begged.

She's anticipating Reht's next move, Triel realized. *She can see that one of his greatest strengths is also his greatest weakness.*

Diawn, disheveled and shaking on the ground, looked at Jaeia with contempt. "What the hell do you know? I'll slit your throat—"

"Baby, that temper of yours—we're going to fix that right now." Reht reached around to the clothing storage unit and pulled out his 6M handgun. Diawn, who had begun to rise, slowly sat back down as Reht pointed it at her head.

"You have to kill her, Reht, or she will kill you," Jaeia whispered.

"She ain't killin' anyone right now. Don't worry, little lady. Now go and take care of your own business."

"Captain—"

"What, your ears all gummed up, kid? Want me to clean 'em out for ya?" Ro yelled, sticking his rifle into Jaeia's ear. She put up her hands and slowly backed away.

As Jaeia turned to go, Triel touched her shoulder to read her biorhythm. Within Jaeia dwelled a strange knowing, intangible and indescribable, that had spread through her body like ripples in water radiating from a dropped stone. *This has set in motion something terrible that we'll one day have to face.*

"She's right, Reht."

"Starfox, love," Reht said, in his most charming voice. "Why don't you mosey back to the *Gallegos*; they already got me on a short enough leash, yeah?"

There was no stopping Reht now. With a heavy heart, Triel followed Jaeia out to the umbilicus that connected the *Wraith* to the *Gallegos*.

"Wait, please," she said.

Jaeia turned her head slightly toward her but continued to decode the hatch lock.

"What just happened?"

Jaeia paused. "That's my unique power—my 'second voice.' I can control people with words."

"It seemed...very powerful," Triel said, choosing her words carefully.

"I'm sorry," Jaeia said, shoulders hunching. "I don't risk using it in full unless it means life or death. I can't really control my talent,

379

and neither can Jetta; they seem to control us. Things always goes too far."

Triel suddenly realized why Jaeia had come to her for help. "Is that how you're planning to defeat Jahx—using a power you can't control?"

Jaeia shook her head as she looked down the dark tunnel of the accessway. "Let's hope it doesn't come to that."

***

"You," the dog-soldier captain said, grabbing Diawn by her hair. "You are through here."

Reht tore the cuff off his shirt and spat on it, then wiped it across his wound, the two fluids together staining the cloth black. He passed the cloth to Ro and Cray, who took turns spitting into it. When Tech and the others finally ran into the room and saw the cloth, they turned their backs to her.

Diawn tried to get to her feet, but not quickly enough for Reht. He grabbed her again by the hair and dragged her to the escape pod access attached to his den.

"Don't ever come back."

"Reht, please!" she begged, clinging to his shirt. Tears streamed from her eyes, smudging her dark makeup. "I love you! I did this for you—the leech is poisoning your mind! You're the only one that ever—"

"You're lucky I don't kill you."

The dog-soldier captain shoved his pilot inside the cramped compartment of the escape pod along with the emblem of her rejection. He knocked the control release panel off with the heel of his boot and ejected the pod manually.

"We should have killed her, Reht," Cray hissed as the pod disappeared into the darkness of space. "It's tradition, you know."

Reht shook his head. If the crew had realized how unstable Diawn was, they probably would have mutinied a long time ago. *But her instability made her a valuable asset. She did things for me that would have sucked the soul out of any other Sentient.*

Somewhere in the depths of his conscience, he felt the truth: *She was my responsibility.*

(I failed her.)

If this was a mistake, he would have to pay for it later.

CHAPTER VII

In less than an hour the *Gallegos* would reach the Alliance Central Starbase. When the admiral summoned Jaeia to his office, she wasn't surprised.

He probably wants to run through battle strategies or review the latest intelligence reports before, she told herself. But when she stepped into his office and discovered he had requested her exclusively, her assumptions turned to dread.

"Admiral," Jaeia said, standing in front of the red fabric chairs positioned around his desk.

He was reviewing a file, his eyes moving back and forth rapidly, the screen turning his face blue and white as he skipped through the pages.

Finally, with a controlled breath, he turned toward her. "Jaeia, please, have a seat."

She did, careful not to make a sound as she listened for his thoughts.

"How are you doing with all this?"

She didn't really understand the question. "Fine, I guess."

The admiral steepled his hands underneath his chin. "This isn't a test. There are no recording devices. They are our only witnesses," he said, tilting his head at the stars streaking past the window as the ship made another jump.

"I don't know what answer you're looking for," Jaeia said.

"Remember when you asked me if your presence bothered me?" Jaeia nodded.

The admiral formed words with his mouth, but there was no sound. Finally, sweeping his hand across the top of his head, he said, "You remind me—you and your sister—of someone that I let down a long time ago. And I can't do that again."

Not knowing what to say, Jaeia waited for him to continue. Unlike her sister who rushed conversations, she found that silence would sometimes trigger the other person to share more.

The admiral cleared his throat. "I am worried about you, Jaeia. You more so than Jetta. The reports I received from Intelligence may differ with me, but I truly believe that you're the one who needs to be in that chair."

Jaeia frowned. "I'm sorry, I don't follow."

The admiral pushed himself away from the desk. He made his way slowly to the window and faced the stars. After a seemingly endless silence a lighter clicked, and the smell of maple spice and burnt hay wafted across the room, making Jaeia's nose wrinkle.

"You and I both know that, in the end, it will be your decision," he said evenly.

Jaeia swallowed hard and rubbed her palms across the fabric of the chair.

"Your sister isn't the type to give up, is she?" he said, taking another drag from his cigar.

Jaeia looked at her feet, but they disappeared in the sudden blur of tears.

"No," Jaeia whispered, her voice catching in her throat.

"That's why I'm worried about you. When the time comes, what will you do to ensure victory? What will you do to beat Jahx?"

She closed her eyes and wished it was all a dream. *If only I could wake up...*

Jaeia always knew the time would come when she and Jetta would be at odds over something that couldn't be resolved with reason or by touching minds. *Jahx told me to be Jetta's anchor, but this time anchoring Jetta might not be enough.*

She wished the admiral would talk, but he patiently waited for her. Before she could tailor her response, the words poured right out of her. "You have no idea how much I love my brother."

Jaeia covered her face with one hand and rubbed the fabric with the other, hard enough to abrade her skin. "I'm always managing my sister's emotions—or at least trying—and she doesn't even ask how I feel. She just assumes she's the only one that cares that he's gone, and somehow it's her responsibility to bring him back. I want him back too, don't you understand that?"

The admiral extinguished the cigar on his boot. "I do, Jaeia, I do."

"I don't want to fight him, and I—I resent that you're asking me to do it."

The admiral moved to the corner of his desk and sat on the edge. He looked as if he wanted to place a hand on her shoulder, but he settled for resting it on a datafile.

"But I will, don't worry," she said, wiping her tears on her sleeve. "Because I know what I saw; he died many months ago, and whatever he is now isn't anything like him. Jahx would never want us to allow him to become somebody's weapon."

383

"How will you do it, Jaeia?" the admiral asked gently. The fatherly look in his eyes was something she both appreciated and resented.

Jaeia shivered. "I will do what I have to in order for the Starways to be safe. I will do what I have to in order to save my sister."

The admiral folded his hands across his lap. His face turned hard and his nostrils flared. "I am giving you command of the Alliance Fleet. I am entrusting you with the lives of all the Sentients of the Starways."

"I know."

"Furthermore, you are a child, a telepath..." he said, trailing off. Doubt crept around the edges of his thoughts. "It was not easy for me to make this happen." He looked straight through her. "Please, tell me I am not wrong to trust you."

The boy in the coolant room appeared by her side, his accusing eyes watching her every move. She wished she could reassure the admiral, but she couldn't.

"May I be excused, Sir?" He didn't give her any indication either way, but when she tried to leave he caught her by the arm. "Do whatever it takes to win, Jaeia. It's what Jahx would have wanted."

***

By the time they had arrived on the Alliance Central Starbase, the admiral had already briefed them three times on what little remained of the Fleet and the Homeworld territories. Jetta's heart sank even further as the admiral outlined the composition of their forces.

"... and the Iuti have one warship, two battleships, and about fifty-two fighters readied at the Homeworld Perimeter. It'll be our last defense. Let it not come to that," the admiral said grimly.

Minister Razar and the chancellor of the General Assembly joined their company in the war room, closely monitoring their discussion from the observation deck. Jetta hated the observers—it just reminded her of her days with the Core. Part of her expected Rogman to come storming out of the crowd, his troop of specialized guards at his heels, ready to dispense the next round of games and punishment.

Jetta, her sister called, *be here now.*

Jetta straightened up. "What about the Deadwalkers?" she asked, studying the projected map of the Homeworlds.

"It's hard to estimate," Unipoesa began, but something made him pause. "Even if they converted all of the Dominion starships into Liiker vessels, it still wouldn't account for the size and mass of their Fleet."

"You mentioned they were abducting Sentients. It would be logical to assume then that they're stealing their technology, too," Jaeia commented, looking at a hologram of a converted Dominion ship.

Tentacles and antennae perforated the hull of the warship. Jaeia rotated the axis of the ship, exposing the bony spires jutting out of fuel tanks. At the stern of the ship, plasma reactors spewed greenish spores into the vacuum of space. The fuselage, deformed by a newly-formed exoskeleton, shimmered with a slick resin.

Jetta could barely keep back her revulsion.

"Yes," the admiral said. "That possibility has been explored. There's some type of distortion field around their vessels blocking our long range sweeps, so we can't get an accurate reading. Even our probes can't get close to their front line."

"What's your best guess?" Jetta asked.

Unipoesa clasped his hands together. "They outmatch us at least ten to one."

Jaeia's doubt rattled around inside her head. *Fighting the Motti's army is near suicide.* Outnumbered and outgunned, they were just two telepaths against an entire army of talented beings with the most powerful telepath in the galaxy at the helm.

It's like I'm four again, and Yahmen's come home drunk, Jetta imagined, seeing his silhouette in the doorway. *How do I defeat an enemy that's so much bigger and stronger than me?*

Rage, unmitigated by time, came alive from memory. *(How can I face an enemy I don't understand?)*

Jetta gnawed on the inside of her cheek, trying not to let the admiral see her increasing uncertainty. *What's left to save, after all? The Motti have obliterated over half the habitable planets in the Homeworld territories.*

Jaeia sighed and put down the list of starcraft she was studying. "How is this going to work?"

"My voice has been recorded into the communications tower. Whatever you say will be filtered and then transmitted to the Fleet."

Admiral Unipoesa must have seen the fear in her eyes. "Remember, the commanding link to the Liiker force is your brother's mind. You understand him and know how he thinks. Use this to your advantage."

Though the admiral meant this as advice, it only made Jetta feel worse. *The Motti are exploiting his ability to predict his enemy. Anything we do is futile.*

In the back of her mind she saw her brother's face. A shy smile and bright blue eyes reminded her of her promise. *No. I'll act quickly, before the part of him that's been taken by the Motti has a chance to react.*

Jetta shot a glance at her sister before moving to sit in one of the two command chairs installed for them in the adjacent campaign room. The area was designed for consultations and private meetings and was ill-equipped to house the bundles of wires, monitors, and projector/processors necessary for combat command.

It's hard to breathe, Jetta heard her sister think. The air, stagnant and hot from all the humming machinery, seemed to press down on them in the cramped space.

Mopping the sweat from her brow, Jetta tried to reassure her sister. *No worse than Fiorah, right?*

"Don't get too close to the war globe," Admiral Unipoesa warned one of the film crew. "And keep all of the shots at my back."

As the news and film teams set up behind the admiral, Jetta breathed a sigh of relief. *At least the cameras aren't trained on us.* She couldn't imagine what it would be like to be in the eye of the public, and even the passing thought of celebrity made her cringe.

No, but look, Jaeia thought, directing Jetta's attention to the Minister and chancellor on the observation deck. Both had changed seats to have a better view of the twins. *You were right. I hate it when people watch. Feels too much like the old days.*

The admiral gave the sisters a nod as he climbed into his chair. Even with his back to the cameras, he made sure to hunch over the Fleet comlink, shielding his mouth.

"I wish Triel was here," Jaeia mumbled to herself.

386

Jetta lifted a brow. "Huh?"

"Nothing."

The admiral gave them their cue. "This is Admiral Damon Unipoesa calling to all Alliance starships. I'm taking over command of the Fleet from CCO Li."

Here we go, Jetta thought as she rang in each of the Alliance ships into their comlink.

The central projector came to life, populating with the various alphanumerics and organized light patterns of starships. Jetta's jaw dropped as a brilliant white tidal wave Liiker vessels descended on the scattering blue orbs of the Alliance Fleet.

Gods—

(Jahx—)

Jaeia initiated the first command. "All warships, position to mark 4.101. Alpha squadron, to strike formation one."

Seeing her sister's angle, Jetta joined the fray. "Red squadron—come about at 7.09. Beta, flank and then break away at mark 5.56."

Even with a synergistic perspective and commands in perfect unison, nothing slowed the avalanche of Liikers riding over their pitiful resistance.

Everything we know, every trick and maneuver, is—

(Anticipated. Expected.)

Jaeia nudged her. *Keep the delta squadron out of range. They're being eaten alive.*

I know, I know. Retreat the starfighters and put out the cruisers.

Jetta—we don't have any reserves—we need to have something to defend the perimeter.

Jetta shook her head and scrolled through different views of the battle. *Formations aren't working. We have to break into smaller teams and root out any weakness.*

"Weakness?" Jaeia exclaimed out loud, covering her microphone as another of the Alliance's orbs intensified and then faded. *We just lost another warship and look—some of our flanking ships are falling back. We're running out of time.*

As Jaeia continued to shout orders, doubt and uncertainty unhinged the last of Jetta's confidence. *I'm making conservative defensive decisions. Why can't I make the attacks?*

387

The revelation hit her like a canon blast. The Dominion Core. The drugs that took away their anxieties and awareness of death. *Because it's never mattered before…*

I'm afraid.

A wave of nausea tightened her abdomen. *I can't do this.*

(Jahx—)

Watch the delta squad! Jaeia yelled across their bond. More Alliance orbs faded into oblivion.

Jaeia can't command alone, but what good am I? Jetta bit her lip. *My mind is blank—I have no voice.*

Gripping the ends of her armrest, Jetta called out silently to her brother. *Why, Jahx? Why didn't you fight?*

Jetta wanted to be angry, to find power in her hatred for the Motti, for all those who had wronged them, but after Tralora, she knew she shouldn't. Her siblings had been right to warn her about relying on those types of feelings. *But without them, how can I win? Not even a thousand years' worth of military knowledge is enough.*

She licked her lips and dug her toes into her boots. As she looked over to her twin shouting commands, she realized her truth. *The Motti are wrong about me. I don't want revenge—I just want my brother back. I want my family to be safe and free. I don't want to hurt anybody ever again.*

An inner voice answered: *(Failing to stop Jahx will hurt others. Jahx wouldn't stand for that.)*

After losing several more ships, Jetta slumped back in her chair, taking her earpiece out and microphone off.

(Find me. Kill him.)

She watched in horror as the battlefield changed. The white orbs that dotted the screen formed a malevolent flame that scorched the optic field, and she reflexively shielded her face.

Jahx, she cried internally, *are you there?*

KILL HIM, echoed in her head over and over again. Something pulled at the back of her mind, dragging her consciousness away from reality. She resisted, fighting to stay grounded.

Please, Jahx, help me, she begged silently, clutching her stomach.

"All units, retreat to mark 2.49," Jaeia called out to the Fleet.

Another failed formation, another retreat. *Jahx, please—*

"Jetta!" Jaeia said, covering the microphone with her trembling hand, "I need you!"

Swallowing the dry lump in her throat, Jetta tried to find her strength. She thought back to other impossible feats: learning a cross-routine for secondary engine when she was only three years old. Fending off child labor gangs and outsmarting laborminders for a cache of bakken. Surviving the brunt of Yahmen's wrath for years. *So why am I surrendering now?*

Her breath came sharply now. *Jahx is impossible to face on this battlefront.*

(But what if I confront him in a different realm?)

"Oh Gods," Jetta whispered. *Is that why I'm having nightmares? He knows we can't defeat what he's become…*

Slamming her fist against her armrest, Jetta refused the implications of her revelation. *No. He's trying to bring his consciousness closer to mine so I can access more than his mind. I can stop all this—I can save him!*

It would be dangerous. A dark presence dominated that reality, and if running from it was dangerous, fighting it would be fatal. How could she expect to keep herself whole and save Jahx in that nightmare?

Jetta bit her lip. She hated herself for even hesitating. *I won't fail him again.*

We can't win this, Jaeia, Jetta said as another squadron went down. Admiral Unipoesa, the Minister and the chancellor all looked up at them with panicked expressions. *Not like this.*

What do you mean? Jaeia asked after commanding the beta-squadron to retreat once again.

She's at the end of her rope, Jetta thought to herself, looking at her sister. Sweat ran down Jaeia's face, and the veins on her forehead bulged with stress. *Besides, I can't risk taking her to that awful place.*

"I figured out my nightmares," Jetta said. Privately, she continued: *Jahx is trying to establish a link between our minds. He wants me to travel to him, to help him—I know it. The time I traveled back voluntarily, I had more control. That's the key!*

As Jetta closed her eyes, Jaeia cried out. "What are you doing?"

389

The connection—now that I understand it, I can see it. I'm going through.

No you're not! Jaeia said. *I saw that place, and I'm not letting you go alone.*

"Jaeia, it's too dangerous—"

Jaeia threw her headset across the room and gripped Jetta by the shoulders, her fingers digging in painfully. "I can't lose you both."

Jetta suddenly recognized the look in her sister's eyes, and a laugh escaped her. "Ow—geez! And here I thought I was the only one."

"When it comes to our family, that part is in both of us," Jaeia said, blushing and backing off.

Well, just keep an eye out for me, okay? Jetta typed in a final set of commands and barked into the mic: "Beta-squadron, hold position!" The remainder of the Fleet surrounded the Gateway Perimeter of the Nine Homeworlds—the last line of defense.

"What are you doing?" the Minister shouted, pulling back the partition. "Get back on those headsets!"

Jetta lifted her arm and warned him to stay back. "Trust me, please," she said.

Before she closed her eyes, Jaeia grabbed her by the hand and kissed her cheek. *Don't let go. Don't forget me.*

"Never."

Holding tight, Jetta allowed herself to fall into the nightmare that existed on the brink of her mind.

***

Jaeia watched as her sister's eyes rolled back in her head, her body stiffening. Her own mind, struggling to stay connected with Jetta's, bent back impossibly, as if she was being swept down an infinitely long drain.

With her body and mind threatening to pull apart, Jaeia felt herself slipping into the darkness. *I can't keep holding on—*

"I'm here," someone said. Slender fingers wrapped around her wrist. Though her mind bridged across two different worlds, Jaeia saw the Healer's blue markings in her periphery.

"Please," Jaeia whispered, "help us."

***

Darkness collapsed all around her as frenzied cries swarmed her mind.

(Jahx, where are you?) *Jetta managed to shout, trying to keep from drowning.*

The wailing faded away, and somehow she found footing, even though she couldn't differentiate between ground and sky in the endless shadow.

(Jahx?!) *she tried again.*

Jetta strained to form a complete body, but there wasn't time. A roar erupted from the murk, and the darkness itself shifted, recombined. Its vibration shook her, growing in intensity by the second until the whole world quaked. She curled in on herself. It's so much stronger—

(Too powerful—I can't—)

The tremors abruptly stopped. Jetta held her breath in the eerie stillness as the seconds ticked away. Finally, she dared to look up. Thousands of lidless, fiery eyes gazed down on her from every direction. Something like the stink of old meat filled her nostrils, and she gagged.

Voices, shrill and frayed, spoke in many different languages: (Where did you come from?)

Panic seized her voice. Something slimy and cold had latched onto the ethereal substance of her body, slithering up her legs toward her stomach. When she tried to pull away, it stabbed her just below the sternum, and pain exploded in her chest. The terrible pain thrashed its way up to her neck until something warm grabbed her hand and jerked her from its clutches.

(Jahx!) *she shouted. Two blue eyes flashed in and out of the shadows as she was pulled along.* (I came to save you!)

His lips did not move, nor did he look back at her, but she could hear his words inside her skull.

(Kill him)

The demon charged after them, closing the distance with every booming step.

391

(Jahx, please!) *she cried, the monster's gnashing teeth only* *centimeters from her head.* (Tell me what I need to do!)

He pushed her, sending her crashing down onto an invisible *surface. Dazed and floating in a sea of hurt, she gritted her teeth and* *willed the rest of body to form. Terror-stricken but determined to* *fight, she rolled over and faced the monster.*

(Not him, take me!), *she tried to say, but her voice would not* *rise above the thunder of the demon's cry. She watched in horror as* *Jahx bowed his head and allowed the demon to retract him with* *spidery fingers into its black maw.*

She heard him one last time, his voice panicked: (KILL HIM)

(Give him back!), *she screamed, lurching for the demon but* *falling short as it began to change. Thousands of red eyes bled into* *one another as the blackness shifted, pulsating dark matter* *transforming into something new. Jetta watched in horror as arms* *and legs emerged from the depths of pitch. Finally, when all of the* *eyes had become just two, a boy with black hair stepped forth from* *the shadows.*

Jetta could not turn away from the hollow gaze of the thing that *mimicked her brother. His eyes, which should have been a vibrant* *blue, turned dead white and glassy.*

Tears filled Jetta's eyes, but she did not move to brush them *away.* (Why did he allow that thing to take him? Doesn't he see that I'm here to save him?)

Jaeia's cry exploded in the back of her mind. Jetta saw flashes *of Jaeia's thoughts and perceptions of the outside world. Explosions,* *screaming, panic. The Motti had broken through their final defenses* *and penetrated the Nine Homeworlds, spreading their plague and* *their madness.* (If I don't do something now, the last worlds of the Starways will be destroyed.)

But she was powerless against the demon before it had *consumed her brother—how could she possibly fight it now? If she* *attacked the demon, she would hurt Jahx.*

He flashed his teeth and lunged at her with incredible speed. *His size was deceptive, his weight nearly crushing her ribs as he* *tackled her. She rolled with the momentum and narrowly flung* *herself away.*

She reared up just in time to avoid his next attack, but his *fingernails scored her arm, carving lines of searing pain. Her entire body shook from the blow, and she tried not to scream as she watched her flesh shear away, blood spraying wildly into the shadows.*

It took everything she had just to dodge his attacks as he came at her from all sides.

(No place to run—I can't get away,) *she panicked. He landed another hit, tearing through her skin as if it were wet paper.*

(Jahx, please!), *she pleaded as he pinned her again. She screamed as his fingers dug into her flesh. His ferocity seeped through her wounds, ripping through her with terrifying desires.*

(I will show you what you are capable of,) *he whispered in a thousand different voices. Rage, pure and unadulterated by any sense of compassion, battered her senses, his need for vengeance poisoning her mind. His smile, once the sunshine that filled her soul, transformed into a pitiless gash in his cold, ghostly face.*

(This isn't you!) *she cried. She tried to counter, slamming her forehead against his jaw, but her face exploded with pain.*

With her skin hanging off her bones in bloody shreds and heartbeat waning, Jetta felt her life teetering on the edge. She couldn't hope to pit herself against the ghastly creature that had once been her brother. Her faith, in herself and in her purpose, once adamant and steadfast, now paled as the thing that was Jahx polluted her with its malice.

(I could make all of this go away,) *she thought, a terrible joy filling her at the idea.* (I can destroy everything that ever hurt me, everything that ever could hurt me, and nothing will ever—)

(*No, that's not who you are!*) *Jaeia cried, her voice faint and remote in the back of her mind.*

Dizziness swooped over her as Jetta struggled against the alien feelings, repeating aloud what her sister had said. (No, this isn't what I am. Jahx would never do this,) *she said through clenched teeth, pushing the implanted thoughts from her mind.* (Jahx would never hurt me or want me to hurt someone else.)

(*That thing is Jahx, but it isn't him!*) *Jaeia shouted hysterically.*

(*It isn't him...*) *Jetta said, making the connection. She remembered Jahx's only words:*

(*Find me, kill him*)

(No…) *Jetta whispered.*

No time left. As her breath left her lungs and her sister's grip faded away, the memory of the perplexing conversation she'd had with Jahx in the hallway of their apartment on Fiorah strummed the last threads of her consciousness.

"I know that Yahmen will kill me," *Jahx had said. She remembered him asking her to make an awful promise:* "…never put my life before yours and Jaeia's…"

To her surprise, the thing let go of her, slinking back a few meters, and she wriggled backward as fast as she could.

(*Why did it do that?*) *she wondered, gasping for air.*

(*Remember Drakken!*) *Jaeia shouted out across their connection.* (*Remember his brother, Xercius!*)

Jetta inhaled sharply as the realization pierced beneath her breastbone, all of her pride and hope crumbling away. She finally understood why he had been so fearful, and the true meaning behind his words. Jahx had known, even back then.

(Please… please don't make me do this,) *Jetta begged.*

Hot tears streaked her face, and she couldn't breathe through her sobs. The thing that stole Jahx moved toward her again, its cold, spectral light wrapping around her as he positioned himself for a final attack. He would swallow her whole—and Jaeia too—if she did not act.

(I am so, so sorry, Jahx. I will never forgive myself for failing you,) *she whispered.*

The terrible demon that ruled this domain was too powerful to fight, strengthened by the minds of untold telepaths, so she fought the only thing she could. She didn't even know if her talents could work here, or what kind of effect they would have if they did, only that she had no other choice.

Jetta closed her eyes and reached out to him, her fingers igniting with pain as they touched his mottled skin. At first all she could think of was the terrible ache worming its way up toward her shoulder, but she held her breath and forced her mind into the monster's.

(I will devour your soul,) *the thing whispered to her. She screamed, her back arching impossibly as its icy grip seized her mind.* (I will make you see.)

Somewhere in the dissonant chorus she heard his voice as the demon slashed away at her from the inside out. *She reached out frantically with her last ounce of strength into the intestinal pit of the creature, hoping that the warm hand she found was her brother's.*

Only seconds remained. With her twin as her anchor, Jetta dug deep into their collective memories to invoke her brother's worst fear. Blossoming forth from the darkest corners of her mind came uncontrolled aggression, rage, and jealousy. Terror clenched her bowels as she tried to recall the precise dimensions of his monstrously large stature, his booming voice, the viciousness behind his blows—

All their worst memories fueling the vision, Yahmen's hulking form began to take shape between her and Jahx, and fear flickered in the eyes of the monster.

(Please don't hurt me.)

She knew the monster mimicked his voice, but it tore straight through her. She buckled and heaved, guilt carving through her resolve.

(*I can't do this—*)

She pulled back.

***

Time slowed to a halt. Jaeia no longer knew what to do. The illusion of Yahmen had shaken her as badly as it had Jetta—and what had been Jahx. Her mind filled with images that twisted her heart: The gratitude in Jahx's eyes when she gave him her third of the bakken, Jetta's giggle as they play-wrestled in a conduit for the first chance to use a laser tool they had lifted off another repairman.

I just want a chance, Jaeia thought. *That's all I want. I want Aunt Lohien to be free again, I want Uncle Galm to smile. I want Jahx to be healthy and Jetta to be happy...*

Jetta withdrew. Only seconds remained. Dread wrapped around her heart as she realized that she had to break her promise to Jetta.

She remembered Jahx's words. *"Be her anchor."*

"Use your talent," the Healer whispered. "It's the only way."

I don't want to hurt her. I don't want to hurt him.

"I am here. I will not leave you."

Jaeia stood on the precipice, starring down into the abyss.

395

Jetta will never forgive me.

* * *

Jetta couldn't do it. It wasn't Jahx she wanted to fight.

Suddenly, something familiar pushed her forward, soothing her pounding heart, forcing her mind through the motions of crafting an illusion that would end it all.

(Don't do this, Jaeia—he needs our help!) *she shrieked, groping for another way out.* (Maybe I can use my talents against the others—)

(*No, Jetta. Jahx was holding himself together for this moment. You're no match for all those other minds. You would lose yourself in their nightmares.*)

(*And I won't in Jahx's?*) *Jetta silently cried back, black-fire hatred filling her heart as she tried to push her sister out of her head.*

(*No, Jetta. Do what must be done.*)

Jetta screamed, trying to fight the mind-bending power of Jaeia's second voice. (How can you forsake Jahx? How can you break your promise?)

Despite her resistance, Jetta's mind built the illusion without her consent.

The world around her changed. Swirling murk solidified into gray and red walls, and the smell of ash was replaced with the stink of stale alcohol and cigarettes. Instead of a cacophony of voices, Jetta could hear a couple arguing just beyond the next room. The afternoon light pouring through the holes in the boarded-up windows confirmed her surroundings.

Home.

As she moved stiffly through the apartment, Jetta spotted evidence of a fight. Their cots, bent and broken, lay in pieces in the corner. The rock dice were gone, and someone had kicked over their soda cans full of water.

"No..." Jetta whispered. *Please, no...*

She rounded the corner, her legs shaking. Bits of couch cushion and broken glass littered the living room floor. Blood painted the wall, and the brown carpet squished beneath her feet.

"You..."

A chill shot up her spine, and she tried to scream, but fear choked her voice.

Yahmen emerged from the shadows, clutching a cigarette and bottle in one hand. His dead eyes, set inside two dark craters, belonged to a cadaver, and his mouth, hanging askew, did not move when he talked.

"You did this," he said, throwing a cloth sack at her. Out spilled pieces of bakken.

This was supposed to be their day of celebration. She had stolen a week's worth of food from one of the galleys on the mining ship, and she and her siblings were finally going to have a full day's worth of meals. But he found out, like he always did.

"You know what the punishment is for stealing," he said, removing his belt slowly, savoring the moment.

Her perspective changed. No longer near the level of his eyes, Jetta's body shrunk into a skeletal form that barely came up to his waist. Grease and scabs covered her tiny hands, and her body, wobbly and tired, protested even the slightest exertion. Unsure of whether to fight or flee, Jetta froze. *I am four years old again.*

Pieces of glass collected and reformed into the decorative figurines that had lined the corkboard table. The couch stuffing picked itself up off the floor and tucked itself back inside the cushions. The blood dotting the walls disappeared, and the carpet no longer oozed beneath her feet.

"No!" she screamed.

She felt movement against her leg, and turned to see her brother and sister crouched at her side. She didn't remember them being so small, or so sickly.

(Jetta, do what must be done!)

"NO!" she screamed, straddling her siblings, placing herself between them and their owner.

(Jetta, do what must be done. For me. For Jahx.)

Her arms and legs turned to lead. She couldn't let Yahmen through. *I can't let him hurt Jahx!*

Her brother looked up at her, his blue eyes wet with tears. "Jetta, please..."

Yahmen's hand reared back, slanted light from the window glinting off the belt buckle.

(Jetta, do what must be done. Do it for Jahx.)

397

"*I warned you!*" Yahmen screamed.

Jaeia stole the choice from her. Jetta's body folded helplessly as Yahmen's arm knocked her backward. He shoved Jaeia's tiny body aside as he grabbed Jahx up by the front of his shirt with his free hand, grinning drunkenly into his terrified face.

"*You'll do,*" he slurred, and then slammed Jahx's head against the wall.

Jetta screamed. *It's supposed to be my blood on the wall, not his!*

Paralyzed by her sister's voice, she watched in horror as Jahx's body bounced lifelessly off the floor. Yahmen's belt came down again and again, even though Jahx no longer struggled.

A cry drowned out the rhythmic strikes of Yahmen's belt. It came from all around her, and as it intensified, the image of Yahmen, their apartment, and her siblings faded into the murk.

Jetta covered her ears. Deafening in its ferocity, the wail rose above the cacophony of the other telepathic minds. The bioelectric energy around her swelled, growing in brightness until the light blinded her, and she covered her eyes. Then all went dark.

(*What have I done?*)

Emptiness. Stillness. A loss that time couldn't measure.

(*I killed my brother.*)

Something inside her broke loose as power snaked through her like living electricity. She had been wrong about how she felt. She did want revenge. And in this realm that fused the psionic and the physical, she could take it. I will wield the dark power of the Motti just as it wielded my brother.

Eyes like burning coals peered down at her from every direction. She closed her eyes, extending her mind to the creature. Jahx's death had left it weakened and wounded. Having severed its bonds, she knew it needed her, and for some reason, she allowed it to come closer. As the eyes drew closer she could feel the attraction, the familiarity between them.

(How do I know you?)

Her mind expanded into the demon's awareness, into its malice and discontent, into the infectious hatred that fueled its every thought. So familiar—

398

(You are a humanoid I do not despise. You are different from the others. You share my disgust for the infectious impurity of the Sentients,) *whispered countless voices.*

(My revenge starts with you,) *Jetta hissed.*

The eyes came closer, and before she could react, the demon slipped beneath her skin, distending her veins with molten fury. She wanted to pull back, but it surrounded her.

(Your brother was weak, and you are too. You are useless as you are.)

(You underestimate me!) *she screamed.*

She tore at the seething entity that surrounded her, freeing all of the unwanted emotion she had once restrained. But the very things she released—all the suffering she had known, all of her anger—was the very thing it hungered for. Instead of retracting, it devoured her. The heat ripped through her chest, braiding itself with the streams of her own power, expanding until her skin felt like it would burst.

Power. Unrestrained power. She could do anything she wanted. Her heart beat rapidly with excitement, her mind tingling with anticipation.

(With eyes open, they burn.)

The alien thought repeated itself over and over again in her mind, until she found herself feeling things she had never felt before with such fervency. (There is so much in the Starways that is useless and unnecessary,) *she realized.* (The Sentients are corrupted by their fleshy desires, freighted by free will and their knowledge of good and evil.)

Her own anger aligned with the collective hunger. (I will take up the reins of power my brother refused, and I will end all of those who have harmed me and my siblings.)

Jetta didn't know where to start. (Yahmen,) *she thought, suddenly thirsting for his death, but that wasn't where it had started. It was Galm's decision to adopt them that had placed them in Yahmen's reach. She would start with him, and Lohien would follow. There were the dog-soldiers, too. They were the ones who sent her back to the Alliance to kill Jahx.*

Of course she would spare no one from the Core, especially Mantri Sebbs. He was the one that gave them the test that exposed them to the Motti in the first place. Every soldier and every officer of the Alliance would pay too, beginning with Tidas Razar and Damon

399

Unipoesa. They put her on this path. It was their fault. It was the fault of every Sentient that had allowed the Dominion Core to arrest telepaths. They killed Jahx.

(Jetta, no!), somebody cried. Somebody familiar. Someone important.

Jaeia. (My sister—)

Jetta screamed, seismic rage burning through her like fire as she remembered what Jaeia had done. It was Jaeia's voice that had guided her powers to create the reality that had killed their brother.

(Why did you do it, Jaeia? Were you that jealous? Jealous enough to kill Jahx? He loved us more than anything and YOU KILLED HIM!) *Power surged into her hands. (I will kill my sister first.)*

(Remember,) Jaeia pleaded, (Jetta, please remember!)

Reaching inwards, Jetta yanked at her psionic connection to her sister, but Jaeia's position seemed unusually grounded. (Jaeia isn't that strong—someone must be helping her—)

(You have to remember,) Jaeia said, using her second voice again. (Remember us.)

Jetta fought viciously against the psionic pull, the dark entity surging within her, giving her the strength to resist.

(Remember me.)

(I will make you pay for what you—)

She gulped for breath as her eyes opened to an entirely different world. Sights and smells long forgotten accosted her senses. Hot and arid air filled her lungs while the green-tiled kitchen, bright and full of energy, chased away the illusion of shadow. Light streamed in from the windows, illuminating her uncle's young face as he smoked his pipe and read from a newsreel at the table.

"Jetta, can you pass me that plate?"

Aunt Lohien? Jetta passed her aunt the last of the dirty dishes before running off to play with her siblings in the other room.

"You're it!" Jaeia squealed as she and Jahx bolted for cover.

"No fair!" Jetta said, running after them. A barrage of pillows followed, along with a scolding from Galm as they tipped over a lamp.

"Come here, you," Galm said, tickling her belly as he righted the lamp. "Be nice to your brother and sister."

Time shifted. The amber rays of night filtered through the windows. Jetta found herself sprawled out on her mattress, trying to fall asleep, but the heat kept her awake.

"Hey, scoot over," Jahx said, gently pushing her with his feet.

"I can't sleep," Jaeia mumbled, rubbing her eyes.

"Just try," Jetta said.

"Well, if you hadn't had that second helping of meatloaf, maybe we could all sleep."

"Whatever. Last night you stunk so bad that I didn't fall asleep—I passed out!" Jetta retorted, playfully hitting her sister in the shoulder. Jaeia returned fire, but Jahx held them both apart until they stopped.

"Jetta, tell us a story," Jahx asked.

"I don't have any," Jetta sighed.

"Then make one up. You've always have the best stories," Jaeia said, propping herself up on her elbows.

Jetta smiled. "Once there was this girl who had an annoying brother and sister..."

Then it became a two on one and Jetta didn't stand a chance. She howled with laughter as her siblings took turns tickling her until their uncle came out of the bedroom to tell them to pipe down.

(I remember,) *Jetta whispered.*

But it wasn't enough. The demon found the connection to her sister, slicing through it layer by layer, eroding her foothold in the physical world. Thrust back into the darkness, Jetta's anger rose up, hot and strong.

(Remember, Jetta—remember why—)

"Thanks," Jaeia said, hugging her.

Jetta found herself back in the red and gray apartment. Boarded up windows blocked out the light. Crushed areas of carpet bespoke of the tables and chairs once furnishing the living room. *Where are Galm and Lohien?*

Jetta remembered the time. Things were starting to get really bad. Yahmen had moved them to a community housing unit and forced Galm out of his job.

"Thanks for always looking out for us. You've always been a good sister."

Jaeia led her back to the entryway, where they had stacked the cots into a fort. Jahx's gaunt frame sat inside, darning what was left of a sock.

"How did you manage to get this?" Jahx said, taking the bakken from Jetta's hand. He took a bite and then gave it to Jaeia.

"I lifted it off one of the miners." Jetta shrugged.

"You're hurt," Jaeia said, pointing to Jetta's knees.

"I fell running down conduit six. No big deal." Jetta wiped at the grease and blood, but that just smeared it across her leg.

"Let me do that," Jaeia said, getting up. She came back from the kitchen with a wet rag.

"Stop it," Jetta said, turning away.

"You stop it," Jaeia said, putting a hand on her shoulder and forcing her to sit.

Jetta grumbled, but the wet rag did feel good on her knees.

"You never let me help. I want to help, you know," Jaeia said when she finished.

"Thanks, Jae," Jetta said, hugging her.

Jaeia kissed her on the cheek and whispered in her ear, "I love you."

(But you made me kill him!) *Jetta cried, sobs wracking her body.*

Jetta stormed back through the threads of their psionic bond, straight into Jaeia's consciousness, and as she moved in for the kill, her sister's resolve collapsed. Unbridled emotions washed down on her, and for the first time in her life, Jetta saw the raw truth through her sister's eyes.

"You and I both know that in the end, it will be your decision."

As she sat in front of Admiral Unipoesa, Jetta rubbed her hands nervously against the fabric of the chair. His words carried the weight of the galaxy, and his eyes conveyed a hard sympathy that drew out her tears. He waited for her to respond, analyzing her every reaction as the moments passed by. Was she strong enough? Could she make that kind of decision?

She heard Jaeia's thoughts as if they were her own: *Jetta will never forgive me; she will hate me forever. I cannot kill my brother—but how can I let him suffer like this? The admiral is right to doubt me. I have to turn against my sister to set my brother free,*

*but she will never see it that way. I love them so much—they are my
life. I will grieve alone, I will be alone, forever, with this decision.*

(Jaeia...)

*Sobering to her sister's pain, Jetta remembered two gray eyes
and a kind smile. She recalled the way their hands fit together and
how Jaeia's embrace gave her hope for more than survival.*

*Calmer, she became aware of another set of eyes, blue and
luminescent, and a familiar, feminine rhythm that amplified her
sister's thoughts, giving her the strength to maintain their
connection across the limbo. She reached out and connected to the
other mind, feeling a vastness beyond anything she could rationalize
or control. Her body reacted to it, seeming to understand what she
had been blinded from in the darkness.*

*Slowly, her rage died, numb exhaustion taking hold. The murk
dissipated, dark layers shifting, retracting, burning eyes winking out
one by one. The inhuman howling subsided to silence, leaving Jetta
alone in the darkness.*

(No...! No, this is all wrong. What have I done?) *Jetta wept,
holding her head in her hands.* (I don't care about the enemy, or
revenge. No more killing; I've done enough.)

*She wanted to close her eyes and forget herself, lose herself in
the vanishing shadow, but someone held fast as the world she ended
slowly faded away.*

***

Jetta drifted in and out of a blur of confusion. Days turned into
weeks without any sense of time's passing, except through a narrow
scope of scrambled impressions. Images formed and reformed in the
haze; dim figures moved in and out of the shadows that surrounded
her. Familiar smells, the feel of warm skin on hers. Cold steel
pressed against her spine as a stinging sensation on the back of her
hand resolved into liquid ice running up her arm.

Voices. Pieces of conversation floated by as Jetta waded in and
out of consciousness.

"I can't keep doing this, Minister, this business of breaking
kids."

"You didn't even know this one."

"It doesn't matter. I won't do it anymore."

403

"I would be careful what you say next, Damon. I don't want to have to worry about you."

Someone held her hand, humming softly. An old memory lay just beyond her reach, but the warm feeling of comfort edged her away from caring.

"Please wake up. Come back to me."

Red eyes in the dark watched her every move, waiting for her, beckoning for her to return. They needed her, but she needed them if she was ever to sate her dark appetites.

A crisp circle of light purged the shadows from Jetta's mind. She relaxed a little. Someone embraced her and pulled her backward.

"Hey, stop cheating!"

A small hand encircled hers and pulled her down into the cot fort, forcing her head to crane at an awkward angle underneath one of the aluminum feet.

"Give me back the dice, it's my turn," he said.

(*Jahx.*)

Her brother looked no older than four, just about the age before their worst year.

Jetta opened her hand and the rock dice clattered onto the cement floor. She didn't want to move. None of this could be real, but she desperately wanted it to be.

(Don't go, Jahx. Don't leave me,) *she whispered.* (I am so, so sorry. I can't—)

"Jetta," Jahx sat back on his heels, his forehead knotting. He twirled a curl of hair with his index finger as he spoke. "You're not playing fair. You have to let me play my turn."

(I can't live—I can't believe—)

Jahx put his arms around her neck and hugged her, his tiny body pressing up tightly against hers. He kissed on her the cheek and whispered in her ear. "It's okay, Jetta, everything's okay. It's time to wake up now."

Tears of release were followed by a slingshot back into hell. Screaming voices, hands holding her down. Fighting only made it worse, but she needed the pain. *Jahx is gone!*

"Please, come back!" she screamed, wanting back the dream. White walls and silver instruments flashed in and out of her limited vision.

"Where's Jaeia?" someone shouted.

404

Warm hands pressed against her chest. An ethereal presence slipped beneath her skin.

I am here, I will not go away.

Foreign essence, something electric she couldn't ignore. Whispering voices on the edge of shadow called out to her, but this time she did not look back at them.

The Healer— Jetta realized. Triel's presence blockaded her fractured thoughts, interlacing with her senses, soothing the bite of her wounds. The magnetic sensation drew her closer, allowing her to forget her grief.

"Jetta, come back to me," Jaeia whispered. "Wake up. Please come back to me."

Her eyes opened against the burning light.

"Hey—hey—"

Someone grabbed her shoulders. "She's coming around!"

"How long...? What happened...?" she mumbled, now feeling the ache in her limbs. She tried to shield her eyes, but straps tethered her arms down.

"Jetta, it's okay, it's okay. You just blacked out for a while. Don't worry, everything's okay. We won. Everybody's safe, you're safe..."

Medics and doctors fluttered over her, measuring and correcting things she didn't care about. Fingers interlocked around hers, and in the back of her mind, Jaeia silently rejoiced at her awakening.

But everything was not okay. She remembered what she had done.

Jetta laid back and closed her eyes. She saw herself in her mind's eye, the crimson expectation of death pooling beneath her body while white tendons, stripped from her limbs like puppet strings, held her upright. A sulphur-skinned creature, drudged up from the stinking swamps of her unconscious, jerked and tugged at the cords.

I cannot escape what I am.

When she looked closer, the image she saw reflected in her own eyes tore her from her grief, sobering her to the truth. She saw her sister, she saw responsibility, and she knew she would have to wake up.

***

405

Jaeia sensed the Healer's presence long before she came to stand beside her in the starbase's observatory.

"Are you all right?" Jaeia asked.

"I'm okay. Jetta's doing better, but part of her is still trying to go back to that awful place."

Jaeia cringed. "I know."

"This has been the strangest experience for me," Triel said, pulling back her long, dark hair into a bun. "Wherever you two went during that battle was far beyond any place that I've ever journeyed. I can't remember much of anything beyond scattered impressions."

"It's probably better that you don't."

The Healer looked up to see what Jaeia had been studying. A muted exclamation escaped her lips as her eyes moved between the magnified views of the nebula under monitor by the astronomy teams.

"Sometimes I need reminders like this—that beauty still exists."

Jaeia silently agreed.

"So," Triel said, turning toward her, eyes earnest and inquiring. "How are you?"

Jaeia squeezed the guardrail as hard as she could. Weeks had passed since the battle against the Deadwalkers, but time hadn't eased the pain. *It's more than the circumstances of Jahx's death,* she thought. *It's what I felt—what I saw—when I pulled Jetta from the other realm.*

"I'm okay," she said, resigning a smile. "I'm just glad you helped out. I couldn't have done it without you."

"No problem," Triel said, brushing the loose hair out of her eyes.

Jaeia chortled. "I was a little worried that you weren't going to show that day."

Triel crossed her arms in front of her chest and took a step back. "It took awhile to get the security clearance."

Deciding not to push the issue any further, Jaeia switched topics. "I never asked—is Reht okay?"

"Yes, I helped him recover from his wound. They're letting him and the crew dock on Trigos. I don't know what's going to happen to him—or me, for that matter. The Alliance considers him—all of us—a security risk. And you know Reht's not exactly the most reasonable person. He tends to make matters worse when he feels cheated."

"He won't sell the device, will he? I have to get that back from him."

Triel blushed. "I don't know, Jaeia. I will do my best to get it back to you. I am sorry about how this ended up. Things never really go according to plan for me."

Jaeia steadied herself against the railing, trying not to show her distress. "I understand why you did it. I just really need to get it back."

Triel nodded. "Like I said, things are hard for him and the crew now. I just hope he keeps his head on his shoulders."

"You two are close, aren't you?" Jaeia said, reading her body language.

Triel massaged the webbing between her fingers. "We have a complicated relationship. I wouldn't try to label it anything else. Rarely is anything normal with a dog-soldier."

"But he isn't going to leave you here, is he?"

Triel shrugged her shoulders. Jaeia could tell she was hiding something from her by the way her lower lip trembled. "I don't know. It depends on a lot of things."

Seeing her discomfort, Jaeia changed the subject. "So how did you find my secret retreat?"

"It wasn't hard. I looked it up. The observatory is separate from the main decks. In other words," she said, absently tracing some of the Prodgy markings on her hand, "it's the quietest place on the ship for a telepath."

"I like that you get that," Jaeia said, looking back to the stars.

"Jaeia," the Healer began hesitantly, "I know what it's like to lose family. But not many people understand how that feels when you had a telepathic bond with the one you lost. It's a different kind of grief altogether."

Jaeia's throat tightened, and she couldn't find the words to reply. She had focused so hard on keeping her sister's emotions in check during the battle and over the last few weeks that she had barely addressed her own.

"I described it once to Reht, but he didn't really understand. I told him being a telepath was like listening to music, and each

407

family member had a different melody. I lost my entire family. Now all I'm left with is silence."

"I'm so sorry," Jaeia whispered. Triel understood her loss, and perhaps even her fear. What would happen if Jetta died? She would be all alone in a gray, tuneless world.

Several moments went by before Jaeia could find her voice again. "Can you ever hear that music again? Could you bond with others?"

Triel wrapped her arms tightly around her chest and sighed. "I hope so. But there are so very few telepaths left. That's why I've decided to stay with the Alliance—to help recover those that survived this massacre, maybe even find some of my people."

Jaeia nodded. She and Jetta had realized the deeper implications of this after Sebbs revealed their past. With so many telepaths impounded by the Core, the possibility of finding any of their original family members was slim. She, Jetta, and Triel were part of a dwindling few.

"When things settle down, Jetta will want to look for our blood relatives and for our uncle and aunt on Fiorah—if, of course, they're still alive. Family has always been important to her, and to me. You could come with us."

"Where would you start?"

Jaeia rolled up the sleeve on her right arm, revealing her tattoo. "With this, I guess. It's our only clue for now."

Triel smiled sadly and turned away from her. "I was wrong about you, Jaeia. I'm so sorry that I ever thought that you were capable of being Volkor. It's funny, in a way. A lot of times you think you know somebody because of what you hear or see, but it's not always true. A lot of times we see what we want to see."

I know, Jaeia worried, hands knotting together. That's why she had come to the observatory—to get away, to clear her mind and answer the question burning inside her every since Jahx's death: *Has love blinded me to the truth about Jetta?*

When Jetta destroyed their brother's mind, an ugly power took her over. Jetta, the most protective person Jaeia had ever known, wanted destruction with a vicious joy that twisted her desire to keep her family safe into pure vengeance.

Jetta's will has always been stronger, she thought. *I'm not capable of standing up to her if she decides to take that power in hand.*

Holding tight to the guardrail, Jaeia embraced her own the dark truth. *...At least not without consequences I couldn't bear to live with.*

Looking up to the stars, Jaeia found them gazing back at her with cold indifference. Somewhere, deep inside her, she heard more than her own subconscious' whisperings: *Jahx had faith in me to be Jetta's anchor. I have to trust his judgment.*

(I have to trust in myself.)

Resolutely, she decided their fate: *It's up to me. Jetta is our fire, but I will be our voice.*

Jaeia sighed and turned to Triel. "I choose to see the best in people. I choose to hope."

* * *

Admiral Unipoesa nursed the last few drops of Old Earth vodka in his glass, watching the stars pass by as the Alliance Central Starbase rotated on its axis. Even though he had turned out the lights and blocked all incoming calls to both his personal com and his desk, he had accurately timed the moment the door to his quarters would be forced open.

"It's not the same galaxy out there. Not anymore," he whispered.

The Minister's hand grazed the top of Unipoesa's desk as he came to stand beside him. "I had my guards sweep your office twice now. By their accounts, you're clean. But I know your resourcefulness."

Unipoesa smirked. "I'm glad you think so."

"And you've stopped using Rai Shar," Razar said. "I thought you of all people would be interested in protecting yourself. The Kyrons seem to trust you."

The admiral stared at his empty glass and grunted. "There's no point. They know we have countermeasures against their mind reading; they'll know we're up to something."

"We can't have them finding out more than they already know," the Minister said, eyes threatening punishment. "You made a mistake showing them that letter."

"I had to give them something. Besides, you know it wasn't the whole thing."

"The Special Missions Team tracked down that Reptili, got him to talk. We have names. Those launnies—there's a significant history there. I want to know what we're dealing with before anything else happens."

"I won't lie to them," the admiral said, squeezing his glass, knuckles turning white. "I made that mistake before. We both did. Look what happened to Li. He's going to start a new war."

A long silence drifted between them as the Minister chose his words. "Then you know what I'll have to do with you."

The admiral looked back at the stars, taking in as much of it in as he could. It would be a long time before he saw them again. *Maria. Tarsha. I'm so sorry.*

"Tidas, don't be foolish," Unipoesa said as two guards emerged from the shadows, guns pulsating. A white flash sent incredible electric pain searing through his chest and down his limbs. Damon flayed wildly, knocking his drink from his desk as he crashed to the ground in convulsions.

The Minister picked up the fallen glass as the guards handcuffed the admiral. "Time for you and me to have a long talk."

***

Jetta sat cross-legged on her bed, quietly contemplating what she and her sister had been through. It had only been a few days since she transitioned out of the medical bay, and her arms and legs still bore the discolored evidence of her ordeal. Triel had offered to heal her wounds, but Jetta refused. *I don't deserve that kindness.*

Through counselors, borrowed memories and newsreels, she put together the broader consequences of what they had done. Though the Alliance had been outnumbered and outclassed, in one battle Jetta and Jaeia had won them the greatest war in the history of the Starways. She should be proud, or so the Minister had told her.

Earlier, the admiral tried to cheer her up with pitiful attempts at redirection. He showed her the newsreels of the crowds on Trigos chanting their names, and the banners running across every holographic broadcast: *The Kyron twins—our heroes! The saviors of the Starways!*

If only they knew who Volkor was, Jetta thought.

"This is your vindication," Unipoesa told her, seeing her disbelief.

If so, it feels hollow.

"At the very least," Unipoesa said. *"You've saved all of us from becoming Deadwalkers. Think of your sister."*

Jetta twisted the bed sheet between her hands and pulled until the fabric tore. *My sister, my twin.* She didn't know what she felt. Her sister had made her do something terrible, something she could never have done alone. Whether or not it was the right decision, it tasted like betrayal. *How can I ever face her again?*

Dumping her despair into someone else's head crossed her mind, but she passed over the idea as quickly as it came. *It won't bring Jahx back. Besides, pain is all that is left of our connection.*

The door chime rang through her chamber, and Jetta stirred. Without acknowledging the call, the doors swished open. She did not have to look up to see her mirror image in the doorframe.

Cheers echoing up from the main assembly rose to a roar of applause, forcing Jaeia to step inside. The door slammed shut on the world outside, locking them in silence.

"Everybody tuned into Admiral Unipoesa's peacetime speech," Jaeia said, voice tremulous. "I wish you could have been there, Jetta—he revealed a lot of classified stuff. It was either incredibly stupid or incredibly brave. The demand for an uplink almost shorted out the interfleet circuitry."

Jetta didn't respond, turning away from her sister.

Dragging her fingers nervously along the top of the chair, Jaeia tried again. "They're waiting for us in reception, you know..."

Jetta shook her head. "I'm not in the mood to celebrate."

"Even the chancellor assembled for the peacetime speech."

"I don't care."

Jaeia did not rustle the bed sheets as she sat next to her, trying not to encroach on her space. "Talk to me. Please."

"Was it easy for you?" Jetta whispered.

Jaeia recoiled as if she had been struck. "You think... you think I wanted to do that?"

411

"You said we couldn't ever use our talent because it's too dangerous—and then you use it against our brother!"

"No—I had to—you wouldn't have—"

"You're right—I would never have hurt Jahx!"

"Jetta—you had to do it! The Motti would have used him to kill us!"

"I hate you!" Jetta screamed, pounding her fist against Jaeia's chest. Her sister grabbed her by the wrists, but Jetta pinned her down with her knees and snapped her arms back. "Didn't Jahx mean anything to you?"

Jaeia stopped struggling, but she turned her face aside so Jetta couldn't see her tears. "He's my brother too, Jetta. Maybe we didn't have the same bond that you two did, but I still loved him, just like I love you."

"Jaeia—"

"It should have been me. Maybe then it wouldn't be so bad for you."

"What? No!" Jetta said. Tears formed in her eyes, but she couldn't wipe them away without letting go of Jaeia, so she let them fall on her sister's face. "Jaeia, no—Gods—I don't wish it was you instead of Jahx. I love you. I do. You are everything to me. You are my sister."

Jaeia inhaled deeply and relaxed a little, but Jetta wasn't done yet.

"It doesn't change the fact that we murdered him, Jaeia."

Jaeia tensed again. "Jetta—we didn't murder him. We set him free."

"There is no difference!"

"There is!" Jaeia shouted back. "It's what he wanted all along. You said it yourself—that's why he made the connection. You did save him, Jetta."

Jetta let her go, but Jaeia didn't get up. Instead, she curled into a ball and her eyes relaxed, not focusing on anything that Jetta could see.

"I love you, Jetta. I would never want to hurt you or manipulate you. I only did what I did because I knew you would have never done anything to harm our brother."

Sitting back on her heels, Jetta wiped away the tears with her sleeve. Jaeia was right, like always, but that didn't justify what they

412

had done. She wanted to scream, to tear the sheets to ribbons, but sheer exhaustion took away the bite of her anger.

"It must have been hard to do what you did," Jetta whispered. "That's what I felt. That's what made me turn back. I felt how much you cared. I felt how much it tore you apart to do that. You risked everything to save us both."

Jaeia sucked in her breath and held it, tears cascading down her cheeks. Jetta reached out and touched her sister's shoulder, unsure if she should, but Jaeia reached back, sitting up and hugging her until Jetta had to pry herself free.

"Okay, okay," Jetta said, wiping away her sister's tears.

Jaeia finally looked at her again, gray eyes puffy and red. "I am so, so sorry, Jetta."

Stomach knotting, Jetta found that she didn't have anything to say. Jaeia wanted her forgiveness for what she had done, but Jetta tightened up at the thought. "Who helped you? It felt like the Healer—but she hates me."

Jaeia tentatively smiled. "It was Triel, and she doesn't hate you. I asked her to help me during the final battle. She helped me before, on Reht's ship, when I used my second voice against one of the dog-soldiers, bringing me back before I went too far."

"What took her so long?"

"She said it was security giving her a hard time, but really, I think she had to get past a few things first. A lot of people have the wrong impression about us. It's going to be a while before things settle down."

"If they ever do," Jetta muttered. "All those people we saved will soon know that 'Kyron' is just another name for 'General Volkor the Slaythe.'"

Jaeia didn't try to talk her out of that one.

"So," Jetta said, breaking the long silence. "What now?"

Jaeia sighed and wiped her eyes. "I don't know exactly. How old are we again?"

Jetta thought about it a moment. "Seven?"

"Well, we should be in second grade, right? Well, I am kind of behind on my barnyard animals."

"You're a giant dork," Jetta said. She grabbed a pillow off the bed and threw it at her, and Jaeia caught it with a smile.

Jetta hung her head. "I don't know if I'll ever be able to accept what happened to Jahx, Jaeia."

Jaeia hugged the pillow and with her free hand held onto the tips of Jetta's fingers. "Jetta—you make sacrifices for those you love. Jahx did for you, and you did for Jahx. You're going to have to accept that. There are those who love you and are willing to make sacrifices, even with your terrible smell."

"Excuse me?" Jetta exclaimed. Jaeia threw the pillow at her, this time hard enough that it burst. As feathers rained down around them, for the first time in a long time, Jaeia laughed.

In seeing her sister laugh, Jetta realized something. Jahx was gone, but Jaeia was safe, alive, and for the first time since they were very little, she had the chance to think of something beyond their immediate survival. Things could be different now, and the thought frightened her.

I can't accept your gift, she thought, hoping that somehow Jahx could still hear her. *I can't accept that you cared that much about us, about me, to sacrifice yourself like that. So I will make you a promise. I will look after Jaeia, and I will honor your life.*

Jetta looked back at her sister. "I want to go back and help our uncle and aunt. I want to find our mother and father. I want to find our families—both the Drachsis and the Kyrons."

Jaeia nodded. "Me too. But we can't just up and leave right now."

"What's more important than finding Galm and Lohien?"

Jaeia cocked her head to the side. "You've been rattling around in my head too long now. I've picked up your street think. We can't expect just to waltz right out of here and go find them. We're on leashes, you know. We're going to need favors to get around now."

"Okay—so what do you want to do?"

Jaeia smiled with a hint of wickedness and firmed her grip on her sister's hand.

"Let's go out there and celebrate. Let's put a few military chubs and politicians in our corner. But while everybody else is cheering for the Alliance's victory, you and I can celebrate something else. We can celebrate what Jahx has given us."

"What exactly is that?"

"A new beginning," Jaeia said, squeezing her hand.

"I don't know if I'm ready to celebrate just yet," Jetta said.

"It'll give you a chance to scare a few senior delegates in the General Assembly. Intimidating authority figures always makes you feel better."

"Haha, Jaeia," Jetta said, folding her arms across her chest. "You think you know me so well. Stop spending so much time in my head—I don't want to become a softie like you."

"Don't worry, you'll always be a sour grump," Jaeia said, pinching her side.

As Jetta readied for their appearance before the public and the entire Fleet, they didn't talk about anything serious. They avoided discussing what Jaeia had rightly observed—that they were on short leashes. Their celebrity status wouldn't last long, and interfederational trials for their crimes against the former United Starways Coalition would be a likely next step.

But for now, Jetta wouldn't think about that. Instead, she listened to her sister's jokes about the designer clothes given to them for their public appearances, her speculation about the gourmet food at the events, and her curiosity about entertainers from worlds they had only dreamed about. As Jaeia remarked on their lack of hairstyle, Jetta realized that they were entering a whole new world together.

She smiled at the thought.

***

Jahx didn't hurt anymore. Everything was okay. When he opened his eyes, he found himself back in the red and gray apartment, holding the hand of his Pao.

(Uncle Galm,) he whispered. Furry eyebrows lifted, and his Pao *wrapped his arms around him and squeezed.*

"My son—I love you very, very much. You know that, don't you?"

He heard two voices, much alike, in a nearby room. He couldn't see them, but he knew they were there, and safe. A woman's voice hummed softly in the kitchen, just loud enough to rise above the sound of dishes being scrubbed.

(Heaven.)

He rested his head on his Pao*'s chest. He was about to close his eyes when the hairs on the back of his neck stood on end and his spine stiffened.* Something's wrong.

Instinctively, he looked toward the entryway. Galm disappeared, as did the other voices. A bare fluorescent bulb flickered overhead, giving hints of the shadowy figure in the doorway. Purple tendrils of smoke rose up to the ceiling from the burning end of a cigarette.

Yahmen—

"Jahx, my boy—I found you. This is only the beginning."
Jahx screamed.

The journey has only begun...

"Hold on, Jetta," Jaeia said, inputting the coordinates for their course heading into the jumpdrive. "This isn't over yet."

Jetta surprised herself with the speed of her attack as she smacked her sister's helmet against the crossbeam. Jaeia mumbled something and slumped in her seat.

She couldn't feel Jaeia anymore. She couldn't even sense her own feelings anymore, except for the emptiness, the fear, the dark seed taking root in the cavity of her chest.

"I'm afraid it is for me," Jetta whispered.

—*Triorion: Abomination (Book Two)*

Now available in stores!
For more information go to: www.triorion.com

Acknowledgements

I owe countless thanks to so many people for the success of this book. First and foremost are my family and friends for their love and continued support over the years as I pursued this dream. Special thanks to my aunt, Irene, for going the extra mile to connect me to the literary world, and to my mother and father, without whom I might never have believed in this project.

To my friends, Linzy Wolman and John Glick, who read the very first draft of the book: thank you. Your enthusiasm gave me a much-needed boost during those early years.

Alice W., Pat R., Patrick K. and Ali Parker—thanks for going that extra mile for me during the final stages of this book. You have no idea how much that meant to me.

A special thanks Erin Cochran, the patient and intrepid editor who gave me invaluable advice and criticisms in the early stages of the series. I would also like to thank my current editor, Vivian Trask, for helping me transform this book to be true to the story I've always wanted to tell.

Last, but certainly not least, thank you to my dearest Nicci, who has helped me in so many ways, both with this book and behind the scenes.

L. J. Hachmeister is a freelance writer, illustrator, and registered nurse originally from Chicago, Illinois. She currently resides in Denver, Colorado with her family and two rambunctious dogs.

Made in the USA
Charleston, SC
01 August 2015